Ernest Rhys

Malory's History of King Arthur and the Quest of the Holy Grail

From the Morte d'Arthur

Ernest Rhys

Malory's History of King Arthur and the Quest of the Holy Grail
From the Morte d'Arthur

ISBN/EAN: 9783743404144

Manufactured in Europe, USA, Canada, Australia, Japa

Cover: Foto ©Andreas Hilbeck / pixelio.de

Manufactured and distributed by brebook publishing software (www.brebook.com)

Ernest Rhys

Malory's History of King Arthur and the Quest of the Holy Grail

MALORY'S HISTORY OF

KING ARTHUR

AND THE

QUEST OF THE HOLY GRAIL.

[FROM THE MORTE D'ARTHUR.]

Edited, with General Introduction to the " Camelot Classics,"

BY ERNEST RHYS.

———◆———

LONDON:

WALTER SCOTT, 24 WARWICK LANE,

PATERNOSTER ROW.

1886.

The Camelot Classics.

INTRODUCTION.

HIS book of King Arthur and his noble Knights of the Round Table, that sets out adventurously in modern guise to-day, has capital claim to be made herald of the great company of prose-writers. This, not so much for its own inherent quality, unique as that is, as for its bearing on the splendid aftergrowth of letters, and its touch of an event which, though compassed bloodlessly amid the rumours and fierce presence of war, was really revolutionary. It was the revolution of Caxton—so peacefully begun in the silence of Westminster; and yet so tremendous, as we see it now. And Sir Thomas Malory's *Morte D' Arthur* was one of the books most directly called into being by Caxton's introduction of printing in the Fifteenth Century.

It is natural to dwell on this link of the literary evolution first; the whole question of the popular approach to letters naturally makes us inclined to think with great interest on Caxton's deliverance. If we pursue this thought now, however, let us not forget the more inward side of things, and the place of the *Morte D' Arthur* on that side. For the inward significance of the book is not slight, and examining it more closely we shall find how typical it is in both matter and method, and how suggestive. Especially we at this time ought to be interested in it, for this prose outcome of the fascinating Middle Age sentiment has direct bearing on the order of prose-writing tyrannically most in vogue with us,—Tale-telling! Across the naive pretence of the word HISTORY printed on its title-page we find *Romance* seductively scribbled, as it were; and indeed no more tempting by-way into English prose literature could well be found for the uninitiated than this first of all favourite English romances. Putting off until later the full considering of the book, however, let us first of all invoke the shade of Caxton,—great forefather of this and all other new editions intended for a Nineteenth Century audience, and try and touch the printing-press afresh with the memory of its picturesque beginning.

It was in the year 1485—four centuries ago exactly— that Caxton imprinted at Westminster the first edition of the *Morte D'Arthur*, eight or ten years later than the first book produced by him. This sounds a commonplace now, with printing one of the commonest of all commonplaces; but it was different then. The successful starting of his press by Caxton in the Almonry at Westminster, "a little enclosure containing a chapel and almshouses, swept away since Caxton's time by later buildings, near the west front of the church," * may be said to have caused a sensation. The audience was still small then, but it was fast growing. The monopoly of letters by the monastic coteries was at an end, and the intellectual appetite of the wider throng of men had been already sharpened in many ways. To this it was the printing-press was directly due, for the demand for books pressed hard upon the slow processes of the scribes and copyists, though these processes had been developed considerably by trade-guilds, such as the Brothers of the Pen at Brussels; and upon the stimulus thus given the genius of Faust and Gutenberg found issue in the printing-press. One can imagine the excitement that the new art aroused in London, when Caxton returned there with it. One sees the stream of students and society

---

* Green's *Short History of the English People*, p. 289.

dilletanti, fair ladies and fine gentlemen—princes, duchesses, priests, merchants—flocking to the Almonry with their patronage and suggestions for new books. And Caxton was equal to the hour : with the love and enthusiasm of a student he had, too, the tact of his trade. Here is his advertisement:—"If it please any man, spiritual or temporal, to buy any pyes of two or three commemorations of Salisbury all emprinted after the form of the present letter, which be well and truly correct, let him come to Westminster, into the Almonry at the red pale, and he shall have them good chepe." The picture this calls up is full of charm. Ladies of quaint costume and bright face, gentlemen of degree, dark-cowled monks, are among the customers there, carrying away with them rare burdens, books of poetry and romance and ritual, one of which would mark a red-letter day for the book-hunter now. "The Almonry—at the red pale!"—a strange and quiet birth-place surely for the violent steam-dragons of modern letters.

It is a far cry from Caxton to the literary activity of to-day ; the recall of four centuries is difficult. But consider for a moment what an immense deliverance was here— what a liberation of forces! Here was another of the mighty strokes with which the human spirit struck its way out of the old imprisonment of time and space, during the Fifteenth Century—a century so barren in many ways as it seems at a first glance. Not long before, Constantinople had fallen to the Turks, and the wealth of Greek culture held for long within its walls was scattered through Europe, the first disciple of the famed Chalcondylas reaching Oxford shortly after Caxton began printing. The effect of this Greek renascence was masterful in the extreme ; the name of Erasmus alone will attest it. The recovery of the perfect culture of that mighty Hellenic world had inestimable influence on the intellectual life of the time. But following this adventure into the past were others more tremendous into the future. At the end of the century came the valiant leap into space of Columbus, and then, even more mighty, that of Copernicus. The old narrow walls of the world fell asunder, and the imagination had a new horizon, vastly extended, opened to it, lit with the radiance of an enchanted promise. It was the first faint dawning of the superb Elizabethan day, when men's souls ran riot at the very access of a sunshine which we with our modern critical discernment of the nice negatives of shadow find so intolerably brilliant and positive.

Thinking of the sudden spiritual escape that these three names betoken, chiefly effected by scientific enlargement of ways and means, it is not extravagant to find in this century a period rather remarkably complementary to that. The obscure little black-letter imp that Caxton unfolded from his cloak has grown out of all knowledge—a very devil in power of mischief, if a ministering angel in power of good. The newspaper is in every obscurest corner of the empire, and it is conceivable that before the present rage for having everything done by law has quieted, the Government may be asked to nationalise the news of the day, and provide each man as his natural right with a morning paper. And with this new provision, such as it is, for the mind, the power to assimilate has increased. Education has gone out; the people have beyond all recall power of knowledge in their hands; and the aspects of a high spiritual destiny may at any time now find the eyes of the vast multitude of men opened to see and look powerfully forward at their high incitement. This as it may, the recent signs of the times proclaim beyond all question a liberation of forces that connects itself suggestively with that of the Fifteenth Century. *The Democracy !*—this is the shape that stands ominously at the gates of Academe, demanding irregular entrance. Well may those to whom the old traditions are sacred tremble somewhat at what to them seems a threatened desecration of the beloved groves! Voices of solemn warning from within have not ceased sounding in our ears, indeed, since Mr. Matthew Arnold uttered years ago his first eloquent protest.

There is a great deal, no doubt, to be said on both sides. The average man, let it be confessed, has rather a suspicion of academic rules and regulations. The vocabularies and the precious distinctions,—what have they to do with him? He reads for the sake of life, and not for the sake of letters. Does it bring solace and courage; does it give stimulus and enlargement to the every-day life; is the pulse that beats for laughter and tears throbbing behind its pages; is it alive, potent, contemporary? These the questions he unconsciously puts to a book, and unless the answer is ready, he will have none of it. And the questions are altogether sane and reasonable. On the other hand, it is pointed out that this verdict is often too hasty, and that a great deal of highest import for every-day life cannot be seized by the impatient hands of men itching for the quick returns of the market-place. There is truth in both sides; and after this it must concern more and more those to whom culture is not a mere luxury for a small coterie of the elect, how best to make the popular approach to the nobler books ready and sure. Here there is the high justification of those who, having watched that reckless pioneer, the newspaper, sally out, wish that the nobler presence of prose should follow.

It is the spirit that imports, the letter is secondary. But the spirit must be naturally embodied in its art-form, in the letter, to really gain the ear of the world. Only by long considering of this art-form by men of genius has our prose utterance become what it now is, and to-day, with the facile opportunities of journalism inviting everyone to speech in print, how greatly important that we should seek earnestly to set a standard of excellence really high in this utterance. For it is not being fantastic altogether to reflect that as the first speech of the lips, so the second speech of the pen may in time become a fluent universal faculty. There will always be, let us hope, the artists of special gift to strike the higher note, but one can conceive a current style—simple, adequate, direct—common to all; capable of expressing with free and manly sincerity the natural relationships of life and thought. Were such a current style the usual acquirement, taught in the schools, of every citizen, it is largely in the matrix of this present half-century that it would most likely be formed. An even wilder flight into the future the imagination takes, indeed, and dreams of still greater destinies, when all languages have become one living whole, and prose and poetry are immortally married, and music is divinely articulate, in the great confederacy of tongues.

The spirit first,—the prime motive impetus,—we ask. And as its test, to save all falseness, let us seek earnestly the literary excellence, asking higher and higher perfection. It is not needed for this test to frame final theories; the final theory of prose indeed is a matter that the good-natured scribbler who would possess his days in peace had better not meddle with. Fortunately for those who have not academic authority to back them, the spiritual test will be found as a rule to connote the literary one. There have been writers who have written excellently about nothing, but they are the rare exceptions; the supreme reach of utterance has been that of the greatest souls. Mere literary quality will not avail for ever. It is the human presence behind the voice, the reliance upon a vision that has fathomed life, and its humours and sorrows, and its greatly celestial import. And what a saving it is, to escape the need of all the thousand classic vocables and categories, and make the simple human heart the test. Only, though exact critical arrangement of the head be done without, the head itself, the intellectually disciplined sense of truth and beauty, which any shepherd on his hillside, or any toiler in the crowd, can attain, is despised at the reader's fatallest peril.

Before attempting therefore to sketch roughly the growth of English prose, let us call up the echoes of two great voices, where the presence behind is indisputable,—pleas separately for the life-inspiration behind the literary, and for the natural direction of art. The first is, as most will at once recognise, from Milton.

> "And long it was not after, when I was confirmed in this opinion, that he, who would not be frustrate of his hope to write well hereafter in laudable things, ought himself to be a true poem . . . ."

There is only one name that naturally appears with

Milton's in the first rank and order, and though it is not as a prose-writer that he whom a recent journalist with a fine faculty for evasion termed "the talented author of 'Hamlet,'" is generally referred to, the excellence of his prose utterance is not likely to be called in question. And the passage, which is of course from "Hamlet," applies suggestively, with a little variation, to the art of prose as well as to the art of acting :—

> "Be not too tame neither, but let your own discretion be your tutor; suit the action to the word, the word to the action, with this special observance, that you o'erstep not the modesty of nature: for anything so overdone is from the purpose of playing, whose end doth at the first and now, was, and is, to hold as 'twere the mirror up to nature; to show virtue her own feature, scorn her own image, and the very age and body of the time his form and pressure."

With these notes of two supreme artists in our ears, giving us a sort of talisman to try the spirit and letter of our prose-writers, we can safely essay the journey of English prose through history.

The story of our prose is indeed most picturesque, full of folk-interest and local colour, as well as of wider historical suggestion. To read it aright we must go back farther even than the monk at his manuscript desk,— to the first life-springs of action, to the battle-field and the castle hall and the cottage hearth, where, on the very edge of adventure, men felt the stirring of that mental appetite which made them call for tale and song. A tale and a song! —there is the beginning : the epic and the lyric instincts lie at the very root of literature, and with them is interwoven the graver one of awe finding voice in prayer. In very subtle ways these first instincts have influenced prose and verse, and the special use of both. Thinking of this special use, and of the qualities and functions which are severally allotted to each, it is a simple and safe way out of a very complicate difficulty to remember that *prose* is primarily the written equivalent of ordinary speech in all its range and variety ; *verse*,—not to confine poetry to metrical utterance only,—of song. This is the fundamental distinction, which, simple as it seems, is often overlooked in the academic deliverances upon the subject. The great virtue of prose is that, like pure speech, it can rise from easiest colloquy to highest eloquence. Beyond this it may not go; for then succeeds song, whose only limitation is one of the music in words. The measure of prose-style is its adequacy to the infinite variety of thought within the written range of speech : there seems no inherent restriction beyond this. The degrees of the approach of speech to song, so inappreciably fine, set one wondering how far a style nobly conjoining the attributes of both can be attained. But this is venturing on dangerous ground, set with many traps for the unwary.

It is ten centuries and more we must turn back for the actual birth of English prose. As Mr. Stopford Brooke has pointed out in his invaluable *English Literature Primer*, it begins with Bæda, the Venerable Bede, who, after writing many important Latin works, gave his last energies to a *Translation of the Gospel of St. John.* "In the story of his death told by his disciple Cuthbert is the first record of English prose-writing. When the last day came the dying man called his scholars to him that he might dictate more of his translation. 'There is still a chapter wanting,' said the scribe, 'and it is hard for thee to question thyself longer.' 'It is easily done,' said Bæda, 'take thy pen and write quickly.' Through the day they wrote, and when evening fell, 'There is yet one sentence unwritten, dear master,' said the youth. 'Write it quickly,' said the master.' 'It is finished now.' 'Thou sayest truth,' was the reply, 'all is finished now;' whereupon he sang the 'Glory to God,' and died. It is to that scene that English prose looks back as its sacred source, as it is in the greatness and variety of Bæda's Latin work that English literature strikes its key-note." The Latin foster-parentage of Bæda's English suggests at once the way in which our language in its growth has been shaped and modified by foreign influence. Like the English people themselves, their prose and poetry are compounded in a very extraordinary way of world-wide elements.

* *Eng. Lit. Primer*, by Stopford Brooke, M.A., p. 19.

To Bæda, the Venerable Bede, succeeds the great name of King Alfred, whose really kingly care and enthusiasm for the cause of the English tongue, proved not only by his own literary work of writing and translating, but by his schools for its propagation, give him the right to be called " The Father of English Prose."   From the reign of Alfred let us take a passage to show what English was in its Anglo-Saxon guise about A.D. 890.   For the sake of easy comparison, let it be the famous first clause of the Lord's Prayer :—

> " Fæder ure thu the eart in heofenum. Si thin nama gehalgod, to-be-come thin rice. Geweorhte thin willa on eorthan, swa swa on heofenum."

The great storehouse of old English prose is the English Chronicle, which continues from Alfred to Stephen.   " The narrative of Alfred's wars with the Danes, written, it is likely, by himself at the end of his reign, enables us to estimate the great weight Alfred himself had in literature." * After Alfred there was a lapse again, but under Athelred and the Danish kings a revival is proved by the growing volume of the English Chronicle, which ends abruptly at last by the death of Stephen, and with it old English prose.   For now followed the Norman invasion, threatening greatly the safety of the language, but after a struggle, often desperate enough as it seemed, the English prevailed, having gained in subtle ways by the adventure. This conflict with foreign influence is repeated with varying circumstance over and over, but all the while the youngest of the languages kept waxing greater and stronger, drawing new qualities from almost every other language in turn. The Normans brought in Romance afresh, and an added zest for tales of all kinds.   The epic instinct moved letters more and more, the Welsh, always masters of romance and song, influencing English literature in a roundabout way through the French.   Geoffrey of Monmouth wrote in Latin, too, twelve books of a romance-history of Britain, collated chiefly from Welsh sources, and these twelve books,

---

* *Eng. Lit. Primer,* by Stopford Brooke, M.A., p. 21.

transmuted and graced by French translation, found their way back into English verse in Layamon's *Brut*. This roundabout process is typical of many other romances in vogue about this time,—from some of which, indeed, by curious evolution, this very book of King Arthur and his Knights is derived. Besides the Arthurian romance as then known, other important romance-cycles were *Charlegmagne*, the *Life of Alexander*, and the *Siege of Troy;* and many more followed as the demand grew.

The second line of development was through religion, and as the romance-cycles culminate in Chaucer and Malory, so the religious element in Langland and Wiclif. The Mendicant Friars had helped to accomplish two things; they had brought about a religious revival, and at the same time mixing with the poorer classes of English speech, had done much to reconcile the conflict between French and English,—the aristocratic and the democratic elements of speech. But presently waxing rich and indolent the religious impulse they had themselves given returned upon their own heads, and with the religious revival that ensued was interwoven a democratic movement of rebellion against oppression of the people by the nobles. It was indeed amid great misery that the English language passed that part of its youth which lies in the Fourteenth Century; and from great misery it learnt new words and new emphasis of bitterness and pain. The Black Death—ominous name!—was in the land, and to the superstitious seeing of the people a great tempest in 1362 gave an added awful significance. In the sorrow and great trouble of their lives men turned eagerly to religion. The best picture of this time is not in prose, but verse; the *Vision of Piers the Plowman* is the monument of the dark interest of these days. But while every one was reading the *Vision*, Wiclif was working at his *Translation of the Bible*, and in his battle with Holy Church sending out tracts and sermons written in stirring popular language, which, with his Bible *Translation*, had great effect upon the popular approach to letters. As we have before taken a short passage from Alfred's time, let us take one from Wiclif—

five hundred years later, be it remembered. The finest examples of Wiclif's English are in his *Translation of the Bible*, and seeing how unspeakably important in our literature is its influence, let us take a line or two from his version of *The Magnificat :—*

> "He hath made myght in his arm, he scatteride proude men with the thoughte of his herte.
> "He sette down mighty men fro secte, and enhaunside meke men.   He hath fulfilled hungry men with goodis, and he has left rich men void."

The master influence in literature during the Fourteenth Century is of course Chaucer, and though his prose work is small in quantity, it is, like that of all our other great poets, remarkable in its own way.   Let us take, therefore, a single example in a short passage from *The Persones Tale*, which ingenious piece of moralising, though probably a free translation from some Latin religious treatise, has yet enough of Chaucer's native quality to make this a warrantable quotation :—

> "Owre swete Lord God of heven, that no man wil perische, but wol that we comen alle to the knowleche of him, and to the blisful life that is perdurable, ammonestith us by the prophet Jeremye, that saith in this wise :—Stondeth upon thi weyes, and seeth and axeth of olde pathes, that is to sayn, of old sentence, which is the good way, and walketh in that way, and ye schul fynde refresshyng for youre soules."

Over and above the Chaucerian grace, which in this passage makes what is really the opening of a long sermon like the breath of a spring wind, there is in the *Persones Tale* an easy power of utterance which is notable at his time.   For, as Mr. George Saintsbury has pointed out in the Introduction to his recent *Anthology of English Prose*, it was not until the Elizabethan era that anything like an adequate art of prose-writing was attained.

In Sir Thomas Malory—to whom we must leap now, the literary path being more familiarly known after Chaucer —the want of the more perfect art is not felt so much, the same demand not arising in narrative prose.   At the same time one cannot read far in the *Morte D' Arthur* without feeling the inadequacy of the modes of expression; awkward confusions and repetitions abound. Happily Malory does not attempt anything in the way of rhetorical demonstrations; he is so simple and natural that the faults themselves have often a certain archaic effect, not unpleasing. The virtues of his style are on the other hand unique in their way, and despite their French derivation in part, merit a better tribute than critics have as a rule paid to them; in one popular and generally admirable account of English literature, indeed, he is scarcely so much as named. Remembering that the *Morte D' Arthur* was largely a translation and a collect from foreign sources, after all deductions are made, there is much with which Malory must be credited that is of the highest importance in prose. He had the literary instinct and genius without a doubt. It is partly for this very reason of its foreign derivation, moreover, that his work is so significant. In no sense of the word absolutely original, translated from sources in probably three different tongues, medley of history and myth, tradition and true report, as it is; the book is eminently typical of English prose generally, with its foreign foster-parentage and its constant foreign modification. The French influence is of course especially dominant in the book, in detail as well as in general treatment. The very idiom of the quaint old romances that Malory drew upon is copied and repeated, often indeed with charming effect. Some of the passages one could not imagine altered in any way so as to be improved. Here, for instance, is one touched with the simplest pathos, describing King Arthur's sorrowful reproach to the Knights on their leaving the court at Camelot on the Quest of the Holy Grail :—

> "And therewith the tears fell into his eyes, and he said, 'Sir Gawaine, Sir Gawaine, ye have set me in great sorrow, for I have great doubt that my true fellowship shall never meet more here again.' 'Ah,' said Sir Launcelot, 'comfort yourself, for it shall be unto us as a great honour, and much more than if we died in other places, for of death we be sure.'"

Such passages abound, but as we have to return to the book later it is best perhaps to resist the temptation to go on quoting now. Of course we do not look to it for many qualities which perfect prose must have, but in its own way, succeeding simply and naturally in that way, the *Morte D' Arthur* is admirable. In the history of prose it is most valuable indeed, as showing the attainment of a taking manner of tale-telling, which has greatly influenced later romancists, not to mention the poets who have been captivated by it.

We are upon more familiar ground in the Fifteenth Century, and it is unnecessary in journeying on to note more than the chief landmarks by the way. Remembering the leading names accordingly, and associating them with all that they suggest, we need only stop at Sir Thomas More before advancing to Tyndale and the red-letter event which is his in English literature. More was really a man of genius, of true literary love and enthusiasm, as interesting in his writings as in his life, and in many ways he links suggestively the Fifteenth and Sixteenth Centuries. Holbein's picture of the circle in the famous house at Chelsea which gives one more association to that renowned old village-suburb by the Thames, carries the imagination actively into the haunted past of More's brilliant and tragic career; and the literary product of that career has no common interest for us. More's style is notable in that it was the style of a writer who wrote first of all and of choice in Latin, turning to English for the sake of reaching the wider audience. His English prose is nervous and wonderfully capable, considering the period at which he wrote. We give a passage describing the character of Richard III., from his history of Edward V. and Richard's usurpation. It will be remembered that Shakespeare followed in his play of "Richard III." More's account :—

> "With large gifts he gat him unsteadfast friendship, for which he was fain to pil and spoil in other places and get him steadfast hatred. He was close and secret; a deep dissimuler, lowly of countenance, arrogant of heart: outwardly coumpinable where he inwardly hated, not letting to kiss whom he thought to kill; dispitious and cruel, not for evil will alway, but oftener for ambition, and either for the surety and increase of his estate."

This will suffice. More's *Utopia* was of course written in Latin, and therefore does not bear directly on English prose. In Tyndale we reach now an important landmark. Tyndale was an ardent believer in the English language and its future, and his "*Translation of the New Testament, 1525, fixed,*" says Mr. Stopford Brooke, "our standard English once for all, and brought it finally into every English home." His version of the Bible throughout, eked out as it was in part from Coverdale's translation, is very much the same as we have in universal use now. "It was this Bible," continues Mr. Brooke, "which, revised by Coverdale, and edited and re-edited as *Cromwell's Bible*, 1539, and again as *Cranmer's Bible*, 1540, was set up in every parish church in England. It got north into Scotland, and made the Lowland English more like the London English. It passed over to the Protestant settlements in Ireland. After its revisal in 1611, it went with the Puritan Fathers to New England, and fixed the standard of English in America. Eighty millions of people now speak the English of Tyndale's Bible, and there is no book which has had so great an influence on the style of English Literature and the standard of English Prose."* In certain orders of prose indeed there is nothing to equal the superb fitness of words and the natural music of some passages in the Old and New Testaments. Turn to almost any of the Books of the Old Testament, to the Gospels and Epistles, and there is truly a wealth of strength and sweetness of utterance that can never fail to splendidly stimulate and refresh our literary processes. For all to whom the virtue of words well used is inestimable, for all who find a mental thrill in the fitness of a great passage, what stimulus, what unspeakable refreshment there is in these fluid, rhythmic sentences. We can open almost anywhere. Here is a passage from *Ecclesiastes*, noble in its thought, hauntingly musical in its expression, and it is but one amid a hundred others :—

"Also when they shall be afraid of that which is high, and fears shall be in the way, and the almond tree shall flourish, and the grasshopper shall be a burden, and desire shall fail : because

* *Eng. Lit. Primer*, p. 59.

man goeth to his long home, and the mourners go about the
streets : or ever the silver cord be loosed, or the golden bowl be
broken, or the pitcher be broken at the fountain, or the wheel
broken at the cistern.   Then shall the dust return to the earth as
it was : and the spirit shall return unto God who gave it."

Turn but a page, and in the *Canticles* we light upon a
passage which has been chosen by such a purist in prose
style as Mr. George Saintsbury, as a perfect example of
prose-rhythm, and which therefore we may admire without
critical misgiving :—

"Set me as a seal upon thine heart, as a seal upon thine arm :
for love is strong as death ; jealousy is cruel as the grave : the
coals thereof are coals of fire, which hath a most vehement flame.
Many waters cannot quench love, neither can the floods drown it :
if a man would give all the substance of his house for love it would
utterly be contemned."

It would be gratuitous to quote further from sources so
returned to,—returned to, indeed, until there is a danger
of the noblest storehouse of English prose becoming so
ordinary a resort as to lose the full influence of its supreme
virtue.   One cannot well lay too much stress on the
unceasing influence the Bible has had upon the language,
unconsciously influencing as it has been, constantly for the
last three hundred years, the everyday ways and means of
expression.

Following the conflicting impulses of the New Learning,
as it has been called,—the recovery, that is, of the immense
literary stimulus of Greek culture, in the Fifteenth Century, and of the Reformation, whose expression is, on its
best side, the Translation of the Bible, and the English
Prayer Book, 1549-52—the throng of great writers makes it
impossible to do more than outline the general line of
advance, and state one or two of the foremost names.
We are on the verge of the Elizabethan era, where the
store of riches is so embarrassing that one might go on
quoting for page after page endlessly, in the vain attempt
to analyse and compare the hundred varying influences.
But the quality and the characteristics of Elizabethan prose
are very much those on the whole of Elizabethan verse,

which every one has, or pretends to have, an understanding
of.   The same tremendous impulse, the same heat and
power, the same intense fusion of thought in passionate
words: these we have in the prose too.   Its virtue was
its energy and imaginative movement ; its lack was a
lack of that intelligent ease which, while preserving the
dignity and earnestness of subject, is able to pass in
turn to all sides of the question.   So we have an eloquence
and an abounding energy which are astonishing ; but we
have not the variety and grace of transition that the
prose equal to the whole range of expression must possess.
Some passages in the Elizabethan prose are as great as,
or greater than, any that have since been written, with
as fine a sense of proportion, as perfect a balance of
the sentence ; but the art is not sustained, is not capable
of a continued, lengthy flight of perfect utterance.   Remembering this, we can choose noble passages in abundance.
Passing by Latimer, who has much that is very tempting,
here is one from Sir Walter Raleigh, the ending of his
History of the World, of which Taine, in his *English Literature*, says :—"The courtier Raleigh, whilst writing of the
fall of empires, and how the barbarous nations had destroyed
this grand and magnificent Roman Empire, ended his book
with the ideas and tone of a Bossuet" :—

> "O eloquent, just, and mightie Death ! whom none could
> advise, thou hast persuaded ; what none hath dared, thou hast
> done ; and whom all the world hath flattered, thou only hast cast
> out of the world and despised : thou hast drawn together all the
> far stretched greatness, all the pride, cruelty, and ambition of
> man, and covered it all over with these two narrow words, *Hic
> jacet.*"

Many others nearly contemporary with Raleigh we must
pass over, but some note must be made on John Lyly,
whose *Euphues* set a fashion in prose, as in the society talk
of the time, which was cleverly caricatured by Shakespeare
in the conceits of Armado in *Love's Labour's Lost.*
Elizabeth herself encouraged the affectation, and for a time it
was all the fashion in court,—a fashion whose influence
may be estimated from such phrases of word-play as "If

she had no sight in descant, desire her to chant it." Lyly's *Euphues*, however, proves a certain artistic devotion to the methods of style which tended greatly to the perfecting of our prose. A tendency to-day, occasionally remarked upon, to a sort of Euphuism in prose and verse gives Lyly an added interest for us moreover. In Sir Philip Sidney we have another of those who have fascinated the popular mind and a much greater writer, who is notable as showing the development of prose in the advance from his Euphuistic *Arcadia* to the noble *Apologie for Poetrie*, from which let us quote this delightful plea for " our Poet the Monarch " .—

> "He beginneth not with obscure definitions, which must blur the margent with interpretations, and load the memory with doubtfulness: but he cometh to you with words sent in delightful proportion, either accompanied with, or prepared for the well inchaunting skill of Musicke; and with a tale forsooth he cometh unto you, with a tale which holdeth children from play, and old men from the chimney corner."

We find the same poetic impulse underlying the Elizabethan prose without. Turn later to Bacon even: his method in the Essays is one of poetic illustration rather than of abstract analysis. As an example of the concrete symbolism with which he expounded his subject there, take this sentence:—

> "Libraries are as the shrines where all the relics of the ancient saints, full of true virtue, and that without delusion or imposture, are preserved and reposed."

The well-known charm of Bacon's *Essays*, in their fulness and fine wisdom, influencing so much all later essayists, and the greatness in matter and form of his *Advancement of Learning*, we can only so far refer to here. And if before Bacon there are many writers whom we must unwillingly pass over, after him how many more? Burton's *Anatomy of Melancholy;* Sir Thomas Browne's *Religio Medici;* Fuller, " quaint and delightful," from whom one wishes to quote if only for his influence on Charles Lamb; Lord Herbert; Clarendon; Jeremy Taylor, whose works, " especially literary, weighty with argument," says

Mr. Stopford Brooke, "are even more read for their sweet and deep devotion, for their rapid, impassioned, and convoluted eloquence." Here is a wealth of choice indeed. One writer, less important in many ways than some we have just mentioned, requires a special note because of his bearing on nature-study in our literature. This is Izaak Walton, whose *Complete Angler* has become the typical book of the citizen's escape to the country, in its simple out-of-door pleasantness and unaffected love of Nature. And this serves to remind us how the love of Nature has affected English literature throughout, how from the first the breath of spring, the welcome gleam of the sun, the shade of trees, the coming of storm, the green pastures and still waters of England have moved those who have interpreted life for us. The feeling for Nature, indeed, has been a dominant influence in our literature throughout, and in its increasing sympathy and truth of description, as shown in White's *Selborne* and in the modern books of nature that derive from White and Walton, throws influence in letters, and in its increasing sympathy and truth of description, throws important light on the development of our prose and verse expression of life generally.

Before turning to Milton, who, following the Elizabethans proper, has much of their characteristic quality and defect in his prose, we must not in our literary quest forget the life-influences of the period in which he had his being. We have traversed so hastily the ground between the date of Tyndale's *Translation of the Bible* and Milton, noticing merely the greater landmarks, that we have overlooked somewhat the signs of human struggle by the way. For conceive the tremendous march of history in this time! Think of the Reformation, the spiritual stimulus to men who up till then had been mainly animal in life; the quickening of the general heart of man, and with the heart, the head! No wonder that the leaders of the time forged new intellectual weapons, and in the violent energies of religion made words newly responsive to and provocative of Thought. Latinists as these writers and preachers were, their sympathies moved always necessarily towards the people; and thus they paved the way to a better adapting of the modes of utterance to the real needs of the human spirit. A wider escape followed the purely theological one. We have but to turn to such a book as Green's *Short History of the English People*, and read the headings of the sections into which his chapter on the Reformation is divided, to feel at once what a time it was for the people. THE PROTESTANTS; THE MARTYRS; ELIZABETH; MARY STUART; THE ARMADA; THE ELIZABETHAN POETS: what a spectacle this connotes! What a drama for the eyes of the multitude, stirring men to apprehend life vividly anew. What an unspeakable widening of the imagination of the people! And then the Puritan epoch, with its moral effort, with its noble spiritual devotion, and its ignoble spiritual selfishness, tragically leading up to the royal scaffold at Whitehall. A drama indeed,—of vast movement!

The grand expression of the heart of this period is of course Shakespeare. The Elizabethan Drama reflects it marvellously, in all its colour and form, in its vast adventure and discovery, in all its exuberance and thriftless splendour. No one can indeed at all understand English prose who does not know intimately the dramatic outcome of this time. All that feeling the way to touch and quicken the human spirit through an art which in any degree made use of words is of the highest importance in the literary advance into Nature and Thought. To all this human comedy and tragedy succeeds well the trumpet challenge and appeal of Milton, behind which one feels an heroic majesty of presence, but not the sweet humanity of the Boar's Head Tavern and the Forest of Arden. The dramatic modes of utterance at this time were necessarily rhythmic beyond the reach of prose, and one feels on turning to Milton that the bearing of verse upon prose was for him imperfectly adjusted. How far his Puritan environment and temper affected this, remembering how great was his artistic sense, we cannot actually determine. But we take Milton as type of the period, and we feel that there is still a great advance to be made in the capable use of words for the hundred purposes of life. Milton's prose is indeed magnificent at its best, great, august; but it is disproportionate, incontinent, without the adequate ease and variety of utterance which the perfect prose-writer must possess. Take that familiar passage from the *Areopagitica*, beginning " Lords and Commons of England ! " What a roll of music; the organ tones are unmistakably there. But read on, and you feel that he is obliged to keep up the *fortissimo* of expression; he has not that grace of transition that it was left to lesser men to discover. But Milton's grandeur and sonorous eloquence have an influence greater than we can estimate. There is something that greatly haunts the ear and the mind in his majestic paragraphs—

> " Lords and Commons of England ! consider what nation it is whereof ye are, and whereof ye are the governors ; a nation not slow and dull, but of a quick, ingenious, and piercing spirit ; acute to invent, subtile and sinewy to discourse, not beneath the reach of any point the human capacity can soar to. . . . "

Enough ; there is no need to complete the passage. One hears the music go rolling on, and realises what power the musician has. The lesser writer who was to bring ease and variety to complete the art of prose was not far behind. Dryden was over forty at Milton's death in 1674 ; it was Dryden who brought balance and sense of form to chasten the Titanic vehemence of Milton's method. Taine, who is peculiarly qualified to deal with a writer like Dryden, says of him :—" He naturally attains a definite prose style ; his ideas are unfolded with breadth and clearness ; his style is well moulded, exact and simple, free from the affectations and the ornaments with which Pope afterwards burdened his own ; his expression is, like that of Corneille, ample and periodic, by virtue simply of the internal argument which unfolds and sustains it." Of course, to judge of the qualities of his prose, and the varied adequacy of his method, one must read him in full, but a sentence or two will show his natural ease of expression :—

"Thoughts, such as they are, come crowding in so fast upon me, that my only difficulty is to choose or to reject, to run them into verses, or to give them the other harmony of prose. I have so long studied and practised both, that they are grown into a habit, and become familiar to me."

After Dryden there is no need to go on particularising. The literary production that follows we are all well familiar with. It is enough to remember generally the influence of the master prose-writers of Pope's time,—Swift, Defoe, Steele, Addison, Berkeley, great respectively in political and social satire, in fiction, in the essay, and in philosophy. Defoe, over and above his immortal distinction as the author of *Robinson Crusoe*, is remarkable as the first pronounced type of journalist. "His *Review*, published twice a-week for a year, was wholly written by himself; but he founded, conducted, and wrote for a host of other newspapers, and filled them with every subject of the day." It is a hundred and fifty years and more now since Defoe was born, and we look back with curious interest to his initiative in journalism, wondering how far it was due to this that his simple appeal as a story-teller to the people was so marvellously successful. Steele and Addison it would be almost an impertinence to comment upon at length, but too much stress can hardly be laid upon the supreme excellence of their style, and their inestimable influence upon the popular mind. Never, indeed, was more clearly shown the great virtue of a real response in letters to life. We find printed in the *Spectator*, indeed, "the whole age of Queen Anne—the political and literary disputes, the fine gentlemen and ladies, the characters of men, the humours of society, the new book, the new play; we live in the very streets and drawing-rooms of Old London." Here again is a large fund of journalistic suggestion, and those who wish to reconcile journalism with literary excellence cannot find a better example than the *Spectator*.

Mr. George Saintsbury, in his recent anthology of the English prose-writers, has pointed out that the Eighteenth Century was reactionary to some extent, against the plain directness and vernacular energy of the writers from Dryden

to Swift. The Latinist influence in its more ponderous
forms was recalled by Dr. Johnson and Gibbon. But at
the same time the popular sense of Fielding and his fellows
in the novel, and the development as a popular literary
influence of the newspaper, acted as an alterative to these
powerful academic draughts. Oliver Goldsmith, with his
exquisite sympathy, and his natural writing, is a very
salutary influence by the side of Johnson's laborious intel-
lectuality. Set Goldsmith on the one side, with his
simplicity and tenderness and idyllic imagination, and
Gibbon, with his historical magnificence and creative
power, on the other, and you have in these the extreme
literary types on either hand of the period. The spirit of
this time is preserved with extraordinary vividness in
Boswell's *Life of Johnson,* a book which will be read
perhaps after the last of Johnson's own writings, and which
artlessly sets a perfect example in the art of biography.
On the whole there can be no doubt of the great advance
in strength and variety in the use of prose during the
Eighteenth Century,—an advance more definitely marked
than that perhaps of our own. If, however, it is true, as
Mr Saintsbury has told us, that the formative period of
English prose ended then, the student who does not possess
any final and exact theory of prose-style will be liable to
imagine that he still sees signs of development in plenty.
He reads Charles Lamb, and De Quincey, and Landor, and
many later writers—not finding everything they do original,
but feeling that there is in them at any rate an immense
further increase in the range and scope of prose.

To take only one of these, Charles Lamb, he alone has
had remarkable effect upon the writing of the present day,
to the end of a capable ease of expression, rising to dignity,
lightly touched with humour, admirably varied in its wit
and wisdom. Deriving as he does from Elizabethan sources
largely, from such choice old spirits as Fuller, he has a
modern touch quite his own, and his sweetness and coy,
kindly wit must have greatly helped to give human quality
to the right British narrowness and arrogance that have so
threatened us, before and after that good old typical

thunderer, Dr. Johnson. Turning from Elia to the utterly different production of Sir Walter Scott again, and considering his immeasurable influence upon the processes of the novel, which forms the most remarkable literary force of our time, we may well feel that the future of English prose must be vast. And with De Quincey and Carlyle and Macaulay—not to speak of such later writers as Mr. Ruskin and Cardinal Newman—powerfully bearing upon literary methods, we may well look sanguinely forward. Not accepting all or any of these as immaculate, discriminating always in our liking for what is best in them, and taking for ensample only what is best, we feel that they mark among them a great advance, and that, apart from the mannerism and slovenliness of many contemporary writers, this advance bids fair to be nobly maintained and improved upon.

It is only a very superficial view that we have been able to take, necessarily, of the growth of English prose. But such as it is, it will help us to relate the present to the past, and the many parts to the great whole of literature. We have seen at any rate how the order of the language has been evoked out of a chaos of diverse elements—how it has grown, struggling always with foreign invasion, losing and gaining in turn, but always gaining in the end. This struggle contributed incalculably, we feel, to the quality and energy of the language; and though it can never have quite the same struggle to go through again, we see how in Carlyle an importation of German, and in more recent writers of French idiom, is having great effect in subtle ways upon power and freedom of expression. With every age, no doubt, new influences will produce new qualities; the strong point of our English tongue is in fact its readiness to assimilate the best from every side. And there are still, one feels, noble qualities to be attained by indefatigable quest in the old empires and the old languages of the world. A little must be taken from every language, to fit for its great future this language of ours, which seems potentially the universal one.

We have in the foregoing sketch of our prose-writers kept

too much to the merely literary standpoint, neglecting rather the active social significance of the different periods. But it will fall to those who take special charge of the several authors in the edition called Camelot to show the full import its volumes have for us. Here it chiefly remains to apply in a general way the gathered suggestion of the past to the contemporary popular need of books, and so to relate it to the present scheme. Lightly as we have gone over the field, it is clear that there are many books of surpassing interest which are hidden away from the everyday reader, but which, by being brought again to light by sympathetic hands, having the right word spoken to put them in touch with the time, can hardly fail to gain new popular vogue. The same holds with many foreign authors, old and new, whom translation would bring familiarly home to us all. By combining these less-known books with others which are already popularly accepted, but which some suggestive word of introduction, showing clearly their contemporary bearing, would do much haply to make more potent in our midst, it may be that we shall be able to help a little in making the higher literature really responsive to everyday life and its needs. As if from the viewless walls of antique Camelot, we call the voices which can affect our lives so greatly to ends of wisdom and happiness.

This first voice, this romance of King Arthur and his Knights, may fairly serve as a test for those to follow. For although the *Morte D' Arthur* has had a certain vogue in time past, it has been found rather diffuse and incoherent as a rule, perhaps, by the modern reader who has turned to it. The present version therefore, revised and divided so as to give it greater coherency and make the leading lines of the romance clearer, may well serve as a test of the acceptance of old books in a new guise. We have dwelt incidentally already on the place of Sir Thomas Malory among our prose-writers, but we must consider the *Morte D' Arthur* apart from pure literature merely if we wish to get at its full significance. The book's history is so remarkable as to seem itself like a romance. The curious parallels in some of its leading incidents with the ancient myths of the Eastern world suggest its genesis in the minds of the remote forefathers of the Welsh who invaded Britain centuries back. Dating back in an indistinguishable degree as far as the Sanskrit *Mahabharata* and other remote records, the story of King Arthur, the Prince who, fatefully environed, sinned his way as it were into heroism and kingdom, won shame and highest honour, and became the romance-type in his weakness and strength of all humanity, has never ceased to fascinate the story-tellers and the people. Its trace is continual in other languages, but especially in our own its history is interwoven, appearing and reappearing, as it does, in a hundred guises, altered in art-form as the literary custom of the day demanded, so that it serves in fact as a sort of touchstone of the different periods. In each version it was modified and added to, and the letter in especial violently revised; but in spite of a hundred re-shapings, the spirit of the book remains virtually the same. The first advent of the story in Britain was probably in the shape of a Welsh bardic epic, sung to a primitive harp in the castle halls and on the battle-fields of old Wales; its first literary appearance was in Geoffrey of Monmouth's romance-history in Latin prose, completed in 1147. These legends of Geoffrey's were translated into French verse, and, coloured and graced by the art of the Norman trouveurs, found their way back again to form one of the great cycles of romance in vogue in the Thirteenth Century. It was then that Walter Map too invented and added, with the insight of true genius, the story of the *Quest of the Grail*. Thus spiritualised, it again passed into France, and was further touched and adorned with French poetry, being told and re-told with all the imaginative feeling of which the French romancists of the day were capable. From these French versions it was that Sir Thomas Malory collated his *Morte D' Arthur*. Since Caxton first issued Malory's English transcript, we know how the book has enthralled the popular heart. Milton, we know, hesitated for long whether he should not make it his life work, instead of the *Paradise Lost*. Its spirit lives in Spenser's *Faery Queen*. Even the

Eighteenth Century felt its fascination, and attempted to adapt it to itself, with what unsuccess need hardly be said. The Nineteenth has been more successful, and it is indeed remarkable how the Arthurian and allied romances have affected modern art of all kinds, not only in England, but elsewhere. Tennyson's *Idylls of the King* naturally occur first to us, and in these poems, nobly perfect in themselves, we see at once an ominous sign of the times in that what has been called our English prose epic should lose its high epic proportion, and its fateful coherency, in the daintier loveliness of an idyllic presentment. Poets of later schools have drawn largely too upon these chivalric romances. Matthew Arnold, William Morris, A. C. Swinburne, and others have touched on one or another of them, and their mediæval romance-spirit has influenced painting still more, as the work of Rossetti, Burne-Jones, G. F. Watts, Millais, and others bears splendid witness. In music and the lyric drama, Wagner stands eminently forward as its exponent. The great trilogy of *Lohengrin, Tristan and Isolde*, and *Parsifal* form indeed by far the most illustrious commentary on the spiritually drawn chivalry of the *Holy Grail* and the mystic walls of Monsalvat that has appeared since the first inception of the legends. All this reflection in modern art is most suggestive. It shows in these times of realism, healthy and morbid, how the artistic spirit inevitably repairs to the Ideal, and tries in this case to solve the problems of Nineteenth Century life by a reference to the romance problems of timeless Camelot.

The book is a romance rather than a history, we have said, but to most of us this is no reproach. Some historians have indeed doubted altogether the existence of King Arthur, but such a doubt to your true reader will always be blasphemous. There may be a want of direct evidence concerning him, but if any distrust the history let them take the book and go to Queen-Camel in Somersetshire, where the legends of the ancient Camelot still remain; or to Carlisle, or Caerleon-upon-Usk, or Bamborough, supposed to be Sir Launcelot's famous castle of Joyous Gard, or best of all, perhaps, to the haunted land of Merlin in South

Wales. There, in the spirit of old romance, go to Merlin's Hill—Mynydd Merlin—where the great prince of magicians is supposed to lie buried, and then striking off from the green pastoral vale of Towey, climb the steep to Cerrig Cennen Castle, within whose lonely walls that were a hopeless sceptic who dared to doubt that King Arthur or some of his knights had listened there to the mysterious tones of Merlin, or the wailing music of minstrel's harp or autumn wind. Cerrig Cennen, with many other spots where the old-time sentiment still lingers, is indeed better than any commentary the libraries can offer on the *Morte D' Arthur*. With its wild surroundings, the Black Mountains, where flows out of the rock the haunted river Loughor, and the mystic tarns, the Llyn yy Fan, lie hid, the castle on its wild steep is eloquent of romance and chivalrous emprise, and it is easy, as the cloud shadows go sweeping by, to imagine the knights of old galloping with hot speed along the mountain sides below.

If the exact letter of the book be doubted, its spirit is happily secure in our hearts for ever. The biography of the material King Arthur will never be catalogued possibly, but the ideal Arthur lives and reigns securely beyond time and space, in that kingdom of old•romance of which Camelot is the capital. In Malory's account he is not immaculate ; he errs and sins and suffers, is defeated and shamed often, and for that reason appeals more closely to the human heart. And so with all his knights, except Sir Galahad, whose honour was without reproach or stain. It is the flower of chivalry which King Arthur typifies, grown in the garden of romance, full of poetic and spiritual symbolism, which charms us to-day, a flower of incomparable setting. The beauty of this setting, so simple, so effective, with all its crudity, is really beyond analysis. How, for instance, this presentment of Merlin in one of his many disguises, pictures him as he came one wild February day to King Arthur at the Castle of Bedegraine, in the forest of Sherwood :—

"And Merlin was so disguised that King Arthur knew him not, for he was all furred in black sheepskins, and a great pair of boots,

> with a bow and arrows, in a russet gown, and brought wild geese in
> his hand, and it was on the morrow after Candlemas Day, but
> King Arthur knew him not."

There is wonderful picturesqueness and colour in Malory's descriptions, and the feeling for the environment of the untiring action of the book is of the highest order of romance. What could be more effective than the episode of the Brachet and the White Hart in the Book of Queen Guenever, or of the Fair Maid of Astolat, so exquisitely reset by Tennyson, or of the Vision of Sir Launcelot in the book we have named after him? The account of Sir Launcelot's death in the last chapters of the last book is full of sorrowful beauty, and contains too the most remarkable prose passage in the *Morte D' Arthur*, that eloquent moral appeal beginning—"Oh, ye mighty and pompous lords!" There is an heroic elevatedness about the last book— the Book of the Morte D' Arthur—throughout, that specially marks it. Malory's practice in the earlier books seemed to have taught him a greater mastery of the means at his command. But in truth, wherever we turn, memorable passages occur tempting us to quote. Here, almost at random, is one from the Book of Balin le Savage, touched with most pathetic grace,—a passage once heard never to be forgotten :—

> "Then he looked by him, and was ware of a damsel that came
> riding as fast as her horse might gallop upon a fair palfrey. And
> when she espied that Sir Launceor was slain, then she made
> sorrow out of measure, and said "O Balin! two bodies hast thou
> slain and one heart, and two hearts in one body, and two souls
> thou hast lost." And therewith she took the sword from her
> love that lay dead, and as she took it she fell to the ground in a
> swoon."

Out of that swoon the damsel only comes to kill herself with her lover's sword, and her fatal fidelity is characteristic of the tragic consistency of the *Morte D' Arthur* episodes throughout.

The whole story of the Quest of the Holy Grail, again, is full of beauty, with its spiritual significance and mysticism woven most imaginatively into the main woof of the book. Walter

Map, when he added this, giving coherency to the diffuse insertion of the various romances, showed true poetic perception. Before it was a mere testament of chivalry,—a chivalry of animal heat and energy; but now upon the knights fell the strange allurement of the Holy Ghost, and following its mystic impulse, they set forth on their new quest with passionate heroism and devotion. Sir Galahad naturally recurs in Tennyson's haunting rhymes as we think of the Sancgreal, which the poet has elsewhere touched on suggestively in his *Idylls:—*

> " Sometimes on lonely mountain meres
>   I find a magic bark :
>   I leap on board ; no helmsman steers,
>   I float till all is dark.
>   A gentle sound, an awful light !
>   Three angels bear the Holy Grail ;
>   With folded-feet, in stoles of white,
>   On sleeping wings they sail !
>   Ah, blessed vision ! blood of God !
>   My spirit beats her mortal bars,
>   As down dark tides the glory glides,
>   And star-like mingles with the stars."

Altogether the romance may be trusted to charm us to-day as it charmed its readers in Caxton's first edition. Its spirit of adventure, the spiritualised reflex of an age of animal energy, is a salutary one to move in our too reflective, critical modern order of literature. There is nothing of the latter-day morbid sentimentalism in it; throughout it is as fresh and breezy as the first west wind of spring. As a romance it is mainly significant; it bears especially upon the processes of tale-telling, and touches the root of the vexed question of romance and realism which is so exercising the present writers of fiction. From a purely literary point of view, it is in this respect that it chiefly commands attention; there is a potent fund of suggestion for the tale-teller in its simple methods and effects. Idealistic and realistic presentment; place and folk interest; dramatic movement: there is curious lore to be learnt in these things from the book.

As collated by Malory, the epic interest of the *Morte D'Arthur* was not kept very strictly in mind, and a certain diffuseness and repetition resulted which have done much to deter the general reader from it. Malory's *Book* really resolves itself into three great divisions: first, the history of King Arthur proper; second, the romances of Sir Launcelot and Sir Tristram de Lyoness, which, chronicling the feats of arms of these two, the most famous of all the knights, become really the story of the long duel in knighthood and chivalry betwixt them; and third, the Quest of the Grail. In the present version it has been thought well to omit the second of these two divisions, which it is·proposed to afterwards issue as a volume by itself, complementary to this of King Arthur and the Quest of the Grail. By this alteration the fateful epic consistency of the book is, it is believed, enhanced, and the tragic movement of the story on through the mysteries of the Holy Grail to the death of Arthur by the hands of Mordred is thrown into clearer outline. What other alterations it has been thought wise to make are explained in the notes at the end of the book, in which will be found, too, other information throwing light upon the present edition.

It is with the idea of making this romance of the age of chivalry more easily available to the modern reader that the present edition has been prepared; and as this book in *Romance*, so it is desired that the volumes of the series named after it shall throughout be representative of the leading sections of prose literature. The idea is not so much to give exact texts for students—there is already admirable provision for this—but to supply books which will meet the larger human need, and thus continue the great work that Caxton began four centuries ago. In their editing and preparation, therefore, which will be entrusted to writers who bring sympathy and enthusiasm as well as intelligence to the work, that only will be said and done which is necessary to make their appeal to the reader contemporary and modernly suggestive for the everyday life. Books for street and field it is hoped to make them, —books which may serve as comrades in the world, speaking greatly for truth and beauty and a natural life, and showing in all the celestial meaning. Not so much for the sake of letters as for the sake of life, then, let us read in their pages, in the spirit of these words of Caxton in the Prologue to the *Morte D' Arthur*, which may be applied in one way or another to the volumes called Camelot throughout :—" For herein may be seen noble chivalry, courtesy, humanity, friendliness, hardiness, love, friendship, cowardice, murder, hate, virtue, and sin. Do after the good and leave the evil, and it shall bring you to good fame and renown. And for to pass the time this book shall be pleasant to read in, but for to give faith and belief that all is true that is contained herein, ye be at your liberty."

EDITOR.

CAXTON'S PROLOGUE.

AFTER that I had accomplished and finished divers histories, as well of contemplation as of other historial and worldly acts of great conquerors and princes, and also of certain books of ensamples and doctrine, many noble and divers gentlemen of this realm of England, came and demanded me, many and ofttimes, why that I did not cause to be imprinted the noble history of the Sancgreal, and of the most renowned Christian king, first and chief of the three best Christian and worthy, King Arthur, which ought most to be remembered among us Englishmen, before all other Christian kings; for it is notoriously known, through the universal world, that there be nine worthy and the best that ever were, that is, to wit, three Paynims, three Jews, and three Christian men. As for the Paynims, they were before the Incarnation of Christ, which were named, the first, Hector of Troy, of whom the history is common, both in ballad and in prose; the second, Alexander the Great; and the third, Julius Cæsar, Emperor of Rome, of which the histories be well known and had. And as for the three Jews, which also were before the Incarnation of our Lord, of whom the first was Duke Joshua, which brought the children of Israel into the land of behest; the second was David, King of Jerusalem; and

the third Judas Maccabeus. Of these three, the Bible
rehearseth all their noble histories and acts. And, since
the said Incarnation, have been three noble Christian men,
stalled and admitted through the universal world, into the
number of the nine best and worthy: of whom was first,
the noble Arthur, whose noble acts I purpose to write in
this present book here following; the second was Charle-
magne, or Charles the Great, of whom the history is had in
many places, both in French and in English; and the third,
and last, was Godfrey of Boulogne, of whose acts and life
I made a book unto the excellent prince and king, of noble
memory, King Edward the Fourth.

The said noble gentlemen instantly required me for to
imprint the history of the said noble king and conqueror,
King Arthur, and of his knights, with the history of the
Sancgreal, and of the death and ending of the said
Arthur, affirming that I ought rather to imprint his acts
and noble feats, than of Godfrey of Boulogne, or any of
the other eight, considering that he was a man born within
this realm, and king and emperor of the same; and that
there be in French divers and many noble volumes of his
acts, and also of his knights. To whom I have answered,
that divers men hold opinion that there was no such Arthur,
and that all such books as be made of him be but feigned
and fables, because that some chronicles make of him no
mention, nor remember him nothing, nor of his knights.
Whereto they answered, and one in especial said, that in
him that should say or think that there was never such a
king called Arthur, might well be aretted great folly and
blindness; for he said there were many evidences to the
contrary. First ye may see his sepulchre in the monastery of
Glastonbury. And also in Policronicon, in the fifth book,
the sixth chapter, and in the seventh book, the twenty-third
chapter, where his body was buried, and after found, and
translated into the said monastery. Ye shall see also in the
History of Bochas, in his book *De Casu Principum,* part
of his noble acts, and also of his fall. Also Galfridus,
in his British book, recounteth his life. And in divers
places of England, many remembrances be yet of him, and

shall remain perpetually of him, and also of his knights. First, in the Abbey of Westminster, at St. Edward's shrine, remaineth the print of his seal in red wax closed in beryl, in which is written — "Patricius Arthurus Britanniæ, Galliæ, Germaniæ, Daciæ Imperator." Item in the castle of Dover ye may see Sir Gawaine's skull, and Cradok's mantle : at Winchester, the Round Table : in other places Sir Launcelot's sword, and many other things. Then all these things considered, there can no man reasonably gainsay but that there was a king of this land named Arthur ; for in all the places, Christian and heathen, he is reputed and taken for one of the nine worthies, and the first of the three Christian men. And also he is more spoken beyond the sea, and more books made of his noble acts, than there be in England, as well in Dutch, Italian, Spanish, and Greek, as in French. And yet of record, remaineth in witness of him in Wales, in the town of Camelot, the great stones, and the marvellous works of iron lying under the ground, and royal vaults, which divers now living have seen. Wherefore it is a great marvel why that he is no more renowned in his own country, save only it accordeth to the word of God, which saith, that no man is accepted for a prophet in his own country. Then all things aforesaid alleged, I could not well deny but that there was such a noble king named Arthur, and reputed for one of the nine worthies, and first and chief of the Christian men. And many noble volumes be made of him and of his noble knights in French, which I have seen and read beyond the sea, which be not had in our maternal tongue. But in Welsh be many, and also in French, and some in English, but nowhere nigh all. Wherefore, such as have late been drawn out briefly into English, I have, after the simple cunning that God hath sent me, under the favour and correction of all noble lords and gentlemen enprised to imprint a book of the noble histories of the said King Arthur, and of certain of his knights after a copy unto me delivered ; which copy Sir Thomas Malory did take out of certain books of French, and reduced it into English. And I, according to my copy, have down set it in print, to the intent that noble men may see and learn the noble acts of chivalry, the gentle and virtuous deeds that some knights used in those days, by which they came to honour, and how they that were vicious were punished, and oft put to shame and rebuke; humbly beseeching all noble lords and ladies, with all other estates of what state or degree they be of, that shall see and read in this present book and work, that they take the good and honest acts in their remembrance, and follow the same. Wherein they shall find many joyous and pleasant histories, and the noble and renowned acts of humanity, gentleness, and chivalry. For, herein may be seen noble chivalry, courtesy, humanity, friendliness, hardiness, love, friendship, cowardice, murder, hate, virtue, and sin. Do after the good, and leave the evil, and it shall bring you unto good fame and renown. And, for to pass the time, this book shall be pleasant to read in, but for to give faith and belief that all is true that is contained herein, ye be at your own liberty. But all is written for our doctrine, and for to beware that we fall not to vice nor sin, but to exercise and follow virtue, by the which we may come and attain to good fame and renown in this life, and after this short and transitory life to come unto everlasting bliss in heaven; the which He grant us that reigneth in heaven, the blessed Trinity. Amen.

THE HISTORY OF KING ARTHUR

AND THE QUEST OF THE HOLY GRAIL.

THE BOOK OF MERLIN, AND THE COMING OF ARTHUR.

I.

T befel in the days of the noble Utherpendragon, when he was king of England, and so reigned, there was a mighty and a noble duke in Cornwall, that held long time war against him ; and the duke was named the duke of Tintagil. And so by means king Uther sent for this duke, charging him to bring his wife with him, for she was called a right fair lady, and a passing wise, and Igraine was her name. So when the duke and his wife were come to the king, by the means of great lords, they were both accorded, and the king liked and loved this lady well, and made her great cheer, in his desire, out of measure. But she was a passing good woman, and would not assent to the king. And then she told the duke, her husband, and said, " I suppose that we were sent for that I should be dishonoured ; wherefore, husband, I counsel you that we depart from hence suddenly, that we may ride all night to our own castle." And like as she had said, so they departed, that neither the king, nor none of his council, were aware of their departing. As soon as king Uther knew of their departing so suddenly, he was

wonderful wrath ; then he called to him his privy council, and told them of the sudden departing of the duke and his wife. Then they advised the king to send for the duke and his wife, by a great charge : "And, if he will not" said they, "come at your commandment, then may ye do your best, for then have you a cause to make mighty war upon him." So that was done, and the messengers had their answers, and that was this, shortly, "That neither he nor his wife would not come at him." Then was the king wondrous wrath. And then the king sent him plain word again, and bade him be ready, and stuff. him, and garnish him ; for within threescore days he would fetch him out of the strongest castle that he had. When the duke had this warning, anon he went and furnished and garnished two strong castles of his, of the which the one was Tintagil, and that other called Terabil. So his wife, dame Igraine, he put in the castle of Tintagil, and he put himself in the castle of Terabil, the which had many issues and posterns out. Then in all haste came Uther, with a great host, and laid a siege about the castle of Terabil, and there he pitched many pavilions. And there was great war made on both parties, and much people slain : then for pure anger and for great love of fair Igraine, king Uther fell sick. Then came to king Uther Sir Ulfius, a noble knight, and asked the king "Why he was sick?" "I shall tell thee," said the king : "I am sick for anger and for love of fair Igraine, that I may not be whole." "Well, my lord," said Sir Ulfius, "I shall seek Merlin, and he shall get you remedy, that your heart shall be pleased." So Ulfius departed, and by adventure he met Merlin in a beggar's array ; and there Merlin asked Ulfius whom he sought? And he said he had little ado to tell him. "Well," said Merlin, "I know whom thou seekest, for thou seekest Merlin, therefore seek no further, for I am he ; and if king Uther will well reward me, and be sworn to me to fulfil my desire, the which shall be his honour and profit more than mine, I shall cause him to have all his desire." "All this will I undertake," said Ulfius, "that there shall be nothing reasonable, but thou shalt have thy desire." "Well," said Merlin, "he shall have his intent and desire ; and, therefore," said Merlin, "ride on your way, for I will not be long behind."

II.

THEN Ulfius was glad, and rode on more than a pace till that he came unto king Utherpendragon, and told him he had met with Merlin. "Where is he?" said the king. "Sir," said Ulfius, "he will not tarry long." Therewithal Ulfius was aware where Merlin stood at the porch of the pavilion's door; and then Merlin was bound to come to the king. When king Uther saw him, he said that he was welcome. "Sir," said Merlin, "I know all your heart, every deal; so you will be sworn to me, as you be a true king anointed, to fulfil my desire, you shall have your desire." Then the king was sworn upon the four Evangelists. "Sir," said Merlin, "this is my desire: by Igraine you shall get a child, and when it is born it shall be delivered to me for to nourish, as I will have it; for it shall be your worship, and the child's avail as much as the child is worth." "I will well," said the king, "as thou wilt have it." "Now make you ready," said Merlin, "this night shall you be with Igraine in the castle of Tintagil, and you shall be like the duke, her husband; Ulfius shall be like Sir Brastias, a knight of the duke's; and I will be like a knight, called Sir Jordains, a knight of the duke's; but beware you make not many questions with her, nor with her men, but say you are weary, and so hie you to bed, and rise not on the morrow till I come to you; for the castle of Tintagil is but ten miles hence." So, as they had devised, it was done; but the duke of Tintagil espied how the king rode from the siege of Terabil; and, therefore, that night he issued out of the castle, at a postern, for to have distressed the king's host; and so through his own issue the duke himself was slain, or ever the king was at the castle of Tintagil. So after the death of the duke, king Uther came unto Igraine more than three hours after his death. And ere day, Merlin came to the king, and bade him make him ready; and so he kissed the lady Igraine, and departed in all haste. But when the lady heard tell of the duke, her husband, and by all record he was dead or ever king Uther came to her, then she marvelled who that might be that came in likeness of her lord; so she mourned privily, and held her peace. Then all the barons, by one assent, prayed the king of accord between the lady Igraine and him. The king gave them leave, for fain would he have been accorded with her. So the king put all his trust in Ulfius to entreat between them; so by that entreaty, at the last, the king and she met together. "Now will we do well," said Ulfius; "our king is a lusty knight, and wifeless, and my lady Igraine is a passing fair lady; it were great joy unto us all and it might please the king to make her his queen." Unto that they were all well agreed, and moved it to the king. And anon, like a lusty knight, he assented thereto with a good will; and so, in all haste, they were married in a morning with great mirth and joy. And king Lot, of Lothian and Orkney, then wedded Margawse, that was Gawaine's mother; and king Nentres, of the land of Garlot, wedded Elaine. All this was done at the request of king Uther. And the third sister, Morgan le Fay, was put to school, in a nunnery; and there she learned so much, that she was a great clerk of necromancy; and after, she was wedded to king Urience, of the land of Gore, that was Sir Ewaine le Blanchemaine's father.

III.

THEN the queen Igraine drew daily nearer her time when the child Arthur should be born, and it fell, within half a-year, that king Uther asked her by the faith she owed unto him, who was father to her child? Then was she sore abashed to give an answer. "Fear you not," said the king; "but tell me the truth, and I shall love you the better by that faith of my body." "Sir," said she, "I shall tell you the truth. The same night that my lord was dead, that hour of his death, there came unto my castle of Tintagil a man like my lord in speech and countenance, and two knights with him in likeness of his two knights, Brastias and Jordains; and so I received him as I ought to do my lord: and that same night, as I shall answer unto God, the child was begotten." "That is truth," said the king, "as you say, for it was I myself that came in his likeness; and, therefore, fear you not, for I am father to the child." And there he told her all the cause how it was by Merlin's counsel. Then the queen made great joy when she knew who was the father of her child. Soon came Merlin unto the king, and said, "Sir, you must provide you for the nourishing of your child." "As thou wilt," said the king, "be it." "Well," said Merlin, "I know a lord of yours, in this land, that is a passing true man, and faithful, and he shall have the nourishing of your child: his name is Sir Ector, and he is a lord of fair livelihood, in many parts of England and Wales. And this lord, Sir Ector, let him be sent for, for to come and speak with you, and desire him yourself, as he loveth you, that he will put his own child to nourishing to another woman, and that his wife nourish yours; and when the child is born, let it be delivered unto me, at yonder postern, unchristened." As Merlin had devised, so it was done. And when Sir Ector was come, he made affiance to the king for to nourish the child, like as the king desired; and there the king granted Sir Ector great rewards. Then when the queen was delivered, the king commanded two knights and two ladies to take the child, bound in rich cloth of gold, "And deliver him to what poor man you meet at the postern gate of the castle." So the child was delivered unto Merlin, and so he bare it forth unto Sir Ector, and made a holy man to christen him, and named him Arthur : and so Sir Ector's wife nourished him with her own breasts.

Then within two years king Uther fell sick of a great malady ; and in the meanwhile his enemies usurped upon him, and did a great battle upon his men, and slew many of his people. "Sir," said Merlin, " you may not lie so as you do, for you must to the field, though you ride in a horse-litter ; for you shall never have the better of your enemies but if your person be there, and then shall you have the victory." So it was done as Merlin had devised, and they carried the king forth in a horse-litter, with a great host towards his enemies. And at Saint Alban's there met with the king a great host of the north ; and that day Sir Ulfius and Sir Brastias did great deeds of arms, and king Uther's men overcame the northern battle, and slew much people, and put the remnant to flight : and then the king returned to London, and made great joy of his victory. And within a while after he was passing sore sick, so that three days and three nights he was speechless, wherefore all the barons made great sorrow, and asked Merlin what counsel were best? "There is none other remedy," said Merlin, "but God will have his will ; but look ye that all his barons be before him to-morrow, and God and I shall make him to speak." So on the morrow all the barons, with Merlin, came before the king ; then Merlin said aloud unto king Uther, " Sir, shall your son Arthur be king after your days of this realm, with all the appurtenances." Then Utherpendragon turned him and said, in hearing of them all, "I give him God's blessing and mine, and bid him pray for my soul, and righteously and worshipfully that he claim the crown upon forfeiture of my blessing." And therewith he yielded up the ghost. And then he was interred as belonged unto a king : wherefore Igraine, the queen, made great sorrow, and all the barons. Then stood the realm in great jeopardy a long while, for every lord that was mighty of men made him strong, and many weened to have been king. Then Merlin went to the Archbishop of Canterbury, and counselled him to send for all the lords of the realm, and all the gentlemen of arms, that they should come to London before Christmas, upon pain of cursing ; and for this cause, that as Jesus was born on that night, that He would of His great mercy show some miracle as He was come to be king of all mankind, for to show some miracle who should be rightwise king of this realm. So the archbishop, by the advice of Merlin, sent for all the lords and gentlemen of arms, that they should come by Christmas eve to London : and many of them made them clean of their lives, that their prayer might be the more acceptable to God. So in the greatest church of London (whether it were Paul's or not the French book maketh no mention) all the estates and lords were long or it was day in the church for to pray. And when matins and the first mass was done, there was seen in the churchyard, against the high altar, a great stone, four-square, like to a marble stone, and in the midst thereof was an anvil of steel, a foot of height, and therein stuck a fair sword, naked by the point, and letters of gold were written about the sword that said thus : "Whoso pulleth out this sword of this stone and anvil is rightwise king born of England." Then the people marvelled and told it to the archbishop. "I command you," said the archbishop, "that you keep you within your church ; and pray unto God still that no man touch the sword till the high mass be all done." So when all the masses were done, all the estates went for to behold the stone and the sword, and when they saw the scripture, some assayed, such as would have been king ; but none might stir the sword, nor move it. "He is not yet here," said the archbishop, "that shall achieve the sword, but doubt not God will make him to be known. But this is my counsel," said the archbishop, "that we let purvey ten knights, men of good fame, and they to keep this sword." And so it was ordained, and then there was made a cry, that every man should assay that would for to win the sword. And, upon new year's day, the barons let make a joust and tournament, that all knights that would joust and tourney there might play : and all this was ordained for to keep the lords together, and the commons, for the archbishop trusted that God would make him known that should win the sword. So, upon new year's day, when the service was done, the barons rode to the field, some to joust, and some to tourney. And so it happened that Sir Ector, that had great livelihood about London, rode to the jousts, and with him rode Sir Kaye, his son, and young Arthur, that was his nourished brother ; and Sir Kaye was made knight at Allhallowmas afore. So as they rode towards the jousts, Sir Kaye had lost his sword, for he had left it at his father's lodging ; and so he prayed young Arthur to ride for his sword. "I will with a good will," said Arthur, and rode fast after the sword ; and when he came home, the lady and all were gone out to see the jousting. Then was

Arthur wrath, and said to himself, " I will ride to the churchyard and take the sword with me that sticketh in the stone, for my brother, Sir Kaye, shall not be without a sword this day."   And so, when he came to the churchyard, Arthur alighted, and tied his horse to the stile, and so went to the tent, and found no knights there, for they were all at the jousting ; and so he handled the sword by the handles, and lightly and fiercely he pulled it out of the stone, and took his horse, and rode his way till he came to his brother, Sir Kaye, and delivered him the sword.   And, as soon as Sir Kaye saw the sword, he wist well that it was the sword of the stone ; and so he rode to his father, Sir Ector, and said, " Sir, lo ! here is the sword of the stone ; wherefore I must be king of this land."   When Sir Ector beheld the sword, he returned again, and came to the church, and there they alighted all three, and went into the church ; and anon he made Sir Kaye to swear upon a book how he came to that sword. " Sir," said Sir Kaye, " by my brother, Arthur, for he brought it to me."   " How gat you this sword ? " said Sir Ector to Arthur. ' Sir, I will tell you ; when I came home for my brother's sword I found nobody at home for to deliver me his sword ; and so I thought my brother, Sir Kaye, should not be swordless, and so I came thither eagerly, and pulled it out of the stone without any pain."   " Found ye any knights about this sword ? " said Sir Ector.   " Nay," said Arthur.   " Now," said Sir Ector to Arthur, " I understand that you must be king of this land."   " Wherefore I ? " said Arthur, " and for what cause ? "   " Sir," said Sir Ector, " for God will have it so ; for there should never no man have drawn out this sword, but he that shall be rightwise king of this land.   Now let me see whether ye can put the sword there as it was, and pull it out again."   " That is no mastery," said Arthur ; and so he put it in the stone.   Therewith Sir Ector assayed to pull out the sword, and failed.

IV.

" Now assay you," said Sir Ector to Sir Kaye.   And anon he pulled at the sword with all his might, but it would not be. " Now shall ye assay," said Sir Ector to Arthur.   " With a good will," said Arthur, and pulled it out easily.   And therewithal Sir Ector kneeled down to the earth, and Sir Kaye also. " Alas ! " said Arthur, " mine own dear father, and my brother, why kneel you to me ? "   " Nay, nay, my lord Arthur, it is not so.   I was never your father, nor of your blood, but I wot well that you are of an higher blood than I weened you were ? "

And then Sir Ector told him all how he was betaken him to nourish, and by whose commandment, and by Merlin's deliverance.   Then Arthur made great moan when he understood that Sir Ector was not his father.   " Sir," said Sir Ector unto Arthur, " will you be my good and gracious lord when you are king ? " " Else were I to blame," said Arthur, " for you are the man in the world that I am most beholden unto, and my good lady and mother, your wife, that, as well as her own, hath fostered and kept me ; and, if ever it be God's will that I be king, as you say, ye shall desire of me what I may do, and I shall not fail you ; God forbid I should fail you."   " Sir," said Sir Ector, " I will ask no more of you but that you will make my son, your fostered brother, Sir Kaye, seneschal of all your lands."   " That shall be done, sir," said Arthur, " and more by the faith of my body, and that never man shall have that office but he while that he and I live."   Therewithal they went unto the archbishop, and told him how the sword was achieved, and by whom.   And, upon the twelfth day, all the barons came thither for to assay to take the sword who that would assay.   But there before them all there might none take it out but only Arthur, wherefore there were many great lords wrath, and said, " It was great shame unto them all and the realm, to be governed with a boy of no high blood born."   And so they fell out at that time, that it was put off till Candlemas, and then all the barons should meet there again.   But always the ten knights were ordained for to watch the sword both day and night ; and so they set a pavilion over the stone and the sword, and five always watched. And at Candlemas many more great lords came thither for to have won the sword, but none of them might prevail ; and right as Arthur did at Christmas he did at Candlemas, and pulled out the sword easily, whereof the barons were sore aggrieved, and put it in delay till the high feast of Easter ; and, as Arthur sped before, so did he at Easter : and yet there were some of the great lords had indignation that Arthur should be their king, and put it off in delay till the feast of Pentecost.   Then the Archbishop of Canterbury, by Merlin's providence, let purvey of the best knights that might be gotten, and such knights as king Utherpendragon loved best, and most trusted in his days ; and such knights were put about Arthur, as Sir Boudwine, of Britain ; Sir Kaye, Sir Ulfius, and Sir Brastias : all these, with many others, were always about Arthur, day and night, till the feast of Pentecost.

V.

AND, at the feast of Pentecost, all manner of men assayed for to pull at the sword that would assay; and none might prevail but Arthur, and he pulled it out before all the lords and commons that were there; wherefore all the commons cried at once, "We will have Arthur unto our king, we will put him no more in delay, for we all see that it is God's will that he shall be our king, and who that holdeth against it we will slay him:" and therewithal they all kneeled down all at once, and cried Arthur mercy because they had delayed him so long. And Arthur forgave it them, and took the sword between both his hands, and offered it up to the altar, where the archbishop was, and was made knight of the best man that was there. And so anon was the coronation made, and there was he sworn to the lords and commons for to be a true king, to stand with true justice from thenceforth all the days of his life: and then he made all the lords that held off the crown, to come in and do him service as they ought to do. And many complaints were made unto king Arthur, of great wrongs that were done since the death of king Utherpendragon, of many lands that were bereaved of lords, knights, ladies, and gentlemen; wherefore king Arthur made the lands for to be rendered again unto them that owed them. When this was done, that the king had established all the countries about London, then he did make Sir Kaye seneschal of England, and Sir Boudwine, of Britain, was made constable, and Sir Ulfias was made chamberlain, and Sir Brastias was made warden, for to wait upon the north from Trent forward; for it was that time, for the most part, enemy unto the king. But within few years after, king Arthur won all the north, Scotland, and all that were under their obeisance: also a part of Wales held against king Arthur, but he overcame them all, as he did the remnant, and all through the noble prowess of himself and his knights of the Round Table.

VI.

THEN king Arthur removed into Wales, and let cry a great feast, that it should be holden at Pentecost after the coronation of him at the city of Carlion. Unto this feast came king Lot, of Lothian and of Orkney, with five hundred knights with him. Also there came unto this feast king Urience, of Gore, which brought with him four hundred knights. Also to this feast there came king Nentres, of Garlothe, and with him seven hundred knights. Also there came unto this feast the king of Scotland, with six hundred knights with him, and he was but a young man. And there came unto this feast a king, that was called the king with the five hundred knights, but he and his men were passing well beseen at all points. Also there came the king of Carados with five hundred knights. Then was king Arthur glad of their coming, for he weened that all the kings and knights had come for great love, and for to have done him worship at his feast; wherefore the king made great joy, and sent unto the kings and knights great present. But the kings would none receive, but rebuked the messengers shamefully, and said they had no joy to receive gifts of a beardless boy that was come of low blood; and sent him word that they would have none of his gifts, and that they were come to give him gifts with hard swords between the neck and the shoulders, and therefore they came thither; so they told the messengers plainly, for it was great shame to all them to see such a boy to have the rule of so noble a realm as this land was. With this answer the messengers departed, and told this answer unto king Arthur; and for this cause, by the advice of his barons, he took him to a strong tower, with five hundred good men of arms with him: and all the kings aforesaid in a manner laid a siege afore him, but king Arthur was well victualled. And within fifteen days after Merlin came among them into the city of Carlion; then all the kings were passing glad of Merlin's coming, and asked him, "For what cause is that beardless boy, Arthur, made your king?" "Sirs," said Merlin, "I shall tell you the cause: for he is king Utherpendragon's son." "Then he is a bastard," said they all. "Nay," said Merlin, "after the death of the duke, was Arthur . begot, and thirteen days after king Utherpendragon wedded fair Igraine; and therefore I prove him he is no bastard, and whosoever sayeth nay, he shall be king, and overcome all his enemies; and or that he die he shall be king of England, and he shall have under his obeisance, Wales, Ireland, and Scotland, and many more realms than I will now rehearse." Some of the kings had marvel at Merlin's words, and deemed well that it should be as he said; and some of them laughed him to scorn, as king Lot and more other called him a witch. But then were they accorded with Merlin, that king Arthur should come out and speak with the kings, and for to come safe and go safe, such assurance was made or Merlin went. So Merlin went unto king Arthur, and told him how he had done, and bade him that he should not fear; but come out boldly and speak with them, and spare them not, but answer them as their king and chieftain : for you shall overcome them all, whether they will or will not.

VII.

THEN king Arthur came out of his tower, and had underneath his gown a jesseraunt of double mail, which was good and sure; and there went with him the Archbishop of Canterbury, and Sir Boudwine, of Britain, and Sir Kaye, the seneschal, and Sir Brastias : these were the men of most worship that were with him ; and when they were met together, there was but little meekness, for there was stout and hard words on both sides. But always king Arthur answered them and said, "That he would make them to bow, and he lived :" wherefore they departed with wrath, and king Arthur bade keep them well, and they bid the king keep him well. So the king returned to the tower again, and armed him and all his knights. "What will ye do?" said Merlin to the kings : "ye are better to stint, for here ye shall not prevail, though ye were ten times so many." "Be we well advised to be afraid of a dream-reader?" said king Lot. With that Merlin vanished away, and came to king Arthur, and bade him set on them fiercely ; and in the meanwhile there were three hundred good-men of the best that were with the kings, that went straight to king Arthur, and that comforted him greatly. "Sir," said Merlin to king Arthur, " fight not with the sword that you had by miracle, till you see that you go to the worst, then draw it out and do your best." So forthwithal king Arthur set upon them in their lodging, and Sir Boudwine, Sir Kaye, and Sir Brastias slew on the right hand and on the left, that it was marvel, and alway king Arthur on horseback laid on with a sword, and did marvellous deeds of arms, that many of the kings had great joy of his deeds and hardiness. Then king Lot brake out cn the backside, and the king with the hundred knights, and king Carados, and set on king Arthur fiercely behind him. With that king Arthur turned with his knights, and smote behind and before, and king Arthur was in the foremost press, till his horse was slain under him. And therewith king Lot smote down king Arthur : with that his four knights received him, and set him on horseback. Then he drew his sword Excalibur ; but it was so bright in his enemy's eyes, that it gave light like thirty torches, and therewith he put them back, and slew much people. And then all the commons of Carlion arose with clubs and staves, and slew many knights ; but all the knights held them together with

the knights that were left alive, and so fled and departed. And
Merlin came to king Arthur, and counselled him to follow
them no farther.

VIII.

So, after the feast and tourney, king Arthur drew him to
London, and by the counsel of Merlin the king did call his
barons to counsel ; for Merlin had told the king that the six
knights that made war upon him would in all haste be avenged
on him and on his lands. Wherefore the king asked counsel
of them all : they could no counsel give, but said, "They were
big enough." "Ye say well," said king Arthur, "and I thank
you for your good courage ; but will ye all that love me speak
with Merlin ? ye know well that he hath done much for me, and
he knoweth many things ; and when he is afore you, I would
that ye prayed him heartily of his best advice." And all the
barons said, "They would pray him and desire him." So
Merlin was sent for, and was fair desired of all the barons to
give them the best counsel. "I shall tell you, sires," said
Merlin ; "I warn you all, that your enemies are passing strong
for you, and they are good men of arms as any that now live ;
and by this time they have gotten four kings more, and a
mighty duke also ; and but if our king had more chivalry with
him than he may make himself within the bonds of his own
realm, and he fight with them in battle, he shall be overcome and
slain." "What were the best to do in this case ?" said all the
barons. "I shall tell you," said Merlin, "mine advice : there
are two brethren beyond the sea, and they be kings both, and
marvellous good men of their hands ; the one hight king Ban
of Benwicke, and that other hight king Bors of Gaul, that is
France ; and on these two kings warreth a mighty man of
men, king Claudas, and striveth with them for a castle ;
but this Claudas is so mighty of goods, whereof he getteth
good knights, that he putteth these two kings for the most part
to the worst : wherefore this is my counsel, that our king send
unto the two kings, Ban and Bors, by two trusty knights with
letters well devised, that if they will come and see king Arthur
and his court, and so help him in his wars, that he will be sworn
to them to help them in their wars against king Claudas. Now,
what say ye unto this counsel ?" said Merlin. "This is well
counselled," said the king and all the barons. Right so in all
the haste were ordained to get two knights upon the message
unto the two kings. So were there made letters in most
pleasant wise, according unto king Arthur's desire. Ulfius and

Brastias were made the messengers, and so rode forth well horsed and well armed, as the guise was that time, and so passed to sea, and rode towards the city of Benwicke, and there besides were eight knights that espied them : and at the straight passage they met with Sir Ulfius and Sir Brastias, and would have taken them prisoners. So they prayed them that they might pass, for they were messengers unto king Ban and Bors, sent from king Arthur. "Therefore," said the eight knights, "ye shall die, or be our prisoners, for we be knights of king Claudas." And therewith two of them dressed their spears, and Ulfius and Brastias dressed their spears, and ran together with great strength, and Claudas' knights brake their spears, and the other two held and bare the two knights out of their saddles unto the earth, and so left them lying, and rode their way ; and the other six knights rode afore to a passage to meet with them again, and so Ulfius and Brastias smote other two down, and so passed on their way. And at the third passage they smote down other two : and at the fourth passage there met with two for two, and both were laid to the earth. So there was none of the eight knights but that he was so hurt or else bruised : and when they came to Benwicke, it fortuned there were both the kings, Ban and Bors. When it was told the kings that there were come messengers, there were sent to them two knights of worship, the one high Lionses, lord of the country of Payarne, and Sir Phariance, a worshipful knight. Anon they asked from whence they came, and they said, "From king Arthur of England : " they then took them in their arms, and made great joy each of other. But anon, as the two kings wist that they were messengers of king Arthur's no tarrying was made ; but forthwith they spake with the knights, and welcomed them in the faithfullest wise, and said, "They were most welcome unto them before all the kings living : " and therewith they kissed the letters, and delivered them straight. And when king Ban and Bors understood the letters, then were they better welcome than before : and after the haste of the letter they gave them this answer, "That they would fulfil the desire of king Arthur's writing." And Ulfius and Brastias tarried there as long as they would, and had as good cheer as might be made them in those marches. Then Ulfius and Brastias told the kings of the adventure of their passage of the eight knights. "Ha ! ha !" said king Ban and Bors, "they were our good friends : I would I had wist of them, they should not have escaped so." So Ulfius and Brastias had good cheer and great gifts, as much as they might bear away, and had their answer by mouth and by

writing, "That those two kings would come to king Arthur in all
the haste that they might." So the two knights rode on afore,
and passed the sea, and came to their lord, and told him how
they had sped, whereof king Arthur was passing glad. "At
what time suppose ye the two kings will be here?" "Sir," said
they, "afore Allhallowmas." Then the king let purvey for a
great feast, and let cry a great joust. And by Allhallowmas the
two kings were coming over the sea, with three hundred knights
well arrayed, both for the peace and for the war. And king
Arthur met with them ten miles out of London, and there was
great joy as could be thought of made; and on Allhallowmas,
at the great feast sate in the hall the three kings, and Sir Kaye,
the seneschal, served in the hall, and Sir Lucas, the butler, that
was duke Corneus' son, and Sir Griflet, that was the son of
Cardol; these three knights had the rule of all the service that
served the kings. And anon as they had washed and were
risen, all knights that would joust made them ready. By when
they were ready on horseback there were seven hundred
knights: and king Arthur, Ban, and Bors, with the Archbishop
of Canterbury, and Sir Ector, Kaye's father, they were in a
place covered with cloth of gold like a hall, with ladies and
gentlewomen, for to behold who did best, and thereon to give
judgment.

IX.

KING Arthur and the two kings let dispart the seven hundred
knights in two parties; and there were three hundred knights
of the realm of Benwicke, and they of Gaul turned on the other
side. Then they dressed their shields, and many good knights
couched their spears. So Sir Griflet was the first that met with
a knight, that was called Ladinas, and they met so eagerly that
all men had wonder; and they fought so that their shields fell
to pieces, and horse and men fell to the earth; and both the
English knight and the French knight lay so long, that all men
weened that they had been dead. And when Lucas, the butler,
saw Griflet lay so, he quickly horsed him again, and they two
did marvellous deeds of arms with many batchelors; and also
Sir Kaye came out of an ambushment with five good knights
with him, and they smote other five down, horse and man. But
Sir Kaye did that day marvellous deeds of arms, that there was
none that did so well as he on that day. Then there came in,
fiercely, Sir Ladinas and Sir Grastian, two knights of France,
and did passing well, that all men praised them. Then came
there Sir Placidas, a good knight, and met with Sir Kaye, and

smote him down, horse and man ; wherefore Sir Griflet was wrath, and met with Sir Placidas so hard, that horse and man fell to the earth. But when the five knights wist that Sir Kaye had a fall, they were wondrous wrath, and there with each of them five bear down a knight. When king Arthur and the two kings saw them begin to wax wrath on both parts, they leaped on small'hackneys, and let cry that all men should depart unto their lodging ; and so they went home and unarmed them, and so to evensong and supper. And after the three kings went into a garden, and gave the prize unto Sir Kaye and to Sir Lucas, the butler, and to Sir Griflet ; and then they went to counsel, and with them Gwenbaus, brother unto Sir Ban and Bors, a wise clerk, and thither went Ulfius and Brastias, and Merlin : and, after they had been in counsel, they went to bed. And on the morrow they heard mass, and after went to dinner, and so their counsel, and made many arguments what were best to do. At the last they were concluded that Merlin should go with a token of king Ban, and that was a ring, unto his men and king Bors ; and Gracian and Placidas should go again and keep their castles and their countries, as king Ban, of Benwicke, and king Bors, of Gaul, had ordained them, and so passed the sea and came to Benwicke. And when the people saw king Ban's ring, and Gracian and Placidas, they were glad, and asked how the king fared, and made great joy of their welfare and accordance ; and, according unto their sovereign lord's desire, the men of war made them ready in all haste possible, so that they had fifteen thousand on horseback and on foot, and they had great plenty of victuals with them, by Merlin's provision. But Gracian and Placidas were left to furnish and garnish the castles, for dread of king Claudas. Right so Merlin passed the sea, well victualled, both by water and by land ; and, when he came to the sea, he sent home the footmen again, and took no more with him but ten thousand men on horseback, the most part men of arms, and so shipped and passed the sea into England, and landed at Dover ; and through the wit of Merlin he led the host northward, the priviest way that could be thought, unto the forest of Bedgraine, and there in a valley he lodged them secretly. Then rode Merlin unto king Arthur and the two kings, and told them how he had sped ; whereof they had great marvel, that man on earth might speed so soon, and go and come. So Merlin told them that ten thousand were in the forest of Bedgraine, well armed at all points. Then was there no more to say, but to horseback went all the host, as king Arthur had afore purveyed. So, with twenty thousand, he passed by night and day, but there was made such an ordinance afore by Merlin, that there should no man of war ride nor go in no country, on this side Trent water, but if he had a token from king Arthur; where the king's enemies durst not ride, as they did before, to espy.

X.

AND so within a little space the three kings came unto the castle of Bedgraine, and found there a passing fair fellowship, and well beseen, whereof they had great joy; and victuals they wanted none. This was the cause of the northern host, that they were reared for the despite and rebuke that the six kings had at Carlion. And those kings, by their means, got to them five other kings, and thus they began to gather their people; and how they swore, that for weal nor woe, they should not leave each other till they had destroyed king Arthur: and then they made an oath. The first that began the oath was the duke of Candebenet, and then swore king Brandegoris of Latangor, and king Clarence of Northumberland, and the king of the hundred knights that was a passing good man and a young, and king Lot, a passing good knight, and Sir Gawaine's father, and king Uriance of the land of Gore, and king Idres of Cornwall, and king Cradelmans, and king Agwisance of Ireland, and king Nentres, and king Carados; to bring each one many thousand men of arms on horseback. So their whole host was of clean men of arms on horseback fifty thousand, and on foot ten thousand, of good men's bodies. Then were they soon ready, and mounted upon horse, and sent forth their fore-riders. For these eleven kings, in their ways, laid siege unto the castle of Bedgraine, and so they departed, and drew toward Arthur, and left few to abide at the siege: for the castle of Bedgraine was holden of king Arthur, and the men that were within were Arthur's. And so, by Merlin's advice, there were sent fore-riders to scour the country, and there met with the fore-riders of the north, and made them tell which way the host came, and then they told it to king Arthur; and by king Ban and Bor's counsel, they let burn, and destroyed all the country afore them, where they should ride. The king with the hundred knights dreamed a wonderful dream, two nights afore the battle: that there blew a great wind, and blew down the castles and their towns, and after that came a water, and bare it all away. All that heard of the dream said it was a token of great battle. Then, by the counsel of Merlin, when they wist which way the eleven kings would ride, and lodge that night, at midnight they set upon them as they were in their pavilions : but the scout watch by their host cried, "Lords, to arms, for here be your enemies at your hand."

XI.

THEN king Arthur, and king Ban, and king Bors, with their good and trusty knights, set upon them so fiercely, that they made them overthrow their pavilions on their heads ; but the eleven kings, by manly prowess of arms, took a fair field. But there was slain that morrow-tide ten thousand of good men's bodies. And so they had afore them a strong passage, yet were they fifty thousand of hardy men. Then it drew toward day. "Now shall you do, by mine advice," said Merlin unto the three kings ; "I would that king Ban and king Bors, with their fellowship of ten thousand men, were put in a wood here beside, in an ambushment, and keep them privy, and that they be led or the light of the day come, and that they stir not till ye and your knights have fought with them long ; and, when it is daylight, dress your battle even afore them and the passage, that they may see all your host ; for then they will be the more hardy when they see you have but twenty thousand, and cause them to be the gladder, to suffer you and your host to come over the passage." All the three kings and the barons said that Merlin had said passing well, and it was done as he had devised. So on the morrow, when either host saw other, the host of the north was well confronted. Then to Ulfius and Brastias were delivered three thousand men of arms, and they set on them fiercely in the passage, and slew on the right hand and on the left hand, that it was wonderful to tell. When the eleven knights saw that there was so few a fellowship, and did such deeds of arms, they were ashamed, and set on them fiercely again ; and there was Sir Ulfius's horse slain under him, but he did well and marvellously on foot. But the duke Eustace of Cambernet, and king Clarence of Northumberland, were always grievous on Sir Ulfius. When Brastias saw his fellow so fared withal, he smote the duke with a spear, that horse and man fell down. That saw king Clarence, and returned to Brastias, and either smote other, so that horse and man went to the earth ; and so they lay long astounded, and their horses' knees broke to the hard bone. Then came Sir Kaye the seneschal with six fellows with him, and did passing well. With that came the eleven kings, and there was Sir Griflet put to the earth, horse and man : and Lucas, the butler, horse and man, by king

Grandegors, and king Idres, and king Agusance. Then waxed the meddle passing hard on both parties. When Sir Kaye saw Sir Griflet on foot, he rode to king Nentres, and smote him down, and led his horse to Sir Griflet, and horsed him again. Also Sir Kaye, with the same spear, smote down king Lot, and hurt him passing sore. That saw the king with the hundred knights, and ran to Sir Kaye, and smote him down, and took his horse, and gave him to king Lot, whereof he said gramercy. When Sir Griflet saw Sir Kaye and Lucas, the butler, on foot, he took a sharp spear, great and square, and rode to Pynell, a good man of arms, and smote down horse and man, and then he took his horse and gave him Sir Kaye. When king Lot saw king Nentres on foot, he ran to Melot de la Roche, and smote him down, horse and man, and gave king Nentres the horse, and horsed him again. Also the king of the hundred knights saw king Idres on foot, then he ran unto Guimiare de Bloi, and smote him down, horse and man, and gave king Idres the horse, and horsed him again. And king Lot smote down Clariance de la Forest Savage, and gave the horse to duke Eustace. And so, when they had horsed the kings again, they drew them all eleven kings together, and said they would be revenged of the damage that they had taken that day. In the meanwhile came in Sir Ector, with an eager countenance, and found Ulfius and Brastias on foot, in great peril of death, which were foul defiled under the horse's feet. Then king Arthur as a lion ran into king Cradelmont, of North Wales, and smote him through the left side, that the horse and the king fell down, and then he took the horse by the reins, and led him unto Ulfius, and said, " Have this horse, mine old friend, for great need hast thou of a horse." " Gramercy 1 " said Ulfius. Then king Arthur did so marvellously in arms, that all men had wonder thereof. When the king with the hundred knights saw king Cradelmont on foot, he ran unto Sir Ector, that was well horsed, Sir Kaye's father, and smote down horse and man, and gave the horse to the king, and horsed him again. And when king Arthur saw the king ride on Sir Hector's horse, he was wrath, and with his sword he smote the king on the helm, that a quarter of the helm and shield fell down, and the sword curved down unto the horse's neck, and so the king and the horse fell down to the ground. The Sir Kaye came to Sir Morganore, the seneschal, with the king of the hundred knights, and smote him down, horse and man, and led the horse unto his father, Sir Ector. Then Sir Ector ran into a knight, that hight Kardens, and smote down horse and man, and led the horse unto Sir Brastias, that had great need of a horse, and was greatly bruised. When Brastias beheld Lucas, the butler, that lay like a dead man under the horse's feet, and to rescue him Sir Griflet did marvellously ; and there were always fourteen knights upon Sir Lucas, and then Brastias smote one of them on the helm, that it went to the teeth ; and he rode to another, and smote him, that the arm flew into the field. Then he went to the third, and smote him on the shoulder, that both shoulder and arm flew into the field. And when Sir Griflet saw him rescued, he smote a knight on the temples, that head and helm went to the earth, and Sir Griflet took the horse of that knight, and led him unto Sir Lucas, and bid him mount upon the horse, and revenge his hurts ; for Brastias had slain a knight before, and horsed Sir Griflet.

XII.

THEN Lucas saw king Agwisance, that late had slain Moris de la Roche ; and Lucas ran to him with a short spear that was great, and he gave him such a fall, that the horse fell down to the earth. Also Sir Lucas found there on foot Bloyas de la Flaundres and Sir Gwinas, two hardy knights ; and in the madness that Sir Lucas was in he slew two bachelors, and horsed them again. Then waxed the battle passing hard on both parties ; but king Arthur was glad that his knights were horsed again : and then they fought together, that the noise and sound rang by the water and the wood ; wherefore king Ban and king Bors made them ready, and dressed their shields and harness, and they were so courageous, that many knights shook and trembled for eagerness. All this while Lucas, and Gwinas, and Briaunt, and Belias of Flanders, held a strong meddle against six kings —that was king Lot, king Nentres, king Brandegoris, king Idres, king Urience, and king Agwisance. So, with the help of Sir Kaye and Sir Griflet, they held these six kings hard, while that they had any power to defend themselves. But when king Arthur saw the battle would not be ended in any manner, he fared like a mad lion, and stirred his horse here and there, on the right hand and on the left, that he stinted not until he had slain twenty knights. Also he wounded king Lot sore on the shoulder, and made him to leave that ground ; for Sir Kaye and Sir Griflet did there, with king Arthur, great deeds of arms ; and then Sir Ulfius, Sir Brastias, and Sir Ector encountered against the duke Eustace, king Cradelmont, king Cardlemans, king Clariance of Northumberland, king Carados, and against the king with the hundred knights. So these knights

encountered with these kings, that they made them to avoid the
ground.   Then king Lot made great dole for his damages and
his fellows, and said unto the eleven kings, "But if ye will not
do as I devise we shall be slain and destroyed.   Let me have
the king with the hundred knights, king Agwisance, king Idres,
and the duke of Cambenet, and we five kings will have fifteen
thousand men of arms with us, and we will go apart while ye six
kings hold the meddle with twelve thousand ; and as we see
that ye have foughten with them long, then will we come on
fiercely, and else shall we never match them," said king Lot,
"but by this mean."   So anon they departed as they had
devised, and the six kings made their party strong against king
Arthur, and made great war long.   In the meanwhile broke the
ambushment of king Ban and Bors, and Lionses and Phariaunce
had the vanguard ; and the two kings met with king Idres and
his fellowship : and there began a great meddle of breaking
of spears, and smiting of swords, with slaying of men and
horses, and king Idres was near at a discomfiture.   That saw
Agwisance, the king, and put Lionses and Phariaunce in point
of death : for the duke of Cambenet came on them with a great
fellowship.   So these two knights were in great danger of their
lives, that they were fain to return, but always they rescued
themselves and their fellowship marvellously.   When king Bors
saw those knights put back, it grieved him sore.   Then he came
on so fast, that his fellowship seemed as black as the men of
Ind.   When king Lot had espied king Bors, he knew him
well : then he said, "O Jesu ! defend us from death and
horrible maims ; for I see well we have been in great peril of
death : for I see yonder a king, one of the most worshipfullest
men, and one of the best knights in the world is joined to his
fellowship."   "What is he ?" said the king with the hundred
knights.   "It is," said king Lot, "king Bors of Gaul : I marvel
how they came into this country without meeting of us all."
"It was by the advice of Merlin," said a knight.   "As for him,"
said king Carados, "I will encounter with king Bors, if ye will
rescue me when it is need."   "Go on," said they all ; "we will
do all that we may for you."   Then king Carados and his host
rode a soft pace till they came as nigh king Bors as a bow-shot.
Then either battle let their horses run as fast as they might ;
and Sir Bleoberis, that was the godson unto king Bors, bore his
chief's standard, which was a passing good knight.   "Now shall
we see," said king Bors, "how these northern Britons can bear
their arms."   And king Bors encountered with a knight, and
smote him throughout with a spear, that he fell down dead unto

the earth, and after drew his sword, and did marvellous deeds of arms, that both parties had great wonder thereof; and his knights failed not, but did their part, and king Carados was smitten to the earth. With that came the king with the hundred knights, and rescued king Carados mightily with force of arms; for he was a passing good knight, and was but a young man.

XIII.

BY then came into the field king Ban as a fierce lion, with bands of green, and thereupon gold. "Ha! ha!" said king Lot, "now shall we be discomfited: for yonder I see the most valiant knight of the world, and the man of most renown. For such two brethren as are king Ban and king Bors are not living: wherefore, we must needs void or die; and but we avoid manly and wisely there is but death." When king Ban came into the battle, he came in so fiercely, that the stroke resounded again from the wood and the water; wherefore king Lot wept for pity and sorrow, that he saw so many good knights take their end. But, through the great force of king Ban, they made both the northern battles that were parted to hurtle together for great dread; and the three kings, with their knights, slew down-right, that it was a pity to behold; and a great multitude fled.

But king Lot, and the king with the hundred knights, and king Morganore, gathered the people together passing knightly, and did great deeds of arms, and held the battle all that day like hard. When the king with the hundred knights beheld the great damage that king Ban did, he thrust unto him with his horse, and smote him a mighty stroke upon the helm, which astonished him sore. Then was king Ban wrath with him, and set upon him fiercely. When that other saw that, he cast up his shield, and spurred his horse forward; but the stroke of king Ban fell down, and carved a cantel of the shield, and the sword slid down by the hawberk behind his back, and cut in twain the trapping of steel, and the horse also, in two pieces, that the sword fell to the ground. Then the king with the hundred knights avoided the horse lightly, and with his sword he broached the horse of king Ban through and through. With that king Ban with great diligence avoided the dead horse, and came and smote at the other so eagerly upon the helm that he fell to the earth. Also in that ire he felled king Morganore, and there was great slaughter of good knights and much people. By that time came in the press king Arthur, that found king Ban standing among dead men and dead horses, fighting on foot as a mad lion, that there came none nigh him as far as he might reach with his sword, but that he caught a grievous buffet, whereof king Arthur had great pity. And king Arthur was so bloody, that by his shield no man might know him ; for all was blood and brains on his sword. And, as king Arthur looked by him, he saw a knight that was passing well horsed ; and therewith he ran to him, and smote him on the helm with such force, that his sword cut him in two pieces, and the one half fell on the one side, and the other on the other side : and king Arthur took the horse and led him unto king Ban, and said, " Fair brother, have this horse ; for ye have great need thereof, and me repenteth sore of your great damage." " It shall be soon revenged," said king Ban ; " for I trust in God mine hurt is not much : but some of them may sore repent this." " I will well," said king Arthur ; " for I saw your deeds full actual : nevertheless, I might not come at you at that time." But, when king Ban was mounted on horseback, then there began a new battle, which was sore and hard, and passing great slaughter.

And so, through great force, king Arthur and king Ban and king Bors made their knights a little to withdraw them ; but always the eleven kings with their chivalry never turned back ; and so withdrew them to a little wood, and so over a little river, and they rested them ; for on the night they might have no rest in the field. And then the eleven kings and their knights assembled them all on a heap together, as men adread and all discomfited. But there was no man that might pass them, they held them so hard together, both behind and before, that king Arthur had marvel of their great deeds of arms, and was passing wrath. " Ah ! Sir Arthur," said king Ban and king Bors, " blame them not ; for they do as good men ought to do : for by my faith," said king Ban, " they are the best fighting men, and knights of most prowess, that ever I saw or heard speak of: and those eleven kings are men of great worship ; and, if they were belonging to you, there were no king under heaven had such eleven knights, and of such worship." " I may not love them," said king Arthur ; " they would destroy me." " That know we well," said king Ban and king Bors ; " for they are your mortal enemies, and that hath been proved aforehand ; and this day they have done their part, and that is great pity of their wilfulness." Then all the eleven kings drew them together ; and then said king Lot, " Lords, ye must take other ways than you do, or else the great loss is behind ; ye may see what people we have lost, and what good men we lose, because always we wait upon those footmen; and ever, in saving one of the horsemen for him. Therefore, this is mine advice: let us put our footmen from us; for it is almost night. For king Arthur will not tarry upon the footmen; therefore, they may save themselves: the wood is near at hand. And, when we horsemen be together, look that every one of you kings make such an ordinance that none break upon pain of death; and who that seeth any man dress him for to flee, lightly that he be slain; for it is better that we slay a coward, than through a coward all we be slain. Now say ye," said king Lot; "answer unto me, all ye kings." "It is well said," quoth king Nentres; and so said the king with the hundred knights; and the same said king Carados and king Urience; so did king Idres and king Brandegoris; and so did king Cardelmans and the duke of Cambenet; the same said king Clariaunce and king Agwisance. And they swore that they would never fail the one unto the other, neither for life nor for death; and who that fled, but did as they did, should be slain. Then anon they amended their harness, and righted their shields, and took new spears, and set them on their thighs, and stood still as it had been a clump of trees.

XIV.

WHEN king Arthur, and king Ban, and king Bors beheld them and all their knights, they praised them greatly for their noble cheer of chivalry, for the hardiest fighters that ever they heard or saw. With that there dressed them a forty noble knights, and said unto the three kings that they would break their battle. These were their names:—Lionses, Phariaunce, Ulfius, Brastias, Ector, Kaye, Lucas, the butler, Griflet le Fise de Dieu, and Meriet of the rock, Gwinas de Bloy, and Briant de la Forrest Savage; Ballaus and Morians, of the castle of Maidens; Flanedrius, of the castle of Ladies; Annecians, which was king Bors' godson, a valiant knight; Ladinas de la Rouse, Emeraus Caulas, and Gracience le Castlein; one Bloise de la Case, and Sir Colgrevaunce, of Cozre. All these forty knights rode on afore with great spears on their thighs, and spurred their horses mightily, as fast as their horses might run. And the eleven kings, with part of their good knights, rushed with their horses as fast as they might with their spears; and there they did, on both parties, marvellous deeds of arms. So came into the thickest of the press king Arthur, Ban, and Bors, and slew downright, on both hands, that their horses went in blood up to the fetlocks. But ever the eleven knights and their host were always in king Arthur's visage ; wherefore king Ban and Bors had great marvel, considering the great slaughter that there was ; but, at the last, they were driven back over a little river. With that came Merlin upon a great black horse, and said to king Arthur, " Ye have never done : have ye not done enough ? Of threescore thousand ye have left on live but fifteen thousand : it is time for to say, Ho ! For God is wrath with you that you will never have done ; for yonder eleven kings, at this time, will not be overthrown ; but, and if ye tarry upon them any longer, all your fortune will turn, and theirs shall increase. And, therefore, withdraw you to your lodging, and there rest you as soon as you may, and reward well your good knights with gold and silver ; for they have right well deserved it. For there may no riches be too dear for them ; for of so few men as ye have, there were never men did more prowess than they have done this day : for ye have this day matched with the best fighters of the world." " That is truth," said king Ban and Bors. " Also," said Merlin, " withdraw you where you list ; for these three years I dare undertake they shall not hurt nor grieve you, and by then ye shall hear new tidings." And then Merlin said to king Arthur, " These eleven kings have more in hand than they are aware of ; for the Saracens are landed in their countries more than forty thousand, that burn and slay, and have laid siege to the castle Vandesborough, and made great destruction : therefore, dread ye not these three years. Also, sir, all the goods that ye have gotten at this battle, let it be searched ; and, when ye have it in your hands, let it be freely given to these two kings that be here, Ban and Bors, that they may reward their knights with all ; and that shall cause strangers to be of a better will to do you service at a need. Also ye be able enough to reward your own knights of your own goods, whensoever it liketh you." " It is well said," quoth king Arthur ; " and as thou hast devised so shall it be done." When it was delivered to king Ban and king Bors, they gave the goods as freely to the knights as it was given them.

Then Merlin took his leave of king Arthur, and of the two kings, for to go to see his master, Blaise, which dwelt in Northumberland, and so departed and came to his master, which was passing glad of his coming ; and there he told him how king Arthur and the two kings had sped at the great battle, and how it was ended, and told him the names of every king and knight of worship that was there. And so Blaise wrote the battle, word by word, as Merlin told him ; how it began, and by whom ;

and in likewise how it was ended, and who had the worst : all
the battles that were done in king Arthur's days, Merlin caused
Blaise, his master, to write them ; also he caused him to write
all the battles that every worthy knight did of king Arthur's
court. After this Merlin departed from his master, and came
to king Arthur, that was in the castle of Bedegraine, that was
one of the castles that stood in the forest of Sherwood ; and
Merlin was so disguised, that king Arthur knew him not ; for
he was all furred in black sheep-skins, and a great pair of boots,
and a bow and arrows, in a russet gown ; and brought wild
geese in his hand, and it was on the morrow after Candlemas-
day ; but king Arthur knew him not. "Sir," said Merlin to
king Arthur, "will ye give me a gift?" "Wherefore," said the
king, "should I give thee a gift, thou churl?" "Sir," said
Merlin, "ye were better to give me a gift, the which is not in
your hands, than to lose great riches ; for here, in the same
place whereas the great battle was, is great treasure hid in the
earth." "Who told thee so, churl?" said king Arthur.
"Merlin told me so," said he. Then Ulfius and Brastias knew him
well enough, and smiled at him. "Sir," said these two knights,
"it is Merlin that speaketh so unto you." Then king Arthur
was greatly abashed, and had marvel of Merlin, and so had
king Ban and king Bors, and so they had great sport at him.
So, in the meanwhile, there came a damsel, which was an earl's
daughter, and her father's name was Sanam, and her name was
Lyonors, a passing fair damsel ; and so she came thither for to
pay homage, as other lords did after the great battle. And
king Arthur set his love greatly upon her, and so did she upon
him ; and in this wise was Borres begotten, that was after a
good knight of the Round Table. Then there came word that
king Rience, of North Wales, made strong war upon king
Leodegraunce of Cameliard ; for the which thing king Arthur
was wrath ; for he loved him well, and hated king Rience,
because he was always against him. So by the ordinance of the
three kings that were sent home to Benwicke, they all would
depart for dread of king Claudas, and Phariaunce, and Antemes,
and Gracians, and Lyonses Payarne, with the leaders of those
that should keep the king's lands.

XV.

THEN king Arthur, and king Ban, and king Bors departed
with their fellowship, about twenty thousand, and came, within
six days, into the country of Cameliard, and there rescued king

Leodegraunce, and slew there much people of king Rience, unto
the number of ten thousand of men, and put him to flight.   And
then had these three kings great cheer of king Leodegraunce, and
thanked them of their great goodness that they would revenge
him of his enemies.   And there had king Arthur the first sight of
Guenever, daughter unto king Leodegraunce, and ever after he
loved her ; and afterward they were wedded, as it shall be
showed hereafter.   So bravely to make an end, these two kings
took their leave to go into their own country ; for king Claudas
did great destruction on both their lands.   "Then," said king
Arthur, "I will go with you."   "Nay," said the two kings, "ye
shall not at this time, for ye have yet much to do in these lands,
therefore we will depart ; and, with the great goods that we
have gotten in these lands, by your gifts, we shall wage many
good knights, and withstand the malice of king Claudas : for
by the grace of God, if we have need, we will send to you for succour.   And if ye have need, send for us, and we will not tarry,
by the faith of our bodies."   "It shall not need," said Merlin,
"that these two kings come again in the way of war ; but I know
well that the noble king Arthur may not be long from you ; for
ere twelve months be passed, ye shall have great need of him,
and then he shall revenge you on your enemies, as ye have revenged him on his : for these eleven kings shall die all in one
day, by the great might and prowess of arms of two valiant
knights, as it shall be showed hereafter, their names Ben Balin
le Savage, and Balan, his brother, which be marvellous good
knights as any be now living.

Now turn we unto the eleven kings which returned to the city,
that hight Sorhaute, which city was within king Urience's land,
and there they refreshed them as well as they might, and made
leeches to search their wounds, and sorrowed greatly for the
death of their people.   With that there came a messenger, and
told them "that there was coming into their lands people that
were lawless, as well as Saracens, forty thousand, and have burnt
and slain all the people that they may come by, without mercy,
and have laid siege unto the castle of Vandesborough."
"Alas !" said the eleven kings, "here is sorrow upon sorrow ;
and if we had not warred against king Arthur, as we have done,
he would soon revenge us ; and as for king Leodegraunce, he
loveth king Arthur better than us ; and as for king Rience, he
has enough to do with king Leodegraunce, for he hath laid siege
unto him."   So they consented to keep all the marshes of Cornwall, of Wales, and of the north.   So first they put king Idres
in the city of Nauntes, in Britain, with four thousand men of

arms, for to watch both the water and the land : also they put in the city of Windesan king Nentres of Garlot, with four thousand knights for to watch both the water and the land.

Also they had, of other men of war, more than eight thousand for to fortify all the fortresses in the marshes of Cornwall ; also they put more knights in all the marshes of Wales, and of Scotland, with many good men of arms. And so they kept them together for the space of three years, and ever allied them with mighty kings, dukes, lords, and gentlemen ; and to them fell king Rience of North Wales, which was a mighty man of men ; and also Nero, that was a mighty man of good men also. And all this while they furnished and garnished them of good men of arms, and victuals, and all manner of ordnance that belongeth to war for to avenge them of the battle of Bedegraine, as it is rehearsed in the book of adventure following.

XVI.

THEN after that king Ban and king Bors were departed, king Arthur rode unto Carlion, and thither came to him Lot's wife, of Orkney, in manner of a messenger ; but she was sent thither to espy the court of king Arthur, and she came richly beseen with her four sons, Gawaine, Gaheris, Agravaine, and Gareth, with many other knights and ladies ; and she was a passing fair lady, wherefore the king cast great love unto her, and in this wise was Mordred begotten. And she was his sister, on the mother's side, Igraine. So there she rested her a month, and, at the last, she departed. Then, on a time, the king dreamed a marvellous dream, whereof he was right sore afraid ; but all this time king Arthur knew not that king Lot's wife was his sister. This was king Arthur's dream. Him thought that there was come into this land many griffins and serpents, and him thought that they burnt and slew all the people in the land, and then him thought that he fought with them, and that they did him passing great damage, and wounded him full sore ; but, at the last, he slew them all. When the king awoke he was passing heavy, and right pensive of his dream ; and so, for to put away all these thoughts, he made him ready, with many knights, to ride on hunting. As soon as he was in the forest the king saw a great hart afore him. "This hart will I chase," said king Arthur. And so he spurred his horse, and rode long after ; and so, by fine force, oft he was like to have smitten the hart : whereas the king had chased the hart so long, that his horse had lost his breath, and fell down dead.

Then a yeoman set the king another horse : the king saw the hart in ambush, and his horse dead, he sat him down by a fountain, and there he fell in great thoughts. And as he sat there alone, him thought he heard a noise of hounds to the number of thirty ; and with that the king saw coming toward him the strangest beast that ever he saw or heard tell of. So the beast went to the fountain, and drank, and the noise was in the beast's belly, like unto the questing of thirty couple of hounds ; but all the while that the beast drank there was no noise in the beast's belly. And therewith the beast departed, with a great noise, whereof the king had great marvel : and so he was in great thought, and therewith he fell on sleep. Right so there came a knight on foot to king Arthur, and said, "Knight, full of thought, and sleepy, tell me if thou sawest a strange beast pass this way ?" "Such a one saw I," said king Arthur unto the knight, "that is past two miles. What would you with that beast ?" said king Arthur. "Sir, I have followed that beast a long time, and have killed my horse, so would God I had another to follow my quest." Right so came one with the king's horse ; and when the knight saw the horse, he prayed the king to give him that horse ; for I have followed the quest these twelve months, and either I shall achieve him, or bleed of the best blood of my body. King Pellinore that time followed the questing beast, and after his death Sir Palomides followed it.

XVII.

"SIR KNIGHT," said king Arthur, "leave that quest, and suffer me to have it, and I will follow it another twelve months." "Ah ! fool," said the knight to king Arthur, "thy desire is vain ; for it shall never be achieved but by me, or by my next kin." Therewith he start to the king's horse, and mounted into the saddle, and said, "Gramercy, this horse is mine." "Well," said king Arthur, "thou mayest take my horse by force ; but, and I might prove thee whether thou wert better on horseback or I, I would be content." "Well," said the knight, "seek me here when thou wilt, and here nigh this well thou shalt find me." And so passed forth on his way. Then sat king Arthur in a great study, and bade his men fetch his horse as fast as ever they might. Right so came Merlin, like a child of fourteen years of age, and saluted the king, and asked him "Why he was so pensive and heavy?" "I may well be pensive and heavy," said the king, "for here even now I have seen the most marvellous sight that ever I saw." "That know I well," said Merlin, "as well as thyself, and of all thy thoughts; but thou art but a fool to take thought, for it will not amend thee; also I know what thou art, and also who was thy father, and also on whom thou wert begotten; king Utherpendragon was thy father, and begat thee on Igraine." "That is false," said king Arthur, "how shouldest thou know it? for thou art not so old of years for to know my father." "Yes," said Merlin, "I know it better than you, or any man living." "I will not believe thee," said king Arthur, and was wrath with the child. So Merlin departed, and came again in the likeness of an old man of fourscore years of age, whereof the king was glad, for he seemed to be a right wise man. "Then," said the old man, "why are you so sad?" "I may well be heavy," said king Arthur, "for divers things; also here was a child, and told me many things that me seemeth he should not know; for he was not of age for to know my father." "Yes," said that old man, "the child told you the truth, and more would he have told you, and you would have suffered him; but you have done a thing late wherefore God is displeased with you; for you have gotten a child by your sister, that shall destroy you and all the knights of your realm." "What are you," said king Arthur, "that tell me these tidings?" "I am Merlin, and I was he in the child's likeness." "Ah!" said king Arthur, "ye are a marvellous man; but I marvel much at thy words, that I must die in battle." "Marvel not," said Merlin, "for it is God's will that your body be punished for your foul deeds; but I may well be sorry," said Merlin, "for I shall die a shameful death and be put into the earth all quick; and ye shall die a worshipful death." As they thus talked came one with the king's horses; and so the king mounted on his horse, and Merlin on another, and so rode to Carlion. And anon the king asked Ector and Ulfius how he was begotten? and they told him that Utherpendragon was his father, and queen Igraine his mother. Then king Arthur said unto Merlin, "I will that my mother be sent for, that I may speak with her; and if she say so herself, then will I believe it." In all haste the queen was sent for; and she came anon, and brought with her Morgan le Fay, her daughter, that was as fair a lady as any might be: and the king welcomed Igraine in the best manner.

XVIII.

RIGHT so came Ulfius, and said openly, that the king and all that were there might hear, "Ye are the falsest lady of the world, and most traitress unto the king's person." "Beware, Ulfius," said King Arthur, "what thou sayest ; for thou speakest a great word." "I am well aware," said Sir Ulfius, "what I speak ; and here is my glove for to prove it upon any man that saith the contrary, that this Queen Igraine is the cause of all your damage, and of your great war that ye have had ; for, and she would have uttered in the life of King Utherpendragon of the birth of you, and how you were begotten, we should never have had half the mortal wars which ye have had. For the most part of your great lords, barons, and gentlemen of your realm knew never whose son ye were, nor of whom you were begotten : and she that bare you of her body should have made it known openly, in excusing of her worship and yours, and in likewise to all the realm. Wherefore, I prove her false to God and you, and to all your realm ; and who will say the contrary, I will prove it upon his body." Then spake Igraine, and said, "I am a woman, and may not fight ; but rather than I should be dishonoured, there would some good man take my quarrel. More," she said, "Merlin knoweth well, and you, Sir Ulfius, how King Uther came to me, in the castle of Tintagil, in the likeness of my lord that was dead three hours before, and thereby was the child Arthur begotten. And, after the thirteenth day, King Uther wedded me, and, by his commandment, when the child was born, it was delivered to Merlin, and nourished by him : and so I saw the child never after, nor wot not what is his name ; for I never knew him yet." And then Sir Ulfius said unto the queen, "Merlin is more to blame than ye." "I wot well," said the queen, "that I bare a child by my lord, King Uther, but I wot not where he is become." Then Merlin took the king by the hand saying, "This is your mother." And therewith Sir Ector bear witness how he nourished him by King Uther's commandment. And therewith King Arthur took his mother, Queen Igraine, in both his arms, and kissed her, and either wept upon other. And then the king let make a feast, which lasted eight days. Then on a day there came into the court a squire on horseback, leading a knight before him, wounded to the death, and told him "There is a knight in the forest that hath reared up a pavilion by the well side, and hath slain my master, a good knight, and his name was Miles : wherefore, I beseech you, that my master may be buried, and that some good knight may revenge my master's death." Then was in the court great noise of the knight's death, and every man said his advice. Then came Griflet, that was but a squire, and he was but young, of the age of King Arthur ; so he besought the king, for all the service he had done, to give him the order of knighthood.

XIX.

"Thou art full young and tender of age," said King Arthur, "for to take so high an order upon thee." "Sir," said Griflet, "I beseech you make me a knight." "Sir," said Merlin, "it were pity to lose Griflet, for he will be a passing good man when he cometh to age, abiding with you the term of his life ; and if he adventure his body with yonder knight at the fountain, he shall be in great peril, if ever he come again, for he is one of the best knights of the world, and the strongest man of arms." "Well," said King Arthur. So at the desire of Griflet, the king made him knight.

"Now," said King Arthur to Griflet, "since that I have made thee knight, thou must grant me a gift." "What ye will, my lord," said Sir Griflet. "Thou shalt promise me, by the faith of thy body, that when thou hast jousted with the knight at the fountain, whether it fall that ye be on foot or on horseback, that in the same manner ye shall come again unto me without any question, or making any more debate." "I will promise you," said Griflet, "as ye desire." Then Sir Griflet took his horse in great haste, and dressed his shield, and took a great spear in his hand ; and so he rode a great gallop till he came to the fountain, and there he saw a rich pavilion, and thereby, under a cloth, stood a fair horse, well saddled and bridled ; and, on a tree, a shield of divers colours, and a great spear. Then Sir Griflet smote upon the shield with the end of his spear, that the shield fell down to the ground. With that came the knight out of the pavilion, and said, "Fair knight, why smote ye down my shield?" "For I will joust with you," said Sir Griflet. "It were better ye did not," said the knight, "for ye are but young, and late made knight, and your might is nothing to mine." "As for that," said Sir Griflet, "I will joust with you." "That is me loth," said the knight, "but sith I must needs, I will dress me thereto ; but of whence be ye?" said the knight. "Sir, I am of King Arthur's court." So they ran together, that Sir Griflet's spear all shivered, and therewithal he smote Sir Griflet through the shield and the left side, and brake his spear, that the truncheon stuck in his body, that the horse and knight fell down.

XX.

WHEN the knight saw him lay so on the ground, he alighted, and was passing heavy, for he weened he had slain him ; and then he unlaced his helm and gave him wind : and so, with the truncheon, he set him upon his horse, and betook him to God, and said, he had a mighty heart, and if he might live, he would prove a passing good knight. And so Sir Griflet rode to the court, whereas a great moan was made for him ; but through good leeches he was healed, and his life saved. Right so came in the court twelve knights, and were aged men, and they came from the Emperor of Rome, and asked of King Arthur truage for this realm, or else the emperor would destroy him and his land. "Well," said King Arthur, "ye are messengers, therefore may ye say what ye will, or else ye would die there-fore ; but this is mine answer : I owe the emperor no truage, nor none will I send him ; but upon a fair field I shall give him my truage, that shall be with a sharp spear, or else with a sharp sword, and that shall be within these few days, by my father's soul." And therewith the messengers departed passingly wrath, and King Arthur was as wrath as they, for in an evil time came they then, for the king was passing wrath for the hurt of Sir Griflet. And by and by he commanded a privy man of his chamber, that, or it be day, his best horse and armour, with all that belonged to his person, that it be without the city or to-morrow day. Right so on the morning, afore day, he met with his man and his horse, and so mounted up and dressed his shield, and took his spear, and bid his chamberlain tarry there till he came again. And so King Arthur rode but a soft pace till it was day, and then was he aware of three churls which chased Merlin, and would have slain him. Then King Arthur rode unto them a good pace, and cried to them, "Flee, churls !" Then were they afraid when they saw a knight, and fled away. "O, Merlin !" said King Arthur, "here hadst thou been slain for all thy craft had I not been." "Nay," said Merlin, "not so, for I could save myself if I would, and thou art more near thy death than I am, for thou goest toward thy death, and God be not thy friend." So as they went thus talking, they came to the fountain, and the rich pavilion by it. Then King Arthur was aware where a knight sat, all armed, in a chair. "Sir knight," said King Arthur, "for what cause abideth thou here,—that there may no knight ride this way but if he do joust with thee ? I rede thee leave that custom," said King Arthur. "This custom," said the knight, "have I used, and will use, maugre who saith nay ; and who is grieved with my custom let him amend it that will." "I will amend it," said King Arthur. "And I shall defend it," said the knight. Anon he took his horse, and dressed his shield, and took his spear ; and they met so hard, either on other's shield, that they all to-shivered their spears. Therewith King Arthur drew his sword. "Nay, not so," said the knight ; "it is fairer that we twain run more together with sharp spears." "I will well," said King Arthur, "and I had any more spears." "I have spears enough," said the knight. So there came a squire and brought two good spears, and King Arthur took one, and he another ; so they spurred their horses, and came together with all their might, that either break their spears in their hands. Then King Arthur set hand to his sword. "Nay," said the knight, "ye shall do better, ye are a passing good jouster as ever I met withal ; for the love of the high order of knighthood let us joust it once again." "I assent me," said King Arthur. Anon there were brought two good spears, and each got a spear, and therewith they ran together, that King Arthur's spear all to-shivered. But the knight hit him so hard in the midst of the shield, that horse and man fell to the earth, wherewith King Arthur was sore angered, and drew out his sword, and said, "I will assay thee, sir knight, on foot, for I have lost the honour on horseback." "I will be on horseback," said the knight. Then was King Arthur wrath, and dressed his shield toward him with his sword drawn. When the knight saw that, he alighted for him. He thought it was no worship to have a knight at such a vantage, he to be on horseback, and that other on foot, and so alighted and dressed him to King Arthur, and there began a strong battle, with many great strokes, and so hewed with their swords, that the cantels flew in the fields, and much blood they bled both, so that all the place where they fought was all bloody, and thus they fought long, and rested them ; and then they went to battle again, and so hurtled together like two wild boars, that either of them fell to the earth. So at the last they smote together, that both their swords met even together. But the sword of the knight smote King Arthur's sword in two pieces, wherefore he was heavy. Then said the knight to the king, "Thou art in my power, whether me list to save thee or slay thee, and but thou yield thee as overcome and recreant, thou shalt die." "As for death," said King Arthur, " welcome be it when it cometh, but as to yield me to thee as recreant, I had rather die than to be so shamed." And there-withal the king leapt unto the knight, and took him by the middle, and threw him down, and rased off his helm. When the knight

felt that, he was a dread, for he was a passing big man of might;
and anon he brought King Arthur under him and rased off his
helm, and would have smitten off his head.

XXI.

THEREWITHAL came Merlin and said, "Knight, hold thy
hand, for and thou slay that knight thou puttest this realm in
the greatest damage that ever realm was in, for this knight is a
man of more worship than thou wottest of." "Why, who is
he?" said the knight. "It is King Arthur." Then would he
have slain him for dread of his wrath, and heaved up his sword,
and therewith Merlin cast an enchantment on the knight, that
he fell to the earth in a great sleep. Then Merlin took up King
Arthur, and rode forth with him upon the knight's horse. "Alas!"
said King Arthur, "what hast thou done, Merlin? Hast thou
slain this good knight by thy crafts? There lived not so worshipful a knight as he was. I had rather than the loss of my land a
year that he were alive." "Care ye not," said Merlin, "for he
is wholer than ye, for he is but asleep, and will awake within
three hours. I told you," said Merlin, "what a knight he was :
here had ye been slain had I not been. Also, there liveth not a
better knight than he is one, and he shall do you hereafter right
good service, and his name is Pellinore ; and he shall have two
sons that shall be passing good men, and, save one, they shall
have no fellow of prowess and of good living ; the one shall be
named Percivale of Wales, and the other Lamoracke of Wales ;
and they shall tell you the name of your own begotten son that
shall be the destruction of all this realm." Right so the king
and he departed, and went unto a hermitage, whereas was a
good man and a great leech. So the hermit searched all his
wounds and gave good salves; and the king was there three
days, and then were his wounds well amended that he might
ride and go. And so Merlin and he departed, and as they
rode King Arthur said, "I have no sword." "No matter," said
Merlin, "hereby is a sword that shall be yours and I may."
So they rode till they came to a lake, which was a fair
water and a broad ; and in the midst of the lake King Arthur
was aware of an arm clothed in white samite, that held a fair
sword in the hand. "Lo," said Merlin unto the king, "yonder
is the sword that I spake of." With that they saw a damsel
going upon the lake. "What damsel is that?" said the king.
"That is the Lady of the Lake," said Merlin, "and within that
lake is a reach, and therein is as fair a place as any is on earth,

and richly beseen ; and this damsel will come to you anon, and then speak fair to her that she will give you that sword." Therewith came the damsel to King Arthur and saluted him, and he her again. "Damsel," said the king, "what sword is that which the arm holdeth yonder above the water? I would it were mine, for I have no sword." "Sir king," said the damsel of the lake, "that sword is mine, and if ye will give me a gift when I ask it you, ye shall have it." "By my faith," said King Arthur, "I will give you any gift that you will ask or desire." "Well," said the damsel, "go ye into yonder barge, and row yourself unto the sword, and take it and the scabbard with you ; and I will ask my gift when I see my time." So King Arthur and Merlin alighted, tied their horses to two trees, and so they went into the barge. And when they came to the sword that the hand held, King Arthur took it up by the handles, and took it with him : and the arm and the hand went under the water, and so came to the land, and rode forth. Then King Arthur saw a rich pavilion. "What signifieth yonder pavilion?" "That is the knight's pavilion, that ye fought with last, Sir Pellinore ; but he is out ; for he is not there ; he hath had to do with a knight of yours, that hight Eglame, and they have foughten together a great while, but at the last Eglame fled, and else he had been dead and Sir Pellinore hath chased him to Carlion, and we shall anon meet with him in the highway." "It is well said," quoth King Arthur, "now have I a sword, and now will I wage battle with him, and be avenged on him." "Sir, ye shall not do so," said Merlin, "for the knight is weary of fighting and chasing ; so that ye shall have no worship to have a do with him. Also he will not lightly be matched of one knight living, and therefore my counsel is, that ye let him pass ; for he shall do you good service in short time, and his sons after his days. Also ye shall see that day in short space, that ye shall be right glad to give him your sister to wife." "When I see him," said King Arthur, "I will do as ye advise me." Then King Arthur looked upon the sword, and liked it passing well. "Whether liketh you better," said Merlin, "the sword or the scabbard?" "Me liketh better the sword," said King Arthur. "Ye are more unwise," said Merlin : "for the scabbard is worth ten of the sword : for while ye have the scabbard upon you, ye shall lose no blood, be ye never so sore wounded, therefore keep well the scabbard alway with you." So they rode on to Carlion, and by the way they met with Sir Pellinore. But Merlin had done such a craft, that Pellinore saw not Arthur, and so he passed by without any words. "I marvel," said the king, "that the knight would not speak." "Sir," said Merlin, "he saw you not ; for and he had seen you, he had not lightly departed." So they came unto Carlion, whereof the knights were passing glad ; and when they heard of his adventures, they marvelled that he would jeopard his person so alone. But all men of worship said it was merry to be under such a chieftain, that would put his person in adventure as other poor knights did.

XXII.

THE meanwhile came a messenger hastily from King Rience, of North Wales, and he was king of all Ireland, and of many isles, and this was his message, greeting well King Arthur in this manner wise, saying, that King Rience had discomfited and overcome eleven kings, and every each of them did him homage ; and that was this : they gave him their beards clean cut off as much as there was, wherefore the messenger came for King Arthur's beard. For King Rience had hemmed a mantle with kings' beards, and there lacked for one place of the mantle, wherefore he sent for his beard, "Or else," said the messenger, "he will enter into thy lands, and burn and slay, and never leave till he have thy head and beard." "Well," said King Arthur, "thou hast said thy message, which is the most villainous and lewdest message that ever man heard sent to a king. Also thou mayest see my beard full young yet for to make a hem of, but tell thou the king this : I owe him no homage, nor none of mine elders, but or it be long, he shall do to me homage on both his knees, or else he shall lose his head, by the faith of my body ; for this is the most shamefullest message that ever I heard speak of. I see well the king met never yet with a worshipful man : but tell him I will have his head without he do homage unto me." Then the messenger departed. "Now is there any here," said King Arthur, "that knoweth King Rience ?" Then answered a knight, that hight Naram, "Sir, I know him well ; he is a passing good man of his body, as few be living, and a passing proud man ; and, sir, doubt ye not, he will make war on you with a mighty puissance." "Well," said King Arthur to the knight, "I shall ordain for him, and that shall he find."

XXIII.

THEN King Arthur let send for all the children that were born on May-day, begotten of lords, and born of ladies. For Merlin told King Arthur that he that should destroy him should be born on May-day; wherefore he sent for them all, upon pain of death. And so there were found many lords' sons, and all were sent unto the king; and so was Mordred sent by King Lot's wife, and all were put in a ship to the sea, and some were four weeks old, and some more. And so, by fortune, the ship drove unto a castle, and was all to riven and destroyed, the most part, save that Mordred was cast up, and a good man found him, and nourished him till he was fourteen years old, and then brought him to the court; as it is rehearsed afterward, toward the end, of the death of King Arthur. So many lords and barons of this realm were sore displeased, because that their children were lost; and many put the blame on Merlin, more than on King Arthur. So, what for dread, and what for love, they held their peace. But when the messenger came to King Rience, then was he moved out of measure for anger, and purveyed him for a great host, as it is rehearsed afterward, in the Book of Balin le Savage, that followeth next after; and how by adventure Balin got the sword.

THE BOOK OF SIR BALIN LE SAVAGE.

I.

AFTER the death of King Utherpendragon reigneth King Arthur his son, which had great wars in his days, for to get all England into his hands; for there were many kings at that time within the realm of England, in Wales, in Scotland, and in Cornwall. So it befel upon a time, when King Arthur was at London, there came a knight that brought the king tidings how that Rience, of North Wales, had reared a great number of people, and were entered into the land, and burnt and slew the king's true liege people. "If that be true," said King Arthur, "it were great shame unto mine estate, but that he were mightily withstanden." "It is truth," said the knight, "for I saw the host myself." Then King Arthur let make a cry, that all the lords, knights, and gentlemen of arms, should draw unto a castle, that was called in those days Camelot, and the king would let make a council general, and a great joust. So when the king was come thither, with all his baronage, and lodged as them seemed best, there came a damsel, which was sent on message from the great Lady Lily, of Avelion; and, when she came before King Arthur, she told him from whom she came, and how she was sent on message unto him for these causes. And she let her mantle fall, that was richly furred, and then she was girded with a noble sword, whereof the king had great marvel, and said, "Damsel, for what cause are ye gird with that sword, it beseemeth you not?" "Now shall I tell you," said the damsel, "This sword, that I am gird withal, doth me great sorrow and remembrance ; for I may not be delivered of this sword but by a good knight ; and he must be a passing good man of his hands, and of his deeds, and without villainy or treachery. If I may find such a knight that hath all these virtues, he may draw out this sword of the scabbard. For I have been at King Rience ; for it was told that there was passing good knights, and he and all his knights have assayed it, and none can speed."

"This is a great marvel," said King Arthur, "and if be sooth, I will myself assay to draw out the sword ; not presuming upon myself that I am the best knight, but that I will begin to draw at your sword, in giving example to all the barons, that they shall assay every one after other, when I have assayed." Then King Arthur took the sword by the scabbard and the girdle, and pulled at it eagerly, but the sword would not out. "Sir," said the damsel, "ye need not pull half so hard ; for he that shall pull it out shall do it with little might." "Ye say well," said King Arthur : "now assay ye, all my barons ; but beware ye be not defiled with shame, treachery, nor guile." "Then it will not avail," said the damsel ; "for he must be a clean knight, without villainy, and of gentle stream of father's side and mother's side." Most of all the barons of the Round Table, that were there at that time, assayed all in turn, but none might speed. Wherefore the damsel made great sorrow out of measure, and said, "Alas ! I weened in this court had been the best knights, without treachery or treason." "By my faith," said King Arthur, "here are as good knights as I deem any be in the world ; but their grace is not to help you, wherefore I am greatly displeased."

II.

IT happened so, at that time, that there was a poor knight with King Arthur, that had been prisoner with him half a year and more, for slaying of a knight, which was cousin to King Arthur. The knight was named Balin le Savage, and by good means of the barons, he was delivered out of prison ; for he was a good man named of his body, and he was born in Northumberland. And so he went privily into the court and saw this adventure, whereof his heart rose, and would assay it as other knights did ; but for because he was poor, and poorly arrayed, he put him not far in press. But in his heart he was fully assured (if his grace happened him) as any knight that was there. And, as that damsel took her leave of King Arthur and the barons, this knight, Balin, called unto her, and said, " Damsel, I pray you of your courtesy, to suffer me as well to assay as these lords ; though I be poorly clothed, in mine heart me seemeth I am fully assured as some of these other lords, and me seemeth in my heart to speed right well." The damsel beheld the poor knight, and saw he was a likely man ; but, because of his poor array, she thought he should be of no worship without villainy or treachery. And then she said to the knight Balin, " Sir, it is no need to put me to any more pain or labour, for it beseemeth not you to speed there, as others have failed." " Ah ! fair damsel " said Balin, " worthiness and good graces, and good deeds, are not all only in raiment, but manhood and worship is hid within man's person ; and many a worshipful knight is not known unto all people ; and therefore worship and hardiness is not in raiment and clothing." " By God ! " said the damsel, " ye say truth ; therefore ye shall assay to do what ye may." Then Balin took the sword by the girdle and scabbard, and drew it out easily ; and when he looked upon the sword, it pleased him well. Then had the king and all the barons great marvel, that Balin had done that adventure ; and many knights had great spite at Balin. " Truly," said the damsel, " that is a passing good knight, and the best man that ever I found, and most of worship, without treason, treachery, or villainy, and many marvels shall he achieve. Now gentle and courteous knight," said the damsel, " give me the sword again." " Nay," said Balin, " for this sword will I keep, but it be taken from me by force." " Well," said the damsel, " ye are not wise to keep the sword from me ; for ye shall slay with the sword the best friend that ye have, and the man that ye most love in this world ; and the sword shall be your destruction." " I shall take the adventure," said Balin, " that God will ordain to me : but the sword ye shall not have at this time, by the faith of my body." " Ye shall repent it within a short time," said the damsel, " for I would have the sword more for your avail than for mine, for I am passing heavy for your sake ; for ye will not believe that the sword shall be your destruction, and that is as great pity as ever I knew." With that the damsel departed, making the greatest sorrow that might be. Anon after Balin sent for his horse and his armour, and so would depart from the court, and took his leave of King Arthur. "Nay," said the king, "I suppose ye will not depart so lightly from this fellowship. I believe ye are displeased, that I have showed you unkindness ; blame me the less, for I was misinformed against you. But I weened you had not been such a knight as ye are of worship and prowess ; and if ye will abide in this court with my good knights, I shall so advance you, that ye shall be well pleased." "God thank your highness," said Balin, "for your bounty and highness may no man praise half to the value ; but now at this time I must needs depart, beseeching you alway of your good grace." "Truly," said King Arthur, "I am right wrath for your departing ; I beseech you, fair knight, that ye will not tarry long, and ye shall be right welcome to me and all my barons, and I shall amend all that is amiss, and that I have done against you." "God thank your lordship," said Balin, and therewith made him ready to depart. Then the most part of the knights of the Round Table said, that Balin did not this adventure all only by might, but by witchcraft.

III.

THE meanwhile that this knight was making him ready to depart, there came into the court a lady, which hight the Lady of the Lake, and she came on horseback richly beseen, and saluted King Arthur, and there she asked him a gift that he had promised her when she gave him the sword.

"That is sooth," said King Arthur, "a gift I promised you ; but I have forgotten the name of the sword which ye gave me." "The name of it," said the lady, "is Excalibur, that is as much to say as cut-steel." "Ye say well," said King Arthur ; "ask what ye will, and ye shall have it, if it lie in my power to give it." "Well," said the Lady of the Lake, "I ask the head of the knight that hath won the sword, or else the damsel's head that brought it ; and though I have both their heads I care not, for he slew my brother, a full good knight and a true, and the gentlewoman was causer of my father's death." "Truly," said King Arthur, "I may not grant you neither of their heads with my worship ; therefore ask what ye will else, and I shall fulfil your desire." "I will ask none other thing of you," said the lady. When Balin was ready to depart, he saw the Lady of the Lake there, by whose means was slain his own mother, and he had sought her three years. And when it was told him that she demanded his head of King Arthur, he went straight to her and said, "Evil be ye found, ye would have my head, and therefore ye shall lose yours :" and with his sword lightly he smote off her head in the presence of King Arthur. "Alas ! for shame," said the king ; "why have you done so? you have shamed me and all my court, for this was a lady that I was much beholden unto, and hither she came under my safe conduct, I shall never forgive you that trespass." "My lord," said Balin, "me fore-thinketh much of your displeasure, for this lady was the untruest lady living ; and by her enchantment and witchcraft she·hath been the destroyer of many good knights, and she was the causer that my mother was burnt through her falsehood and treachery." "What cause soever ye had," said King Arthur, "ye should have forborne her in my presence ; therefore think not the contrary, ye shall repent it, for such another despite had I never in my court afore ; therefore withdraw you out of my court in all the haste ye may." Then Balin took up the head of the lady, and bear it with him to his hostel, and there he met with his squire, that was sorry he had displeased King Arthur ; and so they rode forth out of the town. "Now," said Balin, "we must here depart ; take you this head and bear it to my friends, and tell them how I have sped, and tell my friends in Northumberland that my most foe is dead ; also tell them now I am out of prison, and also what adventure did befall me at the getting of this sword." "Alas," said the squire, "ye are greatly to blame for to displease King Arthur." "As for that," said Balin, "I will hie me with all the haste I may to meet with Rience, and destroy him, or else to die therefore ; and if it may happen me to win him, then will King Arthur be my good and gracious lord." "Where shall I meet with you ?" said the squire. "In King Arthur's court," said Balin. So his squire and he departed at that time. Then King Arthur and all the court made great dole, and had great shame of the death of the Lady of the Lake. Then the king full richly buried her.

IV.

AT that time there was in King Arthur's court a knight that was the king's son of Ireland, and his name was Lanceor ; and he was a proud knight, and he counted himself one of the best knights of the court, and he had great spite at Balin for the achieving of the sword, than any should be accounted of more prowess then he was, and he asked King Arthur, "If he would give him leave to ride after Balin, and to revenge the despite that he hath done." "Do your best," said King Arthur, "for I am right wrath with Balin ; I would he were quit of the despite that he hath done to me and to my court." Then this Lanceor went to his hostel to make him ready : in the meanwhile came Merlin to King Arthur's court, and there it was told him of the adventure of the sword, and of the Lady of the Lake. " Now shall I say to you," said Merlin, " this damsel that here standeth, that brought the sword unto your court, I shall tell you the cause of her coming, she is the falsest damsel that liveth." " Say not so," said they ; " she hath a brother, a passing good knight of prowess, and a full true man ; and this damsel loved another that held her to paramour, and this good knight, her brother, met with the knight that held her to paramour, and slew him by force of his hands. When this false damsel understood this, she went to the lady Lily, of Avelion, and besought her of help to be avenged on her brother. And so this lady Lily, of Avelion, took her this sword, which she brought with her, and told that there should no man draw it out of the scabbard, but if he were one of the best knights of this realm, and he should be hardy and full of prowess, and with that sword he should slay her brother. This was the cause that the damsel came into this court." " I know it as well as ye do," said Merlin ; " would to God she had never come into this court, for she came never in fellowship of worship to do good, but alway great harm, and that knight which hath achieved the sword shall be destroyed by that sword ; wherefore it shall be great damage, for there is not living a knight of more prowess than he is, and he shall do unto you my lord, King Arthur, great honour and kindness ; and great pity it is for he shall not endure but a while, and as for his strength and hardiness, I know not his match living." But the knight of Ireland armed him in all points, and dressed him his shield on his shoulder, and mounted upon horseback, and took his spear in his hand, and rode after as fast as his horse could run : and within a little on a mountain he had a sight of Balin, and with a loud voice he cried to him, and said, " Abide, knight, for ye shall abide, whether ye will or will not : and the shield that is before you, shall not help you." When Balin heard that noise, he turned his horse fiercely, and said, " Fair knight, what will you with me ; will ye joust with me?" " Yes," said the Irish knight, " therefore am I come after you." " Peradventure," said Balin, " it had been better to have holden you at home ; for many a man weeneth to put his enemy to rebuke, and often it falleth to himself. Of what court be ye sent from?" " I am come from the court of King Arthur," said the knight of Ireland, " that am come hither for to revenge the despite that ye have done this day to King Arthur and to his court."

"Well," said Balin, "I see well I must have ado with you, which me forethinketh for to grieve King Arthur or any of his knights, and your quarrel is full simple to me," said Balin; "for the lady that is dead did great damage, and else I would have been as loth as any knight that liveth for to slay a lady." "Make you ready," said the knight Lanceor, "and dress you to me; for one of us shall abide in the field." Then they took their spears in all the haste they might, and came together as fast as their horses might drive, and the king's son of Ireland smote Balin upon his shield, that his spear went all to shivers. And Balin smote him with such a might, that it went through his shield and perished the hawberk, and so pierced through his body and the horse croup; and Balin anon turned his horse fiercely, and drew out his sword, and wist not that that he had slain him, and then he saw him lie as a dead corpse.

<h2 style="text-align:center">V.</h2>

THEN he looked by him, and was ware of a damsel that came riding as fast as her horse might gallop upon a fair palfrey. And when she espied that Sir Lanceor was slain, then she made sorrow out of measure, and said, "O Balin! two bodies hast thou slain and one heart, and two hearts in one body, and two souls thou hast lost." And therewith she took the sword from her love that lay dead, and as she took it she fell to the ground in a swoon: and when she arose, she made great dole out of measure, which sorrow grieved Balin passing sore, and went to her for to have taken the sword out of her hands, but she held it so fast, that in nowise he might take the sword out of her hands; but if he should have hurt her, and suddenly she set the pommel of the sword to the ground, and ran herself through the body. And when Balin saw her dead, he was passing heavy in his heart, and ashamed that so fair a damsel had destroyed herself for the great love she had unto Sir Lanceor. "Alas!" said Balin, "me repenteth sore the death of this knight, for the love of this damsel; for there was much true love between them both," and for sorrow he might no longer behold them, but turned his horse and looked toward a forest, and there he espied the arms of his brother Balan; and when they were met, they put off their helms and kissed together, and wept for joy and pity. "Then," said Balan, "I weened little to have met with you at this sudden adventure; I am right glad of your deliverance out of your dolorous prisoning, for a man told me in the Castle of Fourstones that ye were delivered, and that man had seen you in King Arthur's court ; and therefore I came hither into this country, for here I supposed to find you." And anon Balin told unto his brother of all his adventures of the sword, and of the death of the Lady of the Lake, and how King Arthur was displeased with him ; "wherefore he sent this knight after me that lieth here dead, and the death of this damsel grieveth me full sore." "So doth it me," said Balan ; "but ye must take the adventure that God will ordain unto you." "Truly," said Balin, " I am right heavy of mind that my lord, King Arthur, is displeased with me, for he is the most worshipfullest knight that reigneth now on the earth, and his love I will get, or else I will put my life in adventure ; for King Rience, of North Wales, lieth at a siege at the castle Terabil, and thither will we draw in all haste, to prove our worship and prowess upon him." " I will well," said Balan, "that we do so, and we will help each other as brethren ought to do."

VI.

"BROTHER," said Balin, "let us go hence, and well be we met." The meanwhile as they talked there came a dwarf from the city of Camelot on horseback, as fast as he might, and found the dead bodies ; wherefore he made great dole, and drew his hair for sorrow, and said, "Which of you knights hath done this deed?" "Whereby asketh thou it?" said Balin. "For I would wit," said the dwarf. "It was I," said Balin, "that slew this knight in my defence ; for hither came he to chase me, and either I must slay him or me, and this damsel slew herself for his love, which me sore repenteth, and for her sake I shall owe all women the better love and favour." "Alas!" said the dwarf, "thou hast done great damage unto thyself; for this knight, that is here dead, was one of the most valiantest men that lived, and trust thou well, Balin, that the kin of this knight will chase thee through the world till they have slain thee." "As for that," said Balin, " I fear it not greatly ; but I am right heavy, because I have displeased my sovereign lord, King Arthur, for the death of this knight." So, as they talked together, there came a man of Cornwall riding by them, which was named King Marke ; and when he saw these two bodies dead, and understood how they were dead by one of the two knights abovesaid, then made King Marke great sorrow for the true love that was between them, and said, " I will not depart from hence till I have on this earth made a tomb." And there he pitched his pavilions, and sought through all the country to find a tomb. And in a church they found one was rich and fair, and then the king let put them both in the earth, and put the tomb on them, and wrote both their names on the tomb, " Here lieth Lanceor the king's son, of Ireland ; that at his own request was slain by the hands of Balin, and how his lady Colombe and paramour slew herself with her love's sword, for dole and sorrow."

VII.

THE meanwhile as this was doing, came Merlin unto king Marke, and seeing all his doing, said, " Here in this place shall be the greatest battle between two knights that ever was or ever will be, and the truest lovers, and yet none of them shall slay other ; " and there Merlin wrote their names upon the tomb with letters of gold, that should fight in that place, whose names were Launcelot du Lake, and Tristram de Liones. " Thou art a marvellous man," said King Marke unto Merlin, " that speakest of such marvels ; thou art a boisterous fellow, and an unlikely, to tell of such deeds. What is thy name ?" said King Marke. " At this time," said Merlin, " I will not tell ; but at that time, when Sir Tristram shall be taken with his sovereign lady, then ye shall know and hear my name, and at that time ye shall hear tidings that shall not please you. Then," said Merlin to Balin, " thou hast done thyself great hurt, because thou did not save this lady that slew herself, that might have saved her if thou had would." " By the faith of my body," said Balin, " I could not, nor might not save her : for she slew herself suddenly." " Me repenteth," said Merlin ; "because of the death of that lady, thou shalt strike a stroke the most dolorous that ever man stroke, except the stroke of our Lord ; for thou shalt hurt the truest knight, and the man of the most worship that now liveth, and through that stroke three kingdoms shall be in great poverty, misery, and wretchedness twelve years, and the knight shall not be whole of that wound in many years." And then Merlin took his leave of Balin. " Then," said Balin, " if I wist it were sooth that ye say, I should do such a perilous deed as that I would slay myself to make thee a liar." And therewith anon Merlin suddenly vanished away : then Balin and his brother took their leave of King Marke.

" First," said the king, " tell me your name." "Sir," said Balin, " ye may see he beareth two swords, thereby ye may call

him the knight of the two swords." And so departed King
Marke, and rode to Camelot to King Arthur ; and Balin and his
brother took the way to King Rience, and as they rode together
they met with Merlin disguised, but they knew him not.
"Whither ride ye ? " said Merlin. "We have little to do,"
said the two knights, "for to tell thee." "But what is thy
name ? " said Balin. "As at this time," said Merlin, "I will not
tell thee." "It is full evil seen," said the two knights, "that
thou art a true man, when thou wilt not tell thy name." "As
for that," said Merlin, "be it as it may ; but I can tell you
wherefore ye ride this way, for to meet King Rience : but it will
not avail you, without you have my counsel." "Ah ! " said
Balin, "ye are Merlin : we will be ruled by your counsel."
"Come on," said Merlin ; "ye shall have great worship, and
look that ye do knightly ; for ye shall have great need." "As
for that," said Balin, "dread ye not : we will do what we may."

VIII.

THEN Merlin lodged them in a wood amongst leaves, beside
the highway, and took off the bridles of their horses, and put
them to grass, and laid them down to rest them till it was nigh
midnight. Then Merlin bade them arise and make them ready ;
for the king was nigh them that was stolen away from his host,
with threescore of his best knights : and twenty of them rode
before, to warn the Lady de Vance that the king was coming ;
for that night King Rience should have been with her. "Which
is the king ? " said Balin. "Abide," said Merlin ; "here in a
straight way ye shall meet with him." And therewith he showed
Balin and his brother where he rode. Anon Balin and his
brother met with the king, and smote him down, and wounded
him fiercely, and laid him to the ground ; and there they slew on
the right hand and on the left, and slew more than forty of his
men, and the remnant fled. Then went they again to King
Rience, and would have slain him, if he had not yielded him to
their grace. Then said the king again, "Knights, full of
prowess, slay me not ; for by my life ye may win, and by my
death shall ye win nothing." Then said these two knights,
"Ye say sooth and troth ; " and so laid him on a horse-litter.
With that Merlin was vanished, and came to King Arthur aforehand, and told him how his most enemy was taken and discomfited. "By whom ? " said King Arthur. "By two knights,"
said Merlin, "that would please your lordship, and to-morrow
ye shall know what they be." Anon after came the knight with

the two swords, and Balan, his brother, and brought with them King Rience, and there delivered him to the porters, and charged them with him, and so they two returned again in the springing of the day. King Arthur came to King Rience and said, " Sir king, you are welcome ; by what adventure came ye hither ?" "Sir," said King Rience, " I came hither by a hard adventure." "Who won you ?" said King Arthur. " Sir," said Rience, " the knight with the two swords and his brother, which are two marvellous knights of prowess." " I know them not," said King Arthur ; "but much I am beholden unto them." " Ah ！" said Merlin, " I shall tell you it is Balin that achieved the sword, and his brother, Balan, a good knight ; there liveth not a better in prowess and worthiness, and it shall be the greatest dole of him that ever was of knight, for he shall not long endure." "Alas ！" said King Arthur, " that is a great pity ; for I am greatly beholden unto him, and I have full evil deserved it unto him for his kindness." " Nay," said Merlin, " he shall do much more for you, and that shall ye know ere it be long. But, sir, are ye purveyed ?" said Merlin ; "for to-morrow the host of Nero, King Rience's brother, will set upon you afore dinner with a mighty host : therefore, make you ready, for I will depart from you."

IX.

THEN king Arthur made ready his host in ten battles ; and Nero was ready in the field, afore the Castle Terabil, with a mighty host ; for he had ten battles, with much more people than King Arthur had. So Nero himself had the van-guard with the most party of his people : and Merlin came to King Lot of the Isle of the Orkney, and held him with a tale of prophecy, till Nero and his people were destroyed. And there Sir Kaye, the seneschal, did passing well, that all the days of his life he had thereof worship ; and Sir Hervis de Revel did marvellous deeds with King Arthur : and King Arthur slew that day twenty knights, and maimed forty. At that time came in the knight with the two swords, and his brother, Balan ; but they two did so marvellously, that the king and all the knights had great marvel thereof : and all that beheld them said, that they were sent from heaven as angels, or as devils from hell ; and King Arthur said himself, that they were the best knights that ever he saw ; for they gave such strokes that all men had wonder of them. In the meantime came one to King Lot and told him, that, while he tarried there, Nero was destroyed and slain with all his people. "Alas! I am ashamed," said King Lot, "for, through my default, is slain many a worshipful man : for, if we had been together, there had been no host under heaven that had been able to match us. This flatterer, with his prophecy, hath mocked me." All that did Merlin ; for he knew well that, if King Lot had been there with his body at the first battle, King Arthur and all his people should have been destroyed and slain; and Merlin knew well that one of the kings should be dead that day, and loth was Merlin that any of them both should be slain ; but of the twain he had leaver King Lot had been slain than King Arthur.

"Now what is best to do?" said King Lot, "whether is it better for to treat with King Arthur, or to fight? for the most part of our people are slain and destroyed." "Sir," said a knight, "set upon King Arthur ; for he and his men are weary of fighting, and we be fresh." "As for me," said King Lot, "I would that every knight would do his part as I will do mine." And then they advanced their banners, and smote together, and all to-shivered their spears ; and King Arthur's knights, with the help of the knight of the two swords, and his brother, Balan, put king Lot and his host to the worst. But always King Lot held him in the foremost, and did great deeds of arms ; for all his host was borne up by his hands, for he abode and withstood all knights. Alas! he might not ever endure, the which was great pity that so worthy a knight as he was should be overmatched, and that of late time afore had been a knight of King Arthur's, and had wedded King Arthur's sister ; and, because King Arthur cast his love upon her and therewith begat Mordred, therefore King Lot held against King Arthur. So there was a knight, that was called the knight with the strange beast, and at that time his right name was Pellinore, which was a good man of prowess ; and he smote a mighty stroke at King Lot as he fought with his enemies : and he failed of his stroke, and smote the horse's neck, that he fell to the ground with King Lot. And therewith Sir Pellinore smote him a great stroke through the helm, and hewed him to the brows : then all the host of Orkney fled for the death of King Lot, and there was slain many a mother's son. But King Pellinore bare the blame of the death of King Lot : wherefore, Sir Gawaine revenged the death of his father the tenth year after he was made knight, and slew King Pellinore with his own hands. Also there was slain at the battle twelve kings on King Lot's side with Nero, and all were buried in the church of St. Stevens, in Camelot ; and the remnant of knights, and of others, were buried in a great rock.

X.

So, at the interment, came King Lot's wife, Morgause, with her four sons, Gawaine, Agravaine, Gaheris, and Gareth. Also there came thither King Urience, Sir Ewaine's father, and Morgan le Fay, his wife, that was King Arthur's sister : all these came to the interment. But of all these twelve knights King Arthur let make the tomb of King Lot passing richly, and his tomb stood by itself apart. And then King Arthur let make twelve images of Latin and of copper, and made them to be overgilt with fine gold, in sign and token of the twelve kings; and every image held a taper of wax, which burnt night and day. And King Arthur was made in sign of a figure standing above them all, with a sword drawn in his hand ; and all the twelve figures had countenances like unto men that were overcome. All this made Merlin by his subtle craft, and there he said to King Arthur, "When I am dead the twelve tapers shall burn no longer ; and, soon after this, the adventures of the Holy Sancgreal shall come among you, and shall also be achieved." Also he told unto King Arthur, how Balin, the worshipful knight, should give the dolorous stroke, whereof shall fall great vengeance. "And where is Balin, and Balan, and Pellinore ? " said King Arthur.

"As for Sir Pellinore," said Merlin, " he will meet with you anon ; and as for Balin he will not be long from you : but the other brother, Balan, will depart, and ye shall see him no more." " Now, by my faith," said King Arthur, " they are two marvellous knights, and namely Balin passeth of prowess far of any knight that ever I found ; for I am much beholden unto him. Would to God that he would abide still with me." " Sir," said Merlin, "look that ye keep well the scabbard of Excalibur ; for, as I told you, ye shall lose no blood as long as ye have the scabbard upon you, though ye have as many wounds upon your body as ye may have." So afterwards, for great trust, King Arthur betook the scabbard to Morgan le Fay, his sister ; and she loved another knight better than her husband, King Urience, or King Arthur. And she would have had King Arthur slain : and, therefore, she let make another scabbard like it by enchantment, and gave the scabbard of Excalibur to her love, a knight named Sir Accolon, which after had nigh slain King Arthur. After this Merlin told unto King Arthur of the prophecy that there should be a great battle beside Salisbury, and that Mordred, his own son, should be against him : also he told him, that Basdemegus was his cousin, and german unto King Urience.

XI.

WITHIN a day or two King Arthur was somewhat sick, and he let pitch his pavilion in a meadow, and there he laid him down on a pallet to sleep, but he might have no rest. Right so he heard a great noise of a horse; and therewith the king looked out at the porch of the pavilion's door, and saw a knight coming by him making great sorrow. "Abide, fair sir," said King Arthur, "and tell me wherefore thou makest this sorrow." "Ye may little amend it," said the knight, and so passed forth unto the castle of Meliot. Anon after there came Balin; and, when he saw King Arthur, anon he alighted off his horse, and came to the king on foot, and saluted him. "By my head," said King Arthur, "ye be welcome, sir. Right now came riding this way a knight making great sorrow, and I cannot tell for what cause; wherefore, I would desire you, of your courtesy and gentleness, that ye will fetch that knight again, either by force, or else by his good will." "I will do more for your lordship than that," said Balin, and so rode more than a pace, and found the knight with a damsel in a forest, and said, "Sir knight, ye must come with me unto my lord, King Arthur, for to tell him the cause of your sorrow." "That will I not," said the knight; "for it would scath me greatly, and do you none avail." "Sir," said Balin, "I pray you make you ready; for ye must needs go with me, or else I will fight with you, and bring you by force, and that were I loth to do." "Will ye be my warrant," said the knight to Balin, "if I go with you?" "Yea," said Balin, "or else I will die therefore." And so he make him ready to go with the good knight, Balin, and left there the damsel: and, as they were afore King Arthur's pavilion, there came one invisible, and smote the knight that went with Balin throughout the body with a spear.

"Alas!" said the knight, "I am slain under your conduct and guard, with a traitorous knight, called Garlon; therefore, take my horse, the which is better than yours, and ride to the damsel, and follow the quest that I was in, whereas she will lead you, and revenge my death when ye may best." "That shall I do," said Balin, "and thereof I make a vow to you by my knighthood." And so he departed from this knight, making great sorrow. So King Arthur let bury this knight richly, and made a mention upon the tomb how there was slain Herleus le Berbeus, and also how the treachery was done by the knight, Garlon. But ever the damsel bore the truncheon of the spear with her that Sir Herleus was slain with.

XII.

So Balin and the damsel rode into the forest, and there met with a knight that had been on hunting ; and that knight asked Balin for what cause he made so great sorrow. "Me list not to tell you," said Balin. "Now," said the knight, "and I were armed as ye be I would fight with you." "That should little need," said Balin ; "for I am not afraid to tell it you :" and he told him all the cause how it was. "Ah !" said the knight, "is this all? here I ensure you, by the faith of my body, never to depart from you as long as my life lasteth." And so they went to the hostel and armed him, and so rode forth with Balin ; and as they came by a hermitage, fast by a churchyard, there came the knight Garlon invisible, and smote this good knight, Perin de Mountbelyard, with a spear through the body. "Alas !" said the knight, "I am slain by this traitor knight that rideth invisible." "Alas !" said Balin, "it is not the first despite that he hath done to me." And there the hermit and Balin buried the knight under a rich stone and a tomb royal ; and, on the morrow, they found letters of gold written, how Sir Gawaine shall revenge King Lot's death, his father, upon King Pellinore. And anon, after this, Balin and the damsel rode till they came to a castle ; and there Balin alighted, and he and the damsel weened to have gone into the castle. And anon, as Balin came within the gate, the porticullis fell down at his back : and there came many men about the damsel, and would have slain her. And, when Balin saw that, he was so grieved, because he might not help the damsel : and then he went upon the walls, and leaped over into the ditch, and hurt him not. And anon he pulled out his sword, and would have foughten with them. And they all said "that they would not fight with him ; for they did nothing but the old custom of the castle." And told him how their lady was sick, and had lain many years, and she might not be whole, but if she had a silver dish full of blood, of a clean maid, and a king's daughter ; and, therefore, the custom of the castle is, that there shall none pass this way but she shall bleed of her blood a silver dish full. "Well," said Balin, "she shall bleed as much as she may bleed ; but I will not that she lose her life, while my life lasteth." And so Balin made her to bleed by her good will ; but her blood helped not the lady. And so he and she rested there all that night, and had their right good cheer ; and, on the morrow, they passed on their way. And as it telleth afterwards, in the Sancgreal, that Sir Percivale's sister helped that lady with her blood, whereof she died.

XIII.

THEN they rode three or four days, and never met with adventure; and by hap they were lodged with a gentleman that was a rich man, and well at ease. And, as they sat at their supper, Balin heard one complain grievously by him in a chair. "What noise is this?" said Balin. "Forsooth," said his host, "I will tell you: I was but late at a jousting, and there I jousted with a knight, that is brother unto King Pellam, and twice I smote him down; and then he promised to quit me on my best friend, and so he wounded my son that cannot be whole till I have of that knight's blood: and he rideth always invisible, but I know not his name." "Ah!" said Balin, "I know that knight, his name is Garlon; he hath slain two knights of mine in the same manner, therefore I had rather meet with that knight than all the gold in this realm, for the despite that he hath done me." "Well," said his host, "I shall tell you: King Pellam, of Listenise, hath made a cry, in all this country, of a great feast that shall be within twenty days, and no knight may come there but if he bring his wife with him, or his paramour; and that knight, your enemy and mine, ye shall see that day." "Then I behove you," said Balin, "part of his blood to heal your son withal." "We will be forward to-morrow," said his host. So, on the morrow, they rode all three towards Pellam, and had fifteen days' journey or they came thither: and that same day began the great feast, and they alighted and stabled their horses, and went into the castle: but Balin's host might not be let in, because he had no lady. Then was Balin well received, and brought to a chamber, and unarmed him; and there were brought him robes to his pleasure, and would have had him leave his sword behind him. "Nay," said Balin, "that will I not do; for it is the custom of my country for a knight always to keep his weapon with him, and that custom will I keep, or else I will depart as I came." Then they gave him leave to wear his sword. And so he went to the castle, and was set among knights of worship, and his lady afore him. Soon Balin asked a knight, "Is there not a knight in this court whose name is Garlon?" "Yonder he goeth," said the knight, "he with that black face: he is the marvailest knight that is now living, for he destroyeth many good knights, for he goeth invisible." "Ah! well," said Balin, "is that he?" Then Balin advised him long, "If I slay him here I shall not escape, and if I leave him now, peradventure I shall never meet with him again at such a good time, and much harm he will do, and he live." Therewith this Garlon espied that this Balin beheld him,

and then he came and smote Balin on the face with the back of
his hand, and said, " Knight, why beholdest thou me so ? for
shame ; therefore eat thy meat, and do that thou came for."
" Thou sayest sooth," said Balin ; "this is not the first despite
that thou hast done me ; and, therefore, I will do that I came
for."   And rose .up so fiercely, and cleaved his head to the
shoulders. "Give me the truncheon," said Balin to his lady,
" wherewith he slew your knight." Anon she gave it him, for
always she bear that truncheon with her. And therewith Balin
smote him through the body, and said openly, " With that
truncheon thou hast slain a good knight, and now it sticketh in
thy body." And then Balin called to him his host, saying,
" Now may ye fetch blood enough for to heal your son withal."

XIV.

ANON all the knights rose up from the table for to set on
Balin ; and King Pellam himself arose up fiercely, and said,
" Knight, why hast thou slain my brother? thou shalt die,
therefore, ere thou depart."   " Well," said Balin, "then do it
yourself."   " Yes," said King Pellam, "there shall no man have·
to do with thee but myself, for the love of my brother."   Then
King Pellam caught in his hand a grim weapon, and smote
eagerly at Balin ; but Balin put the sword between his head and
the stroke, and therewith his sword burst in sunder. And when
Balin was weaponless, he came into a chamber for to seek some
weapon, and so from chamber to chamber, and no weapon could
he find ; and always King Pellam followed him, and at the last he
entered into a chamber that was marvellously well dight and
richly, and a bed arrayed with cloth of gold, the richest that
might be thought, and one lying therein, and thereby stood a
table of clean gold, with four pillars of silver that bear up the
table, and upon the table stood a marvellous spear, strangely
wrought. And when Balin saw the spear, he gat it in his hand,
and turned him to King Pellam, and smote him passingly sore
with that spear, that King Pellam fell down in a swoon ; and
therewith the castle rove and walls brake, and fell to the earth,
and Balin fell down, so that he might not stir hand nor foot :
and so the most part of the castle that was fallen down, through
that dolorous stroke, lay upon King Pellam and Balin three
days.

XV.

THEN Merlin came thither and took up Balin, and gat him a
good horse, for his horse was dead, and bade him ride out of that

country. "I would have my damsel," said Balin. "Lo," said Merlin, "where she lieth dead." And King Pellam lay so many years sore wounded, and might never be whole till Galahad, the haughty prince, healed him in the quest of the Sancgreal; for in that place was part of the blood of our Lord Jesus Christ, that Joseph, of Arimathy, brought into this land, and there himself lay in that rich bed. And that was the same spear that Longius smote our Lord to the heart; and King Pellam was nigh of Joseph's kin, and that was the most worshipful man that lived in those days: and great pity it was of his hurt, for the stroke turned him to great dole, vexation, and grief. Then departed Balin from Merlin, and said, "In this world we shall never meet more." So he rode forth through the fair countries and cities, and found the people dead on every side. And all that were alive, cried, "O Balin! thou hast caused great damage in these countries, for the dolorous stroke that thou gavest unto King Pellam, three countries are destroyed; and doubt not but the vengeance will fall on thee at the last." When Balin was past the countries he was passing faint; so he rode eight days ere he met with adventures, and at the last he came into a fair forest, in a valley, and was aware of a tower, and there beside he saw a great horse of war tied to a tree, and there beside sat a fair knight on the ground, and made great mourning: and he was a likely man, and well made. Balin said, "God save you, why be ye so heavy? tell me, and I will amend it, and I may to my power." "Sir knight," said he, "again thou doest me great grief; for I was in merry thoughts, and now thou puttest me to more pain." Balin went a little from him, and looked on his horse. Then Balin heard him say thus: "Ah! fair lady, why have ye broken my promise; for ye promised me to meet me here by noon, and I may curse you that ever ye gave me this sword; for with this sword I will slay myself." And he pulled it out, and therewith Balin started to him, and took him by the hand. "Let go my hand," said the knight, "or else I shall slay thee." "That shall not need," said Balin, "for I shall promise you my help to get you your lady, if you will tell me where she is?" "What is your name?" said the knight. "My name is Balin le Savage." "Ah! sir, I know you well enough; you are the knight with the two swords, and the man of most prowess of your hands living." "What is your name?" said Balin. "My name is Garnish of the Mount, a poor man's son; but, by my prowess and hardiness, a duke hath made me a knight, and gave me lands: his name is Duke Hermel, and his daughter is she that I love, and she me, as I deemed." "How far is she hence?" said Balin. "But five miles," said the knight. "Now ride we hence," said the two knights. So they rode more than a pace till that they came unto a fair castle, well walled and ditched. "I will into the castle," said Balin, "and look if she be there." So he went in, and searched from chamber to chamber, and found her bed, but she was not there; then Balin looked into a fair little garden, and, under a laurel-tree, he saw her lie upon a quilt of green samite, and a knight in her arms, and under their heads grass and herbs. When Balin saw her lie so with the foulest knight that ever he saw, and she a fair lady, then Balin went through all the chambers again, and told the knight how he had found her as she had slept fast, and so brought him to the place where she lay fast sleeping.

XVI.

AND when Garnish beheld her so lying, for pure sorrow his mouth and nose burst out on bleeding, and with his sword he smote off both their heads; and then he made sorrow out of measure, and said, "Oh! Balin, much sorrow hast thou brought to me; for hadst thou not showed me that sight, I should have passed my sorrow." "Forsooth," said Balin, "I did it to this intent, that it should assuage thy courage, and that ye might see and know their falsehood, and to cause you to leave that lady's love. God knoweth I did none other but as I would you did to me." "Alas!" said Garnish, "now is my sorrow double that I may not endure, now have I slain that I most loved in all my life." And therewith suddenly he rove himself on his own sword unto the hilt. When Balin saw that, he dressed him from thence, lest folks should say that he had slain them; and so he rode forth, and within three days he came by a cross, and thereon was letters of gold written, that said, "It is not for a knight alone to ride towards this castle." Then saw he an old hoary gentleman coming toward, that said, "Balin le Savage, thou passeth thy bounds this way; therefore turn again, and it will avail thee." And he vanished away anon, and so he heard a horn blow, as it had been the death of a beast. "That blast," said Balin, "is blown for me; for I am the prize, and yet am I not dead." And therewith he saw a hundred ladies and many knights that welcomed him with fair semblance, and made him passing good cheer unto his sight, and led him into the castle, and there was dancing and minstrelsy, and all manner of joy. Then the chief lady of the castle, said, "Knight with the two swords, ye must have a do and joust with a knight hereby that keepeth an island; for there may no man pass this way, but he may joust, or he pass." "That is an unhappy custom," said Balin, "that a knight may not pass this way, but if he joust." "Ye shall have a do but with one knight," said the lady. "Well," said Balin, "since I shall thereto, I am ready; but travelling men are often weary, and their horses also: but though my horse be weary, my heart is not weary, I would be fain there my death should be." "Sir," said a knight to Balin, "me thinketh your shield is not good, I will lend you a bigger; thereof, I pray you." And so he took the shield that was unknown, and left his own, and so rode unto the island, and put him and his horse in a great boat. And when he came on the other side he met with a damsel, and she said, "O knight, Balin, why have you left your own shield; alas! ye have put yourself in great danger: for by your shield you should have been known. It is great pity of you as ever was of knight, for of prowess and hardiness thou hast no fellow living." "Me repenteth," said Balin, "that ever I came within this country: but I may not turn now again for shame, and what adventure shall fall to me, be it life or death, I will take the adventure that shall come to me." And then he looked on his armour, and understood he was well armed, and therewith blessed him, and mounted upon his horse.

XVII.

THEN afore him he saw come riding out of a castle, a knight, and his horse trapped all in red, and himself in the same colour. And when this knight in the red beheld Balin, him thought that it should be his brother Balin, because of his two swords; but because he knew not his shield, he deemed that it should not be. And so they couched their spears, and came marvellously fast together, and smote either other in the shields; but their spears and their course was so big that it bare down horse and man, so that they lay both in a swoon; but Balin was sore bruised with the fall of his horse, for he was weary of travel. And Balan the first that rose on foot, and drew his sword, and went toward Balin, and he arose and went against him, but Balan smote Balin first, and he put up his shield, and smote him through the shield, and broke his helm; then Balin smote him again with that unhappy sword, and well nigh had felled his brother Balan: and so they fought there together till their breaths failed. Then Balin looked up to the castle, and saw the towers stand full of ladies. So they went to battle again, and wounded each other grievously; and then they breathed often-time, and so went to battle: that all the place there as they fought was red of their blood. And, at that time, there was none of them both but they had smitten either other seven great wounds ; so that the least of them might have been the death of the mightiest giant in the world. Then they went to battle again so marvellously, that doubt it was to hear of that battle ; for the great bloodshedding, and their hawberks unnailed, that naked they were on every side : at the last Balan, the younger brother, withdrew him a little, and laid him down. Then said Balin le Savage, "What knight art thou? for ere now I found never no knight that matched me." "My name is," said he, "Balan, brother to the good knight Balin." "Alas!" said Balin, "that ever I should see this day." And therewith he fell backward in a swoon. Then Balan went on all four, feet and hands, and put off the helm of his brother, and might not know him by the visage, it was so full hewn and bebled ; but when he awoke, he said, "O Balan, my brother, thou hast slain me, and I thee, wherefore all the wide world shall speak of us both." "Alas !" said Balan, "that ever I saw this day, that through mishap I might not know you ; for I espied well your two swords, but because ye had another shield, I deemed you had been another knight." "Alas!" said Balin, "all that made an unhappy knight in the castle, for he caused me to leave mine own shield to the destruction of us both ; and if I might live I would destroy that castle for the ill customs." "That were well done," said Balan, "for I had never grace to depart from them, since that I came hither, for here it happened me to slay a knight that kept this island, and since might I never depart, and no more should ye, brother, and ye might have slain me, as ye have, and escaped yourself with your life." Right so came the lady of the tower with four knights and six ladies, and six yeomen unto them, and there she heard how they made their mourn either to other, and said, "We came both out of one womb, and so shall we lie both in one pit." So Balan prayed the lady of her gentleness, for his true service, that she would bury them both in that place there the battle was done. And she granted them, with weeping cheer, and said, "It should be done richly, and in the best manner." "Now will ye send for a priest, that we may receive the sacrament and blessed body of our Lord Jesus Christ." "Yea," said the lady, "it shall be done." And so she sent for a priest, and gave them their rites. "Now," said Balin, "when we are buried in one tomb, and the inscription made over us how two brethren slew each other, there will never good knight, nor good man, see our tomb, but they will pray for our souls." And so all the ladies and gentlewomen wept for pity. And anon Balan died, but Balin died not till the midnight after,

and so were buried both; and the lady let make an inscription
of Balan, how he was there slain by the hands of his own
brother : but she knew not Balin's name.

XVIII.

ON the morrow came Merlin, and let write Balin's name upon
the tomb, with letters of gold : " Here lieth Balin le Savage,
that was the knight with the two swords, and he that smote the
dolorous stroke."   Merlin let make there also a bed, that there
should never man lie in but he went out of his wit ; yet Launcelot du Lake fordid that bed through his nobleness.   And anon,
after as Balin was dead, Merlin took his sword, and took off
the pommel, and set on another pommel.   Then Merlin had
a knight that stood afore him to handle that sword, and he
assayed, but he could not handle it.   Then Merlin laughed.
" Why laugh ye ? " said the knight.   " This is the cause," said
Merlin : " there shall never no man handle this sword but the
best knight of the world, and that shall be Launcelot, or else
Galahad, his son ; and Launcelot, with his sword, shall slay the
man that in this world he loved best, that shall be Sir Gawaine."
All this he let write in the pommel of the sword.   Then Merlin
let make a bridge of iron and of steel into that island, and it
was but half-a-foot broad : and there shall never man pass that
bridge, nor have hardiness to go over, but if he were a passing
good man, and a good knight, without treachery or villainy.
Also, the scabbard of Balin's sword, Merlin left it on this side
the island, that Galahad should find it.   Also, Merlin let make,
by his subtlety and craft, that Balin's sword was put in marble
stone, standing upright, as great as a millstone, and the stone
hoved always above the water, and did many years : and so,
by adventure, it swam down the stream to the city of Camelot.
And that same day Galahad, the haughty prince, came with
King Arthur ; and so Galahad brought with him the scabbard,
and achieved the sword that was there in the marble stone,
hoving upon the water ; and, on Whitsunday, he achieved the
sword as it is rehearsed in the book of the Sancgreal.   Soon after
this was done Merlin came to King Arthur, and told him of the
dolorous stroke that Balin gave to King Pellam, and how Balin
and Balan fought together the marvailest battle that ever was
heard of, and how they were buried both in one tomb.   " Alas,"
said King Arthur, " this is the greatest pity that ever I heard
tell of two knights ; for in the world I know not such two
knights as they were."   Thus endeth the tale of Balin and
Balan, two brethren, born in Northumberland, good knights.

TIIE BOOK OF TIIE ROUND TABLE AND TIIE THREE QUESTS.

I.

N the beginning of King Arthur, after that he was chosen king by adventure and by grace, for the most part the barons knew not that he was Uther-pendragon's son, but as Merlin made it openly known. But yet many kings and lords made great war against him for that cause, but King Arthur full well overcame them all ; for the most part of the days of his life he was much ruled by the counsel of Merlin. So it befell on a time that King Arthur said unto Merlin, "My barons will let me have no rest, but needs they will have that I take a wife, and I will none take but by thy counsel and by thine advice." "It is well done," said Merlin, "that ye take a wife, for a man of your bounty and nobleness should not be without a wife. Now is there any fair lady that ye love better that another ?" "Yea," said King Arthur, "I love Guenever, the king's daughter,—Leodegraunce, of the land of Cameliard, which Leodegraunce holdeth in his house the Table Round that ye told he had of my father, Uther. And this damsel is the most gentlest and fairest lady that I know living, or yet that I ever could find." "Sir," said Merlin, "as of her beauty and fairness she is one of the fairest that live : but, and ye loved her not so well as ye do, I would find you a damsel, of beauty and of goodness, that should like you, and should please you, and your heart were not set ; but there as a man's heart is set, he will be loth to return." "That is truth," said King Arthur. But Merlin warned the King privily, that Guenever was not wholesome for him to take to wife, for he warned him that Launcelot should love her, and she him again ; and so he turned his tale to the adventures of the Sancgreal. Then Merlin desired of the King to have men with him that should inquire of Guenever : and so the King granted him. And Merlin went forth to King Leodegraunce of Cameliard, and told him of the desire of the King : that he would have to his wife Guenever his daughter. "That is to me," said King Leodegraunce, "the best tidings that ever I heard, that so worthy a king of prowess and nobleness will wed my daughter : and, as for my lands, I will give him, wished I that it might please him, but he hath lands enough, he needeth none ; but I shall send him a gift that shall please him much more, for I shall give him the Table Round, the which Utherpendragon gave me ; and, when it is full complete, there is a hundred knights and fifty : and, as for a hundred good knights, I have myself, but I lack fifty, for so many have been slain in my days." And so King Leodegraunce delivered his daughter, Guenever, unto Merlin, and the Table Round, with the hundred knights : and so they rode freshly, with great royalty, what by water, and what by land, till they came that night unto London.

II.

WHEN King Arthur heard of the coming of Guenever, and the hundred knights of the Round Table, he made great joy for their coming, and said, openly, "This fair lady is passing welcome to me, for I loved her long, and therefore there is nothing so pleasing to me : and these knights with the Round Table please me more than right great riches." Then in all haste the King did ordain for the marriage and coronation, in the most honourable wise that could be devised. "Now, Merlin," said King Arthur, "go thou and espy me in all this land fifty knights, that be of most prowess and worship." Within short time Merlin made the best speed he might, and found twenty-eight good knights, but no more could he find. Then the Archbishop of Canterbury was sent for, and he blessed the sieges of his Round Table with great royalty and devotion ; and there sat the twenty-eight knights in their sieges. And when this was done, Merlin said, "Fair sirs, ye must all arise and come unto King Arthur, for to do him homage ; he will have the better will to maintain you." And so they arose and did their homage ; and, when they were gone, Merlin found in the sieges letters of gold, that told the knights' names that had sitten therein. But two sieges were void. And so anon came young Gawaine, and asked the King a gift. "Ask," said the King, "and I shall grant it you." "Sir, I ask that ye will make me knight the same day that ye shall wed fair Guenever." "I will do it with a good-will," said King Arthur, "and do to you all the worship that I may ; for I must so do, by reason you are my nephew and sister's son."

III.

FORTHWITHAL there came a poor man into the court, and brought with him a fair young man, of eighteen years of age, riding upon a lean mare. And the poor man asked all men that he met, "Where shall I find King Arthur?" "Yonder he is," said the knights; "wilt thou any thing with him ?" "Yea," said the poor man, "therefore I came hither." Anon, as he came before the King, he saluted him, and said, "O King Arthur, the flower of all knights and kings, I beseech Jesus save thee. Sir, it was told me, that at this time of your marriage ye would give any man the gift that he would ask, except it were unreasonable." "That is truth," said the King, "such cries I let make ; and that will I hold, so it impair not my realm nor mine estate." "Ye say well and graciously," said the poor man. "Sir, I ask nothing else but that ye will make my son here a knight." "It is a great thing that thou askest of me," said the King. "What is thy name ?" said the King to the poor man. "Sir, my name is Aries, the cowherd." "Whether cometh this of thee, or of thy son ?" said the King. "Nay, sir," said Aries, "this desire cometh of my son, and not of me. For I shall tell you, I have thirteen sons, and all they will fall to what labour I put them to, and will be right glad to do labour ; but this child will do no labour for me, for any thing that my wife or I may do, but always he will be shooting, or casting of darts, and glad to see battles, and to behold knights : and always, both day and night, he desireth of me that he might be made a knight." "What is thy name ?" said the King to the young man. "Sir, my name is Tor." The King beheld him fast, and saw he was passingly well visaged, and passingly well made of his years. "Well," said King Arthur to Aries, the cowherd, "fetch all thy sons afore me, that I may see them." And so the poor man did, and all were shapen much like the poor man ; but Tor was not like none of them all, in shape nor in countenance, for he was much more than any of them. "Now," said King Arthur unto Aries, the cowherd, "where is that sword that he shall be made knight withal ?" "It is here," said Tor. "Take it out of the sheath," said the King, "and require me to make you a knight." Then Tor alighted off his mare, and pulled out his sword, kneeling, requiring the King that he would make him knight, and that he might be a knight of the Round Table. "As for a knight I will make you," and therewith smote him in the neck with the sword, saying, "Be ye a good knight : and so I pray to God ye may be ; and if ye be of prowess, and of worthiness, ye shall be a knight of the Round Table." "Now, Merlin," said King Arthur, "say whether this Tor shall be a good knight or no." "Yea, sir, he ought to be a good knight, for he is come of as good a man as any is on live, and of king's blood." "How so, sir ?" said the King. "I shall tell you," said Merlin : "this poor man, Aries, the cowherd, is not his father, he is

nothing like to him ; for King Pellinore is his father." "I
suppose nay," said the cowherd. "Fetch thy wife afore me,"
said Merlin, "and she shall not say nay." Anon the wife was
fetched, which was a fair housewife, and there she answered
Merlin full womanly ; and there she told the King and Merlin,
that when she was a maid, and went to milking, "there met
with me a stern knight, and he begot my son Tor ; and he took
from me my greyhound, that I had at that time with me, and
said that he would keep the greyhound for my love." "Ah !"
said the cowherd, "I weened not this ; but I may believe it
well, for the boy had never no likeness to me" "Sir,' said Tor
to Merlin, "dishonour not my mother." "Sir," said Merlin,
"it is more for your worship than hurt ; for your father is a good
man, and a king, and he may right well advance you and your
mother ; for ye were begotten or ever she was wedded." "That
is truth," said the wife. "It is the less grief to me" said the
cowherd.

IV.

So on the morrow King Pellinore came to the court of King
Arthur, which had great joy of him, and told him of Tor, how
he was his son, and how he had made him knight at the request
of the cowherd. When King Pellinore beheld Tor, he pleased
him much. So the King made Gawaine knight, but Tor was the
first that he made at the feast. "What is the cause," said King
Arthur, "that there be two places void in the sieges ?" "Sir,"
said Merlin, "there shall no man sit in those places but they
that shall be of most worship. But in the Siege Perilous, there
shall no man sit therein but one ; and if there be any so hardy
to do it, he shall be destroyed ; and he that shall sit there shall
have no fellow." And therewith Merlin took King Pellinore by
the hand, and, in the one hand next the two sieges and the
Siege Perilous, he said, in open audience : "This is your place,
and best he be worthy to sit therein of any that is here."
Thereat had Sir Gawaine great envy, and said to Gaheris, his
brother, "Yonder knight is put unto great worship ; the which
grieveth me sore, for he slew our father, King Lot, therefore I
will slay him," said Sir Gawaine, "with a sword that was sent
me, which is passing trenchant." "Ye shall not do so," said
Gaheris, " at this time ; for at this time I am but a squire, and,
when I am made knight, I will be avenged on him ; and therefore, brother, it is best ye suffer till another time, that we have
him out of the court, for and we did so now, we should trouble
this high feast." "I will well," said Sir Gawaine, "as ye will."

V.

THEN was the high feast made ready, and the King was wedded at Camelot unto dame Guenever, in the church of St. Stevens, with great solemnity; and, as every man was set after his degree, Merlin went unto all the knights of the Round Table, and bid them sit still, and that none should remove, "for ye shall see a marvellous adventure." Right so as they sat, there came running in a white hart into the hall, and a white brachet next him, and thirty couple of black running hounds came after with a great cry, and the hart went about the Table Round; as he went by the other tables, the white brachet caught him by the buttock, and pulled out a piece, wherethrough the hart leapt a great leap, and overthrew a knight that sat at the table's side; and therewith the knight arose and took up the brachet, and so went forth out of the hall, and took his horse, and rode his way with the brachet. Right soon anon came in a lady on a white palfrey, and cried aloud to King Arthur, "Sir, suffer me not to have this despite, for the brachet was mine that the knight led away" "I may not do therewith," said the King. With this there came a knight riding all armed, on a great horse, and took the lady with him by force; and she cried and made great moan. When she was gone, the King was glad, because she made such a noise. "Nay," said Merlin, "ye may not leave these adventures so lightly, for these adventures must be brought again, or else it would be disworship to you, and to your feast." "I will," said the King, "that all be done by your advice." "Then," said Merlin, "let call Sir Gawaine, for he must bring again the white hart; also, sir, ye must let call Sir Tor, for he must bring again the brachet and the knight, or else slay him; also, let call King Pellinore, for he must bring again the lady and the knight, or else slay him; and these three knights shall do marvellous adventures or they come again." Then were they called all three, as it is rehearsed afore, and every each of them took their charge, and armed them surely. But Sir Gawaine had the first request, and therefore we will begin at him.

VI.

SIR GAWAINE rode more than a pace, and Gaheris, his brother, rode with him instead of a squire, for to do him service. So as they rode they saw two knights fight on horseback passing sore; so Sir Gawaine and his brother rode between them, and asked them for what cause they fought so? The one knight answered and said, "We fight for a simple matter, for we be two brethren, and born and begotten of one man and of one woman." "Alas," said Sir Gawaine, "why do ye so?" "Sir," said the elder, "there came a white hart this way this day, and many hounds chased him, and a white brachet was always near him; and we understood it was adventure made for the high feast of King Arthur; and, therefore, I would have gone after to have won me worship, and here my younger brother said he would go after the hart, for he was a better knight than I, and for this cause we fell at debate; and so we thought to prove which of us both was better knight." "This is a simple cause," said Sir Gawaine; "strange men ye should debate with, and not brother with brother; therefore, and if ye will do by my counsel, I will have ado with you; that is, ye shall yield you unto me, and that ye go unto King Arthur, and yield you unto his grace." "Sir knight," said the two brethren, "we are sore fought, and much blood have we lost through our wilfulness; and, therefore, we would be loth to have ado with you." "Then do as I will have you," said Sir Gawaine. "We will agree to fulfil your will; but by whom shall we say that we be thither sent?" "Ye may say, by the knight that followeth the quest of the white hart. Now what is your names?" said Sir Gawaine." "Sorlouse of the Forest," said the elder: "and my name is," said the younger, "Brian of the Forest." And so they departed and went to the King's court, and Sir Gawaine went in his quest, and as Sir Gawaine followed the hart by the cry of the hounds, even afore him there was a great river, and the hart swam over; and as Sir Gawaine would have followed after, there stood a knight on the other side and said, "Sir knight, come not over after the hart, but if thou wilt joust with me." "I will not fail as for that," said Sir Gawaine, "to follow the quest that I am in." And so he made his horse to swim over the water; and anon they got their spears, and ran together full hard; but Sir Gawaine smote him off his horse, and then he turned his horse, and bid him yield him. "Nay," said the knight, "not so, though thou have the better of me on horseback, I pray thee, valiant knight, alight on foot, and match we together with swords." "What is your name," said Sir Gawaine. "Allardin of the Isles," said the other. Then either dressed their shields and smote together, but Sir Gawaine smote him through the helm so hard, that it went to the brains, and the knight fell down dead. "Ah!" said Gaheris, "that was a mighty stroke of a young knight."

VII.

THEN Sir Gawaine and Sir Gaheris rode more than a pace after the white hart, and let slip at the hart three couple of greyhounds; and so they chased the hart into the castle, and in the chief place of the castle they slew the hart that Sir Gawaine and Gaheris followed after. Right so there came a knight out of a chamber, with a sword in his hand, and slew two of the hounds, even in the sight of Sir Gawaine, and the remnant, he chased them with his sword out of the castle. And when he came again he said, "Oh! my white hart! me repenteth that thou art dead, for my sovereign lady gave thee to me; and evil have I kept thee, and thy death shall be dear bought and I live." And anon he went into his chamber and armed him, and came out fiercely, and there he met with Sir Gawaine. "Why have you slain my hounds?" said Sir Gawaine, "for they did but their kind, and I had rather ye had worked your anger upon me than the dumb beasts." "Thou sayest truth," said the knight, "I have avenged me on thy hounds, and so as I will be on thee or thou go." Then Sir Gawaine alighted on foot, and dressed his shield, and they stroke mightily, and clave their shields, and stunned their helms, and brake their hawberks, that the blood ran down to their feet. At the last, Sir Gawaine smote the knight so hard, that he fell to the earth; and then he cried mercy, and yielded him, and besought him as he was a knight, and gentleman, to save his life. "Thou shalt die," said Sir Gawaine, "for slaying of my hounds." "I will make amends unto my power," said the knight. Sir Gawaine would no mercy have, but unlaced his helm to have stricken off his helm: right so came his lady out of her chamber and fell over him, and so he smote off her head by misadventure. "Alas!" said Gaheris, "that is foul and shamefully done, that shame shall never from you: also, ye should give mercy unto them that ask mercy; for a knight without mercy is without worship." Sir Gawaine was so astonished at the death of this fair lady, that he wist not what he did; and said to the knight, "Arise, I will give thee mercy." "Nay, nay," said the knight, "I take no force of mercy now, for thou hast slain my love and my lady, that I loved best of all earthly things." "Me repenteth it sore," said Sir Gawaine, "for I thought to have stricken at thee: but now thou shalt go unto King Arthur, and tell him of thine adventures, and how thou art overcome by the knight that went in the quest of the white hart." "I take no force," said the knight, "whether I live or die." But, for dread of death, he swore to go unto King

Arthur ; and he made him for to bear one greyhound before him upon his horse, and another behind him also. "What is your name," said Gawaine, "or we depart ?" "My name is," said the knight, "Ablamore of the Marsh." So he departed towards Camelot.

VIII.

AND Sir Gawaine went into the castle, and made him ready to lay there all night, and would have unarmed him. "What will ye do ?" said Gaheris ; "will ye unarm you in this country ? ye may well think that ye have many enemies here about." They had no sooner said that word, but there came four knights well armed, and assailed Sir Gawaine hard, and said thus unto him : "Thou new-made knight, thou hast shamed thy knighthood, for a knight without mercy is dishonoured. Thou hast also slain a fair lady, which is unto thee great shame for evermore ; and, doubt thou not, thou shalt have great need of mercy or thou depart from us." And therewith one of them smote Sir Gawaine such a stroke, that he had nigh felled him to the earth, and Gaheris smote him again sore ; and so they were on the one side, and on the other, that Sir Gawaine and Gaheris were in great jeopardy of their lives, and one of them, with a bow and archer, smote Sir Gawaine through the arm, that it grieved him wondrous sore. And, as they should have been both slain, there came four ladies, and besought the knights of grace for Sir Gawaine. And goodly, at the request of the ladies, they gave Sir Gawaine and Gaheris their lives, and made them to yield them as prisoners ; then Sir Gawaine and Gaheris made great moan. "Alas" said Sir Gawaine, "mine arm grieveth me sore—I am like to be maimed ; " and so made his complaint piteously. On the morrow early came one of the four ladies to Sir Gawaine, which had heard all his complaints, and said, "Sir knight, what cheer ?" "Not good," said he. "It is your own default," said the lady, "for ye have done a passing foul deed in the slaying of the lady, which will be great villainy to you. But be ye not of King Arthur's kin ?" said the lady. "Yes, truly," said Gawaine. "What is your name ?" said the lady, "ye must tell it or that ye pass." "My name is Gawaine, King Lot's son, of Orkney, and my mother is King Arthur's sister." "Ah ! then ye are nephew unto King Arthur," said the lady, "and I shall so speak for you, that ye shall have conduct to go to King Arthur for his love." And so she departed, and told the four knights how their prisoner was King Arthur's nephew, "and his name is Gawaine, King Lot's son, of Orkney." Then they gave him the head of the white hart, because it was in his quest. Then anon they delivered Sir Gawaine under this promise, that he should bear the dead lady with him in this manner: her head was hanged about his neck, and the whole body of her lay before him upon the mane of his horse : and in this manner he rode forth towards Camelot. And anon as he was come to the court, Merlin desired of King Arthur, that Sir Gawaine should be sworn to tell of all his adventures, and so he was : and showed how he slew the lady, and how he would give no mercy to the knight, wherethrough the lady was villainously slain. Then the King and the Queen were greatly displeased with Sir Gawaine for the slaying of the lady : and, thereby, the ordinance of the Queen was set to an inquest of ladies on Sir Gawaine. And they judged him, ever while he lived to be with all ladies, and to fight for their quarrels, and that he should ever be courteous, and never to refuse mercy to him that asketh mercy. Thus was Sir Gawaine sworn upon the four Evangelists, that he would never be against ladies nor gentlewomen, but if he fought for a lady, and his adversary for another. And thus endeth the adventure of Sir Gawaine, which he did at the marriage of King Arthur.

IX.

THEN Sir Tor was ready, and he mounted on horseback, and rode forth his way a good pace after the knight with the brachet. And so as he rode, he met with a dwarf suddenly, which smote his horse on the head with a staff, that he went backward more than his spear's length. "In what intent doest thou smite my horse ?" said Sir Tor. "For thou shalt not pass this way," said the dwarf ; "but that thou shalt first joust with yonder knights, that abide in yonder pavilions that thou seest." Then was Sir Tor ware where two pavilions were, and great spears stood out, and two shields hung on two trees by the pavilions. "I may not tarry," said Sir Tor, "for I am in a quest which I must needs follow." "Thou shalt not pass," said the dwarf; and therewith he blew his horn. Then there came one armed on horseback, and dressed his shield, and came fast toward Sir Tor ; and he dressed him against him, and so ran together, that Sir Tor bare him from his horse. And anon the knight yielded him to his mercy : "But, sir, I have a fellow in yonder pavilion, that will have ado with you anon." "He shall be welcome," said Sir Tor. Then was he ware of another knight coming with great random, and each of them dressed to other, that marvel it was to see ; but the knight smote Sir Tor a great stroke in the midst of the shield, that his spear all to-shivered, and Sir Tor smote him through the shield below, that it went through the side of the knight, but the stroke slew him not. And therewith Sir Tor alight, and smote him upon the helm a great stroke; and therewith the knight yielded him, and besought him of mercy. "I will well," said Sir Tor, "but thou and thy fellow must go unto King Arthur, and yield you prisoners to him." "By whom shall we say that we are thither sent?" "Ye shall say, by the knight that went with the brachet. Now what be your names?" said Sir Tor. "My name is," said the one, "Sir Felot of Langdoc." "And my name is," said the other, "Sir Petipace of Winchelsea." "Now go. ye forth," said Sir Tor: "God speed you and me." Then came the dwarf, and said to Sir Tor, "I pray you to give me a gift." "I will well," said Sir Tor. "I ask no more," said the dwarf, "but that ye will suffer me to do you service, for I will serve no more recreant knights." "Then take a horse anon," said Sir Tor, "and come on and ride with me : I wot ye ride after the knight with the white brachet." "I shall bring you where he is," said the dwarf. And so they rode through the forest, and at the last they were ware of two pavilions by a priory with two shields, and the one shield was renewed with white, and the other shield was red.

X.

THEREWITH Sir Tor alighted, and took the dwarf his spear, and so came to the white pavilion, and saw three damsels lie therein on a pallet sleeping. And then he went unto that other pavilion, and there he found a fair lady sleeping ; and there was the white brachet that bayed at her fast. And therewith anon the lady awoke and went out of the pavilion, and all her damsels : but anon as Sir Tor espied the white brachet, he took it by force, and took it to the dwarf. "What will ye do?" said the lady ; "will ye take away my brachet from me?" "Yea," said Sir Tor ; "this brachet have I sought from King Arthur's court to this place." "Well," said the lady, "sir knight, ye shall not go far with it, but that ye shall be met withal or it be long, and also evil handled." "I shall abide it, what adventure soever cometh by the grace of God :" and so mounted upon his horse, and passed forth on his way toward Camelot ; but it was so near night that he might not pass but little further. "Know ye any lodging?" said Sir Tor. "I know none," said the dwarf; "but here beside is a hermitage, and there ye must take such lodging as ye find." And within awhile they came to the hermitage and took lodging. And there was bread, and grass and oats for their horses ; soon it was sped, and full hard was their supper ; but there they rested them all the night till on the morrow, and heard a mass devoutly, and took their leave of the hermit, and Sir Tor prayed the hermit to pray for him. He said he would, and betook him to God ; and so mounted on horseback, and rode toward Camelot a long while. With that they heard a knight call loud that came after them, and said, "Knight, abide and yield my brachet that thou tookest from my lady." Sir Tor returned again and beheld him, and saw he was a seemly knight, and well horsed and armed at all points : then Sir Tor dressed his shield, and took his spear in his hand, and the other came fiercely upon him, and smote each other that both horse and men fell to the earth. Anon they lightly arose, and drew their swords as eagerly as two lions, and put their shields afore them, and smote through their shields, that the cantels fell off on both parties ; and also they brake their helms that the hot blood ran out, and the thick mails of their halberts they carved and rove asunder, that the hot blood ran to the ground, and they had both many great wounds, and were passing weary. But Sir Tor espied that the other knight fainted, and then he pursued fast upon him, and doubled his strokes, and made him fall to the ground on the one side. Then Sir Tor made him yield him. "That will I not," said Abellius, "while my life lasteth, and the soul within my body, unless that thou wilt give me the brachet." "That will I not do," said Sir Tor, "for it was my quest to bring again the brachet and thee, or else slay thee."

XI.

WITH that came a damsel riding upon a palfrey, as fast as she might drive, and cried with a loud voice unto Sir Tor. "What will ye with me?" said Sir Tor. "I beseech thee," said the damsel, "for King Arthur's love, give me a gift ; I require thee, gentle knight, as thou art a gentleman." "Now," said Sir Tor, "ask a gift, and I will give it you." "Gramercy," said the damsel, "I ask the head of this false knight Abellius, for he is the most outrageous knight that liveth, and the greatest murderer." "I am right sorry and loth," said Sir Tor, "of that gift which I have granted ; let him make you amends in that which he hath trespassed against you." "He cannot make amends," said the damsel, "for he hath slain mine own brother, which was a better knight than ever he was, and he had no mercy upon him ; insomuch that I kneeled half-an-hour afore him in the mire, for to save my brother's life, which had done him no damage, but fought with by adventure of arms as knights adventurous do ; and for all that I could do or say, he smote off my brother's head ; wherefore I require thee, as thou art a true knight, to give me my gift, or else I shall shame thee in all the court of King Arthur, for he is the falsest knight living, and a great destroyer of good knights." Then when Abellius heard this he was sore afraid, and yielded him, and asked mercy. "I may not now," said Sir Tor, "but if I should be found false of my promise ; for when I would have taken you to mercy, ye would none ask, but if ye had the brachet again that was my quest." And therewith he took off his helm, and he arose and fled, and Sir Tor after him, and smote off his head quite. "Now, sir," said the damsel, "it is near night, I pray you come and lodge with me here at my place, it is here fast by." "I will well," said Sir Tor, for his horse and he had fared evil sith they departed from Camelot. And so he rode with her, and had passing good cheer with her ; and she had an old knight to her husband, which made him passing good cheer, and well eased Sir Tor and his horse. And on the morrow he heard mass, and brake his fast, and took his leave of the knight and of the lady, which besought him to tell them his name. "Truly," said he, "my name is Sir Tor, that late was made knight ; and this was the first request of arms that ever I did to bring again that this knight Abellius took away from King Arthur's court." "Oh ! knight," said the lady and her husband, "if ye come again here in our marches, come and see our poor lodging, and it shall be always at your commandment." So Sir Tor departed, and came to Camelot on the third day by noon : and the King and the Queen, and all the court, was passing glad of his coming, and made great joy that he was come again, for he went from the court with little succour ; but that his father, King Pellinore, gave him an old courser, and King Arthur gave him armour and a sword, and else had he none other succour, but rode so forth himself alone. And then the King and the Queen, by Merlin's advice, made him to swear to tell of his adventures, and so he told and made profess of his deeds, as it is afore rehearsed ; wherefore the King and the Queen made great joy. "Nay," said Merlin, "these be but jests to that he shall do ; he shall prove a noble knight of prowess, as good as any is living, and gentle and courteous, and full of good parts, and passing true of his promise, and never shall do outrage." Where, through Merlin's words, King Arthur gave him an earldom of lands that fell unto him : and here endeth the quest of Sir Tor, King Pellinore's son.

XII.

THEN King Pellinore armed him and mounted upon his horse and rode more than a pace after the lady that the knight led away. And so as he rode in the forest, he saw in a valley a damsel sit by a well side, and a wounded knight between her arms, and Sir Pellinore saluted her. And when she was ware of him, she cried overloud, "Help me, knight, for Christ's sake." King Pellinore would not tarry, he was so eager in his quest ; and ever she cried more than a hundred times after help. And when she saw he would not abide, she prayed unto God for to send him as much need of help as she had, and that he might know it or he died. And as the book telleth, the knight died that lay there wounded ; wherefore the lady for pure sorrow slew herself with her love's sword. So as King Pellinore rode in that valley, he met with a poor labouring man. " Sawest thou not," said King Pellinore, "a knight riding and leading away a lady?" "Yes," said the poor man. " I saw that knight, and the lady that made great moan ; and yonder beneath in a valley there shall ye see two pavilions, and one of the knights of the pavilions challenged that lady of that knight, and said, 'she was his near cousin, wherefore he should lead her no farther ;' and so they waged in that quarrel, for the one said, 'he would have her by force ;' and the other said, 'he would have the rule of her, because he was her kinsman, and would lead her to her friends ;' for this quarrel I left them fighting, and if ye ride apace ye shall find them yet fighting, and the lady is in keeping with the squires in the pavilions." "God thank thee," said King Pellinore. Then he rode a gallop till that he had a sight of the two pavilions, and the two knights fighting. Anon rode he to the two pavilions, and saw the lady that was his quest, and said to her, " Fair lady, ye must come with me unto King Arthur's court." " Sir knight," said the two squires that were with her, "yonder be two knights that fight for this lady, go thither and depart them, and be agreed with them, and then may ye have her at your own pleasure." " Ye say well," said King Pellinore. And anon he rode between them, and parted them asunder, and asked the cause why they fought. " Sir knight," said the one, " I shall tell you : this lady is my nigh kinswoman, mine aunt's daughter ; and when I heard her complain that she was with him maugre her head, I waged battle to fight with him." " Sir knight," said the other, whose name was Ontzlake, of Went-land, "this lady I gat by my prowess of arms, this day of King Arthur's court." "That is untruly said," quoth King Pellinore, "for ye came in there all suddenly, as we were at the high feast, and took away this lady or any man might make him ready ; and therefore it was my request for to bring her again, and you also, or else the one of us to abide in the field; therefore the lady shall go with me to King Arthur, or I shall die for it, for I have promised it unto him, and therefore fight no more for her, for none of you both shall have no part of her at this time ; and if ye list to fight for her, fight with me, and I will defend her." "Well," said the knight, "make you ready, and we shall assail you with all our power." And as King Pellinore would have put his horse from them, and alight on foot, Sir Ontzlake run his horse through with the sword, and said, "Now art thou on foot as well as we." And when King Pellinore saw that his horse was so slain, he was wrath, and then fiercely and lightly leapt from his horse, and in great haste drew out his sword and put his shield afore him, and said, "Knight, keep well thy head ; for thou shalt have a buffet for the slaying of my horse." So King Pellinore gave him such a stroke upon the helm that he clove down the head to the chin, and therewith he fell to the earth dead.

XIII.

AND then he turned him to that other knight that was sore wounded ; but when he had seen the buffet that the other had, he would not fight, but kneeled down and said, "Take my cousin, the lady, with you, at your request ; and I require you, as ye be a true knight, put her to no shame nor villainy." "What," said King Pellinore, "will ye not fight for her ?" "No, sir," said the knight, "I will not fight with a knight of prowess as ye be." "Well," said King Pellinore, "ye say well ; I promise you she shall have no villainy by me, as I am a true knight. But now I lack a horse," said King Pellinore, "I will have Ontzlake's horse." "Ye shall not need," said the knight ; "for I shall give you such a horse as shall please you, so that ye will lodge with me, for it is near night." "I will well," said King Pellinore, "abide with you all night." And there he had with him right good cheer, and fared of the best, with passing good wine, and had merry rest that night ; and on the morrow he heard a mass, and after dined, and then was brought him a fair bay courser, and King Pellinore's saddle set upon him. "Now what shall I call you ?" said the knight, "inasmuch as ye have my cousin at your desire of your quest." "Sir, I shall tell you : my name is Pellinore, king of the Isles, and knight of the Round Table." "Now I am glad," said the knight, "that such a noble man as ye shall have the rule of my cousin." "What is now your name?" said King Pellinore: "I pray you tell me." "Sir," said he, "my name is Sir Meliot of Logurs, and this lady, my cousin, hight Nimue; and the knight, that is in that other pavilion, is my sworn brother, a passing good knight, and his name is Brian of the Isles, and he is full loth to do any wrong, and full loth to fight with any man or knight; but if he be sought upon, so that for shame he may not leave." "It is marvel," said King Pellinore, "that he will not have ado with me." "Sir, he will not have ado with no man but if it be at his request." "Bring him one of these to the court of King Arthur," said King Pellinore. "Sir, we will come together." "Ye shall be greatly welcome there," said King Pellinore, "and also greatly allowed for your coming." And so he departed with the lady, and brought her to Camelot. So, as they rode in a valley that was full of stones, the lady's horse stumbled, and threw her down, wherewith her arm was sore bruised, and near she swooned for pain and anguish. "Alas! sir," said the lady, "mine arm is out of joint, wherethrough I must needs rest me." "Ye shall do well," said King Pellinore. And so he alighted under a fair tree, whereas was fair grass, and he put his horse thereto, and so laid him under the tree, and slept till it was nigh night, and when he awoke he would have ridden. "Sir," said the lady, "it is so dark that ye may as well ride backward as forward." So they abode still and make there their lodging. Then King Pellinore put off his armour, and then, a little before midnight, they heard the trotting of a horse. "Be ye still," said King Pellinore, "for we shall hear of some adventure."

XIV.

AND therewith he armed him. So, right even afore him, there met two knights; the one came from Camelot, and the other from the north, and either saluted other. "What tidings at Camelot?" said the one. "By my head," said the other, "there have I been, and espied the court of King Arthur; and there is such a fellowship that they may never be broke, and well nigh all the world holdeth with King Arthur: for there is the flower of chivalry. Now for this cause I am riding into the north to tell our chieftains of the fellowship which is withholden with King Arthur." "As for that," said the other knight, "I have brought a remedy with me, that is the greatest poison that ever ye heard speak of, and to Camelot will I with it; for we have a friend right nigh King Arthur, and well cherished, that shall poison King Arthur: so he hath promised our chieftains,

and hath received great gifts for to do it." "Beware," said the
other knight, "of Merlin, for he knoweth all things by the
devil's craft ; therefore will I not let it," said the knight. And
so they departed in sunder. Anon after King Pellinore made
him ready, and his lady, and rode towards Camelot ; and as
they came by the well, whereas the wounded knight was, and
the lady, there he found the knight and the lady eaten with lions,
or wild beasts, all save the head ; wherefore he made great
mourn, and wept passing sore, and said, "Alas ! her life I
might have saved ; but I was so fierce in my quest, therefore I
would not abide." "Wherefore make ye such dole ?" said
the lady. "I wot not," said King Pellinore ; "but my heart
mourneth sore for the death of this lady, for she was a passing
fair lady, and a young." "Now shall ye do by mine advice,"
said the lady : "take this knight, and let him be buried in a
hermitage, and then take the lady's head and bear it with you
unto King Arthur's court." So King Pellinore took this dead
knight on his shoulders, and had him to the hermitage, and
charged the hermit with his corpse, and that service should be
done for the soul, and take his harness for your labour and pain.
"It shall be done," said the hermit, "as I will answer to God."

XV.

AND therewith they departed, and came whereas the head of
the lady lay with fair yellow hair, which grieved King Pellinore
passing sore when he looked upon it ; for much he cast his
heart on the visage. And so by noon they came to Camelot,
and King Arthur and the Queen were passing glad of his coming
to the court ; and there he was made to swear, upon the four
Evangelists, for to tell all the truth of his quest, from the beginning unto the ending. "Ah ! Sir Pellinore," said the Queen,
"ye were greatly to blame that ye saved not the lady's life."
"Madam," said King Pellinore, "ye were greatly to blame and
if ye would not save your own self and ye might : but, saving
your honour, I was so furious in my quest that I would not
abide, and that repenteth me, and shall do all the days of my
life." "Truly," said Merlin, "ye ought sore to repent it ; for
the lady was your own daughter, born of the Lady of the Rule,
and that knight that was dead was her love, and should have
wedded her, and he was a right good knight of a young man,
and would have proved a good man, and to this court was he
coming, and his name is Sir Miles of the Launds, and a knight
came behind him and slew him with a spear, and his name is
Loraine le Savage, a false knight, and a very coward, and she for

great sorrow slew herself with his sword, and her name was Eleine ; and because ye would not abide and help her, ye shall see your best friend fail you when ye be in the greatest distress that ever ye were, or shall be in : and that penance God hath ordained you for that deed, that he that ye shall most trust to, of any man alive, he shall leave you there as ye shall be slain." "Me forethinketh," said King Pellinore, "that this shall betide me ; but God may well foredo all destinies."

Thus when the quest was done of the white hart that Sir Gawaine followed, and the quest of the brachet followed of Sir Tor, son unto King Pellinore, and the quest of the lady that the knight took away, the which King Pellinore at that time followed, then King Arthur established all his knights, and gave them lands, that were not rich of land, and charged them never to do outrage nor murder, and always to flee treason ; also by no means to be cruel, but to give mercy unto him that asked mercy, upon pain of forfeiture of their worship and lordship of King Arthur for evermore ; and always to do ladies, damsels, and gentlewomen succour, upon pain of death : also that no man take no battles in a wrong quarrel for no law, nor for worldly goods. Unto this were all the knights sworn of the Round Table, both old and young ; and every year they were sworn at the high feast of Pentecost.

———◆———

THE BOOK OF MORGAN LE FAY, AND THE THREE DAMSELS.

I.

THEN after these quests of Sir Gawaine, of Sir Tor, and of King Pellinore, Merlin fell in a dotage on the damsel that King Pellinore brought to the court with him ; and she was one of the damsels of the lake, which hight Nimue. But Merlin would let her have no rest, but always he would be with her in every place ; and ever she made Merlin good cheer, till she had learned of him all manner of things that she desired, and he was so sore assotted upon her that he might not be from her. So, upon a time, he told unto King Arthur, "That he should not endure long, and that, for all his crafts, he should be put in the earth quick." And so he told the king many things that should befall ; but always he warned King Arthur to keep well his sword Excalibur, and the scabbard ; for he told him how the sword and the scabbard should be stolen from him by a woman that he most trusted. Also he told King Arthur that he would miss him, yet had ye rather than all your lands to have me again. "Ah !" said the King, "since I know of your adventure purvey for it, and put away, by your crafts, that mis-adventure." "Nay," said Merlin, "it will not be." And then he departed from King Arthur. And within a while the Lady of the Lake departed, and Merlin went evermore with her wheresoever she went. And oftentimes Merlin would have had her privily away by his subtle crafts ; and then she made him to swear that he should never do none enchantment upon her if he would have his will : and so he swore.

So she and Merlin went over the sea unto the land of Benwick, where King Ban was king, that had great war against King Claudas : and there Merlin spake with King Ban's wife, a fair lady and a good, and her name was Elaine, and there he saw young Launcelot. There the Queen made great sorrow for the mortal war that King Claudas made on her lord and on her lands. "Take no heaviness," said Merlin, "for this child, within these twenty years, shall revenge you on King Claudas, that all Christendom shall speak of it, and this same child shall be the most man of worship of this world ; and I know well that his first name was Galahad, and sith ye have confirmed him Launcelot." "That is truth," said the Queen ; "his first name was Galahad." "Oh ! Merlin," said the Queen, " shall I live to see my son such a man of prowess ?" "Yea, lady, on my peril ye shall see it, and live after many winters." And then, soon after, the Lady of the Lake and Merlin departed ; and by the way as they went Merlin showed her many wonders, and came into Cornwall. And always Merlin lay about the lady ; and she was ever passing weary of him, and fain would have been delivered of him ; for she was afraid of him, because he was a devil's son, and she could not put him away by any means.

And so, upon a time, it happened that Merlin showed to her a rock where was a great wonder, and wrought by enchant-ment, which went under a stone. So, by her subtle craft and working, she made Merlin to go under the stone to let her wit of the marvels there ; but she wrought so there for him, that he came never out, for all the craft that he could do : and so she departed, and left Merlin.

II.

AND then King Arthur rode to Camelot, and there he made a solemn feast, with mirth and joy. So anon after he returned to Carlisle, and there came to King Arthur new tidings, that the

King of Denmark, and the King of Ireland his brother, and the King of Wales, and the King of Soleyse, and the King of the Isle of Longtainse ; all these five knights, with a great host, were entered into King Arthur's land, and burnt and slew all that they found afore them, both cities and castles, that it was great pity to see. "Alas ! " said King Arthur, "yet had I never rest one month, sith I was crowned king of this land. Now shall I never rest till I meet with those kings in a fair field, and to that I make mine avow ; for my true liege people shall not be destroyed in my default, go with me who will, and abide who will." Then the King let write unto King Pellinore, and prayed him in all haste to make him ready, with such people as he might lightliest rear, and hie him after in all haste. All the barons were privily wrath that the King should depart so suddenly : but the King by no means would abide, but made writings unto them that were not there, and bade them hie after him such as were not at that time in the court. Then the King came to Queen Guenever, and said, "Lady, make you ready ; for ye shall go with me, for I may not long miss you : ye shall cause me to be the more hardier, what adventure soever befall me ; I will not wit my lady to be in any jeopardy." "Sir," said she, "I am at your command, and shall be ready what time soever ye be ready." So on the morrow the King and the Queen departed with such fellowship as they had, and came into the north in a forest beside the Humber, and there lodged them. When the tidings came to the five kings above said, that King Arthur was beside the Humber in a forest, there was a knight, brother unto one of the five kings, that gave them this counsel : "Ye know well that King Arthur has with him the flower of chivalry of the world, as it is proved by the great battle he did with the eleven kings ; and, therefore, hie unto him night and day, till that we be nigh him ; for the longer he tarrieth the bigger he is, and we ever the weaker. And he is so courageous of himself, that he is come to the field with little people : and, therefore, let us set upon him or it be day, and we shall so slay of his knights that there shall not one escape."

III.

UNTO this counsel the five kings assented ; and so they passed forth with their host through North Wales, and came upon King Arthur by night, and set upon his host, he and his knights being in their pavilions ; and King Arthur was unarmed, and had laid him to rest with the Queen. "Sirs," said Sir Kaye, "it is not good that we be unarmed." "We shall have no need," said Sir Gawaine and Sir Griflet, that lay in a little pavilion by the King. With that they heard a great noise, and many cried "Treason!" "Alas!" said King Arthur, "we are all betrayed. Unto arms, fellows!" cried he then. So they were anon armed at all points. Then came there a wounded knight unto King Arthur, and said to him, "Sir, save yourself and my lady, the Queen; for our host is destroyed, and much people of ours slain." So anon the King, and the Queen, and three knights, rode towards the Humber to pass over it, and the water was so rough that they were afraid to pass over. "Now may ye choose," said King Arthur, "whether ye will abide, and take the adventure upon this side; for, and ye be taken, they will slay you." "It were me rather," said the Queen, "to die in the water, than for to fall into your enemies' hands, and there to be slain." And as they stood so talking Sir Kaye saw the five kings coming, on horseback, by themselves alone, with their spears in their hands, towards them. "Lo!" said Sir Kaye, "yonder be the five kings; let us go to them, and match them." "That were folly," said Sir Gawaine; "for we are but four, and they be five." "That is truth," said Sir Griflet. "No force," said Sir Kaye. "I will undertake two of them, and may ye three undertake the other three." And therewith Sir Kaye let his horse run as fast as he might, and struck one of them through the shield and the body of a fathom deep, that the king fell to the earth stark dead. That saw Sir Gawaine, and ran unto another king so hard, that he smote him through the body; and therewith King Arthur ran to another, and smote him through the body with a spear, that he fell down to the earth dead; then Sir Griflet ran to the fourth king, and gave him such a fall, that he broke his neck. Anon Sir Kaye ran unto the fifth king, and smote him so hard upon the helm, that the stroke cleaved the helm and the head to the shoulders. "That was well stricken," said King Arthur, "and most worshipfully hast thou holden thy promise; therefore I shall honour thee as long as I live." And therewith they set the Queen in a barge in the Humber; but always Queen Guenever praised Sir Kaye for his noble deeds, and said, "What lady that ye love, and she love you not again, she were greatly to blame; and among ladies," said the Queen, "I shall bear your noble fame; for ye spake a great word, and fulfilled it worshipfully." And therewith the Queen departed. Then the King and the three knights rode into the forest; for there they supposed to hear of them that were escaped, and there King Arthur found the most part of his people, and told them all how

the five kings were dead : "and, therefore, let us hold together till it be day, and when their host espy that their
chieftains be slain, they will make such sorrow that they shall
not be able to help themselves." Right so as the King had said,
so it was ; for when they found the five kings dead, they made
such sorrow, that they fell down from their horses. Therewith
came King Arthur, with a few people, and slew on the right
hand and on the left, that well nigh there escaped no man ; but
all were slain to the number of thirty thousand men. And
when the battle was all ended King Arthur kneeled down and
thanked God full meekly ; and then he sent for the Queen, and
she came anon, and made great joy for the victory of that
dangerous battle.

IV.

THEREWITHAL came one to King Arthur, and told him tha
King Pellinore was within three miles with a great host, and
said, " Go unto him, and let him have knowledge how we have
sped." So within a while King Pellinore came with a great
host, and saluted the people and the King : and there was great
joy made on every side. Then King Arthur let search how
much people of his party there was slain, and there were found
not past a two hundred men slain, and eight knights of the
Round Table in their pavilions. Then the King let rear and
built, in the same place there as the battle was done, a fair
abbey, and endowed it with great livelihood, and let call it the
Abbey of le Beale Adventure. But when some of them came
into their countries, there as the five kings were kings, and told
them how they were slain, there was made great sorrow. And
when all King Arthur's enemies (as the King of North Wales,
and the King of the North) wist of the battle, they were passing
heavy. And so the King returned to Camelot in haste ; and
when he was come to Camelot he called King Pellinore unto
him, and said, " Ye understand well that we have lost eight
good knights of the Table Round ; and, by your advice, we will
choose eight again of the best that we may find in this court."
" Sir," said King Pellinore, " I shall counsel you, after my con-
ceit, the best : there are in your court right noble knights, both
old and young ; and, therefore, by mine advice, ye shall choose
the one half of old, and the other half of young." "Which be
the old ?" said King Arthur. " Sir," said King Pellinore, "me
seemeth that King Urience, that hath wedded your sister,
Morgan le Fay ; and the King of the Lake ; and Sir Hervise de
Revel, a noble knight ; and Sir Galagars, the fourth." " This

is well devised," said King Arthur; "and right so shall it be."
"Sir," said King Pellinore, "the first is Sir Gawaine, your
nephew, that is as good a knight of his time as any is in this
land; and the second, as me seemeth, is Sir Griflet le Fils de
Dieu, that is a good knight, and full desirous in arms, and, who
may see him live, he shall prove a good knight; and the third,
as me seemeth well worthy, is Sir Kaye, the seneschal; for
many time she hath done full worshipful: and now at your last
battle he did full honourably for to undertake to slay two
kings." "By my head," said King Arthur, "he is best worthy
to be a knight of the Round Table of any that ye have
rehearsed, and he had done no more prowess all the days of
my life."

V.

THEN said King Pellinore, "Now shall I put to you two
knights, and ye shall choose which is most worthy, that is, Sir
Bagdemagus and Sir Tor, my son. But because Sir Tor is my
son, I may not praise him; but else and he were not my son, I
durst say that, of his age, there is not in this land a better knight
than he is, nor of better conditions, and loth to do any wrong,
and loth to take any wrong." "By my head," said King
Arthur, "he is a passing good knight as any ye spake of this
day, and that know I full well, for I have seen him proved; and
he saith little, but he doth much more; for I know none in all his
court, and he were as well born on his mother's side as he is on
your side, that is like him of prowess and of might, and therefore I will have him at this time, and leave Sir Bagdemagus till
another time." And when they were so chosen, by the assent of
all the barons, so were there found in their sieges every knight's
name, as is afore rehearsed. And so were they set in their
sieges; whereof Sir Bagdemagus was wondrous wrath, that Sir
Tor was so advanced, and therefore suddenly he departed from
the court of King Arthur, and took his squire with him, and rode
long in a forest, till they came to a cross, and there he alighted,
and said his prayers devotedly. The meanwhile his squire
found written upon the cross that Bagdemagus should never
return again to the court till he had won a knight's body of the
Round Table, body for body. "Lo! sir," said his squire, "here
I find written of you; therefore I bid you return again to the
court." "That shall I never," said Bagdemagus, "till men
speak of me great worship, and that I be worthy to be a knight
of the Round Table." And so he rode forth, and by the way he
found a branch of a holy herb, that was the sign of the

Sancgreal, and no knight found such tokens but he were a good liver. So as Sir Bagdemagus rode to so many adventures, it happened him to come to the rock there as the Lady of the Lake had put Merlin under a stone, and there he heard him make great moan, wherefore Sir Bagdemagus would have helpen him, and went to the great stone, and it was so heavy that a hundred men might not lift it up. When Merlin wist that he was there, he bid him leave his labour, for all was in vain, and might never be helpen but by her that put him there ; and so Sir Bagdemagus departed, and did many adventures, and proved after a full good knight of prowess, and came again to the court of King Arthur, and was made knight of the Round Table. And so on the morrow there fell new tidings, and other adventures.

VI.

THEN it befell that King Arthur, and many of his knights, rode on hunting into a great forest, and it happened King Arthur, King Urience, and Sir Accolon, of Gaul, followed a great hart, for they three were well horsed, and they chased so fast that within awhile they three were ten miles from their fellowship, and at the last they chased so sore, that they slew their horses under them. Then were they all three on foot, and ever they saw the hart afore them, passing weary and ambushed. "What will ye do ?" said King Arthur, "we are hard bested." "Let us go on foot," said King Urience, "till we may meet with some lodging." Then were they ware of the hart, that lay on a great water bank, and a brachet biting upon his throat, and many other hounds came after. Then King Arthur blew the prize, and dight the hart there. Then King Arthur looked about him, and saw afore him, in a great water, a little ship, all appareled with silk, down to the water, and the ship came straight unto them, and landed on the sands. Then King Arthur went to the bank, and looked in, and saw none earthly creature therein. " Sirs," said the king, "come thence, and let us see what is in this ship." So they went in all three, and found it richly hanged with cloth of silk ; and by that time it was dark night, there suddenly were about them a hundred torches, set on all the sides of the shipboards, and gave a great light. And therewith came out twelve fair damsels, and saluted King Arthur on their knees, and called him by his name, and said he was welcome, and such cheer as they had he should have of the best. And the King thanked them fair. Therewith they led the King and his two fellows into a fair chamber, and there was a cloth laid, richly beseen, of all that belonged to a table, and there they were served of all wines and meats that they could think of, that the King had great marvel : for he fared never better in his life for one supper. And so, when they had supped at their leisure, King Arthur was led into a chamber, a richer beseen chamber saw he never none, and so was King Urience served, and led into another chamber ; and Sir Accolon was led into the third chamber, passing rich and well beseen. And so were they laid in their beds right easily, and anon they fell on sleep, and slept marvellously sore all that night. And on the morrow King Urience was in Camelot, a-bed in his wife's arms, Morgan le Fay : and when he awoke he had great marvel how he came there, for on the even afore he was about two days' journey from Camelot. And also, when King Arthur awoke, he found himself in a dark prison, hearing about him many complaints of woeful knights.

VII.

THEN said King Arthur, "What are ye that so complain ?" "We are here twenty good knights prisoners," said they, "and some of us have lain here seven years, and some more and some less." "For what cause ?" said King Arthur. "We shall tell you," said the knights. "The lord of this castle is named Sir Damas, and he is the falsest knight that liveth, and full of treason, and a very coward as any liveth ; and he hath a younger brother, a good knight of prowess, his name is Sir Ontzlake, and this traitor, Damas, the elder, will give him no part of his livelihood, but that Sir Ontzlake keepeth through his prowess, and so he keepeth from him a full fair manor, and a rich ; and therein Sir Ontzlake dwelleth worshipfully, and is beloved of all the people and commonalty. And this Sir Damas, our master, is as evil beloved, for he is without mercy, and he is a very coward, and great war hath been between them both ; but Sir Ontzlake hath ever the better, and ever he proffereth Sir Damas to fight for the livelihood, body for body, but he will do nothing ; or else to find a knight to fight with him, unto that Sir Damas hath granted, to find a knight, but he is so evil, and hated, that there is no knight that will fight for him. And when Sir Damas saw this, that there was no knight that would fight for him, he hath daily lain in a wait, with many knights with him, to take all the knights in this country, to see and espy their adventures ; he hath taken them by force, and brought them into his prison, and so he took us severally, as we rode on our adventures ; and many good knights have died in this prison for hunger, to the number of eighteen knights ; and if any of us all that is here, or hath been, would have foughten with his brother Ontzlake, he would have delivered us ; but because this Sir Damas is so false, and, so full of treason, we would never fight for him to die for it ; and we be so lean for hunger, that we may hardly stand on our feet." "God deliver you, for His mercy," said King Arthur. Anon therewith came a damsel unto King Arthur, and asked him, "What cheer?" "I cannot tell," said he. "Sir," quoth she, "and ye will fight for my lord, ye shall be delivered out of prison, or else ye shall never escape with your life." "Now," said King Arthur, "that is hard ; yet had rather I to fight with a knight than to die in prison : if I may be delivered with this, and all these prisoners," said King Arthur, "I will do the battle." "Yes," said the damsel. "I am ready," said King Arthur, "if I had a horse and armour." "Ye shall lack none," said the damsel. "Me seemeth, damsel, I should have seen you in the court of King Arthur." "Nay," said the damsel, "I came never there ; I am the lord's daughter of this castle." Yet was she false, for she was one of the damsels of Morgan le Fay. Anon she went unto Sir Damas, and told him how he would do battle for him. And so he sent for King Arthur ; and when he came he was well coloured, and well made of his limbs, and that all the knights that saw him said it were a pity that such a knight should die in prison. So Sir Damas and he were agreed that he should fight for him, upon this covenant, that all the other knights should be delivered ; and unto that was Sir Damas sworn unto King Arthur, and also to do this battle to the uttermost. And with that all the twenty knights were brought out of the dark prison into the hall, and delivered ; and so they all abode to see the battle.

VIII.

TURN we unto Sir Accolon of Gaul, that when he awoke he found himself by a deep well side, within half-a-foot in great peril of death, and there came out of that fountain a pipe of silver, and out of that pipe ran water all on high in stone of marble. And when Sir Accolon saw this, he blessed him and said, "Jesus, save my lord, King Arthur, and King Urience, for these damsels in this ship have betrayed us ; they were devils and no women ; and if I may escape this misadventure, I shall destroy all where I may find these false damsels that use enchantments." And with that there came a dwarf with a great mouth and flat nose, and saluted Sir Accolon, and said how he came from Queen Morgan le Fay, " and she greeteth you well, and biddeth you to be strong of heart, for ye shall fight to-morrow with a knight at the hour of prime ; and, therefore, she hath sent you here Excalibur, King Arthur's sword, and the scabbard ; and she desireth you, as you love her, that ye do the battle to the uttermost, without any mercy, like as ye have promised her when ye spake together in private ; and, what damsel that bringeth her the knight's head that ye shall fight withal, she will make her a rich queen for ever." " Now I understand you well," said Sir Accolon, " I shall hold that I have promised her, now I have the sword. When saw ye my lady, Queen Morgan?" " Right late," said the dwarf. Then Sir Accolon took him in his arms, and said, " Recommend me unto my lady, Queen Morgan, and tell her, that all shall be done as I have promised her, or else I will die for it. Now I suppose," said Sir Accolon, " she hath made all these crafts and enchantments for this battle." " Ye may well believe it," said the dwarf. Right so came a knight and a lady with six squires, and saluted Sir Accolon, and prayed him to arise, and come and rest him at his manor. And so Sir Accolon mounted upon a spare horse, and went with the knight into a fair manor by a priory, and there he had passing good cheer. Then Sir Damas sent unto his brother, Sir Ontzlake, and bid him make him ready by to-morrow, at the hour of prime, and to be in the field to fight with a good knight, for he had found a knight that was ready to do battle at all points. When this word came unto Sir Ontzlake he was passing heavy, for he was wounded a little too sore through both his thighs with a spear, and made great moan, but for all he was wounded he would have taken the battle in hand. So it happened at that time, by the means of Morgan le Fay, Sir Accolon was lodged with Sir Ontzlake, and when he heard of that battle, and how Sir Ontzlake was wounded, he said he would fight for him, because Morgan le Fay had sent him Excalibur and the scabbard for to fight with the knight on the morrow. This was the cause Sir Accolon took the battle in hand. Then Sir Ontzlake was passing glad, and thanked Sir Accolon heartily that he would do so much for him. And therewith Sir Ontzlake sent word to his brother, Sir Damas, that he had a knight that for him should be ready in the field by the hour of prime.

So on the morrow King Arthur was armed and well horsed, and asked Sir Damas, " When shall we go to the field?" " Sir," said Sir Damas, "ye shall hear mass." And when mass was done, there came a squire on a great horse, and asked Sir Damas if his knight was ready? "for our knight is ready in the field." Then King Arthur mounted on horseback, and there were all the knights and commons of the country; and so by all advices there were chosen twelve good men of the country for to wait upon the two knights. And, as King Arthur was upon horseback, there came a damsel from Morgan le Fay, and brought unto King Arthur a sword like unto Excalibur, and the scabbard, and said unto King Arthur, " Morgan le Fay sendeth you here your sword for great love." And he thanked her, and weened it had been so, but she was false, for the sword and the scabbard was counterfeit, brittle, and false.

IX.

AND then they dressed them on both parties of the field, and let their horses run so fast, that either smote other in the midst of their shields with their spears, that both horses and men went to the ground, and then they started up both and drew out their swords : and, in the meantime, while that they were thus fighting, came the damsel of the lake into the field that had put Merlin under the stone ; and she came thither for the love of King Arthur, for she knew how Morgan le Fay had so ordained that King Arthur should have been slain that day ; and, therefore, she came to save his life. And so they went eagerly to do their battle, and gave many sad strokes ; but always King Arthur's sword was not like Sir Accolon's ; so that, for the most part, every stroke that Sir Accolon gave he wounded King Arthur sore, that it was marvel that he stood, and always his blood fell fast from him. When King Arthur beheld the ground so sore beblooded he was dismayed, and then he deemed treason that his sword was changed, for his sword was not still as it was wont to do, therefore was he sore adread to be dead, for ever him seemed that the sword in Sir Accolon's hand was Excalibur ; for at every stroke that Sir Accolon struck, he drew blood on King Arthur. "Now, knight," said Sir Accolon to King Arthur, "keep thee well from me." But King Arthur answered not again, and gave him such a buffet on the helm, that he made him to stoop, nigh falling to the ground. Then Sir Accolon withdrew him a little, and came on with Excalibur on high, and smote King Arthur such a buffet, that he fell nigh to the earth. Then were they both wrath, and gave each other many sore strokes ; but always King Arthur lost so much blood,

that it was marvel that he stood on his feet ; but he was so full
of knighthood, that knightly he endured the pain. And Sir
Accolon lost not a drop of blood, therefore he waxed passing
light, and King Arthur was passing feeble, and thought verily to
have died. But, for all that, he made countenance as though he
might endure, and held Sir Accolon as short as he might : but
Sir Accolon was so bold because of Excalibur, that he waxed
passing hardy. But all men that beheld them said they saw
never knight fight so well as did King Arthur, considering the
blood that he bled, and all the people were sorry for him, but
the two brethren would not accord. Then always they fought
together as fierce knights, and King Arthur withdrew him a little
for to rest him, and Sir Accolon called him to battle and said,
" It is no time for me to suffer thee to rest." And therewith he
came fiercely upon King Arthur, and King Arthur was wrath for
the blood that he had lost, and smote Sir Accolon upon the
helm so mightly, that he made him nigh fall to the earth, and
therewith King Arthur's sword brake at the cross, and fell in the
grass among the blood, and the pommel and the handle he held
in his hand. When King Arthur saw that, he was greatly afraid
to die, but always he held up his shield, and lost no ground, nor
abated any cheer.

X.

THEN Sir Accolon began to say thus, with words of treason :
" Knight, thou art overcome, and mayest no longer endure ;
and, also, thou art weaponless, and thou hast lost much of thy
blood, and I am full loth to slay thee ; therefore, yield thee as
recreant." " Nay," said King Arthur, " I may not so, for I
have promised to do thee battle to the uttermost by the faith of
my body while my life lasted ; and, therefore, I had rather
to die with honour than to live with shame ; and if it were
possible for me to die a hundred times, I had rather so often
die than to yield me to thee ; for, though I lack weapon, and
am weaponless, yet shall I lack no worship ; and if thou slay
me weaponless, it shall be to thy shame." " Well," said Sir
Accolon, " as for the shame, I will not spare. Now keep thee
from me," said Sir Accolon, " for thou art but a dead man."
And therewith, Sir Accolon gave him such a stroke, that he fell
nigh to the earth, and would not have King Arthur to cry him
mercy. But King Arthur pressed unto Sir Accolon with his
shield, and gave him, with the pommel in his hand, such a
buffet, that he went three strides back. When the damsel
of the lake beheld King Arthur, how full of prowess and

worthiness his body was, and the false treason that was wrought for him to have slain him, she had great pity that so good a knight, and so noble a man of worship, should be destroyed. And, at the next stroke, Sir Accolon struck him such a stroke, that, by the damsel's enchantment, the sword, Excalibur, fell out of Sir Accolon's hand to the earth ; and therewith King Arthur lightly leapt to it, and quickly gat it in his hand, and forthwith he perceived clearly that it was his good sword, Excalibur, and said, "Thou hast been from me all too long, and much damage hast thou done me." And therewith he espied the scabbard hanging by Sir Accolon's side, and suddenly he leapt to him and pulled the scabbard from him, and anon threw it from him as far as he might throw it. "O knight," said King Arthur, "this day thou hast done me great damage with this sword. Now are ye come to your death ; for I shall not warrant you, but that ye shall be as well rewarded with this sword, or we depart asunder, as thou hast rewarded me ; for much pain have ye made me to endure, and have lost much blood." And therewith King Arthur rushed upon him with all his might, and pulled him to the earth, and then rushed off his helm, and gave him such a buffet on the head, that the blood came out of his ears, nose, and mouth. "Now will I slay thee," said King Arthur. " Slay me ye may," said Sir Accolon, "and it please you, for ye are the best knight that ever I found, and I see well that God is with you ; but for I promised to do this battle," said Sir Accolon, "to the uttermost, and never to be recreant while I lived, therefore shall I never yield me with my mouth, but God do with my body what he will." And then King Arthur remembered him, and thought he should have seen this knight. " Now tell me," said King Arthur, " or I will slay thee, of what country thou art ? and of what court ? " " Sir knight," quoth Sir Accolon, " I am of the court of King Arthur, and my name is Sir Accolon, of Gaul." Then was King Arthur more dismayed than he was before, for then he remembered him of his sister, Morgan le Fay, and of the enchantment of the ship. " Oh ! sir knight," said he, " I pray thee tell me who gave thee this sword, and by whom had ye it ? "

XI.

Then Sir Accolon bethought him, and said, " Woe worth this sword, for by it have I gotten my death." " It may well be," said King Arthur. " Now, sir," said Sir Accolon, " I will tell you : this sword hath been in my keeping the most of these twelve months, and Queen Morgan le Fay, King Urience's wife, sent it me yesterday, by a dwarf, to this intent that I should slay King Arthur, her brother ; for ye shall understand that King Arthur is the man which she most hateth in this world, because that he is the most of worship and of prowess of any of her blood. Also she loveth me out of measure as her paramour, and I her again ; and if she might bring about for to slay King Arthur with her crafts, she would slay her husband, King Urience, lightly, and then had s',e me devised to be king in this land, and so for to reign, and she to be my queen ; but that is now done," said Sir Accolon, "for I am sure of my death." "Well," said King Arthur, "I feel by you ye would have been king in this land : it had been great damage for to have destroyed your lord," said King Arthur. "It is truth," said Sir Accolon : "but now have I told you the truth, wherefore I pray you, that ye will tell me of whence ye are, and of what court ?" "Oh ! Sir Accolon," said King Arthur, "now let thee to wit that I am King Arthur, to whom thou hast done great damage." When Sir Accolon heard that, he cried out aloud, "Oh ! my gracious lord, have mercy on me ; for I knew not." "Oh ! Sir Accolon," said King Arthur, "mercy shalt thou have, because I feel, by thy words at this time, thou knewest not my person ; but I understand well by thy words that thou hast agreed to the death of my person, and therefore thou art a traitor : but I blame thee the less, for my sister, Morgan le Fay, by her false crafts made thee to agree and consent to her false lusts ; but I shall so be avenged upon her, and I live, that all Christendom shall speak of it. God knoweth I have honoured her, and worshipped her more than any of my kin, and more have I trusted her than my own wife, and all my kin after." Then King Arthur called the keepers of the field, and said, "Sirs, come hither, for here we be two knights that have fought unto a great damage of us both, and like each one of us to have slain other, if it had happened so ; and had any of us known other, here had been no battle nor stroke stricken." Then all aloud cried Sir Accolon unto all the knights and men that there were gathered together, and said to them, in this manner wise : "Oh ! my lords, this noble knight that I have fought withal, which me full sore repenteth, is the most man of prowess of manhood and of worship that in all the world liveth ; for it is himself, King Arthur, our most sovereign, liege, lord, and king ; and with great mishap, and great misadventure, have I done this battle against my king and lord that I am holden withal."

XII.

THEN all the people fell down on their knees, and cried King Arthur's mercy. "Mercy shall ye have," said King Arthur; "here may ye see what adventures befalleth oftentimes to errant-knights, how I have fought with one of mine own knights to my great damage and his hurt. But, sirs, because I am sore hurt and he both, and have great need of a little rest, ye shall understand my opinion between you two brethren : as to thee, Sir Damas, for whom I have been champion, and won the field of this knight, yet will I judge, because ye, Sir Damas, are called a very proud knight, and full of villainy, and nothing worth of prowess of your deeds ; therefore I will that ye give unto your brother all the whole manor, with the appurtenance, under this manner of form : that Sir Ontzlake hold the manor of you, and yearly to give you a palfrey to ride upon, for that will become you better to ride on than a courser. Also, I charge thee, Sir Damas, upon pain of death, that thou never distress none errant-knights that ride on their adventures. Also, that thou restore these twenty knights, which thou hast long kept in prison, of all their harness, and that thou content them ; and, if any of them come to my court, and complain of thee, by my head thou shalt die therefore. Also Sir Ontzlake, as to you, because ye are named a good knight, and full of prowess, and true and gentle in all your deeds, this shall be your charge. I will that in all goodly haste ye come to me and to my court, and ye shall be a knight of mine ; and if your deeds be thereafter, I shall so advance you by the grace of God, that ye shall, in a short time, be in ease for to live as worshipfully as doth your brother, Sir Damas." "God thank you of your largess, and of your great goodness," said Sir Ontzlake ; "and I promise you that from henceforth I shall be at all times at your commandment. For, sir, as God would I was hurt but late with an adventurous knight, through both my thighs, which grieved me sore, and else had I done this battle with you." "Would to God," said King Arthur, "it had been so ; for then had not I been hurt as I am. I shall tell you the cause why ; for I had not been hurt as I am, had not it been mine own sword that was stolen from me by treason, and this battle was ordained aforehand for to have slain me, and so it was brought to the purpose by false trickery, and treason, and false enchantment." "Alas !" said Sir Ontzlake, "that is great pity that so noble a man as you are of your deeds and prowess, that any man or woman might find in their hearts to work any treason against your person."   " I shall reward them," said King Arthur, "in short space, by the grace of God.   Now tell me, how far am I from Camelot?"   "Sir, ye are two days' journey therefrom." " I would fain be at some place of worship," said King Arthur, "that I might rest myself."   "Sir," said Sir Ontzlake, "hereby is a rich abbey of nuns, of our elder's foundation, but three miles hence."   So then the King took his leave of all the people, and mounted on horseback, and Sir Accolon with him ; and when they were come to the abbey, he let fetch surgeons and leeches for to search his wounds, and Sir Accolon's both ; but Sir Accolon died within four days after, for he had bled so much blood that he might not live, but King Arthur was well recovered.   And when Sir Accolon was dead, he let send on horseback with six knights of Camelot, and said, " Bear him to my sister, Morgan le Fay, and say that I send him her for a present, and tell that I have my sword, Excalibur, and the scabbard."   So they departed with the body.

XIII.

THE meanwhile Morgan le Fay had weened that King Arthur had been dead.   So on a day she espied King Urience, how he lay in his bed sleeping ; then she called unto her a damsel of her counsel, and said, " Go fetch me my lord's sword, for I saw never better time to slay him than now."   " O madam," said the damsel, " and if ye slay my lord ye can never escape." " Care not thou," said Morgan le Fay, " for now I see my time in the which it is best to do it, and therefore hie thee fast, and fetch me the sword."   Then the damsel departed, and found Sir Ewaine sleeping upon a bed in another chamber ; so she went unto Sir Ewaine, and wakened him, and bade him arise and wait upon my lady, your mother ; " for she will slay the King, your father, sleeping in his bed, for I go to fetch her his sword." " Well," said Sir Ewaine, " go on your way, and let me deal." Anon the damsel brought the sword unto Morgan with quaking hands, and she lightly took the sword and drew it out, and went boldly to the bed's side, and awaited how and where she might slay him best. And as she lift up the sword for to smite, Sir Ewaine came hither and leapt unto his mother, and caught her by the hand, and said, "Ah ! fiend, what wilt thou do ? and thou were not my mother, with this sword I would smite off thy head. Ah !" said Sir Ewaine, " men say that Merlin was begotten of a devil ; but I may say an earthly devil bear me." " Oh ! fair son, Ewaine," said Morgan, " have mercy upon me,

I was tempted with the devil ; wherefore I cry thee mercy, I will never more do so, and save my worship and discover me not." "On this covenant," said Sir Ewaine, "I will give you so you will never be about to do such deeds." "Nay, son," said she, "and thereto I make you assurance."

XIV.

THEN came tidings unto Morgan le Fay, that Sir Accolon was dead, and his body brought to the church, and how King Arthur had his sword again. But when Morgan wist that Sir Accolon was dead, she was so sorrowful that near her heart burst ; but because she would not that it were known, she kept her countenance outward, and made no semblance of sorrow. But well she wist, and if she abode till her brother Arthur came thither, there should no gold save her life. Then she went unto Queen Guenever, and asked her leave to ride into the country. "Ye may abide," said Queen Guenever, "till your brother, the king, come home." "I may not," said Morgan le Fay, "for I have such hasty tidings that I may not tarry." "Well," said Queen Guenever, "ye may depart when ye will." So early on the morrow, or it was day, she took her horse and rode all that day, and the most part of the night ; and, on the morrow, by noon, she came to the same abbey of nuns whereas King Arthur lay, and she knowing that he was there, she asked where he was ; and they answered, and said, "that he had lain him down in his bed to sleep, for he had had but little rest these three nights." "Well," said she, "I charge you that none of you awake him till I awake him myself." And then she alighted from her horse, and thought to steal away Excalibur, his good sword ; and so she went straight unto his chamber, and no man durst disobey her commandment, and there she found King Arthur asleep in his bed, and Excalibur in his right hand naked : when she saw that, she was passing heavy that she might not come by the sword without she had wakened him, and then she wist well that she had been dead. Then she took the scabbard, and went her way on horseback. When the King awoke and missed his scabbard, he was wondrous wrath, and asked who had been there. And they said, his sister Queen Morgan had been there, and had put the scabbard under her mantle, and was gone. "Alas !" said King Arthur, "falsely have ye watched me." "Sir," said they, "all we durst not disobey your sister's commandment." "Ah !" said the King, "let fetch the best horse that may be found, and bid Sir Ontzlake arm him in all haste, and take another good horse, and ride with me."

So anon the King and Sir Ontzlake were well armed, and rode after this lady ; and as they rode they came by a cross, and found a cowherd, and they asked the poor man if there came any lady late riding that way. "Sir," said this poor man, "right late came a lady riding with forty horses, and to yonder forest she rode." Then they spurred their horses, and followed fast after, and within awhile King Arthur had a sight of her, that he chased as fast as he might ; and when she espied him following her, she rode through the forest a great pace, till she came to a plain : and when she saw she might not escape, she rode unto a lake thereby, and said, "Whatsoever becometh of me, my brother shall not have this scabbard." And she let throw the scabbard in the deepest of the water, and it sunk ; for it was so heavy of gold and precious stones. Then she rode into a valley, where many great stones were ; and when she saw that she must needs be overtaken, she turned herself, horse and man, by enchantment into a great marble stone. So anon King Arthur and Sir Ontzlake came whereas the King might not know his sister and her men, and one knight from another. "Ah !" said the King, "here may ye see the vengeance of God ; and now am I sorry that this misadventure is befallen." And then he looked for the scabbard, but it could not be found. So he returned again to the abbey that he came from. When King Arthur was gone, she turned all into the likeness as she and they were before, and said, "Sirs, now may we go wheresoever we will, for my brother Arthur is gone."

XV.

THEN said Morgan, "Saw ye my brother, Sir Arthur?" "Yes," said her knights, "right well, and that ye should have found, and we might have stirred one steed ; for, by his fierce countenance, he would have caused us to have fled." "I believe you well," said Morgan. Anon after she rode she met with a knight leading another knight on his horse before him, bound hand and foot, blindfold, to have drowned him in a fountain. When she saw that knight so bound, she asked what he would do with that knight. "Lady," said he, "I will drown him." "For what cause?" said she. "For I found him with my wife, and she shall have the same death anon." "That were pity," said Morgan. "Now what say you, ye knight, is it truth that he saith of you?" said she to the knight that should be drowned. "Nay, truly, madam, he saith not right of me." "Of whence be ye," said Morgan le Fay, "and of what country?" "I am of the court of King Arthur, and my name is Manassen, cousin unto Sir Accolon, of Gaul." "Ye say well," said she, "and for the love of him ye shall be delivered; ye shall have your adversary in the same case that ye be in." And so Manassen was loosed, and the other knight bound. And anon Manassen unarmed him, and armed himself in his harness, and so mounted on horseback, and the knight afore him, and so threw him into the fountain, and drowned him. And then he rode to Morgan again, and asked her if she would any thing unto King Arthur. "Tell him not that I rescued thee for the love of him, but for the love of Sir Accolon; and tell him that I fear him not, while I can make me and them that be with me in likeness of stones, and let him wit that I can do much more when I see my time." And so she departed, and went into the country of Gore, and there was she richly received, and made her castles and towns passing strong; for always she dreaded much King Arthur. When King Arthur had well rested him at that abbey, he rode to Camelot, and found his Queen and his barons right glad of his coming. And when they heard of his strange adventures, as is afore rehearsed, they all had marvel of the falsehood of Morgan le Fay, and many knights wished her burnt. Then came Manassen to the court, and told the King of his adventure. "Well," said the King, "she is a kind sister: I shall be so avenged on her and I live, that all Christendom shall speak of it." So on the morrow there came a damsel from Morgan to the King, and she brought with her the richest mantle that ever was seen in the court, for it was set as full of precious stones as might stand one by another; and there were the richest stones that ever the King saw. And the damsel said, "Your sister sendeth you this mantle, and desireth you, that ye will take this gift of her, and in what thing she hath offended you, she will amend it at your own pleasure." When the King beheld this mantle, it pleased him much, but he said but little.

XVI.

AND with that came the damsel of the lake unto the King, and said, "Sir, I must speak with you in private." "Say on," said the King, "what ye will." "Sir," said the lady, "put not on you this mantle till you have seen more, and in no wise let it not come upon you, nor on no knights of yours, till ye command the bringer thereof to put it upon her." "Well," said King Arthur, "it shall be done as ye counsel me." And then he said unto the damsel that came from his sister, "Damsel,

this mantle that ye have brought me, I will see it upon you."
"Sir," said she, "it will not beseem me to wear a knight's
garment." "By my head," said King Arthur, "ye shall wear it,
or it come on my back, or any man that is here." And so the
King made it to be put upon her, and forthwith she fell down
dead, and never more spake word after, and was burnt to coals.

Then was the King wondrous wrath, more than he was afore,
and said unto King Urience, "My sister, your wife, is alway
about to betray me ; and well I wot either ye or my nephew,
your son, is of counsel with her, to have me destroyed : but as
for you," said King Arthur to King Urience, "I deem not
greatly that ye be of her counsel : for Sir Accolon confessed to
me, with his own mouth, that she should have destroyed you as
well as me, therefore I hold you excused ; but as for your son,
Sir Ewaine, I hold him suspect, therefore I charge you put him
out of my court." So Sir Ewaine was charged. And when Sir
Gawaine wist of it, he made him ready to go with him, and
said, "Whoso banished my cousin Ewaine shall banish me."
So they two departed, and rode in a great forest ; and so they
came to an abbey of monks, and there were well lodged. But
when the King wist that Sir Gawaine was departed from the
court, there was made great sorrow among all the states.
"Now," said Sir Gaheris, Sir Gawaine's brother, "we have
lost two good knights for the love of one." So on the morrow
they heard mass in the abbey, and so they rode forth till they
came to a great forest ; then was Sir Gawaine ware, in a valley
by a turret, of twelve fair damsels, and two knights armed upon
two great horses, and the damsels went to and fro by a tree.
And then was Sir Gawaine ware how there hung a white shield
on that tree, and ever as the damsels came by it they spit upon
it, and some threw mire upon it.

XVII.

THEN Sir Gawaine and Sir Ewaine went and saluted them,
and asked them why they did that despite to the shield. "Sirs,"
said the damsels, "we shall tell you. There is a knight in this
country that owneth this white shield, and he is a passing good
knight of his hands, but he hateth all ladies and gentlewomen,
and therefore we do all this despite to the white shield." "I
shall say to you," said Sir Gawaine to the ladies, "it beseemeth
evil a good knight to despise all ladies and gentlewomen ; and
also, peradventure, though he hate you, he hath some cause ;
and peradventure that he loveth, in some other places, good
ladies and gentlewomen, and to be loved again, if he be such a

man of prowess as ye speak of. Now, what is his name?"
"Sir," said they, "his name is Marhaus, the king's son of
Ireland." "I know him well," said Sir Ewaine, "he is a
passing good knight as any is living, for I saw him once proved
at a jousting, whereas many knights were gathered, and that
time there might no man withstand him." "Ah!" said Sir
Gawaine, "damsels, me thinketh ye are to blame; for it is to
suppose that he that hung this shield there, he will not be long
therefrom, and then may those knights match him on horseback, and that is more your worship than thus; for I will abide
no longer to see a knight's shield dishonoured." And therewith
Sir Ewaine and Sir Gawaine departed a little from them, and
then they were ware where Sir Marhaus came riding up, on a
great horse, straight toward them. And when the twelve
damsels saw Sir Marhaus, they fled into the turret, as they
had been wild, so that some of them fell by the way. Then the
one of the knights of the turret dressed his shield, and said, on
high, "Sir Marhaus, defend thee." And so they ran together,
that the knight break his spear on Sir Marhaus, and Sir Marhaus smote him so hard that he brake his neck. That saw the
other knight of the turret, and dressed him toward Sir Marhaus,
and they met so eagerly together, that the knight of the turret
was soon smitten down, horse and man, stark dead.

<h2 style="text-align:center">XVIII.</h2>

AND then Sir Marhaus rode unto his shield, and saw how it
was defiled, and said, "Of this despite I am a part avenged;
but for her love that gave me this white shield, I shall wear thee,
and hang mine here in thy stead." And so he hung it about
his neck, and then he rode straight to Sir Gawaine and Sir
Ewaine, and asked them what they did there. They answered,
"that they came from King Arthur's court for to seek adventures." "Well," said Sir Marhaus, "here am I ready, a knight
adventurous, that will fulfil any adventure that ye will desire of
me:" and so departed from them to fetch his range. "Let
him go," said Sir Ewaine to Sir Gawaine, "for he is a passing
good knight as any is living in this world; I would not, by my
will, that any of us two should match with him." "Nay," said
Sir Gawaine, "not so; it were a shame to us if he were not
assayed, were he never so good a knight." "Well," said Sir
Ewaine, "I will assay him afore you, for I am more weaker
than ye are; and, if he smite me down, then may ye revenge."
So these two knights came together with great random, that Sir

Ewaine smote Sir Marhaus that his spear burst in pieces on the shield, and Sir Marhaus smote him so sore, that horse and man he bare to the earth, and hurt Sir Ewaine on the left side. Then Sir Marhaus turned his horse, and rode toward Sir Gawaine with his spear; and when Sir Gawaine saw that, he dressed his shield, and they adventured their spears, and they came together with all the might of their horses, that either smote other so hard in the midst of their two shields, that Sir Gawaine's spear break, and Sir Marhaus's spear held, and therewith Sir Gawaine and his horse rushed down to the earth; and lightly Sir Gawaine arose upon his feet, and drew out his sword, and dressed him toward Sir Marhaus on foot. And Sir Marhaus saw that, and drew out his sword, and began to come to Sir Gawaine on horseback. "Sir knight," said Sir Gawaine, "alight on foot, or else I will slay thy horse." "Gramercy," said Sir Marhaus, "of your gentleness ye teach me courtesy, for it is not according for one knight to be on foot and the other on horseback:" and therewith Sir Marhaus set his spear against a tree and alighted, and tied his horse to a tree, and dressed his shield, and either came to other eagerly, and smote together with their swords, that their shields flew in cantels, and they bruised their helms and their hauberks, and wounded either other. But Sir Gawaine, after it passed nine of the clock, waxed ever stronger and stronger; for then it came to the hour of noon, and thrice his might was increased. All this espied Sir Marhaus, and had a great wonder how his might increased; and so they wounded each other passing sore. And, when it was past noon, and drew toward even-song time, Sir Gawaine's strength waxed passing faint, that scarce he might not endure any longer; and Sir Marhaus waxed bigger and bigger. "Sir knight," said Sir Marhaus, "I have well felt that ye are a passing good knight, and a marvellous man of might as ever I felt any, while it lasteth, and our quarrels are not great, and therefore it were pity to do you hurt: for I perceive ye are passing feeble." "Ah!" said Sir Gawaine, "gentle knight, ye say the words that I should say." And therewith they took off their helms, and either kissed other, and there they swore together, either to love other as brethren. And Sir Marhaus prayed Sir Gawaine to lodge with him that night; and so they took their horses, and rode toward Sir Marhaus's place; and, as they rode by the way, Sir Gawaine said, "Sir knight, I marvel that so valiant a man as ye be love no ladies nor gentlewomen." "Sir," said Sir Marhaus, "they name me wrongfully that give me that name; but well I wot it is the damsels of the turret that so name me,

and others such as they be. Now shall I tell you for what cause
I hate them so ; for they be witches and enchantresses the most
part of them : and be a knight ever so good of his body, and of
prowess as any man may be, they will make him a coward for
to have the better of him ; and this is the principal cause that I
hate them.   And to all good ladies and gentlewomen I owe my
service as a knight ought to do." And, as the French book
rehearseth, there were many knights that overmatched Sir
Gawaine, for all the thrice-might that he had : as Sir Launcelot
du Lake, Sir Tristram, Sir Bors de Gaul, Sir Percivale, and Sir
Marhaus : these five knights had the better of Sir Gawaine.
Then within a while they came to Sir Marhaus's place, the
which was in a little priory, and there they alighted : and ladies
and damsels unarmed them, and hastily looked to their hurts ;
for they were all three hurt.   And so they had there good lodging with Sir Marhaus, and good cheer ; for, when he wist that
they were King Arthur's sister's sons, he made them all the
cheer that lay in his power ; and so they sojourned there about
seven nights, and were right well eased of their wounds, and at
the last departed.   "Now," said Sir Marhaus, "we will not
depart so lightly : for I will bring you through the forest," and
so rode day by day well at seven days or they found any
adventure.   At the last they came into a great forest, which was
named the country and forest of Arroy, and the country of
strange adventures.   "In this country," said Sir Marhaus,
"came never knight, since it was christened, but he found
strange adventures." So long they rode till they came into
a deep valley full of stones, and thereby they saw a fair
stream of water ; and above the head of the stream was a fair
fountain, and three damsels sitting thereby.   And then they
rode unto them, and either saluted the other ; and the eldest
had a garland of gold about her head, and she was threescore
winters of age or more, and her hair was white underneath the
garland.   The second damsel was of thirty winters of age, with
a circlet of gold about her head.   The third damsel was but
fifteen years of age, and she had a garland of flowers about her
head.   When these knights had well beholden them, they asked
them the cause why they sat at that fountain.   "We be here,"
said the damsels, "for this cause: if we may see any errant-
knights, to teach them strange adventures ; and ye be three
knights, that seek adventures, and we three damsels ; and,
therefore, each of you must choose one of us.   And, when ye
have done so, we will lead you unto three highways, and there
each of you shall choose a way, and his damsel with him ; and

this day twelvemonths ye must meet here again, and God spare you your lives; and therefore ye must plight your troth." "This is well said," said Sir Marhaus.

XIX.

"How shall we choose every one of us a damsel?" "I shall tell you," said Sir Ewaine; "I am the youngest and most weakest of you both : therefore I will have the eldest damsel ; for she hath seen much, and can help me best when I have need, for I have most need of help of you both." "Then," said Sir Marhaus, "I will have the damsel of thirty winters of age ; for she falleth best to me." "Then," said Gawaine, "I thank you ; for ye have left me the youngest and the fairest, and she falleth best to me." Then every damsel took her knight by the rein of the bridle, and brought them to the three ways ; and there was their oath made, to meet at the fountain that day twelvemonth, and they lived. So they kissed and departed, and each knight set his lady behind him ; and Sir Ewaine took the way that lay west, and Sir Marhaus took the way that lay south, and Sir Gawaine took the way that lay north. Now will we begin at Sir Gawaine, that held that way till he came to a fair manor, whereas dwelled an old knight and a good householder ; and there Sir Gawaine demanded of the old knight, if he knew any adventures in that country. "I shall show you some to-morrow," said the old knight, "and that marvellous." So on the morrow they rode into the forest of adventures, till they came to a land, and thereby they found a cross ; and, as they stood and halted, there came by them the fairest knight and the seemliest man that ever they saw, making the greatest moan that ever man made. And then he was aware of Sir Gawaine, and saluted him, and prayed to God to send him much worship. "As to that," said Sir Gawaine, "gramercy! Also I pray to God that he send you honour and worship." "Ah" said the knight, "I may lay that on side ; for sorrow and shame cometh to me after worship."

XX.

AND therewith he passed to that one side of the land ; and, on the other side, Sir Gawaine saw ten knights that halted and made them ready with their shields and spears, against that one knight that came by Sir Gawaine. Then this one knight adventured a great spear, and one of the ten knights encountered with him ; but this woeful knight smote him so hard, that he fell over the horse's tail. So this dolorous knight served them all, and smote them down, horse and man ; and all he did it with one spear. And, when they were all ten on foot, they went to that one knight, and he stood stone still, and suffered them to pull him down off his horse, and bound him hand and foot, and tied him under his horse's belly, and so led him with them. "Oh ! Jesus," said Sir Gawaine, "this is a doleful sight, to see yonder knight so to be treated: and it seemeth by the knight, that he suffereth them to bind him so ; for he maketh no resistance." "No, verily," said his host, "that is truth ; for, and if that he would, they were all too weak so to do to him." "Sir," said the damsel unto Sir Gawaine, "me seemeth that it were your worship and honour to help that dolorous knight ; for me thinketh he is one of the best knights that ever I saw." "I would be glad to do for him," said Sir Gawaine : "but it seemeth he will have no help." "Then," said the damsel, "me seemeth ye have no list to help him." Right thus, as they talked, they saw a knight on that other side of the land, all armed save the head ; and on that other side of the land came a dwarf on horseback, all armed save the head, with a great mouth, and a short nose. And the dwarf, when he came nigh to the knight, inquired, "Where is the lady that should meet us here?" And therewithal she came forth out of the wood, and then they began to strive for the lady ; for the knight said he would have her, and the dwarf said he would have her. "Well, ye do well," said the dwarf ; "yonder is a knight at the cross : let us put it to his judgment, and as he deemeth even so be it." "I will well," said the knight. And then they went all three unto Sir Gawaine, and told him wherefore they two strove. "Well, sirs," said he, "will ye put the matter into my hand?" "Yes, sir," said they both. "Now, damsel," said Sir Gawaine, "ye shall stand between them both ; and, whether ye list better to go to, he shall have you." And so, when the damsel was set between them both, she left the knight and went to the dwarf : and the dwarf took her, and went his way singing, and the knight went his way with great mourning. Then came there two knights all armed, and cried on high, "Sir Gawaine, knight of King Arthur, make thee ready in all haste, and joust with me." So they ran together, that either fell down ; and then on foot they drew their swords, and did full actually. In the meanwhile the other knight went unto the damsel, and asked her why she abode with that knight, saying, "And, if ye would abide with me, I will be your faithful knight." "With you will

I be," said the damsel; "for with Sir Gawaine I may not find in mine heart to be with him. For now here was one knight, that discomfited ten knights, and at the last he was cowardly led away; and, therefore, let us two go our way while they fight." And Sir Gawaine fought with the other knight long; but, at the last, they were both accorded, and then the knight prayed Sir Gawaine to lodge with them that night. So, as Sir Gawaine went with this knight, he demanded him, "What knight is he in this country that smote down the ten knights? for, when he had done so manfully, he suffered them to bind him hand and foot, and so led him away." "Ah!" said the knight, "that is the best knight, I trow, in the world, and the man most of prowess; and he hath been served so, as he was even now, more than ten times, and he is named Sir Pelleas; and he loveth a great lady in this country, and her name is Ettarde. And so, when he loved her, there was cried in this country great jousts three days; and all the knights of this country were there, and also the gentlewomen. And who that proved him the best knight should have a passing good sword and a circlet of gold; and the circlet the knight should give it to the fairest lady that was at those jousts. And this knight, Sir Pelleas, was the best knight that was there, and there five hundred knights; but there was never man that ever Sir Pelleas met withal, but that he struck him down, or else from his horse. And every day of the three days he struck down twenty knights; therefore, they gave him the prize. And forthwithal he went there where the Lady Ettarde was, and gave her the circlet, and said openly, that she was the fairest lady that was there, and that would he prove upon any knight that would say nay.

XXI.

"And so he chose her for his sovereign lady, and never to love other but her; but she was so proud that she had scorn of him, and said, that she would never love him, though he would die for her." Wherefore all ladies and gentlewomen had scorn of her because she was so proud; for there were fairer than she, and there was none that was there but, and Sir Pelleas would have proffered them love, they would have loved him for his noble prowess. And so the knight promised the Lady Ettarde to follow her into the country, and never to leave her till she loved him; and thus he is here the most part nigh her, and lodged by a priory, and every week she sendeth knights to fight with him; and when he hath put them to the worst, then will he suffer them wilfully to take him prisoner, because he would have a sight of this lady : and always she doth him great despite ; for sometimes she maketh her knights to tie him to the horse-tail, and sometimes bind him under the horse-belly. Thus in the most shamefullest wise that she can think he is brought to her ; and all this she doth for to cause him to leave this country, and to leave his loving ; but all this cannot make him to leave, for, and he would have fought on foot, he might have had the better of the ten knights, as well on foot as on horseback." "Alas !" said Sir Gawaine, "it is great pity of him ; and after this night, in the morning, I will go seek him in the forest to do him all the help that I can." So, on the morrow, Sir Gawaine took his leave of his host, Sir Carodos, and rode into the forest ; and, at the last, he met with Sir Pelleas making great mourn out of measure : so each of them saluted other, and Gawaine asked him "Why he made such sorrow ?" And, as it is above rehearsed, Sir Pelleas told Sir Gawaine, "But always I suffer her knights to fare so with me as ye saw yesterday, in trust, at the last, to win her love ; for she knoweth well that all her knights should not lightly win me, and me list to fight with them to the uttermost. Wherefore, and I loved her not so sore, I had rather to die a hundred times, and I might die so often, rather than I would suffer this great despite ; but I trust she will have pity upon me at the last, for love causeth many a good knight to suffer for to have his intent : but, alas ! I am unfortunate." And herewith he made so great a mourn and sorrow, that scarce he might hold him on horseback. "Now," said Sir Gawaine, "leave off your mourning, and I shall promise you, by the faith of my body, to do all that lieth in my power to get you the love of your lady, and thereto I will plight you my truth." "Ah ! my good friend," said Sir Pelleas, "of what court are ye ? I pray you that ye will tell me." And then Sir Gawaine said, "I am of the court of King Arthur, and am his sister's son, and King Lot, of Orkney, was my father, and my name is Sir Gawaine." And he then said, "My name is Sir Pelleas, born in the isles, and of many isles I am lord, and never have I loved lady nor damsel till now, in an unhappy time. And, sir knight, sith ye are so nigh a cousin unto King Arthur, and a king's son ; therefore, I pray thee, betray me not, but help me, for I may never come by her but by the help of some good knight : for she is in a strong castle here fast by, within this four miles, and over all this country she is lady of. And so I may never come unto her presence, but as I do suffer her knights for to take me ; and but if I did so that I might have a sight of her I had been dead afore this time, and yet had I never one fair word of her; but when I am brought before her she rebuketh me in the foulest manner that ever she may: and then her knights take me and my horse, and my harness, and put me out of the gates, and she will not suffer me to eat nor drink, and always I offer me to be her prisoner, but so she will not take me; for I would desire no more what pains soever I had, so that I might have a sight of her daily." "Well," said Sir Gawaine, "all this shall I amend, and ye will do as I shall devise: I will have your horse and your armour, and so will I ride to her castle, and tell her that I have slain you; and so shall I come within to her, to cause her to cherish me, and then shall I do my true part, that ye shall not fail to have her love."

XXII.

AND therewithal Sir Gawaine plight his troth unto Sir Pelleas to be true and faithful unto him. When they had plight their troth, the one to the other, they changed their horses and harness, and Sir Gawaine departed and came to the castle, whereas stood the pavilions of this lady without the gate: and as soon as Ettarde had espied Sir Gawaine, she fled towards the castle. Then Sir Gawaine spake on high and bid her abide, for he was not Sir Pelleas; "I am another knight that hath slain Sir Pelleas." "Do off your helm," said the Lady Ettarde, "that I may behold your visage." And when she saw it was not Sir Pelleas, she made him to alight, and led him unto her castle, and asked him faithfully whether he had slain Sir Pelleas? and he said yea. And then Sir Gawaine told her that his name was Sir Gawaine, and of the court of King Arthur, and his sister's son. "Truly," said she, "that is great pity, for he was a passing good knight of his body, but of all men alive I hated him most, for I never could be quiet for him; and for that ye have slain him I shall be your love, and do any thing that may please you." So she made Sir Gawaine good cheer. Then Sir Gawaine said, "That he loved a lady, and by no means she would love him." "She is to blame," said Ettarde, "and she will not love; for that ye be so well born a man, and such a man of prowess, there is no lady in this world too good for you." "Will ye," said Sir Gawaine, "promise me to do all that ye may do, by the faith of your body, to get me the love of my lady?" "Yea, sir," said she, "and that I promise you by the faith of my body." "Now," said Sir Gawaine, "it is yourself that I love so well; therefore, I pray you, hold your promise."

"I may not choose," said the Lady Ettarde : "but if I should be forsworn." And so she granted to fulfil all his desire. And then it was in the month of May that she and Sir Gawaine went out of the castle and supped in a pavilion, and there was a bed made, and in another pavilion she laid her damsels ; and in the third pavilion she laid part of her knights : for then she had no dread nor fear of Sir Pelleas. And there Sir Gawaine was with her, in that pavilion, two days and two nights, against the faithful promise that he made to Sir Pelleas. And, on the third day, in the morning early, Sir Pelleas armed him, for he had not slept since that Sir Gawaine departed from him ; for Sir Gawaine had promised, by the faith of his body, to come unto him to his pavilion by the priory within the space of a day and a night. Then Sir Pelleas mounted on horseback, and came to the pavilions that stood without the castle, and found, in the first pavilion, three knights in their beds, and three squires lying at their feet ; then went he to the second pavilion and found four gentlewomen lying in four beds ; and then he went to the third pavilion, and found Sir Gawaine asleep with his Lady Ettarde, and either clasping other in their arms. And when he saw that his heart almost burst for sorrow ; and said, "Alas ! that ever a knight should be found so false." And then he took his horse, and might no longer abide for sorrow. And when he had ridden nigh half-a-mile, he turned again, and thought to slay them both ; and when he saw them both lie so fast sleeping, scarce he might hold him on horseback for sorrow, and said thus to himself : "Though he be never so false I will not slay him sleeping ; for I will never destroy the high order of knighthood." And therewith he departed again, and left them sleeping. And or he had ridden half-a-mile he returned again, and thought then to slay them, making the greatest sorrow that any man might make ; and when he came to the pavilions, he tied his horse to a tree, and pulled out his sword, naked in his hand, and went straight to them where they lay together, and yet he thought that it were great shame for him to slay them sleeping, and laid the naked sword overthwart their throats, and then he took his horse and rode forth his way, making great and woeful lamentation. And when Sir Pelleas came to his pavilions, he told his knights and squires how he had sped, and said thus to them : "For your true and faithful service that you have done to me I shall give you all my goods ; for I will go unto my bed, and never arise until I be dead. And when I am dead I charge you that ye take the heart of my body, and bear it unto her, between two silver dishes, and tell her how I saw her lie in her pavilion with the false knight, Sir Gawaine." Right so Sir Pelleas unarmed himself and went to bed, making the greatest sorrow that ever man heard. And then Sir Gawaine and the Lady Ettarde awakened out of their sleep, and found the naked sword overthwart both their throats ; then she knew well that it was Sir Pelleas' sword. "Alas !" said she to Sir Gawaine, "ye have betrayed me and Sir Pelleas also ; for ye told me that ye had slain him, and now I know well it is not so, he is alive : and if Sir Pelleas had been as courteous to you as you have been to him ye had been a dead knight, but ye have deceived me and betrayed me falsely, that all ladies and damsels may beware by you and me." And therewith Sir Gawaine made him ready, and went into the forest. Then it happened that the damsel of the lake, Nimue met with a knight of Sir Pelleas, which went on foot in the forest making great moan, and she asked him the cause of his sorrow ; then the woeful knight told her, "how that his master and lord was betrayed through a knight and a lady, and how he would never arise out of his bed till he were dead." "Bring me to him anon, and I will warrant his life, that he shall not die for love ; and she that hath caused him to love, she shall be in as evil a plight as he is now, or it be long : for it is no joy of such a presumptuous lady that will have no mercy of such a valiant knight." Anon the knight brought her unto his lord and master. And when she saw him so lying in his bed, she thought she had never seen so likely a knight, and therewith she threw an enchantment upon him, and he fell asleep. And in the meanwhile she rode to the Lady Ettarde, and charged that no man should waken him till she came again. And so within two hours she brought the Lady Ettarde thither, and both the ladies found him asleep. "Lo !" said the damsel of the lake, "ye ought to be ashamed to murder such a knight." And therewith she cast such an enchantment upon her, that she loved him out of measure, that well nigh she was out of her mind. "Oh ! Lord Jesus," said the Lady Ettarde, "how is it befallen me that I now love him which I before most hated of all men living ?" "This is the right wise judgment of God," said the lady of the lake. And then anon Sir Pelleas awoke, and looked upon the Lady Ettarde ; and when he saw her he knew her, and then he hated her more than any woman alive, and said, "Go thy way hence, thou traitoress ; come no more in my sight." And when she heard him say so, she wept, and made great sorrow out of measure.

XXIII.

"Sir knight, Pelleas," said the damsel of the lake, "take your horse, and come with me out of this country, and ye shall have a lady that shall love you." "I will well," said Sir Pelleas, "for the Lady Ettarde hath done me great despite and shame." And there he told her the beginning, and how he had purposed never to have risen till that he had been dead; "and now God hath sent me such grace, that I hate her as much as ever I loved her, thanked be God." "Thank me," said the damsel of the lake. Anon Sir Pelleas armed him, and took his horse, and commanded his men to bring after his pavilions and his stuff, whereas the damsel of the lake would assign. So the Lady Ettarde died for sorrow, and the damsel of the lake rejoiced Sir Pelleas, and they loved together during their lives.

XXIV.

Now return we unto Sir Marhaus, that rode with the damsel of thirty winters of age southward, and so they came into a deep forest, and by fortune they were benighted, and rode long in a deep way, and at the last they came unto a court-yard, and there they demanded harbour. But the man of the court-yard would not harbour them for no treating that they could treat; but this much the good man said: And ye will take the adventure of your lodging, I shall bring you where ye shall be lodged." "What adventure is that, that I shall have for my lodging?" said Sir Marhaus. "Ye shall wit when ye come there," said the good man. "What adventure soever it be, I require thee bring me thither," said Sir Marhaus, "for I am weary, and my damsel and my horse," so the good man went and opened the gate, and within an hour he brought him unto a fair castle. And then the poor man called the porter, and anon he was let into the castle, and forthwith he showed to the lord how he had brought him an knight-errant, and a damsel that would be lodged with him. "Let him come in," said the lord, "it may happen that they shall repent that they took their lodging here in this castle." So Sir Marhaus was let in with torch-light, and there was a goodly sight of young men that welcomed him. And then his horse was led into the stable, and he and his damsel was brought into the hall: and there stood a mighty duke, and many goodly men about him. Then this lord asked him how he hight, and from whence he came, and with what man he dwelled. "Sir," said he, "I am a knight of King Arthur's, and knight of the

Table Round, and my name is Sir Marhaus, and I was born in Ireland." And then said the duke unto him, "That me sore repenteth, and the cause is this : I love not thy lord, nor none of all thy fellows that be of the Table Round ; and, therefore, ease thyself this night as well as thou mayst, for to-morrow I and my six sons shall match with thee, if God will." "Is there none other remedy but that I must have ado with you and your six sons at once ?" said Sir Marhaus. "No," said the duke, "for this cause I made mine avow : Sir Gawaine slew my seven sons in an encounter ; and, therefore, I made mine avow, that there should never no knight of King Arthur's court lodge with me, or come here as I might have ado with him, but that I should revenge the death of my seven sons." "Sir, I require you," said Sir Marhaus, "that ye will tell me, if it please you, what your name is?" "Wit ye well that I am the Duke of the South Marches." "Ah !" said Sir Marhaus, "I have heard say that ye have been a long time a great foe unto my lord King Arthur, and to his knights." "That shall ye feel to-morrow," said the duke. "Shall I have ado with you ?" said Sir Marhaus. "Yea," said the duke, "thereof thou shalt not choose ; therefore, take thee to thy chamber, where thou shalt have all that to thee belongeth." So Sir Marhaus departed, and was led to a chamber, and his damsel was also led to her chamber. And on the morrow the duke sent to Sir Marhaus, that he should make him ready. And so Sir Marhaus arose and armed him, and then there was a mass sung afore him, and after breakfast, and so mounted on horseback in the court of the castle, where they should do battle. So there was the duke all ready on horseback, clean armed, and his six sons by him, and every one had a spear in his hand ; and so they encountered, whereas the duke, and two of his sons, brake their spears upon him ; but Sir Marhaus held up his spear and touched none of them.

XXV.

THEN came the four sons of the duke by couples, and two of them brake their spears, and so did the other two : and all this while Sir Marhaus did not touch them. Then Sir Marhaus ran to the duke, and so smote him with his spear, that horse and man fell to the earth ; and so he served his sons. And then Sir Marhaus alighted down, and bid the duke yield him, or else he would slay him : and then some of his sons recovered, and would have set upon Sir Marhaus. Then said Sir Marhaus to the duke, "Cease thy sons, or else I will do the uttermost to you all." Then when the duke saw he might not escape death, he

cried to his sons, and charged them to yield them unto Sir
Marhaus. And they kneeled all down, and put the pommels of
their swords unto Sir Marhaus, and he received them ; and then
they helped their father : and there, by a common assent, promised unto Sir Marhaus never to he foes unto King Arthur, and
thereupon, at Pentecost after, the duke to come, and his six
sons, and put them in the King's grace. Then Sir Marhaus
departed ; and, within two days, his damsel brought him whereas was a great tournament that the Lady de Vause had cried ; and
who that did best should have a rich circlet of gold, worth a
thousand besaunts. And there Sir Marhaus did so nobly, that
he was renowned to have smitten down forty knights ; and so the
circlet of gold was rewarded him. Then he departed from
thence with great worship ; and, within seven days after, the
damsel brought him to the earl's place, whose name was called
Fergus, which after was Sir Tristram's knight ; and this earl
was but a young man, and late come to his lands ; and there
was a giant fast by him that hight Taulurd, and he had another
in Cornwall, that hight Taulas, that Sir Tristram slew when he
was out of his mind. So this earl made his complaint unto Sir
Marhaus, that there was a giant by him, that destroyed all his
lands, and how he durst nowhere ride nor go for him. "Sir,"
said Sir Marhaus, "useth he to fight on horseback or on foot?"
"Nay," said the earl, "there may no horse bear him, he is so
great." "Well," said Sir Marhaus, "then will I fight with him
on foot." So on the morrow Sir Marhaus prayed the earl, that
one of his men might bring him whereas the giant was ; and so
he was aware of him, for he saw him sit under a holly tree, and
many clubs of iron and battle-axes about him. So Sir Marhaus
dressed him to the giant, putting his shield afore him, and the
giant started to a club of iron, and came against Sir Marhaus as
fast as he might drive ; and, at the first stroke, he clave Sir
Marhaus's shield all to pieces, and light on a stone and crushed it
into the earth, and there he was in great peril, for the giant was
a wily fighter : but, at the last, Sir Marhaus smote off his right
arm above the elbow. Then the giant fled, and the knight after
him ; and so he drove him to a water, but the giant was so high,
that he could not wade after him : and then Sir Marhaus made
the Earl Fergus's man to fetch stones, and with those stones he
gave the giant many a sore knock, till at the last he made him to
fall down into the water, and so he was there drowned. Then
Sir Marhaus went to the giant's castle, and there he delivered
out of the giant's prison twenty-four ladies, and twenty-two
knights, and there he had riches without number, so that all the

days of his life he was never poor man after. Then he returned to the Earl Fergus, which greatly thanked him, and would have given him half his land, but he would take none. So Sir Marhaus dwelled with the earl nigh half-a-year, for he was sore bruised with the giant, and at the last he took his leave : and as he rode by the way he met with Sir Gawaine and Sir Ewaine : and so by adventure, he met with four knights of King Arthur's court ; the first was Sir Sagramore le Desirous, Sir Osanna, Sir Dodinas le Savage, and Sir Felot of Listinoise ; and there Sir Marhaus, with one spear, smote down these four knights, and hurt them sore. So he departed, and met his day afore set.

XXVI.

NOW turn we unto Ewaine, which rode westward with his damsel of threescore winters of age, and she brought him there as was a tournament, nigh the march of Wales. And at that tournament Sir Ewaine smote down thirty knights, wherefore the prize was given him, and the prize was a gerfalcon and a white steed trapped with cloth of gold. So then Sir Ewaine did many strange adventures, by the means of the old damsel that went with him ; and so she brought him unto a lady that was called the Lady of the Rock, which was a full courteous lady. So there were in that country two knights that were brethren, and they were called two perilous knights ; the one hight Sir Edward, of the Red Castle, and the other hight Sir Hue, of the Red Castle : and these two brethren had disinherited the Lady of the Rock of a barony of lands by their extortion. And, as Sir Ewaine lodged with this lady, she made her complaint unto him of these two knights. "Madam," said Sir Ewaine, "they are to blame, for they do against the high order of knighthood, and the oath that they have made ; and, if it like you, I will speak with them, because I am a knight of King Arthur's, and I will entreat them with fairness ; and, if they will not, I shall do battle with them in the defence of your right." "Gramercy !" said the lady, "and thereas I may not acquit you, God shall." So on the morrow the two knights were sent for, that they should come thither to speak with the Lady of the Rock. And wit it well they failed not, for they came with a hundred horses. But when the lady saw them in this manner so many, she would not suffer Sir Ewaine to go out unto them, neither upon surety, nor for fair language, but she made him to speak with them out of a tower. But, finally, these two brethren would not be entreated, and answered, that they would keep what they had. "Well," said Sir Ewaine, "then will I fight with one of you both, and prove upon your bodies, that ye do wrong and extortion unto this lady." "That will we not do," said the two brethren; "for, and we do battle, we two will fight with one knight at once; and, therefore, if ye will fight so, we will be ready at what hour ye will assign us: and, if that ye win us in plain battle, then the lady shall have her lands again." "Ye say well," said Sir Ewaine, "therefore make you ready, so that ye be here to-morrow in the defence of the lady's right."

XXVII.

THEN was there peace made on both parties, that no treason should be wrought on neither. So then the knights departed and made them ready; and that night Sir Ewaine had great cheer. And, on the morrow, he arose early and heard mass, and broke his fast, and after rode unto the plain without the gates, where halted the two brethren abiding him. Then rode they together passing sore, that Sir Edward and Sir Hue brake their spears upon Sir Ewaine: and Sir Ewaine smote Sir Edward, that he fell over his horse's tail, and yet brake not his spear: and then he spurred his horse and came upon Sir Hue, and overthrew him; but they soon recovered and dressed their shields, and drew their swords, and bid Sir Ewaine alight and do battle to the uttermost. Then Sir Ewaine avoided suddenly his horse, and put his shield afore him, and drew his sword, and so they dressed together, and either gave other great strokes : and there these two brethren wounded Sir Ewaine passing sore, that the Lady of the Rock weened that he would have died. And thus fought they together five hours as men enraged, and without reason: and, at the last, Sir Ewaine smote Sir Edward upon the helm such a buffet, that his sword carved him unto his collar bone; and then Sir Hue abated his courage. But Sir Ewaine pressed fast to have slain him: and when Sir Hue saw that, he kneeled down, and yielded him unto Sir Ewaine. And he of his gentleness received his sword, and took him by the hand, and went into the castle together. Then the Lady of the Rock was passing glad, and Sir Hue made great moan for his brother's death. Then the lady was restored unto her lands, and Sir Hue was commanded to be at the court of King Arthur at the next feast of Pentecost. So Sir Ewaine dwelled with the lady nigh half-a-year, for it was long or he might be whole of his great hurts. And then, when it drew nigh the term day, that Sir Gawaine should meet at the cross way, then every knight drew him thither to hold his promise that they had made ; and Sir Marhaus and Sir Ewaine brought their damsels with them ; but Sir Gawaine had lost his damsel, as it is afore rehearsed.

XXVIII.

AND right at the twelvemonth's end they met all three knights at the fountain, and their damsels : but the damsel that Sir Gawaine had with him could say but little worship of him. So they departed from the damsels and rode through a great forest, and there they met with a messenger that came from King Arthur, which had sought them well nigh a twelvemonth throughout all England, Wales, and Scotland, and was charged, if that he might find Sir Gawaine and Sir Ewaine, to bring them unto the court again : and then were they all glad ; and so they prayed Sir Marhaus to ride with them unto King Arthur's court. And so within twelve days they came to Camelot; and the King was passing glad of their coming, and so were all they of the court. Then King Arthur made them to swear upon a book, to tell him all their adventures that there had been fallen them all the twelvemonths, and so they did. And there was Sir Marhaus well known ; for there were knights that he had matched afore time, and he was named one of the best knights then living. Against the feast of Pentecost came the Damsel of the Lake, and brought with her Sir Pelleas : and at that high feast there was a great jousting of knights, and, of all the knights that were at that jousting, Sir Pelleas had the prize, and Sir Marhaus was named the next. But Sir Pelleas was so strong, that there might but a few knights hit him a buffet with a spear. And, at that feast, Sir Pelleas and Sir Marhaus were made knights of the Table Round, for there were two sieges void, for two knights had been slain in those twelve months. And great joy had King Arthur of Sir Pelleas and Sir Marhaus : but Sir Pelleas loved never after Sir Gawaine, but that he spared him for the love of King Arthur : but often times, at the jousts and tournaments, Sir Pelleas quitted Sir Gawaine ; for so it is rehearsed in the French Book. So Sir Tristram, many days after that, fought with Sir Marhaus in an island, and there they did a great battle ; but at the last Sir Tristram slew him. And Sir Tristram was sore wounded, that hardly he might recover, and lay at a nunnery half-a-year. And Sir Pelleas was a worshipful knight; and was one of the four that achieved the Sancgreal ; and the Damsel of the Lake made by her means, that never he had ado with Sir Launcelot du Lake ; for whereas Sir Launcelot was at any jousts or tournaments she would not suffer him to be there on that day, but if it were on Sir Launcelot's side.

THE BOOK OF SIR LAUNCELOT DU LAKE.

I.

OW leave we of Sir Tristram de Lyons, and speak we of Sir Launcelot du Lake, and Sir Galahad, Sir Launcelot's son, how he was begotten, and in what manner. Afore the time that Sir Galahad was begotten or born, there came in a hermit unto King Arthur, on Whitsunday, as the knights sat at the Round Table: and when the hermit saw the siege perilous, he asked the King and all the knights, why that seat was void? King Arthur and all the knights answered, "There shall never none sit in that siege but one, but if he be destroyed." "Then," said the hermit, "wot ye not what he is?" "Nay," said King Arthur and all the knights, "we wot not who he is that shall sit therein." "Then wot I," said the hermit, "for he that shall sit in that siege is yet unborn and ungotten, and this same year he shall be gotten that shall sit in that siege perilous, and he shall win the Sancgreal." When the hermit had made this mention, he departed from the court of King Arthur. And then after the feast Sir Launcelot rode on his adventures, till upon a time by adventure he passed over the bridge of Corbin: and there he saw the fairest tower that ever he saw, and there under was a fair town full of people, and all the people, men and women, cried all at once, "Ye are welcome, Sir Launcelot du Lake, the flower of all knighthood, for by thee all we shall be holpen out of danger." "What mean ye," said Sir Launcelot, "that ye cry so upon me?" "Ah! fair knight," said they all, "here is within this tower a dolorous lady, that hath been there in pains many winters: for ever she boileth in scalding water. And but late," said all the people, "Sir Gawaine was here, and he might not help her, and so he left her still in pain." "So may I," said Sir Launcelot, "leave her in pain as well as Sir Gawaine hath done." "Nay," said the people, "we know well that it is Sir Launcelot that shall deliver her." "Well," said Sir Launcelot, "then show me what I shall do." Then they brought Sir Launcelot into the tower: and, when he came to the chamber there as this lady was, the doors of iron unlocked and unbolted, and so Sir Launcelot went into the chamber that was as hot as any stew, and there Sir Launcelot took the fairest lady by the hand that ever he saw, and she was all naked as a needle. And, by enchantment, Queen Morgan le Fay and the Queen of Northgalis had put her in there in those pains, because she was called one of the fairest ladies in that country : and there she had been well five years, and never might she be delivered out of her great pains unto the time that the best knight of the world had taken her by the hand. Then the people brought her clothes : and, when she was arrayed, Sir Launcelot thought she was the fairest lady in the world, but if it were Queen Guenever. Then this lady said unto Sir Lancelot, "Sir, if it please you, will ye go with me here by into a chapel, that we may give lauding and praising unto Almighty God?" "Madam," said Sir Launcelot, "come on with me ; I will go with you." So when they came there they gave thanks unto God, and all the people learned and gave thanks unto God, and said, "Sir knight, since ye have delivered this lady, ye shall deliver us from a serpent that is here in a tomb." Then Sir Launcelot took his shield, and said, "Bring me thither ; and what I may do unto the pleasure of God and you, I will do it." So when Sir Launcelot came there, he saw written upon the tomb letters of gold, that said thus : "Here shall come a leopard of king's blood, and he will slay this serpent ; and this leopard shall engender a lion in this foreign country, the which lion shall pass all other knights." So then Sir Launcelot lift up the tomb, and there came out a horrible and fiendly dragon, spitting fire out of his mouth.

Then Sir Launcelot drew out his sword and fought with the dragon long, and at the last with great pain Sir Launcelot slew the dragon. Therewithal came King Pelleas, the good and noble knight, and saluted Sir Launcelot, and he him again. "Fair knight," said the King, "what is your name? I require you of your knighthood tell me."

II.

"SIR," said Sir Launcelot, "wit ye well my name is Sir Launcelot du Lake." "And my name is Sir Pelleas, King of the foreign country, and nigh cousin unto Joseph of Arimathy." Then either of them made much of other, and so they went into the castle for to take their repast : and anon there came in a dove at a window, and in her bill there seemed a little censer of gold, and therewithal there was such a savour, as though all the spicery of the world had been there. And forthwithal there was upon the table all manner of meats and drinks that they could think upon : so there came a damsel passing fair and young, and she bore a vessel of gold between her hands, and thereto the King kneeled devoutly, and said his prayers, and so did all that were there. "Oh Jesu." said Sir Launcelot, "what may this mean ?" "This is," said King Pelleas, "the richest thing that any man hath living. And when this thing goeth about, the Round Table shall be broken : and wit ye well," said King Pelleas, "that this is the Holy Sancgreal which ye have here seen." So King Pelleas and Sir Launcelot led their lives the most part of that day : and full fain would King Pelleas have found the means to have had Sir Launcelot for to have cast his love on his daughter, fair Dame Elaine, and for this intent : the King knew well that Sir Launcelot should get a child upon his daughter, the which should be named Sir Galahad, the good knight, by whom all the foreign country should be brought out of danger, and by him the Holy Grail would be achieved. Then came there forth a lady, which was called Dame Brisen, and she said unto King Pelleas, "Sir, wit ye well that Sir Launcelot loveth no lady in the world, but only Queen Guenever ; and therefore ye must work by my counsel, and I shall make him to come to your daughter Elaine, and he shall not wit but that he is with Queen Guenever." "Oh, the most fairest lady, Dame Brisen," said King Pelleas, "hope ye to bring this about?" "Sir," said she, "upon pain of my life let me deal." For this Dame Brisen was one of the greatest enchantresses that was at that time in the world living. Then anon by Dame Brisen's wit she made one to come to Sir Launcelot that he knew well : and this man brought him a ring from Queen Guenever like as he had come from her, and such a one for the most part as she was wont to wear. And when Sir Launcelot saw that token, wit ye well he was never so fain. "Where is my lady, Queen Guenever?" said Sir Launcelot. "She is in the castle of Case," said the messenger, "but five miles hence." Then Sir Launcelot thought to be there that same night. And then this Dame Brisen, by the commandment of King Pelleas, let send his daughter to that castle with twenty-five knights. Then Sir Launcelot against night rode unto that castle, and there anon he was received worshipfully, with such people unto him seeming as were about Queen Guenever's secret. So when Sir Launcelot was alighted he asked where the Queen was. So Dame Brisen said she was in her chamber. And then the people were avoided, and Sir Launcelot was led unto the chamber : and Dame Brisen brought Sir Launcelot a cup full of wine ; and, as soon as he had drunk that wine he was so besotted, and so mad, that he weened the Lady Elaine had been Queen Guenever. Wit ye well that Sir Launcelot was glad, and so was the lady Dame Elaine ; for well she knew, that the same night Sir Galahad should be begotten that should prove the best knight of the world : and so they lay unto five of the clock on the morrow. And all the windows and holes of that chamber were stopped, that no manner of light might be seen : and then Sir Launcelot remembered him, and he arose and went to the window.

III.

AND anon, as he had unshut the window, the enchantment was gone. "Alas !" said he "that I have lived so long ; now am I shamed." So then he got his sword in his hand, and said, "Thou traitoress, what art thou that hast bewitched me all this night? thou shalt die right here of my hand." Then this fair lady, Dame Elaine, kneeled down before Sir Launcelot, and said, "Fair, courteous knight, come of king's blood, I require you have mercy upon me ; and, as thou art renowned the most noble knight of the world, slay me not, for I shall bear him, by thee, that shall be the most noblest knight of the world." "Ah, thou false traitoress !" said Sir Launcelot, "why hast thou thus betrayed me ? Anon tell me what thou art !" She answered and said, "Sir, I am Elaine, the daughter of King Pelleas." "Well," said Sir Launcelot, "I will forgive you this deed :" and therewith he took her up in his arms, and kissed her ; for she was a fair lady, and thereto lusty and young, and wise as any was at that time living. "So God me help," said Sir Launcelot, "I may not put this blame to you, but her that made this enchantment upon me, as between you and me, and I may find that same Lady Brisen, she shall lose her head for her witchcraft, for there was never knight so deceived as I am this night." And so Sir Launcelot arrayed him and armed him, and took his leave mildly of that young lady, Dame Elaine, and so he departed. Then she said, "My lord, Sir Launcelot, I beseech you, see me as soon as you may, for I have obeyed me unto the prophecy that my father told me, and, by his commandment to fulfil this prophecy, I have given the greatest riches and the fairest flower that ever I had, that is, my maidenhood, which I shall never have again ; and therefore, gentle knight, owe me your good will." And so Sir Launcelot arrayed him, and was armed, and took his leave mildly of that young lady, Dame Elaine, and so he departed, and rode till he came to the castle of Corbin, where her father was. And, as soon as her time came, she was delivered of a fair child, and they christened him, and named him Galahad ; and wit ye well, that child was well kept, and well nourished : and he was thus named Galahad, for because Sir Launcelot was so named at the font stone ; and after

that the Lady of the Lake confirmed him Sir Launcelot du Lake.
Then, after that this Lady Elaine was delivered and churched,
there came a knight unto her, whose name was Sir Bromell le
Plech, which was a great lord, and he had loved that lady long,
and he evermore desired her that he might wed her ; and so by
no means she could put him off ; till, upon a day, she said to
Sir Bromell, "Wit ye well, sir knight, I will not love you, for
my love is set upon the best knight of the world." "Who is
he?" said Sir Bromell. "Sir," said she, "it is Sir Launcelot du
Lake that I love, and none other ; therefore woo me no longer."
"Ye say well," said Sir Bromell ; "and since, ye have told me
so much, ye shall have but little joy of Sir Launcelot ; for I shall
slay him wherever I meet him." "Sir," said the Lady Elaine,
"do him no treason." "Wit ye well, my lady," said Sir Bromell,
"and I promise you these twelvemonths I shall keep the bridge
of Corbin, for Sir Launcelot's sake ; that he shall neither come
nor go to you, but I shall meet with him."

IV.

THEN, as it befel by fortune and adventure, Sir Bors de
Ganis, which was nephew unto Sir Launcelot, came over that
bridge, and there Sir Bromell and Sir Bors jousted ; and Sir
Bors smote Sir Bromell such a buffet, that he bare him over his
horse's tail : and then Sir Bromell, like an hardy knight, pulled
out his sword, and dressed his shield, to do battle with Sir Bors ;
and then Sir Bors alighted and avoided his horse : and there
they dashed together many sad strokes, and long thus they
fought, till at the last Sir Bromell was laid unto the ground ; and
there Sir Bors began for to unlace his helm, for to slay him.
Then Sir Bromell cried Sir Bors mercy, and yielded him.
"Well," said Sir Bors, "upon this covenant thou shalt have
thy life : so thou go unto Sir Launcelot upon Whitsunday that
next cometh, and yield thee unto him as a knight recreant." "I
will do so," said Sir Bromell ; and that he sware upon the cross
of the sword, and so he let him depart. And Sir Bors rode unto
King Pelleas, that was within Corbin, and when the King, and
Dame Elaine, his daughter, knew that Sir Bors was nephew
unto Sir Launcelot, they made him great cheer. Then said
Dame Elaine, "We marvel much where Sir Launcelot is, for
he came never here but once." "Marvel not," said Sir Bors,
"for all this half year he hath been in prison, with Queen Morgan le Fay, King Arthur's sister." "Alas!" said Dame Elaine,
"that me sore repenteth." And ever Sir Bors beheld the child,

that she had in her arms, and ever him seemed it was passing like Sir Launcelot. "Truly," said Dame Elaine, "wit ye well that this child is his." Then Sir Bors wept for joy, and he prayed unto God the child might prove as good a knight as his father was. And so there came in a white dove, and she bare a little censer of gold in her bill : and anon there was all manner of meats and drinks ; and there was a maiden that bare the Sancgreal, and she said openly, "Wit ye well, Sir Bors, that this child is Galahad, that shall sit in the Siege Perilous, and also shall achieve the Sancgreal ; and he shall be much better than ever was Sir Launcelot du Lake, that is his own father." And then they kneeled down and made their devotions ; and there was such a savour, as all the spicery in the world had been there : and when the dove took her flight, the maiden vanished away with the Sancgreal, as she came. "Sir," said Sir Bors unto King Pelleas, "this castle may well be called the Castle Adventurous, for here be many strange adventures." "That is truth," said King Pelleas, "for well may this place be called the adventurous place, for here come but few knights that go away with any worship be he never so strong, here he may be proved : and, but late ago, Sir Gawaine, the good knight, got but little worship here. For I let you to wit," said King Pelleas, "here shall no knight win no worship, but if he be of worship himself, and of good living, and that loveth God, and dreadeth God ; and else he getteth no worship here, be he ever so hardy." "That is a wonderful thing !" said Sir Bors : "what ye mean in this country I wot not ; for ye have many strange adventures : therefore I will lie in this castle this night." "Ye shall not do so," said King Pelleas, "by my counsel, for it is hard that ye escape without a shame." "I shall take the adventure that will befall me," said Sir Bors. "Then I counsel you," said King Pelleas, "for to be confessed clean." "As for that," said Sir Bors, "I will be confessed with a good will." So Sir Bors was confessed ; and, for all women, Sir Bors was a virgin, save for one, which was the daughter of King Brandegoris. And so Sir Bors was led to bed into a fair, large chamber, and many doors were shut about that chamber ; and, when Sir Bors espied all those doors, he made all the people to avoid, for he might have nobody with him ; but in nowise Sir Bors would unarm him, but so laid him upon the bed. And right so he saw come in a light, which he might well see, a spear great and long, which came straight upon him, point long ; and so Sir Bors seemed that the head of the spear burnt like a taper. And anon, or Sir Bors wist, the spear-head smote him into the shoulder an hand's

breadth in deepness ; and that wound grieved Sir Bors passing
sore, and then he laid him down again for pain. And anon
therewithal came a knight, all armed, with his shield on his
shoulder, and his sword drawn in his hand ; and he said to Sir
Bors, "Arise, sir knight! and fight with me." "I am sore
hurt," said Sir Bors ; "but yet I shall not fail thee." And then
Sir Bors started up, and dressed his shield ; and then they
lashed together mightily a great while. And so, at the last, Sir
Bors bare him always backward until he came to a chamber
door ; and there that knight went into that chamber, and there
rested him a great while : and, when he had rested him, he came
out freshly again, and began a new battle with Sir Bors, mightily
and strongly.

V.

THEN Sir Bors thought he should no more go into that
chamber to rest him ; and so Sir Bors dressed him between the
knight and the chamber-door, and there Sir Bors smote him so
sore that he fell down ; and then that knight yielded him to Sir
Bors. "What is your name?" said Sir Bors. "Sir," said that
knight, "my name is Sir Pedivere, of the Straight Marches."
So Sir Bors made him swear, that, at Whitsunday next coming,
for to be at the court of King Arthur, and yield him there as
prisoner, and an overcome knight, by the hands of Sir Bors. So
thus departed Sir Pedivere, of the Straight Marches. And then
Sir Bors laid him down for to rest him ; and then he heard and
felt much noise at that chamber. And then Sir Bors espied that
there came in, he wist not whether at the doors or windows, a
shot of arrows and cross-bow quarels, so thick, that he had great
marvel of it ; and there fell many upon him, and hurt him in
the bare places. And then Sir Bors was aware where came in
an hideous lion. So Sir Bors dressed him unto the lion ; and
anon the lion bereft him of his shield : and with his sword Sir
Bors smote off the lion's head. Right so, Sir Bors forthwith
saw a dragon in the court, passing horrible, and there seemed
letters of gold written in his forehead ; and Sir Bors thought
that the letters made a signification of his lord, King Arthur.
Right so, there came an old and an horrible leopard ; and there
they fought long, and did great battle together. And, at the
last, the dragon spit out of his mouth as it had been well an
hundred dragons ; and lightly all the small dragons slew the old
dragon, and tore him all to pieces. And anon forthwith there
came an old man into the hall, and he sat him down in a fair
chair, and there seemed to be two great adders about his neck ;

and then the old man had a harp, and there he sang an old song, how Joseph of Arimathy came into this land. And when he had sang, the old man bade Sir Bors to go from thence ; "for here shall ye have no more adventures ; and full worshipfully have ye done, and better shall ye do hereafter." And then Sir Bors seemed that there came the whitest dove that ever he saw, with a little golden censer in her mouth ; and anon therewithal the tempest ceased and passeth, that before was marvellous to hear. So was all the court full of good savours. Then Sir Bors saw four fair children, that bare four tapers, and an old man in the midst of the children, with a censer in his own hand, and a spear in his other hand ; and that same spear was called the spear of vengeance.

VI.

"Now," said that old man unto Sir Bors, "go ye unto your cousin Sir Launcelot, and tell him of this adventure, the which had been most convenient for him of all earthly knights. But sin is so foul in him, that he may not achieve such holy deeds ; for, had not his sin been, he had passed all the knights that ever · was in his days. And tell thou Sir Launcelot, that, of all worldly adventures, he passeth in manhood and prowess all other ; but, in these spiritual matters, he shall have many his better." And then Sir Bors saw four gentlewomen coming by him, poorly beseen ; and he saw whereas they entered into a chamber, where was great light, as it were a summer light : and the women kneeled down before an altar of silver, with four pillars ; and he saw as it had been a bishop kneeling down before that table of silver : and, as Sir Bors looked up, he saw a sword like silver, naked, hovering over his head ; and the clearness thereof smote so in his eyes, that, at that time, Sir Bors was blind. And there he heard a voice that said, "Go thou hence, thou Sir Bors ; for as yet thou art not worthy to be in this place." And then he went backward to his bed, till on the morrow ; and, on the morrow, King Pelleas made great joy of Sir Bors : and then he departed, and rode to Camelot ; and there he found Sir Launcelot du Lake, and told. him of the adventures that he had seen with King Pelleas at Corbin.

So the noise sprang to King Arthur's court, that Sir Launcelot had gotten a child by fair Elaine, the daughter of King Pelleas ; wherefore, Queen Guenever was wrath, and gave many rebukes unto Sir Launcelot, and called him false knight. And then Sir Launcelot told the Queen all, and how he was made to come to Elaine by enchantment, in likeness of the Queen : so the Queen held Sir Launcelot excused. And, as the book saith, King Arthur had been in France, and had much war upon the mighty King Claudas, and had won much of his lands, and, when·the King was come again, he let cry a great feast, and all lords and ladies of England should be there, but such as were rebellious against him.

VII.

AND when Dame Elaine, the daughter of King Pelleas, heard of this feast, she sent unto her father, and required him that he would give her leave for to ride unto that feast. The King answered, "I will well that ye go thither; but in anywise, as ye love me, and will have my blessing, that ye be well beseen in the richest wise: and look that ye spare for no cost; ask and ye shall have all that you needeth." Then by the advice if Dame Brisen, her maid, all things were apparelled unto the purpose, and there was never more lady richly beseen than she was. So she rode with twenty knights, and ten ladies, and gentlewomen, to the number of an hundred horses; and, when she came to Camelot, King Arthur and Queen Guenever said, and all the knights, that Dame Elaine was the fairest and best beseen lady that ever was in that court. And anon, as King Arthur wist that she was come, he met her, and saluted her; and so did the most part of the knights of the Round Table, both Sir Tristram, Sir Bleoberis, and Sir Gawaine, and many more that I will not rehearse. But when Sir Launcelot saw her he was sore ashamed, and that because he drew his sword at the Castle of Case, that he would not see her, nor yet speak to her; and yet Sir Launcelot thought she was the fairest woman that he saw in his life days. But when Dame Elaine saw that Sir Launcelot would not speak to her, she was so heavy, that she wend her heart would have burst: for wit ye well that out of measure she loved him. And then Dame Elaine said unto her gentlewoman, Dame Brisen, "The unkindness of Sir Launcelot near hand slayeth me." "A peace, madam!" said Dame Brisen; "I will undertake that this night he shall come to you, and ye would hold you still." "That were me rather," said Dame Elaine, "than all the gold that is above the earth." "Let me deal," said Dame Brisen. So when Dame Elaine was brought unto Queen Guenever, either made other good cheer by countenance, but nothing with hearts. But all men and women spake of the beauty of Dame Elaine, and of her great riches. Then at night the Queen commanded that Dame Elaine should sleep in a chamber, nigh unto her chamber, and all under one roof: and so it was done as the Queen had commanded. Then the Queen sent for Sir Launcelot; and bade him come to her chamber that night, "Or else, I am sure," said the Queen, "that ye will go to your lady, Dame Elaine, by whom ye gat Galahad." "Ah! madam," said Sir Launcelot, "never say ye so; for aforetime it was against my will." "Then," said the Queen, "look that ye will come to me when I send for you." "Madam," said Sir Launcelot, "I shall not fail you, but I shall be ready at your command." This bargain was not so soon done and made between them, but Dame Brisen knew it by her crafts, and told it to her lady, Dame Elaine. "Alas!" said she, "how shall I do?" "Let me deal," said Dame Brisen; "for I shall bring him by the hand to you, and he shall ween that I am Queen Guenever's messenger." "Now well is me," said Dame Elaine, "for of all the world I love none so much as I do Sir Launcelot."

VIII.

So, when the time came that all the folks were asleep, Dame Brisen came unto Sir Launcelot, and said, "Sir Launcelot du Lake, be ye asleep? my lady, Queen Guenever, waiteth upon you." "O, fair lady!" said Sir Launcelot, "I am ready to go with you where ye will have me." So Sir Launcelot threw upon him a long gown, and took his sword in his hand; and then Dame Brisen took him by the finger, and led him unto Dame Elaine: and then she departed, and left them together. Wit ye well the lady was glad, and so was Sir Launcelot; for he weened that it was the Queen. Now leave we them, and speak we of Queen Guenever, that sent one of her gentlewomen unto Sir Launcelot; and, when she came there, she found Sir Launcelot away. So she came again unto the Queen, and told her all, how she had sped. "Alas!" said the Queen, "where is that knight become?" Then the Queen was nigh out of her wits, and then she writhed and weltered as a mad woman, and might not sleep a four or five hours. Then Sir Launcelot had a condition that he used of custom, he would clatter in his sleep, and speak oft of his lady, Queen Guenever. So Sir Launcelot had waked so long as it had pleased him; then by course of kind he slept. And in his sleep he talked and clattered as a jay of the love that had been between Queen Guenever and him; and so, as he talked so loud, the Queen heard him there as she lay in her chamber: and when she heard him so clatter, she was nigh out of her mind, and for anger and pain wist not what to do ; and then she coughed so loud that Sir Launcelot awaked, and he knew her hemming ; and then he knew well that he was not with the Queen. And therewith he leapt out of his bed as he had been a madman in his shirt, and the Queen met him in the floor, and thus she said : "False traitor knight thou art, look thou never abide in my court, and avoid my chamber ; and be not so hardy, thou false traitor knight that thou art, that ever come in my sight." "Alas," said Sir Launcelot, and therewith he took such a hearty sorrow at her words, that he fell down to the ground in a swoon ; and therewith Queen Guenever departed. And when Sir Launcelot awaked of his swoon he leapt out at a bay window into a garden, and there with thorns he was all to scratched in his visage and his body ; and so he ran forth he wist not whither, and was mad as ever was man. And so he ran two years, and never man might have grace to know him.

IX.

Now turn we unto Queen Guenever, and unto Dame Elaine. Then, when Dame Elaine heard Queen Guenever so rebuke Sir Launcelot, and also she saw how he swooned, and after leapt out of a bay window, then she said unto Queen Guenever, " Madame, ye are greatly to blame for Sir Launcelot, for now ye have lost him ; for I saw and heard by his countenance that he is mad for ever. Alas, madam, ye do great sin, and to yourself great dishonour, for ye have a lord of your own, and therefore it is your part for to love him above all other ; for there is no Queen in all this world that hath such another King as ye have ; and if it were not, I might have the love of my lord, Sir Launcelot ; and because I have to love him, for by him I have borne a fair son, and his name is Galahad, and he shall be in his time the best knight in the world." " I warn and charge you, Dame Elaine," said the Queen, "that when it is daylight, to avoid my court ; and, for the love ye owe to Sir Launcelot, discover not your counsel, for and ye do it will be his death." "As for that," said Dame Elaine, " I dare undertake he is marred for ever, and that have ye made ; for ye nor I are like to rejoice him, for he made the most piteous groan when he leapt out at yonder bay window that ever I heard man make." "Alas!" said Queen Guenever, "for now I wot well we have lost him for ever." "Alas!" said fair Elaine. So on the morrow Dame Elaine took her leave to depart, and she would no longer abide. Then King Arthur brought her on her way, with more than a hundred knights, through a great forest : and by the way she told Sir Bors de Ganis all how it betide that same night, and how Sir Launcelot leapt out at a bay window, distraught out of his wit. "Alas!" said Sir Bors, "where is my lord, Sir Launcelot, become?" "Sir," said Dame Elaine, "I cannot tell you." "Alas," said Sir Bors, "between you both ye have destroyed that good knight." "As for me," said Dame Elaine, "I said never, nor did never thing that should in anywise displease him; but with the great rebuke that Queen Guenever gave him, I saw him swoon to the ground; and when he awoke he took his sword in his hand, naked, save his shirt, and leapt out at a window, with the grisliest groan that ever I heard any man make." "Now farewell, Dame Elaine," said Sir Bors, "and hold my lord, King Arthur, with a tale as long as ye may, for I will turn again unto Queen Guenever, and give her an heat; and I require you, as ye will have my service, make good watch, and espy if ye may see my lord, Sir Launcelot." "Truly," said Dame Elaine, "I will do all that I may, for as fain would I know where he is become as you or any of his kin, or as Queen Guenever, and a good cause I have thereto, as well as any other. And wit ye well, I would lose my life for him rather than he should be hurt. But, alas! I fear me that I shall never see him, and the chief causer of all this is Dame Guenever." "Madam," said Dame Brisen (the which had made the enchantment before between Sir Launcelot and her), "I pray you heartily let Sir Bors depart, and hie him with all his might as fast as he may to seek Sir Launcelot, for I warn you he is clean out of his mind, and yet he shall be well helped, and but by miracle." Then wept Dame Elaine, and so did Sir Bors de Ganis, and so they departed; and Sir Bors rode straight unto Queen Guenever: and when she saw Sir Bors, she began to weep as she had been mad. "Fie upon your weeping," said Sir Bors, "for ye weep never but when there is no boot. Alas, that ever Sir Launcelot's kin saw you; for now have ye lost the best knight of all our blood, and he that was the leader of us all, and our succour: and, I dare well say, and make it good, that all kings, Christian or heathen, may not find such a knight, for to speak of his nobleness and courtesy, with his beauty and gentleness. Alas!" said Sir Bors, "what shall we do that be of his blood?" "Alas!" said Sir Ector de Maris. "Alas!" said Sir Lionel.

X.

AND when the Queen heard them say so, she fell to the ground in a deadly swoon. And then Sir Bors took her and roused her; and when she was come to herself again, she kneeled before the three knights, and held up both her hands, and besought them to seek him, and not to spare for no goods but that he be found, for I wot well he is out of his mind. And Sir Bors, Sir Ector, and Sir Lionel departed from the Queen, for they might not abide no longer for sorrow. And then the Queen sent them treasure enough for their expenses : and so they took their horses and their armour, and departed, and then they rode from country to country, in forests, and in wildernesses, and in ways, and ever they laid watch as well both at forests and at all manner of men as they rode to hearken and to inquire after him, as he that was a naked man in his shirt, with a sword in his hand. And thus they rode well nigh a quarter of a year endlong and overthwart in many places, forests, and wildernesses, and oftentimes were evil lodged for his sake, and yet for all their labour and seeking could they never hear word of him ; and, wit ye well, these three knights were passing sorry. So then, at the last, Sir Bors and his fellows met with a knight that hight Sir Melion de Tartare. "Now, fair knight," said Sir Bors, "whither be ye going?" for they knew either other beforetime. "Sir," said Sir Melion, "I am in the way towards the court of King Arthur." "Then we pray you," said Sir Bors, "that ye will tell my lord, King Arthur, and my lady, Queen Guenever, and all the fellowship of the Round Table, that we cannot in no wise tell where Sir Launcelot is become." Then Sir Melion departed from them, and said that he would tell the King, and the Queen, and all the fellowship of the Round Table, as they had desired him. So when Sir Melion was come unto the court of King Arthur, he told the King, and the Queen, and all the fellowship of the Round Table, what Sir Bors had said of Sir Launcelot. Then Sir Gawaine, Sir Ewaine, Sir Sagramore le Desirous, Sir Aglovale, and Sir Percivale de Galis took upon them, by the great desire of King Arthur, and in especial by the Queen, to seek throughout all England, Wales, and Scotland, to find Sir Launcelot ; and with them rode eighteen knights more to bear them fellowship ; and, wit ye well, that they lacked no manner of spending, and so were they twenty-three knights. Now return we unto Sir Launcelot, and speak we of his care and woe, and what pain that he endured ; for cold, hunger, and thirst, he had plenty. And thus, as these noble knights rode together, they by one assent departed asunder, and then they rode by two, by three, by four, and by five ; and ever they assigned where they should meet. And so Sir Aglovale and Sir Percivale rode together unto their mother, which was a Queen in those days : and when she saw her two sons, for joy she wept right tenderly, and then she said unto them, "Ah, my dear sons, when your father was slain he left me four sons, of the which now be two slain, and for the death of my noble son, Sir Lamoracke, shall my heart never be glad." And then she kneeled down upon both her knees before Sir Aglovale and Sir Percivale, and besought them to abide at home with her. "Ah, sweet mother," said Sir Percivale, "we may not abide here, for we be come of King's blood on both parties; and therefore, mother, it is our kind to hunt at arms and noble deeds." "Alas! my sweet sons," said she, "for your sakes I shall lose my liking and lust, and wind and weather I may not endure, what for the death of your father, King Pellinore, that was shamefully slain by the hands of Sir Gawaine, and his brother, Sir Gaheris; and they slew him not manfully, but by treason. And, my dear sons, this is a piteous complaint for me of your father's death, considering also the death of Sir Lamoracke, which of knighthood had but few fellows : now, my dear sons, have this in your minds." Then there was great weeping and sobbing in the court when they should depart, and she fell down in a swoon in the midst of the court.

XI.

As soon as she came again to herself, she sent a squire after them with spending enough for them. And when the squire had overtook them, they would not suffer him to ride with them, but sent him home again to comfort their mother, praying her meekly of her blessing. And so this squire was benighted, and, by misfortune, he happened to come unto a castle where dwelled a baron ; and so when the squire was come into the castle, the lord asked him from whence he came, and whom he served. "My lord," said the squire, "I serve a good knight, that is called Sir Aglovale." The squire said it to a good intent, weening unto him to have been the more forborne for Sir Aglovale's sake, than that he had answered he had served the Queen, Sir Aglovale's mother. "Well, my fellow," said the lord of the castle, "for Sir Aglovale's sake thou shalt have an evil lodging; for Aglovale slew my brother, and therefore thou shalt die on part of payment." And then the lord commanded his men to have him out of his castle, and there they slew him out of mercy. Right so on the morrow came Sir Aglovale and Sir Percivale riding by a churchyard where men and women were busy, and beheld the dead squire, and thought to bury him. "What is there," said Sir Aglovale, "that ye behold so fast ?" A good man started forth and said, " Fair knight, here lieth a squire slain shamefully this night." " How was he slain, fair fellow ?" said Sir Aglovale. "My fair sir," said the man, " the lord of this castle lodged the squire this night ; and because he said he was servant unto a good knight that is with King Arthur, his name is Sir Aglovale, therefore the lord commanded to slay him, and for this cause he is slain." "Gramercy," said Sir Aglovale, "and lightly shall ye see his death revenged, for I am the same knight for whom this squire was slain." Then Sir Aglovale called unto him Sir Percivale, and bid him alight quickly, and so they alighted both. And so they went on foot into the castle, and as soon as they were within the castle-gate Sir Aglovale bid the porter go into his lord, and tell him that I am Sir Aglovale, for whom this squire was slain this night. Anon, the porter told this unto his lord, whose name was Sir Goodwin, and anon he armed him, and then he came into the court and said, "Which of you is Sir Aglovale." " Here am I," said Sir Aglovale : "for what cause," said Sir Aglovale, "slewest thou this night my mother's squire ?" " I slew him," said Sir Goodwin, "because of thee ; thou slewest my brother, Sir Gawdelyn." "As for thy brother," said Sir Aglovale, " I avow it I slew him ; for he was a false knight, and a betrayer of ladies and of good knights, and for the death of my squire thou shalt die." " I defy thee," said Sir Goodwin : and then they lashed together as eagerly as it had been two wild lions ; and Sir Percivale fought with all the remnant that would fight : and so within awhile Sir Percivale had slain all that would withstand him ; for Sir Percivale dealed so his strokes, that were so rude, that there durst no man abide him. And, within a little while, Sir Aglovale had down Sir Goodwin to the earth, and there he unlaced his helm, and struck off his head. And then they departed and took their horses ; and then they let carry the dead squire unto a priory, and there they buried him.

XII.

AND when this was done, they rode into many countries, ever inquiring after Sir Launcelot, but in nowise they could hear of him. And at the last they came to a castle hight Cardigan, and there Sir Percivale and Sir Aglovale were lodged together ; and privily, about midnight, Sir Percivale came to Sir Aglovale's squire, and said, "Arise, and make thee ready, for thou and I will ride away secretly." " Sir," said the squire, " I would fain ride with you where ye would have me, but, and my lord your brother take me, he will slay me." "As for that, care thou not," said Sir Percivale, "for I shall be thy warrant." And so they rode till it was afternoon, and then they came upon a bridge of stone, and there he found a knight that was bound with a chain fast about the waist unto a pillar of marble. "O, fair knight," said that bound knight, "I require thee loose me of my hands." "What knight are ye," said Sir Percivale, "and for what cause are ye so bound?" "Sir, I shall tell you," said that knight ; "I am a knight of the Round Table, and my name is Sir Persides, and thus by adventure I came this way, and here I lodged in this castle at the bridge foot, and therein dwelleth an uncourteous lady ; and, because she proffered me to be my paramour, and that I refused her, she set her men upon me suddenly or that I might come to my weapon, and thus they bound me, and here, and wot well I shall die, but if some man of worship break my hands." "Be ye of good cheer," said Sir Percivale, " and because ye are a knight of the Round Table as well as I, I trust to God to break your hands ;" and therewith Sir Percivale drew out his sword, and stroke at the chain with such a might, that he cut in two the chain, and went through Sir Persides' hawberk, and hurt him a little. " O Jesu," said Sir Persides, "that was a mighty stroke as ever I felt, for had not the chain been ye had slain me." And therewithal Sir Persides saw a knight coming out of the castle all that he might, flying. "Beware," said Sir Persides, "yonder cometh a man that will have to do with you." "Let him come," said Sir Percivale. And so he met with that knight in the midst of the bridge, and Sir Percivale gave him such a buffet, that he smote him quite from his horse, and over a part of the bridge, that had not been a little vessel underneath the bridge that knight had been drowned. And then Sir Percivale took the knight's horse, and made Sir Persides to mount upon him. And so they rode unto the castle, and bid the lady deliver Sir Persides' servants, or else he would slay all that he might find. And so for fear she delivered them all. Then was Sir Percivale aware of a lady that stood in a tower. "Ah, madam," said Sir Percivale, " what use is that in a lady for to destroy good knights but if they will be your paramour forthwith ; it is a shameful custom of a lady ; and if that I had not a great matter in hand, I should undo your evil customs." And so Sir Persides brought Sir Percivale unto his own castle, and there he made him the best cheer that he could devise all that night. And, on the morrow, when Sir Percivale had heard- mass. and broken his fast, he bid Sir Persides ride unto King Arthur, "and tell the King how ye met with me, and tell my brother, Sir Aglovale, how I rescued you, and bid my brother that he seek not after me ; for tell him that I am in the quest for to seek Sir Launcelot du Lake, and though he seek me, he shall not find me ; and tell him that I will never see him nor the court till I have found Sir Launcelot. Also, tell Sir Kaye, the seneschal, and Sir Mordred, that I trust unto Jesu to be of as great worthiness as either of them ; for tell them, that I shall never forget their mocks and scorns that they did to me that day when I was made knight ; and tell them, that I will never see that court till men speak of me more worship than ever man did of any of them both." And Sir Persides departed from Sir Percivale, and then he rode unto King Arthur, and told there of Sir Percivale ; and when Sir Aglovale heard him speak of his brother, Sir Percivale, he said, " He departed from me unkindly."

XIII.

"SIR," said Sir Persides, "on my life he shall prove a noble knight as any is now living." And when he saw Sir Kaye and Sir Mordred, Sir Persides said thus : " My fair lords both, Sir Percivale greeteth you well both, and he sendeth you word by me, that he trusteth unto God, or ever he cometh to the court again to be of as great nobleness as ever ye were both, and more men to speak of his nobleness than ever did of yours." " It may well be," said Sir Kaye and Sir Mordred, " but at that time when he was made knight he was full unlikely to prove a good knight." " As for that," said King Arthur, " he must needs prove a good knight, for his father and his brethren were noble knights." Now will we return unto Sir Percivale, that rode long, and in a forest he met a knight with a broken shield and a broken helm ; and as soon as either saw other readily, they made them ready to joust, and so hurtled together with all the might of their horses, and met together so hard, that Sir Percivale was smitten to the earth. And then Sir Percivale arose lightly, and cast his shield upon his shoulder, and drew his sword, and bade the other knight alight and do battle to the uttermost. " Will ye more ? " said the knight ; and therewith he alighted and put his horse from him, and then they came together an easy pace, and there they lashed together with their swords ; and sometimes they stroke, and sometimes they feigned, and either gave other many great wounds. Thus they fought near half-a-day, and never rested them but little ;

and there was none of them both that had less wounds than fifteen, and they bled so much, that it was marvel that they stood upon their feet. But this knight that fought with Sir Percivale was a proved knight, and a well fighting, and Sir Percivale was young and strong, not knowing in fighting as the other was. Then Sir Percivale spake first, and said—"Sir knight, hold thy hand a little while still, for we have fought for a simple matter and quarrel ever long, and therefore I require thee of gentleness tell me thy name, for I was never or this time matched." "So God me help," said the other knight, "and never before this time was there never no manner of knight, the which wounded and hurt me so dangerously as thou hast done; and yet have I fought in many battles, and now shalt thou wit that I am a knight of the Round Table, and my name is Sir Ector de Maris, brother unto the good knight, Sir Launcelot du Lake." "Alas!" said Sir Percivale, "and my name is Sir Percivale de Galis, that have made my quest for to seek Sir Launcelot: now am I seeker that I shall never finish my quest, for ye have slain me." "It is not so," said Sir Ector, "for I am slain by your hands, and may not live; therefore I require you," said Sir Ector unto Sir Percivale, "ride ye hereby unto a priory, and bring me a priest, that I may receive my Saviour, for I may not live. And when ye come unto the court of King Arthur, tell not my brother Sir Launcelot how ye have slain me, for then he will be your mortal enemy; but ye may say, that I was slain in my quest as I sought him." "Alas!" said Sir Percivale, "ye say that thing that never will be, for I am so faint for bleeding, that unless I may stand, how should I then take my horse."

XIV.

THEN they made both great dole out of measure. "This will not avail," said Sir Percivale; and then he kneeled down and made his prayers devoutly unto Almighty God, for he was one of the best knights of the world that was at that time, in whom the very faith stood most in. Right so there came by the holy vessel of the Sancgreal, with all manner of sweetness and savour, but they could not readily see who bear that holy vessel; but Sir Percivale had a glimmering of that vessel, and of the maiden that bear it; for she was a perfect clean maid. And forthwith they were both as whole of limb and hide as ever they were in their life days; wherefore, they gave thanks unto Almighty God right devoutly. "O Jesu!" said Sir Percivale, "what may this mean, that we be thus healed, and right now we were at a point of dying." " I wot well," said Sir Ector, "what it is : it is an holy vessel that is borne by a maiden, and therein is a part of the holy blood of our Lord Jesus Christ, blessed might He be ; but it may not be seen," said Sir Ector, "but if he be by a perfect man." " So God me help," said Sir Percivale, " I saw a damsel as me, though all in white, with a vessel in both her hands, and forthwithal I was whole." So then they took their horses and their harness, and amended it as well as they might, that was broken, and so they mounted upon their horses, and rode talking together ; and there Sir Ector told Sir Percivale how he had sought his brother Sir Launcelot, and never could have knowledge of him. In many strange adventures have I been in this quest : and so either told other of their adventures.

XV.

AND now leave we a little of Sir Ector and Sir Percivale, and speak we of Sir Launcelot, that suffered and endured many sharp showers, which ever ran wild wood from place to place, and lived by fruit, and such as he might get, and drank water two years : and other clothing had he but little, save his shirt and his breeches. And thus, as Sir Launcelot wandered here and there, he came into a fair meadow, where he found a pavilion, and there upon a tree hung a white shield, and two swords hung thereby, and two spears there leaned against a tree. And when Sir Launcelot saw the swords, anon he leapt to the one sword, and took it in his hand, and drew it out, and then he lashed at the shield, that all the meadow rang of the dints that he gave, with such a noise as ten knights had fought together. Then there came forth a dwarf, and leapt unto Sir Launcelot, and would have had the sword out of his hand ; and then Sir Launcelot took him by both the shoulders, and threw him to the ground upon his neck, that he had almost broken his neck ; and therewithal the dwarf cried for help. Then came forth a little knight, and well apparelled in scarlet, furred with minever ; and anon as he saw Sir Launcelot, he deemed that he should be out of his wits, and then he said with fair speech, " Good friend, lay down that sword, for as me seemeth thou hast more need to sleep, and of warm clothes, than to wield that sword." " As for that," said Sir Launcelot, " come thou not nigh me ; for and thou do, wit thou well I will slay thee." And when the knight of the pavilion saw that, he started backward within the pavilion ; and then the dwarf armed him lightly, and so the knight thought by force and might to take the sword from Sir Launcelot : and so he came stepping out ; and when Sir Launcelot saw him come all armed with his sword in his hand, Sir Launcelot flew upon him with such a might, and hit him upon the helm such a buffet, that the stroke troubled his brains. And therewith the sword brake in three, and the knight fell to the ground as though he had been dead, and the blood burst out at his mouth, nose, and ears. And then Sir Launcelot ran into the pavilion, and there he crept into the warm bed ; and in that bed there was a lady, and lightly she gat her smock, and ran out of the pavilion. And when she saw her lord lie on the ground, like to be dead, then she cried and wept as though she had been mad. Then with her noise the knight awaked out of his swoon, and looked up quickly with his eyes, and then he asked her where the madman was that had given him such a buffet ; "for such a buffet had I never of man's hand." "Sir," said the dwarf, "it is no worship to hurt him ; for he is a man out of his wits, and doubt ye not he hath been a man of great worship, and for some heartily sorrow that he hath taken he is fallen mad." "And me seemeth," said the dwarf, "that he resembleth much unto Sir Launcelot du Lake, for him I saw at the great tournament beside Lonazep." "Jesu defend," said that knight ; "that ever the noble knight Sir Launcelot should be in such a plight : but whatsoever he be," said that knight, "harm will I none do him." And this knight's name is Sir Bliaunt ; then he said unto the dwarf, "Go thou in all haste, on horseback, unto my brother Sir Selivant, that is at the castle Blanche, and tell him of mine adventure, and bid him bring with him a horse litter, and then will we bear this knight unto my castle."

XVI.

So the dwarf rode fast and came again, and brought Sir Selivant with him, and six men with a horse-litter. And so they took up the feather-bed with Sir Launcelot, and carried all with them to the castle Blanche, and he never awakened until he was within the castle ; and then they bound his hands and his feet, and gave him good meals and good drink, and brought him again to his strength and his fairness ; but in his wits they could not bring him again, nor to know himself. Thus Sir Launcelot was there more than a year and a-half, honestly arrayed, and fair faring withal. Then upon a day, this lord of that castle, Sir Bliaunt, took his arms on horseback, with a spear to seek adventures ; and as he rode in a forest there met him two knights adventurous ; the one was Sir Breuse Sans Pitie, and his brother, Sir Bertlot ; and these two ran both at once upon Sir Bliaunt, and break both their spears upon his body, and then they drew out their swords, and made a great battle, and fought long together : but at the last Sir Bliaunt was sore wounded, and felt himself faint, and then he fled on horseback towards his castle.   And as they came hurtling under the castle, where Sir Launcelot lay in a window, and saw two knights laid upon Sir Bliaunt with their swords ; and when Sir Launcelot saw that, yet as mad as he was, he was sorry for his lord Sir Bliaunt. And then Sir Launcelot break his chains from his legs, and from his arms, and in his breaking he hurt both his hands : and so Sir Launcelot ran out at a postern, and there he met with the two knights that chased Sir Bliaunt, and there he pulled down Bertlot with his bare hands from his horse, and therewithal he writhed his sword out of his hands ; and as he leapt up to Sir Breuse, and gave him such a buffet upon the head, that he tumbled backward over the horse's croup.   And when Sir Bertlot saw his brother have such a fall, he gat a spear in his hand, and would have run Sir Launcelot through : that saw Sir Bliaunt, and struck off the hand of Sir Bertlot ; and then Sir Breuse and Sir Bertlot gat their horses, and fled away.   When Sir Selivant came, and saw what Sir Launcelot had done for his brother, then he thanked God, and so did his brother, that ever they did him any good ; but when Sir Bliaunt saw that Sir Launcelot was hurt, with the breaking of his chains, then he was sorry that he had bound him.   " Bind him no more," said Sir Selivant, " for he is happy and gracious."   Then they made great joy of Sir Launcelot, and they bound him no more.   And so he abode there half-a-year and more ; and in a morning early Sir Launcelot was aware where came a great boar, with many hounds nigh him ; but the boar was so big, that there might no hounds tear him, and the hunters came, after blowing their horns both on horseback and on foot ; and, at the last, Sir Launcelot was aware where one of them alighted and tied his horse to a tree, and leaned his spear against the tree.

XVII.

So came Sir Launcelot and found the horse bound to a tree, and a spear leaning against a tree, and a sword tied unto the saddle bow : and then Sir Launcelot leapt into the saddle, and gat that spear in his hand, and then he rode after the boar ; and then Sir Launcelot was aware where the boar set his back unto a tree fast by a hermitage. Then Sir Launcelot ran at the boar with his spear: and therewith the boar turned him suddenly, and tore out the lungs and the heart of Sir Launcelot's horse: so Sir Launcelot fell to the earth, and or ever Sir Launcelot might get from his horse, the boar tore him on the brawn of the thigh up to the huckle bone: and then Sir Launcelot was wrath, and up he gat him on his feet, and drew out his sword, and he smote off the boar's head at one stroke. And therewith came out the hermit; and, when he saw him have such a wound, then the hermit came unto Sir Launcelot, and bemoaned him, and would have had him unto his hermitage: but when Sir Launcelot heard him speak, he was so wrath with his wound, that he ran upon the hermit to have slain him. And then the hermit ran away: and when Sir Launcelot might not overtake him, he threw his sword after him; for Sir Launcelot might not go farther for bleeding. Then the hermit turned again, and asked Sir Launcelot how he was hurt? "Fellow," said Sir Launcelot, "this boar hath bitten me right sore." "Then come with me," said the hermit, "and I shall heal you." "Go thy way," said Sir Launcelot, "and deal not with me." And then the hermit ran his way fast, and in his way he met with a good knight with many men. "Sir," said the hermit, "here is fast by my place the goodliest man that ever I saw, and he is sore wounded with a boar, and yet he hath slain the boar; but well I wot," said the hermit, "and he be not holpen, that goodly man shall die of that wound, and that were full great pity." Then that knight, at the desire of the hermit, gat a cart, and in that cart that knight put the boar and Sir Launcelot; for Sir Launcelot was so feeble that they might right easily deal with him. And so Sir Launcelot was brought to the hermitage, and the hermit healed him of his wounds. But the hermit might not find Sir Launcelot sustenance, and so he impaired and waxed feeble, both of his body and of his wit for default of sustenance, and waxed more weaker than he was aforehand. And then upon a day Sir Launcelot ran his way into the forest, and by adventure came into the city of Corbin, where Dame Elaine was that had borne Galahad, Sir Launcelot's son. And so when he was entered into the town, he ran through the town into the castle, and then all the young men of the city ran after Sir Launcelot, and there they threw turfs at him, and gave him many sad strokes: and, as Sir Launcelot might reach any of them, he threw them, so that they would never more come into his hands; for of some he break their legs, and some their arms, and so fled into the castle. And then came out knights and squires for to rescue Sir Launcelot, and when they beheld him, and looked upon his person, they thought they saw never so goodly a man ; and when they saw so many wounds upon him, they all deemed that he had been a man of worship. And then they ordained clothes unto his body, and straw underneath him, and a little house, and then every day they would throw him meat, and set him drink ; but there were few or none that would bring meat to his hands.

XVIII.

So it befell, that King Pelleas had a nephew, whose name was Castor, and he desiréd of the King, his uncle, to be made a knight ; and so, at the request of this Castor, the King made him knight at the feast of Candlemas. And when Castor was made knight, that same day he gave many gowns ; and so Sir Castor sent for the fool, that was Sir Launcelot ; and when he was come afore Sir Castor, he gave Sir Launcelot a robe of scarlet, and all that belonged unto him : and when Sir Launcelot was arrayed like a knight, he was the seemliest man in all the court, and none so well made. So, when he saw his time, he went into the garden, and there Sir Launcelot laid him down by a well, and slept. And so, at afternoon, Dame Elaine and her maidens came into the garden for to play them ; and, as they ran up and down, one of Dame Elaine's maidens espied where lay a goodly man by the well sleeping, and anon showed him unto Dame Elaine. "Peace," said Dame Elaine, "say no word :" and then she brought Dame Elaine where as he lay. And when Dame Elaine beheld, anon she fell in remembrance of him, and knew him verily for Sir Launcelot, and therewith she fell on weeping so heartily, that she sunk down to the ground ; and when she had wept a great while, then she arose and called her maidens, and said she was sick. And so she went out of the garden, and went straight unto her father, and there she took him apart by himself, and then she said, "Oh, father, now have I need of your help : and but if that ye help me, farewell my good days for ever." "What is that, daughter?" said King Pelleas. "Sir," said she, "thus it is : in your garden I went to sport me, and there, by the well, I found Sir Launcelot du Lake sleeping." "I may not believe it," said King Pelleas. "Sir," said she, "truly he is there : and me seemeth that he should be defraught of his wit." "Then hold you still," said King Pelleas, "and let me deal." Then the King called unto him such as he most trusted a four persons, and Dame Elaine, his daughter ;

and when they came to the well, and beheld Sir Launcelot, anon Dame Brisen knew him. "Sir," said Dame Brisen, "we must be wise and ware how we deal with him, for this knight is out of his mind ; and if that we awake him rudely, what he will do we all know not, but ye shall abide, and I shall throw such an enchantment upon him, that he shall not awake within the space of an hour." And so she did. Then, within a little while after, King Pelleas commanded that all the people should avoid, that none should be in that way there as the King should come : and so, when all this was done, these four men, and these ladies, laid hand upon Sir Launcelot, and so they bear him into a tower, and so into the chamber, where as was the holy vessel of Sancgreal ; and, by force, Sir Launcelot was laid by that holy vessel. And then there came a holy man and uncovered the vessel : and so, by miracle, and by virtue of that holy vessel, Sir Launcelot was all healed and recovered : and, when he was awaked, he groaned and sighed sore, and complained greatly that he was passing sore.

XIX.

AND when Sir Launcelot saw King Pelleas and Dame Elaine, he waxed ashamed, and thus he said : "O, good Lord Jesu ! how came I here : for God's sake, my lord, let me wit how I came here." "Sir," said Dame Elaine, "into this country ye came like a madman, all out of your wit, and here ye have been kept as a fool, and no creature here knew what ye were, till that, by fortune, a maid of mine brought me unto you, where, as ye lay sleeping by a well side ; and anon, as I verily beheld you, I knew you, and then I told my father; and so ye were brought before this holy vessel, and, by the virtue of it, thus were ye healed." "O, Jesu ! mercy," said Sir Launcelot, " if this be sooth, how many be there that know of my weakness ? " "So God help me," said Dame Elaine, "no more but my father and I, and Dame Brisen." "Now, for Christ's love," said Sir Launcelot, "keep it secret, and let no man know it in the world. For I am sore ashamed that I have been thus miscarried : for I am banished out of the country of Logris for ever ; that is to say, out of the country of England." And so Sir Launcelot lay more than a fortnight or ever he might stir for soreness, and then, upon a day, he said unto Dame Elaine these words : "Fair lady, for your sake I have had much travel, care, and anguish ; I need not to rehearse it, ye know well how, notwithstanding I know well that I have done foul to you, when I drew my sword upon you, for to have slain you on the morrow, when I had been with you : and all was the cause that ye and Dame Brisen made me to come to you, maugre my head ; and, as ye say, that night Galahad, your son, was gotten." "That is truth," said Dame Elaine. "Now will ye, for my love," said Sir Launcelot, "go unto your father, and get me a place of him, wherein I may dwell ; for in the court of King Arthur may I never come." "Sir," said Dame Elaine, "I will live and die with you, and only for your sake, if my life might not avail you, and that my death might avail you : wit ye well, I would die for your sake. And I will go to my father, and I am sure there is nothing that I can desire of him but I shall have it : and where ye be, my lord, Sir Launcelot, doubt ye not but I will be with you, with all the service that I may do." So forthwith she went unto her father, and said, "Sir, my lord, Sir Launcelot, desireth to be here by you, in some castle of yours." "Well, daughter," said the King, "sith it is his desire to abide in these Marches, he shall be in the castle of Bliaunt, and there shall ye be with him, and twenty of the fairest ladies that be in this country, and they shall be of the greatest blood ; and also ye shall have ten knights with you ; for, daughter, I will that ye wit, we all be honoured by the blood of the noble knight Sir Launcelot."

XX.

THEN went Dame Elaine unto Sir Launcelot, and told him how her father had devised for him and her. Then came the knight Sir Castor (that was nephew unto King Pelleas) unto Sir Launcelot, and asked him what was his name. "Sir," said Sir Launcelot, "my name is le Chevalier mal Fet : this is as much to say, the knight that hath trespassed." "Sir," said Sir Castor ; "it may well be so, but me seemeth that your name should be Sir Launcelot du Lake ; for, or now I have seen you." "Sir," said Launcelot, "ye are not as a gentle knight ; I put, case my name were Sir Launcelot, and that it list me not to discover my name, what should it grieve you to keep my counsel, and ye not hurt thereby. But wit ye well, and ever it lie in my power, I shall grieve you, and that I promise you truly." Then Sir Castor kneeled down, and asked Sir Launcelot mercy ; "for I shall never utter what ye be, as long as ye be in these parts." Then Sir Launcelot pardoned him. And then after this King Pelleas, with ten knights, and Dame Elaine, and twenty ladies, rode unto the castle of Bliaunt, that stood in an island, enclosed with iron, with a fair water, deep and large. And, when they were there, Sir Launcelot let call it the Joyous Isle ; and there he was called none otherwise but le Chevalier mal Fet, the knight that hath trespassed. Then Sir Launcelot let make him a shield all of sable, and a queen crowned in the midst, all of silver, and a knight clean armed, kneeling before her ; and every day once, for any mirths that all the ladies might make him, he would look towards the realm of Logris, where as King Arthur and Queen Guenever were, and then would he fall on a-weeping, as though his heart should all to break. So it befell that time, that Sir Launcelot heard of a jousting fast by his castle, within six miles : then he called unto him a dwarf, and bid him go unto that jousting, and, or ever the knights depart, look that thou make there a cry, in hearing of all the knights that be there, " that there is a good knight in Joyous Isle, that is, the castle Bliaunt, and say that his name is le Chevalier mal Fet, that will joust against all knights that will come, and who that putteth that knight to the worst shall have a fair maiden and a ger-falcon."

XXI.

So when this cry was made, unto Joyous Isle drew many knights, to the number of five hundred : and, wit ye well, that there was never seen in King Arthur's days one knight that did such deeds of arms as Sir Launcelot did three days together. For he had the better hand of five hundred knights, and yet there was none slain of them ; and after that Sir Launcelot made them all a great feast. And, in the meanwhile, came Sir Percivale de Galis and Sir Hector de Maris under the castle that was called the Joyous Isle, and so, as they beheld that fair castle, they would have gone into it, but they might not for the broad water, and bridge could they none find. Then they saw, on that other side, a lady, with a sparrow-hawk upon her hand, and Sir Percivale called unto her, and asked her who was within that castle. " Fair knight," said the lady, " here within this castle is the fairest lady in this land, and her name is Dame Elaine ; also we have in this castle the fairest knight and the mightiest man that is (I dare well say) now living, and he calleth himself le Chevalier mal Fet." " How came he into this Marches ? " said Sir Percivale. " Truly," said the damsel, " he came into this country like a madman, with dogs and boys chasing him throughout the city of Corbin ; and, by the holy vessel of the Sancgreal, he was brought into his wit again, but he will not do battle with no knight but by nine of the clock at morning or by noon. And. if ye list to enter into the castle," said the damsel, "ye must ride unto the further side of the castle, and there shall ye find a vessel that shall bear you and your horses." Then they departed, and came unto the vessel ; and then Sir Percivale alighted, and said unto Sir Ector de Maris, " Ye shall abide me here, until I know what manner of knight he is, for it were a great shame unto us, inasmuch as he is but one knight, and we should both do battle with him." "Do as ye list," said Sir Ector de Maris, "here shall I abide you, until that I hear of you again." Then Sir Percivale passed the water, and when he came to the castle gate, he said to the porter, " Go thou unto the good knight within the castle, and tell him that there is come an errant-knight to joust with him." "Sir," said the porter, "ride ye within the castle, and there shall ye find a common place for jousting, that lords and ladies may behold you." So anon, as Sir Launcelot had warning, he was soon ready. And there Sir Percivale and Sir Launcelot encountered with such a might, and their spears were so rude, that both the horses and the knights fell to the ground ; and then they avoided their horses and drew out their swords, and hewed away cantels of their shields, and hurtled together with their shields like two wild boars, and either wounded other passing sore ; and at the last Sir Percivale spake first, when they had fought more than two hours : " Fair knight," said Sir Percivale, " I require thee tell me thy name ? for I met never with such a knight as ye are." " Sir," said Sir Launcelot, "my name is le Chevalier mal Fet. Now tell me your name," said Sir Launcelot, " I require you as ye are a gentle knight." " Truly," said Sir Percivale, "my name is Sir Percivale de Galis, which is brother unto the good knight Sir Lamoracke de Galis, and King Pellinore was our father, and Sir Aglavale is my brother." " Alas !" said Sir Launcelot, " what have I done, to fight with you, that are a knight of the Round Table, that sometime was your fellow in King Arthur's court."

XXII.

AND therewithal Sir Launcelot kneeled down upon his knees, and threw away his shield and his sword from him. When Sir Percivale saw him do so, he marvelled what he meant, and thus he said unto him : " Sir knight, whatsoever thou be, I require thee, upon the high order of knighthood, tell me your right name." Then Sir Launcelot answered and said, " So God me help, my name is Sir Launcelot du Lake, King Ban's son, of

Benwick." "Alas!" said Sir Percivale, "what thing have I done: I was sent by Queen Guenever for to seek you, and so I have sought you near this two years; and yonder is Sir Ector de Maris, your brother, abideth me on the other side of the water. Now, sir, I pray you, for God's sake," said Sir Percivale, "forgive me mine offence that I have done." "It is soon forgiven," said Sir Launcelot. Then Sir Percivale sent for Sir Ector de Maris. And when Sir Launcelot had a sight of him, he ran unto him, and took him in his arms; and then Sir Ector kneeled down, and either wept upon other, that all had great pity to behold them. Then came Dame Elaine, and there she made them the greatest cheer that she could devise; and there she told Sir Ector and Sir Percivale how and in what manner Sir Launcelot came into that country, and how he was there healed. And there it was known how long Sir Launcelot was with Sir Bliaunt and with Sir Selivant, and how he first met with them, and how he departed from them because of a boar; and how the hermit healed Sir Launcelot of his great wounds, and how that he came to Corbin.

XXIII.

Now leave we of Sir Launcelot in Joyous Isle, with the fair lady, Dame Elaine, and Sir Percivale and Sir Ector playing with them; and return we unto Sir Bors de Ganis, and Sir Lionel, which had sought Sir Launcelot nigh by the space of two years, and never could they hear of him. And so, as they rode thus by adventure, they came unto the house of King Brandegore, and there Sir Bors was well known; for he had gotten a child of the King's daughter fifteen years before, and his name was Helaine le Blancke. And, when Sir Bors saw that child, it liketh him passing well: and so those two knights had good cheer of King Brandegore. And, on the morrow after, Sir Bors came before King Brandegore and said: "Here is my son, Helaine le Blancke, that, as it is said, he is my son; and, sith it is so, I will that ye wit I will have him with me unto King Arthur's court." "Sir," said the King, "ye may well take him with you; but he is over tender of age." "As for that," said Sir Bors, "I will have him with me, and bring him unto the house of most worship in the world." So, when Sir Bors should depart, there was made great sorrow for the departing of Helaine le Blancke, and great weeping was there made. But Sir Bors and Sir Lionel departed: and, within short space after their departing, they came to Camelot, whereas at that time was King Arthur. And when King

Arthur understood that Helaine le Blancke was Sir Bors' son, and nephew unto King Brandegore, then King Arthur let make him knight of the Round Table : and so he proved a good knight and an adventurous.

Now will we turn unto our matter of Sir Launcelot. It befell upon a day Sir Ector and Sir Percivale came unto Sir Launcelot, and asked him what he would do, and whether he would go with them unto King Arthur or not? "Nay," said Sir Launcelot, "that may not be by any means ; for I was so evil entreated at that court, that I cast me never to come there more." "Sir," said Sir Ector, "I am your own brother, and ye are the man in the world that I love most ; and, if I understood that it were your disworship, ye may right well understand that I would never counsel you thereto : but King Arthur and all his knights, and in especial Queen Guenever, made such dole and sorrow that it was marvellous to hear and see. And ye must remember the great worship and renown that ye be of, how that ye have been more spoken of than any other knight that is now living : for there is none that beareth the name now but ye and Sir Tristram. Therefore, brother," said Sir Ector, "make you ready to ride unto the court with us ; and I dare well say, there was never knight better welcome unto the court than ye. And I wot well, and can make it good," said Sir Ector, "it hath cost my lady, the Queen, twenty thousand pounds the seeking of you." "Well, brother," said Sir Launcelot, "I will do after your counsel, and ride with you." So then they took their horses, and made them ready, and took their leave of King Pelleas, and of Dame Elaine. And when Sir Launcelot should depart, Dame Elaine made great sorrow. "My lord, Sir Launcelot," said Dame Elaine, "at this same feast of Pentecost shall your son and mine, Galahad, be made knight ; for he is full fifteen winters old." "Do as ye list," said Sir Launcelot ; "God give him grace to prove a good knight." "As for that," said Dame Elaine, "I doubt not but he will prove the best man of his kin, except one." "Then shall he be a man good enough," said Sir Launcelot.

XXIV.

THEN they departed, and, within five days' journey, they came to Camelot, which is called, in English, Winchester ; and, when Sir Launcelot was come among them, the King and all the knights made great joy of him. And there Sir Percivale de Galis, and Sir Ector de Maris, began to tell of all the adventures, how Sir Launcelot had been out of his mind all the time of his absence; how he called himself le Chevalier mal Fet; as much as to say, the knight had trespassed. And in three days Sir Launcelot smote down five hundred knights. And ever, as Sir Ector and Sir Percivale told these tales of Sir Launcelot, Queen Guenever wept as she would have died: then, afterwards, the queen made great joy. "O Jesu!" said King Arthur, "I marvel for what cause ye, Sir Launcelot, went out of your mind: I, and many others, deemed that it was for the love of fair Elaine, the daughter of King Pelleas, by whom it is noised that ye have gotten a child, and his name is Galahad; and men say he shall do marvels." "My lord," said Sir Launcelot, "if I did any folly, I have found that I sought." And so the King held him still, and spake no more; but all Sir Launcelot's kin knew for whom he went out of his mind. And then there were great feasts made, and great joy; and many great lords and ladies, when they heard that Sir Launcelot was come to the court again, made great joy.

◆

THE BOOK OF SIR GALAHAD.

I.

T the vigil of Pentecost, when all the fellowship of the Round Table were come unto Camelot, and there they all heard their service, and then all the tables were covered, ready to set thereon the meat, right so entered into the hall a full fair gentlewoman on horseback, that had ridden full fast, for her horse was all besweat. Then she there alighted, and came before King Arthur and saluted him. And then the King said, "Damsel, God bless you." "Sir," said she, "for God's sake show me where Sir Launcelot is." "Yonder may ye see him," said King Arthur. Then she went unto Sir Launcelot, and said, "Sir Launcelot, I salute you on King Pelleas' behalf, and I require you to come with me hereby into a forest." Then Sir Launcelot asked her with whom she dwelled. "I dwell," said she "with King Pelleas." "What is your will with me?" said Sir Launcelot. "Ye shall know and understand," said she, "when ye come thither." "Well," said he, "I shall gladly go with you." So Sir Launcelot bade his squire to saddle his horse, and bring his armour: and in all the haste he did his commandment. Then came the Queen unto Sir Launcelot, and said, "Will ye leave us at this high feast?" "Madam," said the gentlewoman, "wit

ye well he shall be with you to-morrow by dinner-time." "If I wist," said the Queen, "that he should not be with us here to-morrow, he should not go with you by my good will." Right so departed Sir Launcelot with the gentlewoman, and rode till they came into a forest, and into a great valley, where he saw an abbey of nuns, and there was a squire ready to open the gates : and so they entered in and descended from their horses, and there came a fair fellowship about Sir Launcelot and welcomed him, and were passing glad of his coming ; and then they led him into the abbess's chamber, and unarmed him. Right so he saw, lying upon a bed, two of his cousins, Sir Bors and Sir Lionel, and then he awaked them ; and when they saw him they made great joy. "Sir," said Sir Bors unto Sir Launcelot, "what adventure hath brought you hither, for we weened to-morrow to have found you at Camelot." "So God me help," said Sir Launcelot, "a gentlewoman hath brought me hither, but I know not the cause." In the meanwhile, as they stood thus talking together, there came in twelve nuns, which brought with them Galahad, the which was passing fair and well made, that scarcely men in the world might not find his match. And all those ladies wept. "Sir," said the ladies, "we bring here this child, the which ye have nourished ; and we pray you for to make him a knight, for of a more worthier man's hand may he not receive the order of knighthood." Sir Launcelot beheld that young squire, and saw he was seemly and demure as a dove, with all manner of good features, that he weened of his age never to have seen so fair a man of form. Then said Sir Launcelot, "Cometh this desire of himself?" He and all, they said, "Yea." "Then shall he," said Sir Launcelot, "receive the high order of knighthood as to-morrow at the reverence of the high feast." That night Sir Launcelot had passing good cheer, and on the morrow, at the hour of prime, at Galahad's desire, he made him a knight, and said, "God make him a good man, for beauty faileth him not as any that liveth."

II.

"Now, fair sir," said Sir Launcelot, "will ye come with me unto the court of my lord King Arthur?" "Nay," said he, "I will not go with you as at this time." Then he departed from them, and took his two cousins with him; and so they came unto Camelot, by the hour of nine on Whitsunday morning. By that time the King and the Queen were gone to the minister to hear their service : then the King and the Queen were passing glad of Sir Bors and Sir Lionel, and so was all the fellowship.

So when the King and all the knights were come from the service, the barons espied in the sieges of the Round Table all about written with letters of gold, "Here ought to sit he ;" and "He ought to sit here." And thus they went so long, until they came unto the Perilous Siege, where they found letters newly written of gold, and said : "Four hundred winters, and four and fifty accomplished, after the passion of our Lord Jesus Christ, ought this siege to be fulfilled." Then they all said, "This is a full marvellous thing, and an adventurous." "In the name of God !" said Sir Launcelot ; and then he accounted the term of the writing, from the birth of our Lord unto that day. "It seemeth me," said Sir Launcelot, "this Siege ought to be fulfilled this same day ; for this is the feast of Pentecost, after the hundred and four and fiftieth year ; and if it would please all parties, I would that none of these letters were seen this day, till he be come that ought to achieve this adventure." Then made they for to ordain a cloth of silk for to cover these letters in the Perilous Siege. Then the King had haste unto dinner. "Sir," said Sir Kaye, the steward, "if ye go now unto your meat, ye shall break the old custom of your court ; for ye have not used upon this day to sit at your meat, or that ye have seen some adventure." "Ye say truth," said King Arthur, "but I had so great joy of Sir Launcelot and of his cousins, which be come to the court whole and sound, that I bethought me not of mine old custom." So as they stood speaking, in came a squire, and said unto the King, "Sir, I bring unto you marvellous tidings." "What be they ?" said King Arthur. "Sir, there is here beneath, at the river, a great stone, which I saw float above the water, and therein saw I a sword sticking." "Then," said the King, "I will see that marvel." So all the knights went with him, and when they came unto the river, they found there a stone floating, as if it had been of red marble, and therein stuck a fair and a rich sword, and in the pommel thereof were precious stones wrought with subtle letters of gold. Then the barons read the letters, which said in this wise :—"Never shall man take me hence, but only he by whom I ought to hang, and he shall be the best knight of the world." When the King had seen these letters, he said unto Sir Launcelot, "Fair sir, this sword ought to be yours ; for I am sure that ye be the best knight of the world." Then Sir Launcelot answered soberly, "Certainly, sir, it is not my sword : also, sir, wit ye well I have no hardiness to set my hand to it, for it belongeth not to hang by my side : also, who assayeth for to take that sword, and faileth of it, he shall receive a wound by that sword, that he shall not be whole long after. And I will that ye wit that this same day will be the adventures of the Sancgreal (that is called the holy vessel) begin."

III.

"Now, my fair nephew," said the King unto Sir Gawaine, "assay ye once for my love." "Sir," said he, "save your grace, I shall do that." "Sir," said the King, "assay to take the sword at my command." "Sir," said Sir Gawaine, "your command I will obey." And therewithal he took the sword by the handle, but he might not stir it. "I thank you," said King Arthur unto Sir Gawaine. "My lord Sir Gawaine," said Sir Launcelot, "now wit ye well this sword shall touch you so sore, that ye shall will ye had never set your hand thereto, for the best castle of this realm." "Sir," said Sir Gawaine, "I might not withstand mine uncle's will and commandment." But when King Arthur heard this, he repented it much : and then he bade Sir Percivale that he should assay for his love, and he said gladly for to bear Sir Gawaine fellowship. And therewithal he set his hand upon the sword, and drew at it strongly ; but he might not once move it. Then were there no more that durst be so hardy to set their hands thereto. "Now may ye go unto your dinner," said Sir Kaye unto King Arthur, "for a marvellous adventure have ye seen." So the King and all his knights went unto the court, and every knight knew his own place, and set them therein : and the young men that were no knights served them. So then they were served, and all the sieges fulfilled, save only the Perilous Siege. And there befel a marvellous adventure, that all the doors and the windows of the palace shut by themselves ; but, for all that, the hall was not greatly darkened, and therewith they were all abashed both one and other. Then King Arthur spake first and said : "By God, fair fellows and lords, we have seen this day marvels.; but or night I suppose we shall see greater marvels." In the meanwhile came in a good old man and an ancient, clothed all in white ; and there was no knight that knew from whence he came. And with him he brought a young knight, both on foot, in red arms, without sword or shield, save a scabbard hanging by his side, and these words he said : "Peace be with you, fair lords." Then the old man said unto King Arthur, "Sir, I bring you here a young knight that is of king's lineage, and of the kindred of Joseph of Arimathy : wherefore the marvels of this court, and of strange realms, shall be fully accomplished."

IV.

THE King was right glad of his words, and said unto the good man, "Sir, ye be right heartily welcome, and the young knight with you." Then the old man made the young knight to unarm him, and he was in a coat of red sandal, and bear a mantle upon his shoulder, that was furred with fine ermines, and put that upon him : and the old man said unto the young knight, "Sir, follow after." And anon he brought him unto the Perilous Siege, where beside sat Sir Launcelot ; and the good old man lift up the cloth, and found there letters that said, "This is the siege of Sir Galahad, the good knight." "Sir," said the old man, "wit ye well this place is yours." And then he set him down surely in that siege, and then he said to the old man, "Sir, ye may now go your way, for ye have well done that ye were commanded to do : and recommend me unto my grandsire King Pelleas, and unto my Lord Pechere, and say unto them on my behalf, 'that I shall come and see them as soon as I may.'" So the good man departed, and there met him twenty noble squires, and so they took their horses and went their way. Then all the knights of the Round Table marvelled them greatly of Sir Galahad, that he durst sit there in that Perilous Siege, and was so tender of age ; and wist not from whence he came, but only by God, and said he, "This is by whom the Sancgreal shall be achieved, for there sat never none but that he were mischieved." Then Sir Launcelot beheld his son, and had great joy of him. Then Sir Bors told his fellows, "Upon pain of my life, this young knight shall come unto great worship." This noise was great in all the court, so that it came to the Queen : then she had great marvel what knight it might be, that durst adventure him to sit in the Perilous Siege. Many said unto the Queen, that he resembled much unto Sir Launcelot. "I may well suppose," said the Queen, "that Sir Launcelot begat him upon King Pelleas' daughter, which was by enchantment, and his name is Sir Galahad : I would fain see him," said the Queen, "for he must needs be a nobleman, for so is his father that him begat ; I report me unto all the knights of the Round Table." So when dinner was done, and that the King and all were risen, the King went unto the Perilous Siege, and lift up the cloth, and found there the name of Sir Galahad ; and then he showed it unto Sir Gawaine, and said, "Fair nephew, now we have among us Sir Galahad, the good knight, that shall worship us all ; and upon pain of my life, he shall achieve the Sancgreal,

as Sir Launcelot hath done us to understand." Then came
King Arthur unto Sir Galahad, and said, "Sir, ye be welcome,
for ye shall move many good knights unto the quest of the
Sancgreal, and ye shall achieve that never knight might bring
to an end." Then the King took him by the hand, and went
down from the palace, to show Sir Galahad the adventure
of the stone.

V.

THE Queen heard thereof, and came after with many ladies,
and showed the stone which hoved on the water. "Sir," said
the King to Sir Galahad, "here is a great marvel as ever I saw,
and right good knights have assayed and failed." "Sir," said
Sir Galahad, "that is no marvel, for this adventure is not theirs,
but mine ; and for the surety of this sword I brought none with
me, for here by my side hangeth the scabbard." And anon he
laid his hand on the sword, and lightly drew it out of the stone,
and then he put it into the scabbard, and said unto the King :
"Now it goeth better than it did aforehand." "Sir," said the
King, "then a shield God shall send unto you." "Now have
I," said Sir Galahad, "that sword that sometime was belonging
unto the good knight Sir Balin le Savage, and he was a passing
good man of his hands ; and with that sword he slew his
brother Balan, and that was great pity, for he was a good
knight, and either slew other through a notorious stroke that
Sir Balan gave unto my grandfather, King Pelleas, the which is
not yet whole, nor shall not be till I heal him." Therewith the
King and all other espied where came riding down the river a
lady on a white palfrey, toward them, and she saluted the King
and the Queen, and asked if Sir Launcelot was there : and then
Sir Launcelot answered himself—"I am here, fair lady." Then
she said, all weeping, "Your great doings be changed since to-
day in the morning." "Damsel, why say ye so ?" said Sir
Launcelot. "I say you sooth," said the damsel, "for ye were
this day the best knight in the world ; but who should say so now
should be openly proved a liar, for there is one better than ye,
and well is it proved by the adventure of the sword, whereto ye
durst not set your hand, and that is the change and leaving of
your name ; wherefore I make unto you a remembrance, that
ye shall not ween from henceforth that ye be the best knight of
the world." "As touching that," said Sir Launcelot, "I know
well I was never the best." "Yes," said the damsel, "that
were ye, and yet are of any sinful man of the world : and, sir,
King Nacien, the hermit, sendeth thee word that to thee shall

befall the greatest worship that ever befell king in Britain, and shall tell you wherefore, for this day the Sancgreal appeared in this thy house, and fed thee and all thy fellowship of the Round Table." And so the damsel took her leave, and departed the same way that she came.

VI.

"Now," said the King, "I am sure at this quest of the Sancgreal, shall all ye of the Round Table depart, and never shall I see you again whole together; therefore I will see you all whole together in the meadow of Camelot, for to joust and to tourney, that after your death men may speak of it, that such good knights were wholly together such a day." And unto that counsel, and at the King's request, they accorded all, and took on their harness that longed to jousting. But all the meaning of the King was to see Sir Galahad proved, for the King deemed he should not lightly come again unto the court after his departing: so were they all assembled in the meadow, both more and less. Then Sir Galahad, by the prayer of the King and the Queen, did upon him a noble jesserance, and also he did on his helm, but shield would he take none, for no prayer of the King. And then Sir Gawaine and other knights prayed him for to take a spear, and so he did: and the Queen was in a tower with all her ladies to behold that tournament. There Sir Galahad dressed him in the middest of the meadow, and there he began to break spears marvellously, that all men had wonder of him, for he there surmounted and exceeded all other knights, for within a little while he had thrown down many good knights of the Round Table, save twain, that was Sir Launcelot and Sir Percivale.

VII.

Then the King, at the Queen's request, made him to alight and to unlace his helm, that Queen Guenever might see him in the visage: and when she beheld him she said, "Soothly I dare say that Sir Launcelot begat him, for never two men resembled more in likeness, therefore it is no marvel though he be of great prowess." So a lady that stood by the Queen said, "Madam, for God's sake ought he of right to be so good a knight." "Yea forthwith," said the Queen, "for he is of all parties come of the best knights of the world, and of the highest lineage, for Sir Launcelot is come but of the eighth degree from our Lord, Jesu Christ, and Sir Galahad is of the ninth degree of our Lord, Jesu

Christ, therefore I dare well say that they be the greatest gentlemen of all the world." And then the King and all the estate
went home unto Camelot's minster: and so, after that they
went to supper, and every knight sat in their place as they were
before-hand, then anon they heard cracking and crying of
thunder, that they thought the place should all to rive. In the
midst of the blast entered a sunbeam more clear by seven times
than ever they saw day, and all they were alighted of the grace
of the Holy Ghost. Then began every knight to behold other,
and either saw other by their seeming fairer than ever they saw
other, not for then there was no knight that might speak any
word a great while; and so they looked every man on other as
they had been dumb. Then there entered into the hall the
Holy Grail covered with white samite, but there was none that
might see it, nor who bare it, and there was all the hall fulfilled
with great odours, and every knight had such meat and drink as
he best loved in this world, and when the Holy Grail had been
borne through the hall, then the holy vessel departed suddenly,
that they wist not where it became. Then had they breath to
speak, and then the King yielded thanks unto God of his grace
that he had sent them. "Certainly," said King Arthur, "we
ought greatly to thank our Lord, Jesus Christ, for that he hath
showed us this day at the reverence of this high feast of Pentecost." "Now," said Sir Gawaine, "we have been served this
day of what meats and drinks we thought on, but one thing be-
guiled us, we might not see the Holy Grail, it was so preciously
covered, wherefore I will make here a vow, that to-morrow,
without any longer abiding, I shall labour in quest of the
Sancgreal, that I shall hold me out a twelvemonth and a day,
or more if need be, and never shall I return again unto the court
till I have seen it more openly than it hath been seen here.
And if I may not speed I shall return again, as he that may not
be against the will of our Lord, Jesus Christ." When they of
the Round Table heard Sir Gawaine say so, they arose the most
part of them and avowed the same. And anon as King Arthur
heard this, he was greatly displeased, for he wist well that they
might not gainsay their vows. "Alas," said King Arthur unto
Sir Gawaine, "ye have nigh slain me with the vow and promise
that ye have made, for through you ye have bereft me of the
fairest fellowship, and the truest of knighthood, that ever were
seen together in any realm of the world, for when they shall
depart from hence I am sure that all shall never meet more in
this world, for there shall many die in the quest, and so it forethinketh me a little, for I have loved them as well as my life;

wherefore it shall grieve me right sore the separation of this fellowship, for I have had an old custom to have them in my fellowship."

VIII.

AND therewith the tears fell into his eyes, and he said, " Sir Gawaine, Sir Gawaine, ye have set me in great sorrow, for I have great doubt that my true fellowship shall never meet more here again."   "Ah," said Sir Launcelot, " comfort yourself, for it shall be unto us as a great honour, and much more than if we died in any other places, for of death we be sure."   "Ah, Sir Launcelot," said the king, " the great love that I have had unto you all the days of my life, maketh me to say such doleful words ; for never Christian king had never so many worthy men at his table as I have had this day at the Round Table, and that is to me great sorrow."   When the Queen, ladies, and gentlewomen wist these tidings, they had such sorrow and heaviness, that no tongue might tell it, for those knights had holden them in honour and charity ; but among all other Queen Guenever made great sorrow.   " I marvel," said she, " my lord will suffer them to depart from him."   Thus was all the court troubled, because those knights should depart ; and many of those ladies that loved knights would have gone with their lovers : and so had they done, had not an old knight come among them in religious clothing, and then he spake all on high and said, " Fair lords, that have sworn in the Quest of the Sancgreal, thus sendeth your nation the hermit word, that none in this quest lead lady nor gentlewoman with him, for it is not to do in so high a service as they labour in ; for I warn you plain, he that is not clean out of sin, he shall not see the mysteries of our Lord Jesu Christ."   For this cause they left their ladies and gentlewomen.   After this the Queen came unto Sir Galahad, and asked him of whence he was, and of what country.   He told her of whence he was, and son unto Sir Launcelot she said he was ; as to that he said neither yea nor nay.   " So God me help," said the Queen, " of your father ye need not to shame you, for he is the goodliest knight, and of the best men come, and of the race of all parts of kings, and of so therefore ye ought of right to be of your deeds a passing good man, and certainly," she said, " ye resemble him much."   Then was Sir Galahad a little ashamed, and said unto the Queen, " Madam, inasmuch as ye know it of a certainty, wherefore do ye ask it of me ? for he that is my father shall be known openly, and all betimes." And then they went to rest them ; and, in the honour of the highness of Sir Galahad, he was led into King Arthur's chamber, and there he rested him in his own bed. And, as soon as it was daylight, the king arose ; for he had taken no rest of all that night for sorrow. Then went he unto Sir Gawaine, and unto Sir Launcelot, that were risen for to hear mass. And then King Arthur said again, "Ah ! Sir Gawaine, Sir Gawaine ! ye have betrayed me ; for never shall my court be amended by you, but ye will never be sorry for me as I am for you." And therewith the tears began to run down by his visage, and therewith the King said, "Ah ! knight, Sir Launcelot ! I require thee that thou wilt counsel me, for I would this quest were undone, and it might be." "Sir," said Sir Launcelot, "ye saw yesterday so many worthy knights that then were sworn, that they may not leave it in no manner of wise." "That wot I well," said the King, "but it shall so heavy me their departing, that I wot well that there shall no manner of joy remedy me." And then the King and the Queen went to the minster: so anon Sir Launcelot and Sir Gawaine commanded their men to bring their arms ; and when they were all armed, save their shields and their helms, then they came to their fellowship, which all were ready in the same wise for to go to the minster to hear their service. Then, after the service was done, the king would wit how many had taken the quest of the Sancgreal, and to account them he prayed them all. Then found they by tale an hundred and fifty, and all were knights of the Round Table : and then they put on their helms and departed, and recommended them all wholly unto the Queen, and there was weeping and great sorrow. Then the Queen departed into her chamber, so that no man should perceive her great sorrows. When Sir Launcelot missed the Queen he went into her chamber, and when she saw him, she cried aloud, "O ! Sir Launcelot ! ye have betrayed me and put me to death, for to leave thus my lord." "Ah ! madam," said Sir Launcelot, " I pray you be not displeased, for I shall come again as soon as I may with my worship." "Alas !" said she, "that ever I saw you ; but He that suffered death upon the cross for all mankind be to you good conduct and safety, and all the whole fellow-ship." Right so departed Sir Launcelot, and found his fellowship that abode his coming : and so they mounted upon their horses, and rode through the streets of Camelot, and there was weeping of the rich and poor, and the King returned away, and might not speak for weeping. So within a while they came to a city and a castle that hight Vagon ; there they entered into the castle. And the lord of that castle was an old man, that hight Vagon, and he was a good man of his living, and set open the gates, and made them all the good cheer that he might. And so, on the morrow, they were all accorded that they should depart every each from other. And then they departed on the morrow with weeping and mourning cheer, and every knight took the way that him best liked.

IX.

Now rideth Sir Galahad yet without shield, and so he rode four days without any adventure ; and, at the fourth day, after even-song, he came to a white abbey, and there he was received with great reverence, and led to a chamber, and there he was unarmed ; and then was he ware of two knights of the Round Table, one was King Bagdemagus, and the other was Sir Uwaine ; and when they saw him they went unto him, and made of him great solace, and so they went to supper. "Sir," said Sir Galahad, "what adventure brought you hither?" "Sir," said they, "it is told us that within this place is a shield that no man may bear about his neck, but if that he be mischieved or dead within three days, or else maimed for ever." "Ah ! sir," said King Bagdemagus, "I shall bear it to-morrow for to essay this strange adventure." "In the name of God," said Sir Galahad. "Sir," said King Bagdemagus, "and I may not achieve the adventure of this shield, ye shall take it upon you, for I am sure ye shall not fail." "Sir," said Sir Galahad, "I agree right well thereto, for I have no shield." So on the morrow they arose and heard mass ; then King Bagdemagus asked where the adventurous shield was. Anon a monk led him behind an altar, where the shield hung as white as any snow, but in the midst was a red cross. "Sir," said the monk, "this shield ought not to hang about any knight's neck, but he be the worthiest knight's of the world, and therefore I counsel you knights to be well advised." "Well," said King Bagdemagus, "I wot well that I am not the best knight of the world, but yet shall I essay to bear it." And so he bare it out of the monastery, and then he said unto Sir Galahad, "If it will please you, I pray you abide here still, till ye know how I shall speed." "I shall abide you here," said Sir Galahad. Then King Bagdemagus took with him a squire, the which should bring tidings unto Sir Galahad how he sped. Then when they had ridden a two mile, and came in a fair valley before a hermitage, then they saw a goodly knight come from that party in white armour, horse and all, and he came as fast as his horse might run, with his spear in the rest, and King Bagdemagus dressed his spear against him, and brake it upon the white knight; but the other struck him so hard, that he brake the mails, and thrust him through the right shoulder, for the shield covered him not as at that time; and so he bear him from his horse, and therewith he alighted, and took the white shield from him, saying, ."Knight, thou hast done thyself great folly, for this shield ought not to be borne but by him that shall have no peer that liveth." And then he came to King Bagdemagus' squire and said, "Bear this shield unto the good knight, Sir Galahad, that thou left in the abbey, and greet him well from me." "Sir," said the squire, "what is your name?" "Take thou no heed of my name," said the knight, "for it is not for thee to know, nor none earthly man." "Now, fair sir," said the squire, "at the reverence of Jesu Christ tell me for what cause this shield may not be borne, but if the bearer thereof be mischieved." "Now sith thou hast conjured me so," said the knight, "this shield behoveth to no man but unto Sir Galahad." Then the squire went unto King Bagdemagus, and asked him whether he were sore wounded or not. "I am sore wounded," said he, "and full hardly I shall escape from the death." Then he set his horse, and brought him with great pain to an abbey: then was he taken down softly and unarmed, and laid in a bed, and his wound was looked unto; for he lay there long, and escaped hard with his life.

X.

"Sir Galahad," said the squire, "that knight that wounded King Bagdemagus sendeth you greeting, and bid that ye should bear this shield, wherethrough great adventures shall befall." "Now blessed be God and fortune," said Sir Galahad, and then he asked for his armour, and mounted upon his horse, and hung the white shield about his neck, and commended them to God. And Sir Uwaine said he would bear him fellowship if it please him. "Sir," said Sir Galahad, "that may ye not, for I must go alone, save this squire, that shall bear me fellowship:" and so departed Sir Uwaine. Then within awhile came Sir Galahad there as the white knight abode him by the hermitage, and every each saluted other courteously. "Sir," said Sir Galahad, "by this shield have been full many marvels." "Sir," said the knight, "it befell after the passion of our Lord Jesu Christ thirty years that Joseph of Arimathy, the gentle knight that took down our Lord from the cross, and at that time he

departed from Jerusalem with a great part of his kindred with
him.   And so they laboured till they came to a city, that hight
Sarras; and, at that same hour that Joseph came unto Sarras,
there was a king, that hight Evelake, that had great war against
the Saracens, and in especial against one Saracen, the which
was King Evelake's cousin, a rich and mighty king ; the which
marched nigh this land, and his name was called Tollome le'
Feintes : so upon a day these two met to do battle.

"Then Joseph, the son of Joseph of Arimathy, went unto King
Evelake, and told him that he would be discomfited and slain, but
if he left his belief of the old law, and believed upon the new law.
And then he showed him the right belief of the Holy Trinity,
the which he agreed with all his heart, and then this shield
was made for King Evelake, in the name of Him that died upon
the cross.   And then, through his good belief, he had the
better of King Tollome ; for when King Evelake was in the
battle, there was a cloth set before the shield ; and, when he
was in the greatest peril, he let put away the cloth, and then
anon his enemies saw a figure of a man upon the cross, wherethrough they were discomforted.   And so it befell that a man of
King Evelake's had his hand smitten off, and bear his hand in
his other hand.   And Joseph called that man unto him, and bid
him go with good devotion and touch the cross : and as soon
as that man had touched the cross with his hand, it was as whole
as ever it was before.   Then soon after there befell a great marvel
that the cross of the shield at one time vanished away, that no
man wist where it became.   And then was the King Evelake
baptised, and, for the most part, all the people of that city.   So,
soon after, Joseph would depart, and King Evelake would go
with him, whether he would go or not.   And so by fortune they
came into this land, which at that time was called Great
Britain, and there they found a great felon paynim that put
Joseph in prison.   And so, by fortune, tidings came unto a
worthy man, that hight Mondrames, and he assembled all his
people, for the great renown that he had heard of Joseph, and
so he came unto the land of Great Britain, and deserted his
felon paynim, and consumed him, and therewith delivered
Joseph out of prison ; and after that all the people were turned
to the Christian faith.

XI.

"NOT long after that Joseph was laid in his death-bed, and
when King Evelake saw that he made great sorrow and said,
"For thy love I have left my country, and sith thou shall

out of this world, leave me some token that I may think on thee." "That will I do right gladly," said Joseph: "now bring me the shield that I took from you when ye went into the battle against King Tollome." Then Joseph bled sore at the nose, that he might not by no means be stenched ; and thereupon that same shield he made a cross of his own blood. "Now may ye see a remembrance that I love you ; for ye shall never see this shield but ye shall think of me, and it shall be always as fresh as it is now, and never shall no man bear this shield about his neck but he shall repent it, unto the time that Sir Galahad, the good knight, bear it, and the last of my lineage shall have it about his neck, the which shall do many marvellous deeds." "Now," said King Evelake, "where shall I put this shield, that this worthy knight may have it ?" "Ye shall have it there at Nacien, where the hermit shall be put after his death ; for thither shall the good knight come the fifteenth day after that he shall receive the order of knighthood, and so that day that they set, is this time that ye have his shield ; and in the same abbey lieth Nacien, the hermit." And then the white knight vanished away. Anon as the squire had heard these words, he alighted from his hackney, and kneeled down at Sir Galahad's feet, and besought him that he might go with him till that he had made him a knight. "If I would not refuse you, and then will ye make me a knight," said the squire, "and that high order, by the grace of God, shall be well set upon me." And Sir Galahad granted him, and then they returned again unto the abbey that they came from. And there men made full great joy of Sir Galahad : and anon as he was alighted, there was a monk brought him unto a tomb in a churchyard, whereas was such a noise that who heard it should very nigh be made to lose his strength. "And, sir," said he, "I deem it is a fiend."

XII.

"Now lead me thither," said Sir Galahad. And so they did, all armed save his helm. "Now," said the good man, "go to the tomb, and lift it up." And so he did, and heard a great noise, and piteously he said, that all men might hear it, "Sir Galahad, the servant of God, come thou not near me, for thou shalt make me go again there where I have been so long." But Sir Galahad was nothing afraid, but quickly lift up the stone, and there came out a foul smoke, and after he saw the foulest figure leap out thereof that ever he saw in the likeness

of a man, and then he blest him, and wist well that it was
a fiend of hell. Then heard he a voice that said, "Galahad, I
see thereabout thee so many angels, that my power may not
hurt thee." Right so Sir Galahad saw a body, all armed, lie in
the tomb, and beside him there lay a sword. "Now, fair
brother," said Sir Galahad, "let us remove this cursed body;
for it is not worthy to lie in the churchyard, for he was a false
Christian man." And therewith they all departed and went to
the abbey. And anon as he was unarmed, a good man came
and set him down by him, and said, "Sir, I shall tell you what
betokeneth all that ye saw. That covered body betokeneth the
hardness of the world, and the great sin that our Lord found in
the world; for there was such wretchedness, that the father
loved not the son, nor the son loved not the father, and that was
one of the causes that our Lord took flesh and blood of a clean
maiden; for our sins were so great at that time, that well
nigh all was but wickedness." "Truly," said Sir Galahad, "I
believe you right well." So Sir Galahad rested him there
all that night, and on the morrow he made the squire a knight,
and asked him his name, and of what kindred he was come.
"Sir," said he, "men call me Melias de Lile, and I am the son
of the King of Denmark." "Now, fair sir," said Sir Galahad,
"sith ye be come of kings and queens, now look that knighthood be well set upon you, for ye ought to be a mirror unto all
chivalry." "Sir," said Melias, "ye say sooth; but, sir, sith ye
have made me a knight, ye must of right grant me my first desire
that is reasonable." "Ye say sooth," said Sir Galahad.
"Then," said Sir Melias, "that ye will suffer me to ride with
you in this Quest of the Sancgreal, till some adventure do
part us." "I grant you," said Sir Galahad.

Then men brought Sir Melias his armour, and his spear, and
his horse; and so Sir Galahad and he rode forth all that week
ere they found any adventure. And then upon a Monday, in
the morning, as they were departed from an abbey, they came
unto a cross which departed two ways; and on that cross were
letters written, that said thus: "Now ye knights-errant, the
which goeth for to seek adventures, see here two ways, that
one way defendeth thee, that thou go not that way, for he shall
not go out of that way again, but if he be a good man, and a
worthy knight; and if thou go on the left hand, thou shalt not
there lightly win prowess, for thou shalt in this way be soon
assayed." "Sir," said Sir Melias unto Sir Galahad, "if liketh
you to suffer me for to take the way on the left hand, tell it me,
for there I shall well prove my strength." "It were better,"

said Sir Galahad, "that ye rode not that way, for I deem I should better escape in that way than ye." "Nay, I pray you, my lord, let me have that adventure." "Take it in God's name," said Sir Galahad.

XIII.

AND then Sir Melias rode into an old forest, and therein he rode two days and more, and then he came into a fair meadow, and there was a fair lodge of boughs, and then he espied in that lodge a chair, wherein was a crown of gold, subtly wrought ; also there were cloths covered upon the earth, and many delicious meats were set thereon. Sir Melias beheld this adventure, and thought it marvellous, but he had no hunger ; but of the crown of gold he took much keep, and therewith he stooped down and took it up, and rode his way with it. And anon he saw a knight come riding after him, that said, "Knight, set down that crown which is not yours, and therefore defend you." Then Sir Melias blessed him, and said, "Fair Lord of heaven, help and save thy new-made knight." And then they let their horses run as fast as they might, so that the other knight smote Sir Melias through the hawberk and through the left side, that he fell to the earth nigh dead ; and then he took the crown and went his way, and Sir Melias lay still, and had no power to stir.

In the meanwhile, by fortune, there came Sir Galahad, and found him there in peril of death, and then he said, "Ah ! Sir Melias, who hath wounded you? therefore it had been better to have ridden that other way." And when Sir Melias heard him speak, he said, "Sir, for God's love, let me not die in this forest, but bear me unto the abbey here beside, that I may be confessed and have my rites." "It shall be done," said Sir Galahad, "but where is he that hath wounded you?" With that Sir Galahad heard in the leaves cry on high, "Knight, keep thee from me." "Ah ! sir," said Sir Melias, "beware, for that is he that hath slain me." Sir Galahad answered, "Sir knight, come on at your peril." Then either dressed them to other, and came together as fast as their horses might run ; and Sir Galahad smote him so that his spear went through his shoulder, and smote him down off his horse, and in the falling Sir Galahad's spear broke. With that came out of the leaves another knight, and broke a spear upon Sir Galahad, or he might turn him ; and then Sir Galahad drew out his sword, and smote off the left arm of him, so that it fell unto the ground, and then he fled, and Sir Galahad followed fast after him. And then he returned again unto Sir Melias, and there he alighted and dressed him softly upon his horse before him ; for the truncheon of the spear was in this body, and Sir Galahad started up behind him, and held him in his armour, and so brought him to an abbey, and there he unarmed him, and brought him to his chamber, and then he asked for the Sacrament of his Saviour. And when he had received him, he said unto Sir Galahad, " Sir, let death come when it pleaseth God." And therewith he drew out the truncheon of the spear out of his body, and then he swooned. Then came there an old monk, which had been sometime a knight, and beheld Sir Melias, and anon he ransacked him, and he said unto Sir Galahad, " I shall heal him of his wound, by the grace of God, within the space of seven weeks." Then was Sir Galahad glad, and unarmed him, and said, " He should abide there three days." And he asked Sir Melias " how it stood with him ?" Then he said he was turned unto healing, God be thanked.

XIV.

" Now will I depart," said Sir Galahad, " for I have much in hand ; for many good knights be full busy about it ; and this knight and I were in the same quest of the Sancgreal." " Sir," said a good man, " for his sin he was thus wounded ; and I marvel," said the good man to Sir Melias, " how ye durst take upon you so rich a thing as the high order of knighthood without clean confession, and that was the cause ye were so bitterly wounded : for the way on the right hand betokeneth the high way of our Lord Jesus Christ, and the way of a true and good liver ; and the other way betokeneth the way of sinners and misbelievers : and, when the devil saw your pride and presumption for to take you in the quest of the Holy Sancgreal, that made you for to be overthrown ; for it may not be achieved but by virtuous living : also, the writing on the cross was a significa- tion of heavenly deeds, and of knightly deeds in God's works ; and pride is the head of all deadly sins, that caused this knight to depart, Sir Galahad ; and where thou tookest the crown of gold thou sinned in covetousness and in theft, and these were no knight's deeds : and the two knights which fought with this holy knight, Sir Galahad, doth signify the two deadly sins which were entirely in you, but they might not withstand Sir Galahad, for he is without deadly sin." Now departed Sir Galahad from thence, and commended them all unto God. Sir Melias said, " My lord, Sir Galahad, as soon as I may ride I shall see you."

"God send you good help," said Sir Galahad. And so he took his horse and departed, and rode many journeys forward and backward, as adventure would lead him ; and at the last it happened him to depart from a place or a castle, that was named Abblasour, and he had not heard no mass, the which he was always wont to hear or that he depart out of any castle or place, and kept that for a custom. Then Sir Galahad came unto a mountain, where he found an old chapel, and found there nobody ; for all was desolate. And there he kneeled before the altar, and besought God of wholesome counsel. So as he prayed he heard a voice that said thus : "Go now, thou adventurous knight, unto the Castle of Maidens, and there do thou away all the wicked customs."

XV.

Then as Sir Galahad heard this he thanked God, and took his horse, and he had not ridden but half-a-mile, when he saw in a valley before him a strong castle with deep ditches ; and there ran beside a fair river, the which hight Severn, and there he met with a man of great age, and either saluted other, and Sir Galahad asked him what was the castle's name. "Fair sir," said he, "it is the Castle of Maidens." "That is a cursed castle," said Sir Galahad, "and all they that have been conversant therein ; for all pity is out thereof, and all hardiness and mischief is therein." "Therefore I counsel you, sir knight," said the old man, "to return again." "Sir," said Sir Galahad, "wit ye well I shall not return again." Then looked Sir Galahad on his armour that nothing failed him, and then he put his shield afore him, and anon there met him seven maidens, that said unto him, "Sir knight, ye ride herein a great folly, for ye have the waters for to pass over." "Why should I not pass here over this water?" said Sir Galahad. And so he departed away from them, and then he met with a squire that said, "Sir knight, those knights in the castle defy you, and forbid you that ye go no farther, till that they wit what ye would." "Fair fellow," said Sir Galahad, "I am come to destroy the wicked custom of this castle." "Sir," said the squire, "and ye will abide by that, ye shall have enough to do." "Go ye now," said Sir Galahad, "and haste my matters."

Then the squire entered into the castle. And anon after there came out of the castle seven knights, and all were brethren ; and, when they saw Sir Galahad, they cried, "Knight keep thee ; for we assure thee nothing but death." "Why," said

Sir Galahad, "will ye all have to do with me at once?" "Yea," said they all; "for thereto mayest thou trust." Then Sir Galahad put forth his spear, and smote the foremost to the earth, that almost he had broken his neck; and therewith all the others smote on his shield great strokes, so that all their spears break. Then Sir Galahad drew out his sword, and set upon them so hard, that it was a marvel to see it; and so through great force, he made them to forsake the field: and Sir Galahad chased them until they entered into the castle, and so passed through the castle at another gate. And there met Sir Galahad an old man, clothed in religious clothing, the which said to him, "Sir, have here the keys of the castle." Then Sir Galahad opened the gates, and saw so much people in the street, that he might not number them; and they said, "Sir, ye be welcome; for long have we been forbidden our deliverance." And then there came unto him a gentlewoman, and said, "These knights be fled; but they will come again this night, and here begin again their evil and wicked custom." "What will ye that I shall do?" said Sir Galahad. "Sir," said the gentlewoman, "that ye send after all those knights hither, that hold their lands of this castle, and make them swear for to use the customs that were used heretofore of old time." "I will well," said Sir Galahad. And then the gentlewoman brought him a horn of ivory, richly bound with gold, and said, "Sir, blow ye this horn, which will be heard two miles about this castle." And when Sir Galahad had blown the horn, he set him down upon a bed. Then came there a priest unto Sir Galahad, and said, "Sir, it is past a seven year since that these seven brethren came into this castle, and harboured with the lord of this castle, which hight the Duke Lianour; and he was lord of all this country. And, so, when they espied the duke's daughter, that was a fair woman, then by their false cunning they made debate between themselves, and the duke of his goodness would have departed them. And there they slew him and his eldest son; and then they took the maiden, and the treasure of the castle. And then, by great force, they held all the knights of this castle, against their will, under their obeisance, and in great servage and truage, robbing and pillaging the poor common-people of all that they had. So it happened upon a day that the duke's daughter said, "Ye have done to me great wrong, to slay mine own father and my brother, and thus to hold our lands. For them," said she, "ye shall not hold this castle for many years; for by one knight ye shall be overcome." Thus she prophesied seven years before. "Well," said the seven knights, "since ye say so, there shall never lady nor knight pass this castle, but they shall abide, maugre their heads : die, therefore, till that knight be come by whom we shall lose this castle."   And, therefore, it is called the Maidens' Castle ; for they have devoured many maidens."   "Now," said Sir Galahad, "is she here for whom this castle was lost ?"   "Nay," said the priest, "she died within three nights after she was thus enforced ; and since they have kept her young sister, which endureth great pains with more other ladies."   By this were the knights of the country come ; and then he made them to do homage and fealty to the duke's daughter, and set them in great ease of heart.   And, on the morrow, there came one unto Sir Galahad, and told him how Sir Gawaine and Sir Gareth and Sir Uwaine had slain the seven brethren.   "I suppose well," said Sir Galahad.   And then he took his armour and his horse, and commended them to God.

XVI.

Now (saith the story) after that Sir Gawaine was departed, he rode many divers journeys, both toward and froward ; and so, at the last, he came unto the abbey whereas Sir Galahad had the white shield : and there Sir Gawaine learned the very way for to follow after Sir Galahad.   And so he rode unto the abbey whereas Sir Melias lay sick : and there Sir Melias told Sir Gawaine of the marvellous adventure that Sir Galahad had done.   "Truly," said Sir Gawaine, "I am not happy that I took not the way that he went ; for and I may meet with him, I will not depart from him lightly : for all the marvellous adventures Sir Galahad achieveth."   "Sir," said one of the monks, "he will not be of your fellowship."   "Why ?" said Sir Gawaine.   "Sir," said he, "for ye be wicked and sinful, and he is blissful."   Right, as they stood thus talking together, there came in riding Sir Gareth ; and then they made great joy either of other.   And on the morrow they heard mass, and so departed ; and, by the way, they met with Sir Uwaine le Avoutres ; and there Sir Uwaine told Sir Gawaine how he had met with no adventure sithence he departed from the court. "Nor we," said Sir Gawaine.   And either promised other of these three knights not to depart, while that they were in the quest, but if fortune caused it.   So they departed and rode by fortune till that they came unto the Castle of Maidens ; and there the seven brethren espied the three knights.   And then they said, "Sithence we be banished by one knight from this castle, we shall destroy all the knights of

King Arthur's, that we may overcome, for the love of Sir Galahad." And therewith the seven knights set upon the three knights. And by fortune Sir Gawaine slew one of the seven brethren, and each of his fellows slew another, and so slew the remnant. And then they took their way unto the castle ; and there they lost the way that Sir Galahad rode, and every one of them departed from the other. And Sir Gawaine rode till he came to a hermitage ; and there he found the good man saying his even-song of our Lady. And there Sir Gawaine asked harbour for charity ; and the good man granted it him gladly. Then the good man asked him what he was, and from whence he came ? "Sir," said he, "I am a knight of King Arthur's court, that am in the quest of the Sancgreal, and my name is Sir Gawaine." "Sir," said the good man, "I will wit how it standeth between God and you." "Sir," said Sir Gawaine, "I will with a good will show you my life, and it please you." And there he told him how the monk of an abbey called him a wicked knight. "He might well say it," said the good man ; "for, when ye were first made knight, ye should have taken you unto knightly deeds and virtuous living ; and ye have done the contrary, for ye have lived mischievously many winters. And the noble knight, Sir Galahad, is a maiden, and never sinned ; and that is the cause he shall achieve whersoever he goeth, that ye nor none such shall ever attain, nor any of your fellowship : for ye have used the most untruest life that ever I heard knight live. For, truly, had ye not been so wicked as ye are, never had the seven brethren been slain by you, and by your two fellows ; for Sir Galahad himself, all alone, bet them all seven that day before : but his living is such, that he shall slay no man lightly. Also I may say to you, the Castle of Maidens betoken the good souls that were in prison before the incarnation of Christ ; and the seven knights betoken the seven deadly sins which reigned that time in the world. And I may liken the good knight, Sir Galahad, unto the Son of the high Father, that light within a maiden, and brought all the souls out of thraldom ; so did Sir Galahad deliver all the maidens out of the woeful castle. Now, Sir Gawaine," said the good man, "thou must do penance for thy sins." "Sir, what penance shall I do ?" "Such as I will give," said the good man. "Nay," said Sir Gawaine, "I may do no penance ; for we knights adventurous often suffer great woe and pain." "Well," said the good man ; and then he held his peace, and commended him unto God. And by adventure he met with Sir Aglovale and Sir Griflet, two knights of the Round Table ; and they two had ridden four days without finding of any adventure. And at the fifth day they departed, and every each held as fell them by adventure.

XVII.

So when Sir Galahad was departed from the Castle- of Maidens, he rode till he came unto a vast forest, and there he met with Sir Launcelot and Sir Percivale ; but either of them knew him not, for he was new disguised. Right so Sir Launcelot, his father, dressed his spear, and break it upon his son, Sir Galahad ; and Sir Galahad smote him so hard again, that he smote down both horse and man. And then he drew his sword, and dressed him unto Sir Percivale, and smote him so on his helm, that it rove the coif of steel, and, if the sword had not swerved, Sir Percivale had been slain ; and, with the stroke, he fell out of his saddle. These jousts were done before the hermitage, where a recluse dwelled ; and, when she saw Sir Galahad ride, she said, " God be with thee, the best knight of the world. Ah! certainly," said she all aloud, that Sir Launcelot and Sir Percivale might hear it, "and yonder two knights had known thee as well as I do, they would not have encountered with thee." When Sir Galahad heard her say so, he was sore adread to be known : therewithal he smote his horse with his spurs, and rode a great pace froward them. Then perceived they both that it was Sir Galahad, and up they gat on their horses, and rode fast after him ; but, within a while, he was out of their sight, and then they turned again with a heavy cheer. " Let us ask some tidings," said Sir Percivale, " at yonder recluse." " Do as ye list," said Sir Launcelot. When Sir Percivale came unto the recluse, she knew him well enough, and in likewise she knew Sir Launcelot. But Sir Launcelot rode overthwart and endlong in a wild forest, and held no path, but as wild adventure led him. And at the last he came unto a stone cross, which departed two ways in waste land ; and by the cross was a stone that was of marble ; but it was so dark, that Sir Launcelot might not well know what it was. Then Sir Launcelot looked by him, and saw an old chapel, and there he weened to have found much people. And so Sir Launcelot tied his horse to a tree, and there he put off his shield, and hung it upon a tree ; and then he went unto the chapel door, and found it wasted and broken : and within he found a fair altar, full richly arrayed with cloth of silk ; and their stood a fair candlestick, which bare six great candles, and the candlestick was of silver. And when Sir Launcelot saw this light, he had a great will for to enter into the chapel, but he could find no place where he might enter. Then was he passing heavy and dismayed; then he returned and came again to his horse, and took off his saddle and his bridle, and let him pasture; and unlaced his helm, and ungirded his sword, and laid him down to sleep upon his shield before the cross.

XVIII.

AND so he fell on sleep, and, half waking and half sleeping, he saw come by him two palfreys, both fair and white, the which bear a litter, therein lying a sick knight; and, when he was nigh the cross, he there abode still. All this Sir Launcelot saw and beheld, for he slept not verily, and he heard him say, "Oh, sweet Lord, when shall this sorrow leave me, and when shall the holy vessel come by me, wherethrough I shall be blessed? for I have endured thus long for little trespass;" and thus a great while complained the knight, and always Sir Launcelot heard it. With that Sir Launcelot saw the candlestick with the fire tapers come before the cross, but he could see nobody that brought it; also there came a table of silver, and the holy vessel of the Sancgreal, the which Sir Launcelot had seen before that time in King Petchour's house. And therewithal the sick knight sat him upright, and held up both his hands, and said, "Fair sweet Lord, which is here within the holy vessel, take heed to me that I may be whole of this great malady;" and therewith, upon his hands and upon his knees, he went so nigh that he touched the holy vessel, and kissed it: and anon he was whole; and then he said, "Lord God I thank thee, for I am healed of this malady." So when the holy vessel had been there a great while, it went unto the chapel again, with the candlestick and the light; so that Sir Launcelot wist not where it became, for he was overtaken with sin, that he had no power to arise against the holy vessel; wherefore afterward many men said of him shame: but he took repentance afterward. Then the sick knight dressed him upright, and kissed the cross. Then anon his squire brought him his arms, and asked his lord how he did. "Certainly," said he, "I thank God right heartily, for through the holy vessel I am healed. But I have right great marvel of this sleeping knight, which hath had neither grace nor power to awake during the time that this holy vessel hath been here present." "I dare it right well say," said the squire, "that this same knight is befouled with some manner of deadly sin, whereof he was never confessed." "By my faith," said the knight, "whatsoever he be, he is unhappy; for, as I deem, he is of the fellowship of the Round Table, the which is entered into the quest of the Sancgreal." "Sir," said the squire, "here I have brought you all your arms, save your helm and your sword; and therefore, by mine assent, now may ye take this knight's helm and his sword;" and so he did. And when he was clean armed, he took Sir Launcelot's horse, for he was better than his own : and so they departed from the cross.

XIX.

THEN anon Sir Launcelot awaked, and set himself upright, and bethought him what he had there seen, and whether it were dreams, or not right so, he heard a voice that said, "Sir Launcelot, more hardy than is the stone, and more bitter than is the wood, and more naked and bare than is the leaf of the fig-tree, therefore go thou from hence, and withdraw thee from this holy place." And when Sir Launcelot heard this, he was passing heavy, and wist not what to do; and so he departed, sore weeping, and cursed the time that he was born. For then he deemed never to have had more worship : for the words went unto his heart, till that he knew wherefore that he was so called. Then Sir Launcelot went to the cross, and found that his helm, his sword, and his horse, were taken away; and then he called himself a very wretch, and most unhappy of all knights. And there he said, "My sin and my wretchedness hath brought me unto great dishonour : for when I sought worldly adventures, and worldly desires, I ever achieved them, and had the better in every place, and never was I discomfited in any quarrel, were it right or wrong ; and now I take upon me the adventures of holy things : and now I see and understand that mine old sin hindereth me, and also shamed me, so that I had no power to stir, nor to speak, when the holy blood appeared before me." So thus he sorrowed till it was day, and heard the fowls of the air sing ; then was he somewhat comforted. But when Sir Launcelot missed his horse and his harness, then wist ye well that God was displeased with him. Then he departed from the cross on foot, into a wild forest, and so by prime he came unto a high mountain, and there he found a hermitage, and a hermit therein, which was going to mass. And then Sir Launcelot kneeled down upon both his knees, and cried our Lord mercy, for his wicked works that he had done. So when mass was done, Sir Launcelot called the hermit to him, and prayed him for charity to hear his confession. "With a good will," said the good man. "Sir," said he, "be ye of King Arthur's court, and of the noble fellowship of the Round Table?" "Yea, forsooth, and my name is Sir Launcelot du Lake, which hath been right well said of, and greatly magnified; and now it is so, my good fortune is changed, for I am the most wretch and captive of the world." Then the hermit beheld him, and had great marvel how he was so sore abashed. "Sir," said the hermit, "ye ought to thank God more than any knight living; for he hath caused you to have more worldly worship than any knight that now liveth. And, for your presumption to take upon you, in deadly sin, for to be in his presence, where his flesh and his blood was, that caused you ye might not see it with your worldly eye : for he will not appear where such sinners be, but if it be unto their great hurt, and unto their great shame. And there is no knight living that ought for to give unto God so great thanks as ye : for he hath given unto you beauty, seemliness, and great strength, above all other knights, and therefore ye are the more beholding unto God than any other man, to love him, and to dread him, for your strength and manhood will little avail you, and God be against you."

XX.

THEN Sir Launcelot wept, and made full heavy cheer, and said, "Now I know well, ye tell me truth." "Sir," said the good man, "hide none old sin from me." "Then," said Sir Launcelot, "that were me full loth to discover : for this fourteen years I never discovered any thing which I have used, and that may I now wit my shame, and my misadventure." And then he told there that good man all his life, and how he had loved a Queen unmeasurably many years ; "and all my great deeds of arms that I have done, I did for the most part for the Queen's sake ; and for her sake would I do battle, were it right or wrong ; and never did I battle at all only for God's sake, but for to win worship, and to cause me to be the better beloved, and little or nought I thanked God of it." Then Sir Launcelot said, "I pray you counsel me." "I will counsel you," said the hermit, "if ye will ensure me that ye will never come into that Queen's fellowship as much as ye may forbear." And then Sir Launcelot promised the hermit, by his faith, that he would no more come into her company. "Look that your heart and your mouth accord," said the good old man, "and I shall ensure you that ye shall have more worship than ever ye had." "Holy father," said Sir Launcelot, "I marvel of the voice that said to me marvellous words, and ye have heard here before." "Have ye no marvel thereof," said the good man, "for it seemeth well that God loveth you, for men may understand that a stone is hard of kind, and namely one more than another; and that is to understand, by Sir Launcelot, for thou wilt not leave thy sin for no goodness that God hath sent thee, therefore thou art more harder than any stone; and never would thou be made soft, neither by water nor by fire, and that is the heat of the Holy Ghost may not enter into thee. Now take heed in all the world, men shall not find one knight to whom our Lord hath given so much grace, as our Lord hath given you: for he hath given you fairness with seemliness; he hath given you wit and discretion, for to know good from evil; he hath given you prowess and hardiness, and hath given you to work so largely, that ye have had at all times the better, wheresoever ye came. And now our Lord will suffer you no longer, but that ye shall know him whether ye will or not; and why the voice called thee bitterer than wood; for where overmuch sin dwelleth there may be but little sweetness, wherefore thou art likened to an old rotten tree. Now I have showed thee why thou art harder than the stone, and bitterer than the tree; now I shall show thee why thou art more naked and bare than the fig tree. It befell that our Lord Jesus Christ preached on Palm Sunday in Jerusalem, and there he found in the people that all hardness was harboured in them, and there he could not find one in all the town that would harbour him, and then he went without the town, and found in the midst of the way a fig tree, the which was right fair and well-garnished with leaves, but fruit had it none; then our Lord cursed the tree that bare no fruit, that betokeneth the fig tree unto Jerusalem, that had leaves and no fruit. So thou, Sir Launcelot, when the Holy Grail was brought before thee, he found in thee no fruit, neither good thought, nor good will, and defouled with lechery." "Certainly," said Sir Launcelot, "all that ye have said is true, and from henceforward, I cast me, by the grace of God, never to be so wicked as I have been, but as to follow knighthood, and to do feats of arms." Then the good man enjoined Sir Launcelot such penance as he might do, and to show knighthood; and so he assailed Sir Launcelot, and prayed him to abide with him all that day. "I will well," said Sir Launcelot, "for I have neither helm, nor horse, nor sword." "As for that," said the good man, "I shall help you or to-morrow at even of a horse, and all that belongeth unto you." And then Sir Launcelot repented him greatly.

XXI.

NOW when the hermit had kept Sir Launcelot three days, the hermit got him a horse, a helm, and a sword, and then he departed, about the hour of noon, and then he saw a little house; and when he came near he saw a chapel, and there beside he saw an old man, that was clothed all in white, full richly: then Sir Launcelot said, "God save you." "God keep you well," said the good man, "and make you a good knight." Then Sir Launcelot alighted, and entered into a chapel, and there he saw an old man dead, in a white shirt, of passing fine cloth. "Sir," said he, "this good man, that is here dead, ought not to be in such clothing as ye see him in, for that he break the oath of his order; for he hath been more than a hundred winters a religious man." And then the good man and Sir Launcelot went into the chapel, and the good man took a stole about his neck, and a book, and then he conjured on that book, and with that they saw a hideous figure, and a horrible, that there was no man so hard-hearted, nor so hardy, but that he would have been afraid. Then said the fiend, "Thou hast travailed me greatly; now tell me what thou wilt with me." "I will," said the good man, "that thou tell me how my fellow became dead, and whether he be saved or damned." Then he said, with a horrible voice, "He is not lost, but saved." "How may that be," said the good man, "it seemed to me that he lived not well, for he break his order, for to wear a shirt, whereas he ought to wear none: and who that trespasseth against our order doth not well." "Not so," said the fiend, "this man, that lieth here dead, was come of great lineage; and there was a lord, that hight the Earl de Vale, that held great war against this man's nephew, which hight Aguarus. And so this Aguarus saw that earl was bigger than he, then went he for to take counsel of his uncle, which lieth now dead, as ye may see; and then he asked leave, and went out of his hermitage, for to maintain his nephew, the mighty earl; and so it happened, that this man, that lieth here dead, did so much by his wisdom and hardiness, that the earl was taken, and three of his lords, by force of this dead man.

XXII.

"THEN was there peace between the earl and this Aguarus, and great surety, that the earl should never war against him. Then this dead man, that there lieth, came to this hermitage again: and then the earl made two of his nephews to be avenged upon this man. So they came upon a day, and found this dead man at the sacring of the mass, and they abode till he had said his mass, and then they set upon him, and drew out their swords for to have slain him. But there would no sword bite on him, no more than upon a gad of steel ; for the high Lord, which he served, preserved him. Then made they a great fire, and did off his clothes, and the hair of his back : and then this dead man, the hermit, said unto them, "Ween ye to burn me, it shall not lie in your power, nor to perish me as much as a thread, and there were any upon my body." "No," said one of them, "it shall be essayed." And then they spoiled him, and put upon him this shirt, and threw him in the fire, and he lay all that night, till it was day, in that fire, and yet was he not dead. And so on the morrow I came and found him dead, but I found neither thread nor skin perished, and so took him out of the fire with great fear, and laid him here, as you may see : and now ye may suffer me to go my way, for I have told you the truth." And then he departed, with a horrible tempest. Then was the good man and Sir Launcelot more gladder than they were before, and then Sir Launcelot dwelled with the good man that night. "Sir," said the good man, "be ye not Sir Launcelot du Lake ?" "Yea, sir," said he. "What seek ye in this country?" said the good man. "Sir," said Sir Launcelot, "I go to seek the adventures of the Sancgreal." "Well," said he, "seek it may ye well ; but, though it were here, ye shall have no power to see it, no more than a blind man should see a bright sword, and that is long of your sin, and else were ye more abler than any man living." And then Sir Launcelot began to weep. Then said the good man, "Were ye confessed sith ye entered into the quest of the Sancgreal?" "Yea," said Sir Launcelot. Then on the morrow, when the good man had sung his mass, they buried the dead man. Then said Sir Launcelot, "Father, what shall I do?" "Now," said the good man, "I require you to take this hair, that was this holy man's, and put it next your skin, and greatly shall it prevail you." "Sir, and I will do it," said Sir Launcelot. "And I charge you," said the good man, "that ye eat no flesh as long as ye be in the quest of the Holy Sancgreal, nor ye shall drink no wine, and that ye hear mass daily ; and he may do it." So he took the hair and put it upon him, and so he departed at even-song time ; and so he rode into a forest, and there he met with a gentlewoman riding upon a white palfrey, and she asked him, "Sir knight, whither ride ye ?" "Certainly, damsel," said Sir Launcelot, "I wot not whither I ride but as fortune leadeth me." "Ah ! Sir Launcelot," said she, "I wot not what adventure ye seek, for ye were aforetime more nearer than ye be now ; and yet shall ye see it more openly than ever ye did, and that shall ye understand in short time." Then Sir Launcelot asked her where he might be harboured that night. "Ye shall none find this day nor night, but to-morrow ye shall find good harbour, and ease you of that ye be in doubt of." And then he commended her unto God. Then he rode till that he came to a cross, and took that for his host, as for that night.

XXIII.

AND he put his horse to pasture, and took off his helm and his shield, and made his prayers to the cross, that he might never again fall in deadly sin. And so he laid him down to sleep : and anon as he was asleep it befell him that he had a vision. That him thought there came a man before him all encompassed of stars, and that man had a crown of gold on his head, and that man led in his fellowship seven kings and two knights, and all these worshipped the cross, kneeling upon their knees, holding up their hands toward heaven, and all they said, "Fair, sweet father of heaven, come and visit us, and yield unto us every one as we have deserved." Then Sir Launcelot looked up to heaven, and him seemed that the clouds opened, and that an old man came down with a company of angels and alight among them, and gave unto every each his blessing, and called them his servants, and good and true knights. And when this old man had said thus, he came to one of those knights and said, "I have lost all that I have set in thee ; for thou hast ruled thee against me as a warrior, and used wrong wars with vain glory, more for the pleasure of the world than to please me ; therefore thou shalt be confounded without thou yield me my treasure." All this vision saw Sir Launcelot at the cross. And on the morrow he took his horse and rode till mid-day, and there by adventure he met with the same knight that took his horse, his helm, and his sword, when he slept, when the Sancgreal appeared afore the cross. And when Sir Launcelot saw him, he saluted him not fair, but cried on high, "Knight, keep thee ; for thou hast done to me great unkindness." And then they put before them their spears, and Sir Launcelot came so fiercely upon him, that he smote him and his horse down to the earth, that he had almost broken his neck. Then Sir Launcelot took the knight's horse, that was his own beforehand, and descended from the horse that he sat upon, took his horse, and then tied the knight's own horse to a tree, that he might find that horse when he was risen. Then Sir Launcelot rode till night, and by adventure he met a hermit, and each of them saluted other ; and there he rested with that good man all night, and gave his horse such as he might get. Then said the good man unto Sir Launcelot, "Of whence be ye ?" "Sir," said he, "I am of King Arthur's court, and my name is Sir Launcelot du Lake, that am in quest of the Sancgreal ; and, therefore, I pray you to counsel me of a vision, the which I had at a cross." And so he told him all.

XXIV.

"Now, Sir Launcelot," said the good man, "there thou mightest have understood the high lineage that thou art come of, and thy vision betokeneth this : after the passion of Jesu Christ forty years, Joseph of Arimathy preached the victory of King Everlake, that he had in the battle the better of his enemies, and of the seven kings and the two knights. The first of them it called Napus, a right holy man, and the second hight Nacien, in remembrance of his grandsire, and in him dwelled our Lord Jesu Christ ; and the third was called Pelias le Grose, and the fourth hight Licias, and the fifth hight Ionas, he departed out his country and went into Wales, and took the daughter of Manuel, whereby he had the land of Gaul, and he came to dwell in this country, and of him came King Launcelot thy grandsire, which there wedded the king's daughter of Ireland, and he was as worthy a man as thou art, and of him came King Ban thy father, the which was the last of the seven kings. And by thee, Sir Launcelot, it signifieth that the angels said, that thou were none of the seven fellowships : and the last was the ninth knight, he was signified to a lion, for he should pass all manner of earthly knights, that is Sir Galahad, which thou begat upon King Pelleas' daughter, and thou ought to thank God more than any man living, for an earthly sinner thou hast no peer in knighthood, nor never shall be ; but little thanks hast thou given unto God for all the great virtues that God hath lent thee." "Sir," said Sir Launcelot, "ye say that the good knight is my son." "That oughtest thou to know," said the good man, "and no man better, for thou knewest the daughter of King Pelleas, and begattest Galahad, and that was he that at the feast of Pentecost sat in the Perilous Siege ; and, therefore, make thou it known openly that he is one of thy begetting on King Pelleas' daughter, for that will be thy worship and honour unto thy kindred ; and I counsel you in no place press not upon him to have to do with him." "Well," said Sir Launcelot, "me seemeth that good knight should pray for me to the high Father, that I fall not to sin again." "Trust thou well," said the good man, "that thou farest much the better for his prayer, but the son shall not bear the wickedness of the father, nor the father shall not bear the wickedness of the son, but every one shall bear his own burthen; and, therefore, pray you only unto God, and he will help thee in all thy deeds." And then Sir Launcelot and he went to supper and laid him to rest, and the hair pricked so Sir Launcelot's skin, that it grieved him full sore, but he took it meekly, and suffered the pain. And so on the morrow he heard his mass, and took his arms, and so took his leave.

<h2 style="text-align:center">XXV.</h2>

AND then he mounted upon his horse and rode into a forest, and held no highway; and as he looked before him he saw a fair plain, and beside that plain stood a fair castle, and before that castle were many pavilions of silk, and of divers hue. And him seemed that he saw there five hundred knights riding on horseback, and there were two parties: they that were of the castle were all in black, their horses and their trappings black: and they that were without were all upon white horses with white trappings. And every each hurled to other, whereas Sir Launcelot marvelled greatly: and, at last, he thought that they of the castle were put unto the worst: and then thought Sir Launcelot to help the weaker party, in increasing of his chivalry. And so Sir Launcelot thrust in among the parties of the castle, and smote down a knight, both horse and man to the earth; and then he rushed here and there, and did marvellous deeds of arms. And then he drew out his sword, and struck many knights to the earth, so that all those that saw him marvelled that ever one knight might do such deeds of arms. But always the white knights held them nigh about Sir Launcelot, for to weary him and wind him.

And, at the last, as a man might not ever endure, Sir Launcelot waxed so faint of fighting and of travelling, and was so weary of great deeds, that he might not lift up his arms for to give one stroke, so that he weened never to have borne arms. And then all they took him and led him away into a forest, and there they made him to alight and to rest him. And then all the fellowship of the castle were overcome for the default of him: and then all they said unto Sir Launcelot, "Blessed be God that he be now of our fellowship, for we shall hold you in our prison." And so they left him with few words; and then Sir Launcelot made great sorrow and said, "Never till now was I at tournament nor jousts but that I had the better, and now I am shamed;" and then he said, "Now I am sure that I am more sinful than ever I was." Thus he rode sorrowing, and half a day he was in despair, till that he came into a deep valley; and when Sir Launcelot saw he might not ride up into the mountain, he alighted there under an apple-tree, and there he left his helm and his shield, and put his horse to pasture, and then he laid him down to sleep, and then he thought there came an old man before him which said, "Ah, Sir Launcelot, of evil faith and poor belief, wherefore is thy will turned toward thy deadly sin." And when he had thus said, he vanished away, and Sir Launcelot wist not where he became. Then he armed him, and took his horse, and as he rode that way, he saw a chapel where was a recluse, which had a window that she might see up to the altar, and all aloud she called Sir Launcelot, because he seemed a knight-errant. And then he came, and she asked him what he was, and of what place, and what he seeked.

XXVI.

AND then he told her altogether, word by word, and the truth how it befell him at the tournament, and after he told her his vision that he had that night in his sleep, and prayed her for to tell him what it might mean, for he was not well content with it. "Ah, Sir Launcelot," said she, "as long as ye were knight of earthly knighthood, ye were the most marvellous man of the world, and the most adventurous. Now," said the lady, "since that ye be set among the knights of heavenly adventures, if adventure fell the contrary of that tournament, have thou no marvel, for that tournament yesterday was but a tokening of our Lord Jesus Christ, and not for then there was none enchantment, for they at the tournament were earthly knights. The tournament was a token for to see who should have most knights, either Eliazar, the son of good King Pelleas, or Augustus, the son of King Harlon. But Eliazar was all clothed in white, and Augustus was clothed in black, the which were come : all what this betokeneth I shall tell thee. On the day of Pentecost, when King Arthur held his court, it befell that earthly kings and knights took a tournament together, that is to say, the quest of the Sancgreal. The earthly knights were they the which were clothed all in black, and the covering betokeneth the sins, whereof they be not confessed ; and they with the covering of white betokeneth virginity, and they that choose chastity, and thus was the quest began in them.   Then thou beholdest the sinners and the good men ; and when thou sawest the sinners overcome, thou inclinest unto that part, for pomp and pride of the world, and all that must be left in the quest ; for in this quest thou shalt have many fellows, and thy betters, for thou art so feeble of evil trust and good belief. This made it when thou were there where they took thee and led thee into the forest.   And anon there appeared the Sancgreal unto the white knights, but thou wert so feeble of good belief and faith, that thou might not abide it, for all the teaching of the good man, but anon thou turned unto the sinners ; and thou caused thy misadventure that thou shouldst know good from evil, and the vain glory of the world, the which is not worth a pear.   And for great pride thou madest great sorrow thou hadst not overcome all the white knights with the covering of white, by whom was betokened virginity and chastity ; and, therefore, God was wrath with thee, for God loveth not such deeds in his quest.   And this vision signifieth that thou were of evil faith, and of poor belief, the which will make thee to fall into the deep pit of hell, if thou keep thee not.   Now have I warned thee of thy vain glory, and of thy pride, that thou hast many times erred against thy Maker. Beware of everlasting pain, for of all earthly knights I have most pity of thee ; for I know well thou hast not thy peer of any earthly sinful man." And so she commanded Sir Launcelot to dinner: and after dinner he commended her unto God, and took his horse, and so rode into a deep valley, and there he saw a river and a high mountain, and through the water he must needs pass, the which was full hideous ; and then, in the name of God, he took the water with a good heart : and when he came over he saw an armed knight, horse and man as black as any deer, and without any word speaking, he smote Sir Launcelot's horse to the earth ; and so he passed forth, and wist not where he became.   And then he took his helm and his shield, and thanked God of his adventure.

THE BOOK OF SIR PERCIVALE.

I.

NOW, saith the tale, that when Sir Launcelot was ridden after Sir Galahad, his son, the which had all these adventures here above rehearsed, Sir Percivale returned again unto the recluse, where he deemed to have tidings of that knight which Sir Launcelot followed : and so he kneeled at her window, and anon the recluse opened it, and asked Sir Percivale what he would. "Madam," said he, " I am a knight of King Arthur's court, and my name is Sir Percivale de Galis." So when the recluse heard his name, she made passing great joy of him, for greatly she loved him before all other knights of the world ; for so of right she ought to do, for she was his aunt. And then she commanded that the gates should be opened to him, and there Sir Percivale had all the cheer that she might make him, and all that was in her power was at his commandment. So on the morrow Sir Percivale went unto the recluse, and asked her if she knew that knight with the white shield. "Sir," said she, " why would ye wit?" "Truly, madam," said Sir Percivale, "I shall never be well at ease till that I know of that knight's fellowship, and that I may fight with him; for I may not leave him so lightly, for I have the shame yet." "Ah ! Sir Percivale," said she, "would ye fight with him? I see well ye have great will to be slain, as your father was through outrageousness." " Madam," said Sir Percivale, "it seemeth by your words that ye know me." "Yea," said she, "I well ought to know you, for I am your aunt, although I be in a priory place : for I was sometime called the Queen of the Waste Lands, and I was called the Queen of most riches in the world; and it pleased me never so much my riches as doth my poverty." Then Sir Percivale wept for very great pity, when he knew she was his aunt. "Ah ! fair nephew," said she, "when heard you any tidings from your mother?" " Truly," said he, "I heard not of her in a great while, but I have dreamed of her much in my sleep, and therefore I wot not whether she be dead or alive." " Certainly, fair nephew," said she, "your mother is dead ; for after your departing from her she took such a sorrow, that anon, after she was confessed, she died." " Now God have mercy upon her soul," said Sir Percivale, "it sore forethinketh me : but all we must change our life.

Now, fair aunt, tell me what is the knight? I deem it be he that bear the red arms on Whit Sunday." "Wit ye well," said his aunt, "that is he ; for otherwise he ought not to do but to go in red arms, and that same knight hath no peer, for he worketh all by miracle : and he shall never be overcome of no earthly man's hands.

II.

"Also," said his aunt, "Merlin made the Round Table in token of the roundness of the world : for by the Round Table is the world signified by right. For all the world, Christian and heathen, resort unto the Round Table ; and when they are chosen to be of the fellowship of the Round Table, they think them more blessed, and more in worship, than if they had gotten half the world, and ye have seen that they have lost their fathers and their mothers, and all their kin, and their wives and their children, for to be of your fellowship, it is well seen by you ; for sith ye departed from your mother, ye would never see her, ye found such a fellowship at the Round Table. When Merlin had ordained the Round Table, he said, by them that should be fellows of the Round Table the truth of the Sancgreal shall be well known. And men asked him how men might know them that should best do to the achieving of the Sancgreal. Then said he, there should be three white bulls that should achieve it : and the two should be maidens, and the third should be chaste ; and that one of the three should pass the father, as much as the lion passeth his leopard, both of strength and of hardiness. They which heard Merlin say so, said thus unto Merlin : Since there shall be such a knight, thou shouldst ordain by thy craft a siege that no man should sit thereto, but he only which shall pass all other knights. And then Merlin answered that he would do so ; and then he made the Siege Perilous, in which Sir Galahad sat at his meat upon Whit Sunday last past." "Now, madam," said Sir Percivale, "so much have I heard of you, that by my good will I will never have to do with Sir Galahad, but by way of kindness. And for God's love, fair aunt, can ye teach me some way where I may find him, for much would I love the fellowship of him?" "Fair nephew," said she, "ye must ride unto a castle the which is called Goothe, where he hath a cousin-german, and there may ye be lodged this night. And as he teacheth you, sue after as fast as ye can, and if he can tell you no tidings of him, ride straight unto the castle of Carbonek, where the maimed King is there lying, for there shall ye hear true tidings of him."

III.

THEN departed Sir Percivale from his aunt, either making great sorrow. And so he rode till even-song time. And then he heard a clock smite. And then he was ware of a house closed well with walls and deep ditches, and there he knocked at the gate, and was let in, and he alight, and was led unto a chamber, and soon he was unarmed. And there he had right good cheer all that night, and on the morn he heard his mass, and in the monastery he found a priest ready at the altar. And on the right side he saw a pew closed with iron, and behind the altar he saw a rich bed and a fair, as of cloth of silk and gold. Then Sir Percivale espied that therein was a man or a woman, for the visage was covered. Then he left off his looking, and heard his service. And when it came to the sacring, he that lay within that perclose dressed him up, and uncovered his head, and then him beseemed a passing old man, and he had a crown of gold upon his head, and his shoulders were naked and uncovered unto his middle. And then Sir Percivale espied his body was full of great wounds, both on the shoulders, arms, and visage. And ever he held up his hands unto our Lord's body, and cried, "Fair sweet Father Jesu Christ, forget not me," and so he lay down, but always he was in his prayers and orisons : and him seemed to be of the age of three hundred winters. And when the mass was done, the priest took our Lord's body, and bare it to the sick King, And when he had used it, he did off his crown, and commanded the crown to be set on the altar. Then Sir Percivale asked one of the brethren, what he was. "Sir," said the good man, "ye have heard much of Joseph of Arimathy, how he was sent by Jesu Christ into this land, for to teach and preach the holy Christian faith, and therefore he suffered many persecutions, the which the enemies of Christ did unto him. And in the city of Sarras he converted a King whose name was Evelake. And so this King came with Joseph into this land : and always he was busy to be there as the Sancgreal was, and on a time he nighed it so nigh that our Lord was displeased with him, but ever he followed it more and more, till God struck him almost blind. Then this King cried mercy, and said, 'Fair Lord, let me never die till the good knight of my blood of the ninth degree be come, that I may see him openly that he shall achieve the Sancgreal, that I may kiss him.'

IV.

"WHEN the King had thus made his prayers, he heard a voice that said, 'Heard be thy prayers, for thou shalt not die till he have kissed thee: and when that knight shall come, the clearness of your eyes shall come again, and thou shalt see openly, and thy wounds shall be healed, and erst shall they never close.' And this befell of King Evelake: and this same King hath lived this three hundred winters this holy life. And men say the knight is in the court that shall heal him." "Sir," said the good man, "I pray you tell me what knight that ye be, and if ye be of King Arthur's court and of the Table Round?" "Yea, forsooth," said he, "and my name is Sir Percivale de Galis." And when the good man understood his name, he made great joy of him. And then Sir Percivale departed, and rode till the hour of noon. And he met in a valley about twenty men of arms, which bear in a bier a knight deadly slain. And when they saw Sir Percivale, they asked him of whence he was? and he answered, "Of the court of King Arthur." Then they cried all at once, "Slay him." Then Sir Percivale smote the first to the earth, and his horse upon him. And then seven of the knights smote upon his shield all at once, and the remnant slew his horse, so that he fell to the earth. So had they slain him or taken him, had not the good knight, Sir Galahad, with the red arms, come there by adventure into those parts. And when he saw all those knights upon one knight, he cried, "Save me that knight's life." And then he dressed him toward the twenty men of arms as fast as his horse might drive, with his spear in the rest, and smote the foremost horse and man to the earth. And when his spear was broken, he set his hand to his sword, and smote on the right hand and on the left hand, that it was marvel to see. And at every stroke he smote one down, or put him to a rebuke, so that they would fight no more, but fled to a thick forest, and Sir Galahad followed them. And when Sir Percivale saw him chase them so, he made great sorrow that his horse was away. And then he wist well it was Sir Galahad. And then he cried aloud, "Ah, fair knight, abide and suffer me to do thankings unto thee, for much have ye done for me!" But ever Sir Galahad rode so fast, that at the last he passed out of his sight. And as fast as Sir Percivale might he went after him on foot, crying. And then he met with a yeoman riding upon an hackney, the which led in his hand a great black steed, blacker than any bier. "Ah, fair friend," said Sir Percivale, "as ever I may do for you, and to be your true knight in the first place ye will require me, that ye will lend me that black steed, that I might overtake a knight, the which rideth afore me." "Sir knight," said the yeoman, "I pray you hold me excused of that, for that I may not do. For wit ye well, the horse is such a man's horse, that, and I lent it you or any other man, that he would slay me." "Alas," said Sir Percivale, "I had never so great sorrow as I have had for losing of yonder knight." "Sir," said the yeoman, "I am right heavy for you, for a good horse would beseem you well, but I dare not deliver you this horse, but if ye would take him from me." "That will I not do," said Sir Percivale, and so they parted. And Sir Percivale sat him down under a tree, and made sorrow out of measure; and, as he was there, there came a knight riding on the horse that the yeoman led, and he was clean armed.

V.

AND anon the yeoman came riding after as fast as ever he might, and asked Sir Percivale "if he saw any knight riding on his black steed?" "Yea, forsooth," said he, "why ask ye that of me?" "Ah! sir," said the yeoman, "that steed he hath taken from me by strength, wherefore my lord will slay me in what place soever he findeth me." "Well," said Sir Percivale, "what wouldst thou that I should do? thou seest well that I am on foot: but, and I had a good horse, I should bring him soon again." "Sir," said the yeoman, "take mine hackney, and do the best ye can, and I shall follow you on foot, to wit how ye shall speed." Then Sir Percivale mounted upon that hackney, and rode as fast as he might; and at the last he saw that knight, and then he cried, "Knight, turn again." And he turned and set his spear against Sir Percivale, and he smote the hackney in the midst of the breast, that he fell down dead to the earth, and there he had a great fall; and the other rode his way. And then Sir Percivale was waxed wrath, and cried, "Abide thou wicked knight, coward, and false-hearted knight, turn again and fight with me on foot." But he answered not, but passed forth his way. When Sir Percivale saw he would not turn, he cast away his helm and his sword, and said, "Now am I a very wretch; cursed and most unhappy above all other knights." So in this sorrow he abode all that day till it was night, and then he was faint, and laid him down and slept till it was midnight; and then he awaked, and saw before him a woman, that said unto him right fiercely, "Sir Percivale, what doest thou here?" He answered and said, "I do neither good nor evil." "If thou wilt ensure me," said she, "that thou wilt fulfil my will when I shall summon thee, I shall lend thee mine own horse, which shall bear thee whither thou wilt." Sir Percivale was glad of her proffer, and ensured her to fulfil all her desire. "Then abide ye here," said she, "and I shall go and fetch you a horse." And so she came soon again and brought a horse with her that was black. When Sir Percivale beheld that horse, he marvelled that he was so great and so well apparelled, and then he was so hardy that he leapt upon him, and took no heed to himself. And so anon as he was upon him, he thrust to him with his spurs, and so rode by a forest, and the moon shone clear, and within an hour and less he bore him four days' journey thence, till he came to a rough water that roared, and his horse would have borne him into it.

VI.

AND when Sir Percivale came nigh the brim, and saw the water so boisterous, he doubted to pass over it ; and then he made the sign of the cross on his forehead. When the fiend felt him so charged, he shook off Sir Percivale, and he went into the water crying and roaring, and making great sorrow, and it seemed to him that the water burnt. Then Sir Percivale perceived that it was a fiend, which would have brought him unto his perdition. Then he commended himself unto God, and prayed our Lord to keep him from all such temptations ; and so he prayed all that night, till on the morrow that it was day. Then saw he that he was on a wild mountain, which was closed with the sea nigh all about, that he might see no land about him which might relieve him, but wild beasts. And then he went in a valley, and there he saw a young serpent bring a young lion by the neck, and so he came by Sir Percivale : with that there camē a lion crying and roaring after the serpent ; and as soon as Sir Percivale saw this, he marvelled and hied him thither. But anon the lion had overtaken the serpent, and began battle with him ; and then Sir Percivale thought to help the lion, for he was the most natural beast of the two, and there gave the serpent such a buffet, that he had a deadly wound. When the lion saw that, he made no semblance to fight with him, but made him all the cheer that a beast might make a man. When Sir Percivale perceived that, he cast down his shield, the which was broken, and then he put off his helm for to gather wind, for he was greatly chafed with the serpent, and the lion went alway about him fawning

like a spaniel ; and then he stroked him with his hand upon
the neck, and upon the shoulders, and gave thanks unto God
of the fellowship of the beast. And, about noon, the lion took
his little whelp and trussed him, and bear him unto the place
that he came from. And then was Sir Percivale alone ; and,
as the story telleth, he was one of the men of the world, at that
time, that most believed in our Lord Jesu Christ. For in
those days there were but few folk that believed perfectly in
Almighty God, our Saviour and Redeemer Jesus Christ : for in
those days the son spared not the father, no more in con-
sideration than a stranger. And so the noble knight Sir
Percivale comforted himself in our Lord Jesus Christ, and
besought God that no temptation should bring him, nor
pervert him out of God's service, but for to endure and persevere
as his true champion. Thus, when Sir Percivale had prayed,
he saw the lion come toward him, and then he couched down at
his feet ; and all that night the lion and he slept together. And
when Sir Percivale slept, he dreamed a marvellous dream : that
there met with him two ladies, and the one sat upon a lion, and
that other sat upon a serpent ; and the one of them was young,
and the other was old, and the youngest he thought said, " Sir
Percivale, my lord saluteth thee, and sendeth thee word that
thou array thee and make thee ready, for to-morrow thou must
fight with the strongest champion of the world ; and if thou be
overcome, thou shalt not be quit for losing of any of thy members,
but thou shalt be ashamed to the world's end." And then he
asked her who was her lord ? and she said, " The greatest lord
of the world." And so she departed suddenly, and wist not
where she became.

<h2 style="text-align:center">VII.</h2>

THEN came forth the other lady that rode upon the serpent,
and she said, " Sir Percivale, I complain me of you that ye have
done to me, that have not offended you." "Certainly, madam,"
said he, "unto you, nor no lady I never offended." "Yes,"
said she, " I will tell you why : I have nourished in this place a
great while a serpent, which served me a great while, and
yesterday ye slew him, for the lion was not yours." "Madam,"
said Sir Percivale, "I know well that the lion is not mine ; but
I did it, for the lion is of a more gentler nature than the serpent,
and therefore I slew him ; me seemeth I did not amiss against
you. Madam," said he, "what would ye that I did ?" "I
would," said she, "that for the amends of my beast, that ye
become my man." And then he answered, "That will I not

grant you." "No," said she, "truly ye were never but my servant, save since ye received the homage of our Lord Jesu Christ ; and therefore I ensure you that, in what place soever I may find you without keeping, I shall take you as he that sometime was my man." And so she departed from Sir Percivale, and left him sleeping, the which was sore travailed of his vision ; and on the morrow he rose and blessed him, and he was passing feeble. Then was Sir Percivale ware in the sea, and saw a ship come sailing toward him ; and Sir Percivale went unto the ship, and found it covered within and without with white samite, and at the border stood an old man clothed in a surplice, in the likeness of a priest. " Sir," said Sir Percivale, " ye be welcome." " God keep you," said the good man. " Sir," said the old man, " of whence be ye ?" " Sir," said Sir Percivale, " I am of King Arthur's court, and a knight of the Round Table, the which am in the quest of the Sancgreal ; and here I am in great duress and misery, and never am I like to escape out of this wilderness." " Doubt ye not," said the good man, " and if ye be so true a knight as the high order of knighthood requireth, and also of heart as ye ought and should be, ye should not doubt nor mistrust that none enemy should hurt nor fear you." " What are ye ?" said Sir Percivale. " Sir," said the old man, " I am of a strange country, and hither I come to comfort you." " Sir," said Sir Percivale, " what signifieth my dreams that I dreamed this night ?" And there he told him altogether. " She that rode upon the lion," said the good man, " betokeneth the new law of Holy Church, that is to understand faith, good hope, belief, and baptism : for she seemed younger than the other, it is great reason, for she was born in the resurrection and the passion of our Lord Jesu Christ ; and for great love she came to thee to warn thee of the great battle that shall befall thee." " With whom shall I fight ?" said Sir Percivale. " With the most champion of the world," said the old man : " for as the lady said, but if thou quit thee well thou shalt not be quit by losing of one member, but yet thou shalt be ashamed to the world's end. And she that rode upon the serpent signifieth the old law, and that serpent betokeneth a fiend, and why she blamed thee that thou slewest her servant, it betokeneth nothing. The serpent that thou slewest betokeneth the devil that thou rodest upon to the rock ; and when thou madest the sign of the cross, there thou slewest him, and put away his power. And then she asked thee amends, and to become her man, and thou saidest thou wouldest not, that was to make thee to believe on her, and leave thy baptism." So he commanded Sir Percivale to depart ; and so he leapt over the board, and the ship and all went away he wist not whither. Then he went up unto the rock, and found the lion that alway kept him fellowship, and had great joy of him.

VIII.

By that Sir Percivale had abidden there till mid-day, he saw a ship come rowing in the sea, as all the wind of the world had driven it. And so it drove under that rock ; and when Sir Percivale saw this, he hied him thither, and found the ship covered with silk more blacker than any bier ; and therein was a gentlewoman of great beauty, and she was richly beseen, that none might be better. And when she saw Sir Percivale, she said, " Who brought you into this wilderness, where ye be never like to pass hence, for ye shall die here for hunger and mischief." " Damsel," said Sir Percivale, " I serve the best man in the world, and in his service he shall not suffer me to die ; for who that knocketh shall enter, and who that asketh shall have, and who that seeketh him he hideth him not." And then she said, " Sir Percivale, wot ye what I am." " Yea," said Sir Percivale. " Now, who told ye my name ? " said she. " Damsel," said Sir Percivale, " I know you better than ye ween." " And I come out of the vast forest where I found the red knight with the white shield," said the damsel. " Ah ! damsel," said he, " with that knight would I meet passing fair." " Sir," said she, " and ye will ensure me, by the faith ye owe unto knighthood, that ye shall do my will what time I shall summon you, I bring you to that knight." " Yea," said he, " I shall promise you your desire." " Well," said she, " I shall tell you : I saw him in the forest chasing two knights to a water, the which is called Mortraise, and he drove them into the water for dread of death. And the two knights passed over, and the red knight passed after, and there was his horse drowned, and he with great strength escaped unto the land." Thus she told him, and Sir Percivale was passing glad thereof. Then she asked him if he had eaten any meat lately : " Nay, truly madam," said he ; " I have eaten no meat nigh these three days, but late here I spake with a good man that fed me with his good and holy words, and refreshed me greatly." " Ah ! sir knight," said she, " that same man is an enchanter and a multiplier of words, for and ye believe him ye shall plainly be ashamed, and die in this rock for pure hunger, and be eaten by wild beasts : and ye be a young man and a goodly

knight, and I shall help you, and ye will." "What are ye,"
said Sir Percivale, "that proffereth me this great kindness ?"
" I am," said she, "a gentlewoman that am disinherited, which
was sometime the richest woman of the world." "Damsel,"
said Sir Percivale, "who hath disinherited you? for I have
great pity of you." "Sir," said she, "I dwelled with the
greatest man of the world, and he made me so fair and so clean,
that there was none like me ; of that great beauty I had a little
pride, more than I ought to have had. Also, I said a word that
pleased him not, and then he would not suffer me to be any
longer in his company, and so drove me from mine heritage,
and so disinherited me ; and he had never no pity of me, nor
of none of my counsel, nor of my court ; and since, sir knight, it
hath befallen me so, through me and mine I have taken from
him many of his men, and made them become my men, for
they ask never nothing of me but I give it them, that and much
more. Thus I and all my servants war against him night and
day ; therefore I know now no good knight, nor no good man,
but I get them on my side and I may : and, because I know
that thou art a good knight, I beseech thee to help me, and for
ye be a fellow of the Round Table, wherefore ye ought not to
fail no gentlewoman that is disinherited, and if she besought
you of help."

IX.

THEN Sir Percivale promised her all the help that he might,
and then she thanked him : and at that time the weather was
hot, and then she called unto her a gentlewoman, and bade her
to bring forth a pavilion ; and so she did, and pitched it upon
the gravel. "Sir," said she, "now may ye rest you in this heat
of the day." Then he thanked her, and she put off his helm
and his shield, and there he slept a great while. And then he
awoke, and asked her if she had any meat ; and she said, "Yea,
ye shall have meat enough." And so there was set upon the
table much meat ; and there was so great plenty, that Sir Percivale had great marvel thereof, for there was all manner of
meats that he could think on ; also, he drank there the strangest
wine that ever he drank, as him thought, and therewithal he
was a little chafed more than he ought to be : with that he
beheld the gentlewoman, and him thought that she was the fairest
creature that ever he saw. And then Sir Percivale proffered
her love, and prayed her that she would be his love ; and then
she refused him in a manner when he required her, for because
he should be the more ardent on her ; and he ceased not to

pray her of love. And when she saw him well chafed, then she said, " Sir Percivale, wit ye well that I shall not fulfil your will, but if ye swear from henceforth ye shall be my true servant, and to do nothing but that I shall command you : will ye ensure me this, as ye be a true knight ? " " Yea, fair lady," said he, " by the faith of my body." " Well," said she, " now shall ye do with me whatsoever shall please you : and now wit ye well that ye are the knight in the world that I most desired." But then by adventure and grace Sir Percivale saw his sword lie upon the ground all naked, in whose pommel was a red cross, and the sign of the cross therein, and he bethought him of his knighthood, and on his promise made beforehand unto the good man. Then he made a sign of the cross on his forehead, and therewithal the pavilion turned upside down ; and then it changed unto a smoke and a black cloud, and then he was dread, and cried out aloud,

X.

" FAIR sweet Father, Jesu Christ, let me not be shamed, that was near lost, had not thy grace been." And then he looked into the ship, and saw her enter therein, which said, " Sir Percivale, ye have betrayed me." And so she went, with the wind roaring and crying, that it seemed that all the water burnt after her. Then Sir Percivale made great sorrow, and drew his sword unto him, saying, " Since my flesh will be my master, I shall punish it," and therewith he rove himself through the thigh, that the blood started about him, and he said, " Oh, good Lord, take this in compensation of that I have done against thee, my good Lord." So then he clothed him, and armed him, and called himself wretch, saying, " How nigh I had lost that which I should never have gotten again, which is my virginity ; for that may never be recovered after it be once lost." And then he stopped his bleeding wound with a piece of his shirt. And thus, as he made his moan, he saw the same ship from the Orient come, that the good man was in the day before ; and then was the noble knight ashamed with himself, and therewith he fell into a swoon ; and when he awoke he went unto him weakly, and there he saluted this good man. And then he asked Sir Percivale how he had done since he departed from him. " Sir," said he, " here was a gentlewoman, that led me into deadly sin," and told him all. " Know ye not her ? " said the old man. " Nay," said he, " but well I wot the fiend sent her hither, to shame me." " Oh, good knight," said he, " thou art a fool ; for that gentlewoman was the master fiend of hell ; the which hath power over all devils, and that was the old lady that thou sawest in thy vision, riding upon a serpent." Then he told Sir Percivale how our Lord Jesu Christ beat him out of heaven for his sin, the which was the most brightest angel of heaven ; and therefore he lost his heritage, "and that was the champion that thou foughtest withal, the which had overcome thee, had not the grace of God been. Now beware, Sir Percivale, and take this for an ensample." And then the good man vanished away. Then Sir Percivale took his armour, and entered into the ship, and so departed from thence.

THE BOOK OF THE ACHIEVEMENT OF THE HOLY GRAIL.

I.

AS, saith the history, that when Sir Galahad had rescued Sir Percivale from the twenty knights, he rode unto a waste forest, wherein he rode many journeys, and found there many adventures, which he brought to an end. Then he took his way to sea on a day; and it befell that he passed by a castle where was a tournament; but they without had done so much, that they within were put to the worst, yet they within were knights good enough. And when Sir Galahad saw that those within were at so great a mischief, that men slew them at the entry of the castle, then he thought to help them, and put forth his spear, and smote the first that he fell to the earth, and the spear brake all to pieces: then he drew his sword, and smote there as they were thickest ; and so he did there wonderful deeds of arms, that they all marvelled thereof. Then it happened that Sir Gawaine and Sir Ector de Maris were with the knights without ; but when he espied the white shield with the red cross, the one said to the other, " Yonder is the good knight, Sir Galahad : now he should be a great fool that would meet with him to fight." So, by adventure, he came by Sir Gawaine, and he smote him so hard, that he cleave his helm, and the coif of the iron unto his head, so that Sir Gawaine fell to the earth ; but the stroke was great, that it slanted down to the earth, and carved the horse's shoulder in two. When Sir Ector saw Sir Gawaine down, he drew him aside, and thought it no wisdom for to abide him, and also for natural love, because he was his uncle. Thus, through his great hardiness, he beat back all the knights without ; and then they within came out and chased them all about. But when Sir Galahad saw that there would none turn again, he stole away privily, so that no man wist where he became. "Now, by my head," said Sir Gawaine unto Sir Ector, "the words are true that were said of Sir Launcelot du Lake, that the sword which stuck in the stone should give me such a buffet, that I would not have it for the best castle that is in the world ; and, certainly, now it is proved true, for never before had I such a stroke of man's hand." "Sir," said Sir Ector, "me seemeth your quest is done." "And yours is not," said Sir Gawaine, "but mine is done, I shall seek no further." Then Sir Gawaine was borne into a castle and unarmed him, and laid him in a rich bed, and a leech found, that he might live, and be whole within a month. Thus Sir Gawaine and Sir Ector abode together, for Sir Ector would not away till Sir Gawaine were whole. And the good knight Sir Galahad rode so long till that he came that night to the castle of Carbnecke, and it befell him that he was benighted in a hermitage ; and so the good knight was full glad when he saw that it was a knight-errant. So when they were at rest, there came a gentlewoman knocking at the door, and called Sir Galahad. And so the good man came to the door to wit what she would. Then she called the hermit Sir Ulfin : "I am a gentlewoman that would speak with the knight that is with you." Then the good man awaked Sir Galahad, and bid him arise and speak with a gentlewoman, which seemeth hath great need of you. Then Sir Galahad went to her, and asked her what she would. "Sir Galahad," said she, "I will that ye arm you, and mount upon your horse and follow me, for I will show you within these three days the highest adventure that ever any knight saw." Anon Sir Galahad armed him, and took his horse and commended him to God, and bid the gentlewoman go, and he would follow there as she liked

<h2 style="text-align:center">II.</h2>

So the damsel rode as fast as her palfry might gallop, till that she came to the sea that was called Collibe : and at night they came unto a castle in a valley, that was closed with running water, and with high and strong walls : and she entered into the castle with Sir Galahad, and there had he great cheer, for the lady of that castle was the damsel's lady. So when he was unarmed, the damsel said to the lady, " Madam, shall we abide here this night?" " Nay," said she, " but till he hath dined and slept a little." So he eat, and slept till the maid called him, and armed him by torch-light. And when the maid and he were both horsed, the lady took Sir Galahad a fair shield and a rich. And so they departed from the castle, and rode till they came to the sea-side ; and there they found a ship where Sir Bors and Sir Percivale were in, the which cried on the ship-board, " Sir Galahad, ye be welcome, we have abidden you long." And when he heard them, he asked them what they were. " Sir," said the damsel, " leave your horse here, and I shall leave mine ;" and took their saddles and their bridles with them, and made a cross on them, and so entered into the ship ; and the two knights received him with great joy, and every one knew the other. And so the wind arose and drove them through the sea unto a marvellous place, and within a while it dawned ; then Sir Galahad took off his helm and his sword, and asked of his fellows from whence the fair ship came. " Truly," said they, " ye wot as well as we, but of God's grace." And then they told every one to other of their adventures, and of their great temptation. " Truly," said Sir Galahad, " ye are much bounden to God, for ye have escaped great adventures ; and had not the gentlewoman been, I had not come hither ; for as for you, I weened never to have found in this strange country." " Ah, Sir Galahad," said Sir Bors, " if that Sir Launcelot, your father, were here, then were we well at ease, for then me seemeth we should lack nothing." . " That may not be," said Sir Galahad, " but if it please our Lord." And by then the ship went from the land of Logris, and, by adventure, it arrived between two rocks, passing great and marvellous, but there they might not land, for there was a whirlpool of the sea, but there was another ship, and upon it they might go without danger. " Go we thither," said the gentlewoman, " and there shall we see adventures ; for so it is our Lord's will." And when they came thither, they found the ship rich enough, but they found neither man nor woman therein, but they found in the end of the ship two fair letters written, which said a dreadful word and a marvellous. " Thou man which shall enter into this ship, beware thou be in steadfast belief, for I am faith ; and, therefore, beware how thou enterest, for and thou fail, I shall not help thee." " Then," said the gentlewoman, " wot ye what I am." " Certainly," said he, " not of my witting." " Wit ye well," said she, " I am thy sister, that am daughter to King Pellinore ; and, therefore, wit ye well that ye are the man in the world that I most like : and, if ye be not in perfect belief of Jesu Christ, and enter not to no manner of wise, for then should ye perish in the ship, for it is so perfect it will suffer no sin in it." And when Sir Percivale knew that she was his sister, he was inwardly glad, and said, " Fair sister, I shall enter therein, for if I be a miscreature, or an untrue knight, there shall I perish."

III.

IN the meanwhile Sir Galahad blessed him and entered therein, and then next the gentlewoman, and then Sir Bors and Sir Percivale. And when they were therein, they found it so marvellous fair and rich, that they had great marvel thereof ; and in the midst of the ship was a fair bed, and Sir Galahad went thereto, and found there a crown of silk, and at the feet was a sword, fair and rich, and it was drawn out of the scabbard half-a-foot and more, and the sword was of divers fashions, and the pommel was of stone, and there was in it all manner of colours, that any man might find, and every one of the colours had divers virtues ; and the scales of the haft were of two ribs of divers beasts ; the one beast was a serpent, which was conversant in Calidone, and is called the serpent of the fiend ; and the bone of him is of such a virtue, that there is no hand that handled it shall never be weary or hurt ; and the other beast is a fish, which is not right great, and haunteth the flood of Ousrates ; and that fish is called Ortanar : and his bones be of such a manner of kind, that who that handleth them he shall have so much courage, that he shall never be weary, and he shall not think on joy nor sorrow that he hath had, but only the thing which he beholdeth before him. And as for this sword, there shall never no man begripe it to the handle but one, but he shall pass all other. " In the name of God," said Sir Percivale, " I shall essay to handle it." So he set his hand to the sword, but he might not begripe it. " By my faith," said he, " now have I failed." Sir Bors set his hand to it and failed. Then Sir Galahad beheld the sword, and saw the letters as red as blood, that said, " Let see who shall essay to draw me out of my scabbard ; but if he be more hardier than other ; and who that draweth me, wit ye well that he shall never fail of shame of his body, or be wounded unto the death." " By my faith," said Sir Galahad, " I would draw this sword out of the scabbard, but

the offending is so great that I shall not send my hand thereto."
"Now, sir," said the gentlewoman, "wit ye well that the drawing of this sword is warned unto all men, save unto you."   And
then beheld they the scabbard, which seemed to be of a serpent's
skin, and thereon were letters of gold and silver ; and the girdle
was but poorly to account, and not able to sustain such a rich
sword, and the letters said, "He that shall wield me ought to
be more hardier than any other, if that he bear me as truly as I
ought to be borne ; for the body of him which I ought to hang
by, he shall not be shamed in no place while he is girded with
this girdle, nor never none shall be so hardy to do away this
girdle, for it ought not be done away but by the hands of a
maid, and that she be a King and Queen's daughter, and she
must be a maid all the days of her life, both in will and in deed ;
and, if she break her virginity, she shall die the most villainous
death that ever did any woman."   "Sir," said Sir Percivale,
"turn this sword, that we may see what is on the other side."
And it was as red as blood, with black letters as any coal, which
said, "He that shall praise me most, most shall he find me to
blame at a great necessity, and to whom I shall be most
debonair, shall I be most felon, and that shall be at one time."

IV.

"Sir," said she, "there was a King, that hight Pelleas, the
maimed King ; and, while he might ride, he supported much
Christendom, and the holy church.   So upon a day he hunted
in a wood of his, which lasted unto the sea, and at the last he
lost his hounds and his knights, save only one, and there he and
his knight went till that they come towards Ireland, and there he
found the ship.   And when he saw the letters, and understood
them, yet he entered, for he was right perfect of his life.   But
his knight had no hardiness to enter, and there he found this
sword, and drew it out as much as ye may see ; so therewithal
entered a spear, wherewith he was smitten through both his
thighs, and never sith might he be healed, nor nought shall
before we come to him.   Thus," said she, "was not King
Pelleas, your grandsire, maimed for his hardiness."   "In the
name of God, damsel," said Sir Galahad.   So they went toward
the bed to behold all about it, and above the bed's head there
hung two fair swords ; also there were two spindles which were
as white as any snow ; and there were other that were as red
as any blood, and other above as green as any emerald : of

these colours were the spindles, and of natural colour within, and without any painting. "These spindles," said the damsel, "were when sinful Eve came to gather fruit, for which Adam and she were put out of paradise, she took with her the bough on which the apple hung : then perceived she that the branch was fair and green, and she remembered her of the loss that came from the tree ; then she thought to keep the branch as long as she might, and because she had no coffer to keep it in, she put it into the ground ; so by the will of our Lord, the branch grew to a great tree, within a little while, and was as white as any snow, branches, boughs, and leaves, that it was a token a maid planted it. But after God came unto Adam, and bade him know his wife. So was Adam with his wife under the same tree ; and anon the tree that was white became as green as any grass, and all that came of it. And in the same time was Abel begotten. Thus was the tree long of green colour. And so it befell, a long time after, under the same tree Cain slew his brother Abel, whereof befell full great marvel ; for anon as Abel had received the death under the green tree, it lost the green colour and became red, and that was in tokening of the blood. And anon all the plants died thereof ; but the tree grew, and waxed marvellous fair, and it was the fairest tree, and the most delectable that any man might behold ; and so died the plants that grew out of it before the time that Abel was slain under it. So long endured the tree till that Solomon, King David's son, reigned, aed held the land after his father. This Solomon was wise, and knew the virtues of stones and of trees : and so he knew the course of the stars, and many other things. This Solomon had an evil wife, where-through he weened that there had never been no good woman ; and so he despised them in his books. So a voice answered him once, 'Solomon, if heaviness come unto a man by a woman, yet reck thou never ; for there shall come a woman, whereof there shall come greater joy unto man a hundred times more than the heaviness giveth sorrow or heaviness ; and the same woman shall be born of thy lineage.'

"Then when King Solomon heard these words, he held himself but a fool, and the truth he perceived by old books ; also the Holy Ghost showed him the coming of the glorious Virgin Mary. Then asked he of the voice, 'If it should be in the line of his lineage. "Nay,' said the voice ; 'but there shall come a man which shall be of a pure maid, and the last of your blood, and he shall be as good a knight as was Duke Josue, thy brother-in-law.'

V.

"'Now have I certified thee of that thou stoodest in doubt.' Then was Solomon glad that there should come such a one of his lineage, but ever he marvelled and studied who that should be, and what his name might be. His wife perceived that he studied, and thought that she would know it at some season ; and so she awaited her time, and asked of him the cause of his studying ; and there he told her all together how the voice told him. 'Well,' said she, 'I shall let a ship be made of the best wood, and most durable that men may find.' So Solomon sent for all the best carpenters of the land. And when they had made the ship, the lady said unto Solomon, 'Sir,' said she, 'since it is so that this knight ought to pass all other knights of chivalry, which have been before him, and also that shall come after him, moreover I shall tell you,' said she, 'ye shall go into our Lord's temple, whereas is King David's sword, your father, the which is the marvellest and the sharpest that ever was taken in any knight's hand : therefore take that, and take ye off the pommel, and thereto make ye a pommel of precious stones, that it be so subtly made that no man perceive it, but that they be all one ; and after make a hilt so marvellously and wondrously, that no man may know it, and after make a marvellous sheath. And when you have made all this, I shall let a girdle be made thereto, such as shall please you.' And this King Solomon made it as she devised, both the ship and all the remnant. And when the ship was ready in the sea for to sail, the lady let make a great bed, and marvellous rich, and set herself upon the bed's head, covered with silk, and laid the sword at the bed's feet ; and the girdles were of hemp. And therewith was the King angry. 'Sir, wit ye well,' said she, 'that I have none so high a thing that were worthy to sustain so big a sword, and a maid shall bring other knights thereto ; but I wot not when it shall be, nor what time.' And there she let a covering be made to the ship of cloth, that shall never rot for no manner of weather. Yet went that lady and made a carpenter to come to that tree which Abel was slain under. 'Now,' said she, 'carve me out of this tree as much wood as will make me a spindle.' 'Ah ! madam,' said the carpenter, 'this is the tree, the which our first mother planted.' 'Do it,' said she, 'or else I shall destroy thee.' Anon as the carpenter began to work, there came out drops of blood, and then would he have left ; but she would not suffer him. And so he took away as much wood as might well make a spindle ; and so she made him take as much of the green tree, and of the white tree. And when these three spindles were shapen, she made them to be fastened on the canopy of the bed. When Solomon saw this, he said to his wife, 'Ye have done marvellously; for, though all the world were here now, they could not tell wherefore all this was made, but our Lord himself, and thou that hast done it, wottest not what it shall betoken.' 'Now let it be,' said she, 'for ye shall hear tidings sooner than ye ween.'

VI.

"THAT night lay King Solomon before the ship with a small fellowship. And when King Solomon was asleep, he thought there came from heaven a great company of angels and alighted into the ship, and took water which was brought by an angel in a vessel of silver, and besprent all the ship; and after he came to the sword, and drew letters in the hilts; and after went to the ship-board, and wrote there other letters which said, 'Thou man that wilt enter within me, beware that thou be full within of faith, for I am but faith and belief.' When King Solomon espied these letters, he was sore abashed, so that he durst not enter, and so drew him back; and anon the ship was shoven into the sea, and it went so fast that he lost the sight of it within a little while. And then a little voice said, 'Solomon, the last knight of thy lineage shall rest in this bed.' Then went King Solomon and awaked his wife, and told her the adventures of the ship."

Now saith the history, that a great while the three fellows beheld the bed and the three spindles; then they were of natural colours, without any manner of painting. Then they lift up a cloth which was above the ground, and there they found a rich purse by seeming; and Sir Percivale took it, and therein he found a writing, and so he read it, and spake of the manner of the spindles, and of the ship from whence it came, and by whom it was made. "Now," said Sir Galahad, "where shall we find the gentlewoman that shall make new girdles to the sword?" "Fair sir," said Sir Percivale's sister, "dismay you not, for by the leave of God I shall let a girdle be made to the sword, such a one as shall belong thereto." And then she opened a box and took out girdles, which were seemly wrought with golden threads; and thereupon were set full of precious stones, and a rich buckle of gold. "Lo! lords," said the gentlewoman, "here is a girdle that ought to be set about the sword ; and wit ye well that the greatest part of this girdle was made of my hair, the which I loved full well while I was a woman of the world ; but as soon as I wist that this adventure was ordained me, I clipped off my hair, and made this girdle in the name of God." "Ye are well found," said Sir Bors, "for truly ye have put us out of a great pain, wherein we should have entered, nor had your teaching been." Then went the gentlewoman, and set it up on the girdle of the sword. "Now," said the three fellows, "what is the right name of the sword, and what shall we call it?" "Truly," said she, "the name of the sword is, the Sword with the Strange Girdles, and the scabbard, Mover of Blood ; for no man that hath blood in him shall never see the one part of the scabbard which was made of the Tree of Life." Then they said unto Sir Galahad, "In the name of Jesu Christ we pray you that ye gird you with this sword, which hath been so much desired in the realm of Logris." "Now let me begin," said Sir Galahad, "to gripe this sword for to give you courage ; but wit ye well that it belongeth no more to me than it doth to you." And then he griped about it with his fingers a great deal : and then she girded him about the middle with the sword. "Now reck I not, though I die ; for now I hold me one of the blessed maidens of the world, which hath made thee now the worthiest knight of the world." "Fair damsel," said Sir Galahad, "ye have done so much, that I shall be your knight all the days of my life." Then they went from that ship, and went into the other ship. And anon the wind drove them into the sea a great pace, but they had no victuals. But it happened that they came on the morrow to a castle that men call Carteloise, that was in the marshes of Scotland ; and, when they had passed the port, the gentlewoman said, "Lords here be arriven, that and they wist that ye were of King Arthur's court, ye should anon be essayed." "Damsel," said Sir Galahad, "he that cast us out of the rock shall deliver us from them."

VII.

So it befell, as they spake thus, there came a squire by them, and asked what they were ; and they said they were of King Arthur's court. "Is that sooth ?" said he. "Now, by my head," said he, "ye are evil arrived." And then returned he again unto the chief fortress ; and within a while they heard a horn blow. Then a gentlewoman came to them and asked them, of whence they came? and they told her. "Fair lords," said she, "return again if ye may, for God's love ! for ye be come to your death." "Now," said they, "we will not turn again ; for he shall help us in whose service we be entered." Then, as they stood thus talking, there came knights well armed, and bid them yield them, or else they would die. "That yielding," said they, "shall be evil to you." And therewithal they let their horses run together ; and Sir Percivale smote the foremost to the earth, and took his horse and mounted upon him ; and in likewise did Sir Galahad. Also Sir Bors served another so ; for they had no horses in the country ; for they had left their horses, when they took their ship, in other countries. And so, when they were horsed, then they began to set upon them. And the knights of the castle fled into the strongest fortress, and the three knights followed after them into the castle ; and so they alighted on foot, and with their swords slew them downright, and gat them into the hall. So, when they beheld the great multitude of people which they had slain, they held themselves great sinners. "Certainly," said Sir Bors, "I ween and God had loved them, we should not have had power to have slain them thus ; but they have done so much against our Lord, that he will not suffer them to reign any longer." "Say ye not so," said Sir Galahad, "for, if they misdid against God, the vengeance is not ours, but to him which hath power thereof." So came there out of a chamber a good man, which was a priest, and bare God's body in a cup ; and, when he saw the which lay dead in the hall, he was all abashed. And Sir Galahad put off his helm, and kneeled down, and so did his two fellows. "Sir," said they, "have ye no dread of us ; for we be of the court of King Arthur?" Then asked the good man, how they were slain so suddenly? and they told him. "Truly," said the good man, "if ye might live as long as the world shall endure, nor might ye never have done so great an alms-deed as this." "Sir," said Sir Galahad, "I repent me much, inasmuch as they were christened." "Nay, repent ye not," said he, "for they were not christened : and I shall tell you how I wot of this castle. Here was the Earl Hernox but one year, and he had three sons, good knights of arms, and a daughter, the fairest gentlewoman that men knew. So those three knights loved their sister so sore, that they grew full fain, and dishonoured her ; and because she cried to her father they slew her, and took their father and put him in prison, and wounded him nigh unto the death. But a cousin of her's rescued him. And then did they great untruth ; for they slew priests and clerks, and made to beat down chapels, that our Lord's service might not be served nor said : and this same day their father sent to me for to be confessed and houseled. But such shame had never man as I had this day with the three brethren. But the earl bade me suffer ; for he said that they should no longer endure : for three servants of our Lord God should destroy them. And now it is brought to an end : and by this may ye wit, that our Lord is not displeased with your deeds." "Certainly," said Sir Galahad, "and it had not pleased our Lord, never would we have killed so many men in so little a while." And then they brought the Earl Hernox out of prison into the midst of the hall, which knew Sir Galahad anon ; and yet he never seen him before, but by revelation of our Lord.

VIII.

THEN began he to weep full tenderly, and said, "Long have I abidden your coming ; but, for God's love, hold me in your arms, that my soul may depart out of my body in so good a man's arms as ye be." "Gladly," said Sir Galahad. And then one said on high that all heard it, "Sir Galahad, well hast thou avenged me on God's enemies. Now behoveth thee to go to the maimed King, as soon as thou mayest ; for he shall receive by thee his health, the which had bidden so long," And therewith the soul departed from the body ; and Sir Galahad made him to be buried as he ought to be. So departed the three knights, and Sir Percivale's sister with them ; and so they came into a waste forest, and there they saw before them a white hart, which four lions led. Then they took them to assent for to follow after, for to know whether they repaired. And so they rode after a great pace, till that they came to a valley, and thereby was a hermitage, whereas a good man dwelled ; and the hart and the lions entered in also. So, when they saw all this, they turned unto the chapel, and saw the good man in a religious mood, and in the armour of our Lord ; for he would sing mass of the Holy Ghost : and so they entered and heard mass ; and, at the secrets of that mass, they three saw the hart become a man, the which marvelled them, and set upon the altar in a rich seat ; and saw the four lions changed, the one to the form of a man, and the other unto the form of a lion, and the third unto an eagle, and the fourth was changed unto an ox. Then took they their seat where the hart sat, which went out through a glass window, and there was nothing perished nor broken. And they heard a voice that said thus :—" In such a manner entered the Son of God into the womb of the maid Mary, whose virginity was not perished nor hurt." And, when they heard these words, they fell down to the ground, and were astonished : and therewith was a great clearness : and, when they were come to themselves again, they went to the good man, and prayed him that he would tell them the truth. "What thing have ye seen?" said he. And they told him all that they had seen. "Ah ! lords," said he, " ye are welcome. Now wot I well ye be the good knight, the which shall bring the Sancgreal to an end ; for ye be they to whom our Lord shall show great secrets. And well ought our Lord to be signified unto a hart ; for the hart, when he is old, weareth young again into his white skin : right so cometh again our Lord from death to life ; for he lost earthly flesh, that was the deadly flesh, which he had taken in the womb of the blessed Virgin Mary : and for that cause appeared our Lord as a white hart, without a spot. And the four that were with him is to understand the four evangelists, which set in writing part of Jesu Christ's deeds, that he did sometimes when he was among you an earthly man. For wit ye well, that never erst nor might no knight know the truth ; for oftentimes or this our Lord showed him unto good men, and unto good knights, in likeness of a hart : but, I suppose that, from henceforth, ye shall see him no more." And then they joyed much, and dwelled there all that day ; and, on the morrow, when they had heard mass, they departed, and commended the good man unto God. And so they came unto a castle, and passed by ; so there came a knight armed, and said, "Lords, hearken what I shall say unto you.

IX.

"This gentlewoman that ye lead with you is a maid." "Sir," said she, " a maid I am." Then he took her by the bridle and said, " By the holy cross, ye shall not escape me, before ye have yielded the custom of the castle." "Let her go," said Sir Percivale, " ye be not wise : for a maid, in what place soever she cometh, she is free." So, in the meanwhile, there came out of the castle a ten or twelve knights, armed ; and with them came a gentlewoman which held a dish of silver. And then, "This gentlewoman must yield us the custom of this castle." " Sir," said a knight, " what maid that passeth hereby shall give this dish full of blood of her right arm." "Blame have ye," said

Sir Galahad, "that brought up such customs : and, so God me save, I ensure you, that of this gentlewoman ye shall fail as long as I live." "So God me help," said Sir Percivale, "I had rather be slain." "And I also," said Sir Bors. "By my faith," said the knight, "then shall ye die ; for ye may not endure against us, though ye were the best knights of the world." Then let they run each to other ; and the three fellows beat the ten knights, and then set their hands unto their swords, and beat them down, and slew them. Then there came out of the castle well a threescore knights all armed. "Fair lords," said the three fellows, "have mercy upon yourselves, and have not to do with us." "Nay, fair lords," said the knights of the castle, "we counsel you to withdraw you ; for ye are the best knights of the world ; and, therefore, do ye no more. We will let you with this harm ; but we must needs have the custom." "Certainly," said Sir Galahad ; "for nought speak ye well." Said they, "Will ye die ?" "We be not come thereto," said Sir Galahad. Then began they to meddle together ; and Sir Galahad, with the strange girdles, drew his sword, and smote on the right hand and on the left hand, and slew whom that would abide him, and did such marvel, that there was none that saw him but that they weened he had been none earthly knight, but a monster. And his two fellows helped him passing well : and so they held their journey every each in like hard, till that it was night. Then must they needs depart. So there came a good knight, and said to the three fellows, "If ye will come in to-night, and take such harbour as here is, ye shall be right welcome ; and we shall ensure you, by the faith of our bodies, as we are true knights, to leave you in such estate to-morrow as we find you, without any falsehood : and, as soon as ye know of the custom, we dare say that ye will accord thereto." "Therefore, for God's love," said the gentlewoman, "go thither, and spare not for me." "Go we," said Sir Galahad. And so they entered into the castle ; and, when they were alighted, they made of them great joy. So, within a while, the three knights asked the custom of the castle, and wherefore it was. "What it is," said they, "we will say you the truth.

X.

"THERE is in this castle a gentlewoman, which we have : and this castle is hers, and many other more. So it befell, many years ago, there fell upon her a malady ; and, when she had lain a great while, she fell into a leprosy, and of no leech she could have no remedy. But at the last an old man said, 'And she might have a dish full of the blood of a maid and a clean virgin, in will and in work, and a king's daughter, that blood would be her health, and for to anoint her therewith.' And for this thing was this custom made." "Now," said Sir Percivale's sister, "fair knights, I see well that this gentlewoman is but dead, but if she have so much of my blood." "Certainly," said Sir Galahad, "and if ye bleed so much as ye may die." "Truly," said she, "and I die for to heal her, then shall I get me great worship and soul's health, and worship unto my lineage. And better is one harm than twain ; and, therefore, there shall be no more battle : but, to-morrow, I shall yield you the custom of the castle."

And then there was great joy, more than ever there was afore : for else had there been mortal war on the morrow, notwithstanding she would none other, whether they would or not. All that night were the three fellows eased with the best ; and, on the morrow, they heard mass. And Sir Percivale's sister bid bring forth the sick lady : so she was brought forth before her, which was full evil at ease. Then said she, "Who shall let me blood ?" So anon there came one forth to let her blood ; and she bled so much, that the dish was full. Then she lift up her hand and blessed her. And then she said unto the lady, "Madam, I am come by my death to make you whole ; for God's love, pray for me." With that she fell into a swoon. Then Sir Galahad, Sir Percivale, and Sir Bors started up to her, and lift her up, and staunched her blood : but she had bled so much, that she might not live. Then, when she was awake, she said, "Fair brother, Sir Percivale, I must die for the healing of this lady ; so I require you that ye bury not me in this country ; but, as soon as I am dead, put me in a boat at the next haven, and let me go as adventure will lead me ; and as soon as ye three come to the city of Sarras, there to achieve the Holy Grail, ye shall find me under a tower arrived, and there bury me in the spiritual place. For, I say you so much, there shall Sir Galahad be buried, and ye also in the same place." So when Sir Percivale understood these words, he granted it her, weeping. And then said a voice : "Lords and fellows, to-morrow at prime ye three shall depart from other, till the adventure bring you unto the maimed King." Then asked she her Saviour, and, as soon as she had received him, the soul departed from the body. So the same day was the lady healed, when she was enjointed with all. Then Sir Percivale made a letter, of all that she had holpen them, as in strange adventures, and put it in her right hand, and so laid her in a barge, and covered it with silk ; and so the wind arose, and drove the barge from the land, and all knights beheld it, till it was out of their sight. Then they drew all unto the castle ; and so forthwith there fell a sudden tempest of thunder, lightning, and rain, as all the earth would have broken. So half the castle turned upside down ; so it passed even-song or the tempest was ceased. Then they saw before them a knight armed, and wounded hard in the body and in the head, that said, "O, Lord God, succour me, for now it is need." After this knight came another knight and a dwarf, which cried to him afar, "Stand, ye may not escape." Then the wounded knight held up his hands unto God, that he should not die in such tribulation. "Truly," said Sir Galahad, "I shall succour him, for his sake that he calleth upon." "Sir," said Sir Bors, "I shall do it ; for it is not for you : for he is but one knight." "Sir," said he, "I grant." So Sir Bors took his horse, and commended him to God, and rode after to rescue the wounded knight.

XI.

THE story saith, that all night Sir Galahad and Sir Percivale were in a chapel, in their prayers, for to save Sir Bors. So on the morrow they dressed them in their harness, toward the castle, for to wit what was betide of them therein ; and, when they came there, they found neither man nor woman but what they were dead, by the vengeance of the Lord. With that they heard a voice, which said, "This vengeance is for bloodshedding of maidens." Also they found, at the end of the chapel and churchyard, and therein they might see forty fair tombs. And that place was so fair, and so delectable, that it seemed them there had been no tempest : for there lay the bodies of all the dead maidens, which were martyred for the sick ; also they found the name of every each of them, and of what blood they were come. And were all of kings' blood ; and twelve of them were knights' daughters. Then they departed, and went into a forest. "Now," said Sir Percivale unto Sir Galahad, "we must depart ; so pray we our Lord that we may meet together in short time." Then took they off their helms, and kissed together, and wept at their departing.

———

XII.

THE story saith, that when Sir Launcelot was come to the water of Morteise, as it is rehearsed before, he was in great peril, and so he laid him down and slept, and took his adventure that God would send him. So when he was asleep, there came a vision unto him, and said, " Launcelot, arise up, and take thine armour, and enter into the first ship that thou shalt find." And when he had heard these words he started up, and saw a great clearness about him, and then he lift up his hand, and blessed him ; and so took his armour, and made him ready. And by adventure he came by a strand, and found a ship, the which was without sail and oars ; and, as soon as he was within the ship, there he felt the most sweetest savour that ever he felt, and he was filled with all things that he thought on or desired. Then he said, " Fair Father, Jesu Christ, I wot not in what joy I am, for this joy passeth all earthly joys that ever I was in ;" and so in this joy he laid him down on the ship-board, and slept till daylight. And when he awoke, he found there a fair bed, and therein lying a gentlewoman dead, the which was Sir Percivale's sister. And as Sir Launcelot beheld her, he espied in her right hand a writing, the which he read, wherein he found all the adventures as ye have heard before, and of what lineage she was come. So with this gentlewoman Sir Launcelot was a month and more. If ye would ask me how he lived, he that fed the people of Israel with manna in the desert in likewise fed him. For every day, when he had said his prayers, he was sustained with the grace of the Holy Ghost.

So upon a night he went to play him by the water's side, for he was somewhat weary of the ship, and then he listened, and heard a horse come, and one riding upon him ; and, when he came nigh, he seemed a knight, and so he let him pass, and went there as the ship was ; and there he alighted, and took the saddle and bridle, and put the horse from him, and went into the ship. And then Sir Launcelot went toward him, and said, " Sir, ye be welcome." And he answered and saluted him again, and asked him his name, " for much my heart giveth unto you." " Truly," said he, " my name is Sir Launcelot du Lake." " Sir," said he, " then ye be welcome ; for ye were the beginning of me in this world." " Ah !" said Sir Launcelot, " are ye Sir Galahad ?" " Yea, forsooth," said he. And so he kneeled down and asked him his blessing, and after took off his helm, and kissed him. And so there was great joy between them; for there is no tongue can tell the joy that they made either of other, and many a friendly word was spoken between them, as kind would, the which is no need here to be rehearsed ; and there each one told other of their adventures and marvels that were befallen them in many journeys, since they departed from the court. And anon as Sir Galahad saw the gentlewoman dead in the bed, he knew her well enough, and told great worship of her, and that she was the best maid living, and it was great pity of her death. But when Sir Launcelot heard how the marvellous sword was gotten, and who made it, and all the marvels rehearsed before, then he prayed Sir Galahad, his son, that he would show him the sword ; and so he did. And anon he kissed the pommel, the hilts, and the scabbard. "Truly," said Sir Launcelot, "never till now knew I of so high adventures done, and so marvellous and strange." So dwelled Sir Launcelot and Sir Galahad within that ship half-a-year, and served God daily and nightly, with all their power. And oft they arrived in isles, far from folk, where were but wild beasts ; and there they found many strange adventures, and perilous, which they brought to an end. But because those adventures were with wild beasts, and not in the quest of the Sancgreal, therefore the tale maketh here no mention, for it would be long to tell that befell them.

XIII.

So after, upon a Monday, it befell that they arrived in the edge of a forest, before a cross of stone, and then saw they a knight armed all in white, and was richly horsed, and led in his right hand a white horse, and so he came to the ship, and saluted the two knights upon the high Lord's high behalf, and said, "Sir Galahad, ye have been long enough with your father ; come out of the ship, and leap upon this horse, and ride where adventures shall lead thee in the quest of the Sancgreal." Then he went unto his father, and kissed him full courteously, and said unto him, "Fair father, I wot not when I shall see you any more, till that I see the body of our Lord Jesu Christ." "I pray you," said Sir Launcelot, "pray you unto the high Father, that he hold me in his service." And so he took his horse, and there they heard a voice, that said, "Think for to do well, for the one shall never see the other till the dreadful day of doom." "Now my son, Sir Galahad," said Sir Launcelot, "sith we shall depart, and never see other more, I pray unto the high Father of heaven for to preserve both you and me." "Sir," said Sir Galahad, "no prayer availeth so much as yours." And therewith Sir Galahad entered into the forest; and the wind arose, and drove Sir Launcelot more than a month throughout the sea, where he slept but little, and prayed unto God that he might have a sight of the Holy Sancgreal. So it befell, upon a night, at midnight, he arrived afore a castle, on the back side, which was rich and fair; and there was a postern that opened toward the sea, and was open without any keeping, save two lions kept the entry; and the moon shined clear. Anon Sir Launcelot heard a voice, that said, "Launcelot, go out of this ship, and enter into the castle, where thou shall see a great part of thy desire." Then he ran to his arms, and armed him, and so he went unto the gate, and saw the two lions; then he set hands to his sword, and drew it. Then came there suddenly a dwarf, that smote him upon the arm so sore, that the sword fell out of his hand. Then he heard a voice, that said, "Oh, man of evil faith and poor belief, wherefore believest thou more in thy harness than in thy Maker; for he might more avail thee than thine armour, in whose service thou art set." Then said Sir Launcelot, "Fair Father, Jesu Christ, I thank thee, of thy great mercy, that thou reprovest me of my misdeed. Now see I well that thou holdest me for thy servant." Then took he again his sword, and put it upon his shield, and made a cross on his forehead, and came to the lions; and they made attempt to do him harm; notwithstanding, he passed by them without hurt, and entered into the castle, to the chief fortress, and there were they all at rest. Then Sir Launcelot entered in so armed, and he found no gate, nor door, but it was opened; and so at the last he found a chamber, whereof the door was shut, and he set his hand thereto, for to have opened it, but he might not.

XIV.

THEN he enforced him much for to undo the door. Then he listened, and heard a voice, which sung so sweetly, that it seemed none earthly thing; and thought that the voice said, "Joy and honour be to the Father of heaven." Then Sir Launcelot kneeled down before the chamber, for well he wist that there was the Sancgreal in that chamber. Then said he, "Fair sweet Father, Jesu Christ, if ever I did thing that pleased the Lord, for thy pity, nor have me not in despite for my foul sins done here before time, and that thou show me something of that which I seek." And with that he saw the chamber-door open, and with that there came out a great clearness, that the house was as bright as though all the torches of the world had been there. So came he to the chamber-door, and would have entered, and anon a voice said unto him, "Flee, Sir Launcelot, and enter not, for thou oughtest not to do it ; and, if thou enter, thou shalt forethink it." And he withdrew him back, and was right heavy in his mind. Then he looked up in the midst of the chamber, and saw a table of silver, and the holy vessel covered with red samite, and many angels about it, whereof one of them held a candle of wax burning, and the other held a cross, and the ornaments of the altar. And before the holy vessel he saw a good man, clothed like a priest ; and it seemed that he was at the consecrating of the mass. And it seemed unto Sir Launcelot that above the priest's hands there were three men, whereof the two put the youngest, by likeness, between the priest's hands, and so he lift it up on high : and it seemed to show so to the people. And then Sir Launcelot marvelled not a little ; for him thought that the priest was so greatly changed of the figure, that him seemed that he should have fallen to the ground. And when he saw none about him that would help him, then he came to the door a great pace, and said, "Fair Father, Jesu Christ, nor take it for no sin, though I help the good man, which hath great need of help." Right so he entered into the chamber, and came toward the table of silver. And when he came nigh he felt a breath, that him thought was intermeddled with fire, which smote him so sore in the visage, that him thought it all to break his visage ; and therewith he fell to the ground, and had no power to arise. As he was so enraged, that he had lost the power of his body, and his hearing, and his saying, then he felt many hands about him, which took him up, and bear him out of the chamber, without any amendment of his swoon, and left him there, seeming dead, to all the people. So on the morrow, when it was fair daylight, they within were arisen, and found Sir Launcelot lying before the chamber-door ; and they marvelled how he came in. And so they looked upon him, and felt his pulse, to wit whether there were any life in him ; and so they found life in him, but he might neither stand nor stir no member that he had ; and so they took him by every part of the body, and bear him into a chamber, and laid him in a rich bed, far from all folk : and so he lay four days. Then the one said he was alive, and the other said nay. "In the name of God," said an old man, "for I do verily to wit he is not dead, but he is so full of life as the mightiest of you all, and therefore I counsel you that he be well kept, till God send him life again."

XV.

In such a manner they kept Sir Launcelot twenty-four days, and as many nights, which lay still like a dead man, and at the twenty-fifth day befell him, after midnight, that he opened his eyes, and when he saw folk, he made great sorrow, and said, "Why have ye wakened me ; for I was better at ease than I am now. Oh, Jesu Christ, who might be so blessed, that might see openly the great marvels of secretness there, where no sinner may be." "What have ye seen ?" said they about him. "I have seen," said he, "great marvels, that no tongue can tell, and more than any heart can think ; and if my son had not been here before me, I had seen much more." Then they told him how he had lain there twenty-four days, and as many nights. Then him thought how it was a punishment for the twenty-four years he had been a sinner ; wherefore our Lord put him in penance twenty-four days and nights. Then looked Sir Launcelot before him, and saw the hair, which he had borne nigh a year ; for that he forethought him right much that he had broken his promise unto the hermit, which he had vowed to do. Then they asked him how it stood with him. "Forsooth," said he, "I am whole of my body, thanked be our Lord ; therefore, sirs, for God's love, tell me where I am." Then said they all, he was in the castle of Garboneck. Therewith came a gentle-woman, and brought him a shirt of fine linen cloth ; but he changed not there, but took the hair to him again. "Sir," said they, "the quest of the Sancgreal is achieved right now in you; that never shall ye see more of the Sancgreal than ye have seen." "Now, I thank God," said Sir Launcelot, "of his great mercy, of that I have seen, for it sufficeth me : for, as I suppose, no man in this world hath lived better than I have done, to achieve that I have done." And therewith he took the hair, and clothed him in it, and above that he put a linen shirt, and after a robe of scarlet, fresh and new ; and when he was so arrayed, they marvelled all ; for they knew that he was Sir Launcelot, the good knight. And then they said all, "O Lord, Sir Launcelot, be that ye ?" And then he said, "Truly, I am he." Then came word to King Pelleas, that the knight which had lain so long dead was Sir Launcelot. Then was King Pelleas wondrous glad, and went to see him. And when Sir Launcelot saw him come, he dressed him against him. And there the King made great joy of him : and there the King told him tidings that his fair daughter was dead. Then was Sir Launcelot right heavy of it, and said, "Sir, it forethinketh me thy daughter, for she was a full fair lady, fresh and young ; and well I wot she bare the best knight that is now on the earth, or that ever was since God was born." So King Pelleas held Sir Launcelot there four days, and on the morrow he took his leave of King Pelleas, and of all the fellowship that were there, and thanked them of their great labour. Right so, they sat at their dinner in the chief hall ; then it was so that the Sancgreal had filled the table with all manner of meats, that the heart might think. So, as they sat, they saw all the doors and windows of the place were shut without man's hand, whereof they were all abashed, and none wist what to do. And then it happened, suddenly, that a knight came unto the chief door, and knocked mightily, and cried, " Undo the door !" But they would not. And ever he cried, " Undo ;" but they would not. And, at the last, it annoyed him so much, that the King himself arose, and came to a window, where the knight called ; then he said, " Sir knight, ye shall not enter at this time, while the Sancgreal is here, and therefore go into another ; for certainly ye be none of the knight of the quest, but one of them that hath served the fiend, and hath left the service of our Lord." Then was he wondrous wrath at the King's words. " Sir knight," said the King, " since ye would so fain enter, tell me of what country ye be." " Sir," said he, " I am of the country and realm of Logris, and my name is Sir Ector de Maris, and brother unto the noble knight Sir Launcelot." " In the name of God," said King Pelleas, " me forethinketh that I have, for your brother is here within." And when Sir Ector de Maris understood that his brother was there, for he was the man in the world that he most dread and loved, and then he said, " Ah ! Lord God, now doubleth my sorrow and shame. Full truly said the good man of the hill unto Sir Gawaine and me of our dreams." Then went he out of the court as fast as his courser might run, and so throughout the castle.

XVI.

AND then King Pelleas came to Sir Launcelot, and told him tidings of his brother, whereof he was sorry, that he wist not what to do. So Sir Launcelot departed, and took his armour, and said "That he would go to see the realm of Logris, which I have not seen these twelve months." And therewith he commended the King unto God, and so rode through many realms ; and at the last he came unto an abbey, and there he had great cheer. And on the morrow he arose and heard mass, and afore

an altar he found a rich tomb which was newly made, and then
he took heed and saw the sides written with letters of gold,
which said—"Here lieth King Bagdemagus, of Gore, the which
King Arthur's nephew slew, and named him Sir Gawaine."
Then was he not a little sorry, for Sir Launcelot loved him
more than any other; and if it had been any other than Sir
Gawaine, he should not have escaped from death, and said to
himself, "Ah! Lord God, this is a full great damage to King
Arthur's court, the loss of such a man." And then he departed,
and came unto the abbey, whereas Sir Galahad did the adventure of the tombs, and won the white shield with the red cross,
and there had he great cheer all that night. And on the
morrow he turned to Camelot, whereas he found King Arthur
and Queen Guenever : but many of the knights of the Round
Table were slain and destroyed more than half. And so three
of them were come home again ; that were Sir Gawaine, Sir
Ector, and Sir Lionel, and many other which needeth not to
be rehearsed. Then all the court was passing glad of Sir
Launcelot, and King Arthur asked him what tidings of his son
Sir Galahad. And there Sir Launcelot told the King of his
adventures that had befallen him sithence he departed ; and
also he told him of the adventures of Sir Galahad, Sir Percivale,
and Sir Bors, which he knew by the letter of the dead damsel,
and as Sir Galahad had told him. "Now would God," said the
King, "that they were all three here." "That shall never be,"
said Sir Launcelot ; "for two of them shall ye never see, but one
of them shall come again."

XVII.

Now that Sir Galahad rode many journeys in vain ; and at
the last he came unto the abbey where King Mordrains was,
and when he heard that, he thought he would abide to see him.
And on the morrow, when he had heard mass, Sir Galahad
came unto King Mordrains, and anon the King saw him, which
had lain blind a long time. And then he dressed him against
him, and said, "Sir Galahad, the servant of Jesu Christ, whose
coming I have abidden long, now embrace me, and let me rest
on thy breast, so that I may rest between thine arms ; for thou
art a clean virgin above all knights, as the flower of the lily, in
whose virginity is signified, and thou art the rose, the which is
the flower of all good virtues, and in the colour of fire ; for the
fire of the Holy Ghost is so taken in thee that the flesh which
was of dead oldness is become young again." When Sir

Galahad heard his words, he embraced him in his arms.   Then
said King Mordrains, "Fair Lord Jesu Christ, now I have my
will ; now I require thee in this point that I am in, that thou
come and visit me." And anon our Lord heard his prayer ;
therewith the soul departed from the body.   And then Sir
Galahad put him in the earth as a king ought to be, and
so departed and came into a perilous forest ; whereas he found
the well that boiled with great waves, as the tale telleth before.
And so soon as Sir Galahad set his hand thereto it ceased ; so
that it burnt no more, and the heat departed.   For that it burnt,
it was a sign of lechery, the which was at that time much used :
but that heat might not abide his pure virginity.   And this was
taken in the country for a miracle, and so ever after was it
called Sir Galahad's Well.   Then by adventure he came into
the country of Gore, and into the abbey where Sir Launcelot
had been beforehand, and found the tomb of King Bagdemagus,
but Joseph of Arimathy's son was the founder thereof ; and
there he found the tomb of Simeon, where Sir Launcelot had
failed.   Then he looked into a cross under the minster, and
there he saw a tomb, the which burned full marvellously.   Then
asked he the doctor what it was : "Sir," said he, "it is a
marvellous adventure that may not be brought to an end, but
by him that passeth of bounty and of knighthood all the knights
of the Round Table."   "I would," said Sir Galahad, "that ye
would lead me thereto."   "Gladly," said they.   And so they
led him unto a cave, and he went down upon a pair of stairs,
and came nigh the tomb, and then the flaming failed, and
the fire staunched, the which many a day had been great.
Then came there a voice that said, "Much are ye beholden to
thank our Lord, that hath given you a good hour, that ye may
draw your souls out of earthly pain, and put them into the joys
of paradise.   I am of your kindred, the which hath dwelled
in this heat these three hundred and four and fifty years, for
to be purged of the sin that I did to Joseph of Arimathy."
Then Sir Galahad took the body in his arms and bear it to the
minster, and that night lay Sir Galahad in the abbey.   And
on the morrow he gave him service, and put him in the earth,
before the high altar.

XVIII.

So departed he from thence, and commended the brethren to
God.   And so he rode five days, till that he came to the
maimed King ; and ever followed Sir Percivale the five days,

asking where he had been, and so one told him how the adventures of Logris were achieved. So upon a day it befell that there came out of a great forest, and there they met at a travers with Sir Bors that rode alone. It is no need to tell if they minded. And then he saluted, and they yielded him honour and good adventure, and they told each other their adventures. Then said Sir Bors, " It is more than a year and a-half, that I never lay ten times where men dwelled, but in wild forests and in mountains, but God was ever my comfort." Then rode they a great while, till they came to the castle of Corbonek, and when they were entered within the castle, King Pelleas knew them all. Then was there made great joy, for he knew well by their coming that they had fulfilled the quest of the Sancgreal. Then Eliazar, King Pelleas' son, brought before them the broken sword, wherewith Joseph was smitten through the thigh. Then Sir Bors set his hand thereto, if he might have forced it again together, but it would not be. Then he took it to Sir Percivale, but he had no more power thereto than he. " Now have ye it," said Sir Percivale unto Sir Galahad, " for and it be ever achieved by one bodily man, ye must do it." And then took he the pieces and set them together, and they seemed that they had never been broken, and as well as it had been first forged. And then they within espied that the adventure of the sword was achieved; then they gave the sword unto Sir Bors, for he might not be better set, for he was a full good knight and a worthy man : and a little before even the sword arose great and marvellous, and was full of great heat, that many men fell for dead. And anon light a voice among them said, " They that ought not to sit at the table of our Lord Jesu Christ arise; for now shall very knights be fed." So they went thence all, save King Pelleas and Eliazar his son, the which were holy men, and a maid which was his niece : and so these three fellows and they three were there, and no more. Anon they saw knights all armed come in at the hall door, and did off their helms and their harness, and said unto Sir Galahad, " Sir, we have hied sore to be with you at this table, where the holy meat shall be parted." " Then," said he, " ye be welcome, but of whence be ye ?" So three of them said they were of Gaul, and other three said they were of Ireland, and other three said they were of Denmark. So as they sate thus, there came a bed of wood out of a chamber, the which four gentlewomen brought; and in that bed lay a good man sick, and a crown of gold upon his head, and there in the midst of the place they sat them down and went their way again. Then he lift up his head and said, "Sir Galahad, knight, ye be welcome, for much have I desired your coming, for in such pain and anguish as ye see have I been long; but now I trust to God the time is come that my pain shall be allayed, that I shall pass out of this world, so as it was promised me long ago." Therewith a voice said, "There be two among you that be not in the quest of the Sancgreal, and therefore depart ye."

XIX.

THEN King Pelleas and his son departed; and therewith it seemed them that there came a man and four angels from heaven, clothed in the likeness of bishops, and had a cross in his hand; and the four angels bear him up in a chair, and set him down before the table of silver, whereupon the Sancgreal was, and it seemed that he had in the midst of his forehead letters that said, "See ye here, Joseph, the first bishop of Christendom, the same which our Lord succoured in the city of Sarras, in the spiritual place." Then the knights marvelled, for that bishop was dead more than three hundred years before. "Oh, knights!" said he, "marvel not, for I was sometime an earthly man." With that they heard the chamber-door open, and there they saw angels, and two bear candles of wax, and the third a towel, and the fourth a spear, which bled marvellously, that the drops fell within a bier, the which he held with his other hand. And then they set their candles upon the table, and the third put the towel upon the vessel, and the fourth set the holy spear even upright upon the vessel. And then the bishop made semblance as though he would have gone to the consecrating of the mass; and then he took a wafer, which was made in the likeness of bread, and at the lifting up there came a figure in the likeness of a child, and the visage was as red and as bright as any fire, and smote himself into that bread, so that they all saw that the bread was formed of a fleshy man. And then he put it into the holy vessel again; and then he did that belonged unto a priest to do at mass. And then he went unto Sir Galahad and kissed him, and then went and bade him go and kiss his fellows; and as he was bidden so he did. "Now," said he, "ye servants of Jesu Christ, ye shall be fed before this table with sweet meats, which never no knights tasted." And when he had said, he vanished away, and they set them in great dread, and made their prayers. Then looked they and saw a man come out of the holy vessel, that had all the signs of the passion of Jesus Christ, bleeding all openly, and said, " My knights and my servants, and my true children, which be come out of deadly life, I will now no longer hide me from you ; but ye shall see now a part of my secrets and of my hidings. Now hold and receive the high meat which ye have so much desired." Then took he himself the holy vessel, and came to Sir Galahad, and he kneeled down, and there he received his Saviour ; and so after him received all his fellows, and they thought it so sweet that it was marvel to tell. Then he said, " Galahad, son, wottest thou what I hold between my hands ? " " Nay," said Sir Galahad, " but if ye tell me." " This is," said he, " the holy dish wherein I eat the lamb on Shrove-Thursday, and now hast thou seen that thou desirest most to see ; but yet hast thou not seen it openly as thou shalt see it in the city of Sarras, in the spiritual place. Therefore thou must go hence, and bear with thee this holy vessel : for this night it shall depart from the realm of Logris, that it shall never be seen more here, and wottest thou therefore, for it is not served nor worshipped to his right, by them of this land, for they be turned unto evil living. Therefore I shall disinherit them ; and therefore go ye three to-morrow unto the sea, whereas ye shall find your ship ready, and with you take the sword with the strange girdles, and no more with you but Sir Percivale and Sir Bors. And also I will ye take with you of the blood of this spear for to anoint the maimed King, both his legs and all his body, and he shall have his health." " Sir," said Sir Galahad, " why shall not these other fellows go with us ? " " For this cause ; for right as I parted mine apostles, one here and another there, so will I that ye part ; and two of you shall die in my service, but one of you shall come again, and tell tidings." Then gave he them his blessing, and vanished away.

XX.

THEN Sir Galahad went anon to the spear which lay upon the table, and touched the blood with his fingers, and came to the maimed King, and anointed his legs. And therewith he clothed him anon, and started upon his feet, out of his bed, as a whole man, and thanked our Lord that he had healed him, and that was not to the world ward ; for anon he yielded him unto a place of religion of white monks, and was a full holy man. That same night, about midnight, there came a voice among them, that said thus : "Mine own sons, and not my chief sons, my friends, and not my warriors, go ye hence whither ye hope best to do, and as I bade you." "Ah! thanked be thou, Lord," said they, "that thou wilt vouchsafe to call us so ; now may we prove that we have not lost our pain." And anon in all haste they took their harness and departed ; but the three knights of Gaul, one of them hight Claudine, King Claudas' son, and the other two were great gentlemen. Then prayed Sir Galahad unto every each of them, "If ye come unto King Arthur's court, that ye will salute my lord, Sir Launcelot, my father, and all the fellowship of the Round Table ; and pray them that if they come in these parts that they should not forget it." Right so departed Sir Galahad, and Sir Percivale and Sir Bors with him. And so they rode three days, and then they came to a strand, and found the ship, whereof the tale speaketh before. And when they came within board, they found in the midst the table of silver which they had left with the maimed King, and the Sancgreal, which was covered with red samite. Then they were passing glad for to have such things in their fellowship : and so they entered and made great reverence thereto. And Sir Galahad fell in his prayers a long time unto our Lord, that at what time he asked he might pass out of this world ; and so much he prayed, till at the last a voice said to him, "Galahad, thou shalt have thy request, and when thou askest the death of thy body, thou shalt have it, and then shalt thou find the life of thy soul." Sir Percivale heard this, and prayed him of fellowship that was between them, for to tell him wherefore he asked such things. "That shall I tell you," said Sir Galahad. "The other day when we saw the part of the adventures of the Sancgreal, I was in such a joy of heart, that I trow never man was that was earthly ; and, therefore, I wot well that when my body is dead my soul shall be in great joy for to see the blessed Trinity every day, and the majesty of our Lord Jesus Christ." So long were they in the ship, that they said unto Sir Galahad, "Sir, in this bed ought ye to lie ; for so saith the Scripture." And then he laid him down, and slept a great while ; and when he awoked, he looked afore him, and saw the city of Sarras ; and as they would have landed, they saw the ship wherein Sir Percivale had put his sister. "Truly," said Sir Percivale, "in the name of God well hath my sister held us covenant." Then took they out of the ship the table of silver ; and he took it to Sir Percivale and to Sir Bors to go before, and Sir Galahad came behind. Right so they went into the city ; and at the gate of the city they saw an old man sit crooked. Then Sir Galahad called him, and bade him help to bear this heavy thing. "Truly," said the old man, "it is ten years ago that I might not go but with crutches." "Care thou not," said Sir Galahad, "arise up, and show thy good-will." And so he essayed and found himself as whole as ever he was; then he ran to the table, and took one part against Sir Galahad. And anon there arose a great noise in the city, that a cripple was made whole by a knight's marvellous, that were entered into the city. Then anon after they three knights went to the water, and brought up into the palace Sir Percivale's sister, and buried her as richly as a king's daughter ought to be. And when the king of the city, which was called Estourause, saw the fellowship, he asked them of whence they were, and what thing it was that they had brought upon the table of silver; and they told him the truth of the Sancgreal, and the power that God had set there. Then the king was a tyrant, and was come of the lineage of Paynims, and took them and put them in prison in a deep hole.

XXI.

BUT as soon as they were there, our Lord sent them the Sancgreal, through whose grace they were always filled while they were in prison. So at the year's end, it befell that this King Estourause lay sick, and felt that he should die; then he sent for the three knights, and they came before him, and he cried them mercy of that he had done to them; and he forgave him goodly, and he died anon. When the king was dead, all the city was dismayed, and wist not who might be their king. Right so, as they were in counsel together, there came a voice among them, and bid them choose the youngest knight of the three to be their king, for he shall maintain you and all yours. So they made Sir Galahad king by all the assent of the holy city, and else they would have slain him. And when he was come for to behold the land, he let make about the table of silver a chest of gold and of precious stones, that covered the holy vessel; and every day in the morning the three fellows would come before it, and said their devotions. Now, at the year's end, and the same day after that Sir Galahad had borne the crown of gold, he arose up early, and his fellows, and came unto the palace, and saw before them the holy vessel, and a man kneeling upon his knees in the likeness of the bishop, which had about him a great fellowship of angels, as it had been Jesu Christ himself: and then he arose and began a mass of our Lady. And when he came to the consecrating of the mass, and had done, anon he called Sir Galahad, and said unto him, " Come forth, the servant of Jesu Christ, and thou shalt see that which thou hast much desirèd to see." And then Sir Galahad began to tremble right sore when the deadly flesh began to behold the spiritual things. Then he held up both his hands towards heaven and said, "Lord, I thank thee, for now I see that which hath been my desire many a day : now, blessed Lord, would I no longer live, if it might please thee, good Lord." And therewith the good man took our Lord's body between his hands, and proffered it unto Sir Galahad ; and he received it right gladly and meekly. "Now," said the good man, "wottest thou whom I am ?" "Nay," said Sir Galahad. "I am Joseph of Arimathy, which our Lord hath sent here to thee to bear thee fellowship. And wottest thou wherefore he hath sent me more than any other ? for thou hast resembled me in two things : one is, that thou hast seen the Sancgreal, and the other is, in that thou hast been a clean maiden as I am." And when he had said these words, Sir Galahad went to Sir Percivale and kissed him, and commended him to God, and said, "Fair lord, salute me to my lord, Sir Launcelot, my father ; and soon as ye see him, bid him remember this unstable world." And therewith he kneeled down before the table and made his prayers ; and then suddenly his soul departed unto Jesus Christ, and a great multitude of angels bear his soul up to heaven that his two fellows might behold it : also, his two fellows saw come from heaven a hand, but they saw not the body, and then it came right to the vessel and took it, and the spear, and so bear it up to heaven. Since then was there never no man so hardy for to say that he had seen the Sancgreal.

XXII.

WHEN Sir Percivale and Sir Bors saw Sir Galahad dead, they made as much sorrow as ever did two men, and if they had not been good men, they might lightly have fallen in despair ; and the people of the country and of the city were right heavy. And as soon as he was buried, Sir Percivale yielded him to a hermitage out of the city, and took a religious clothing, and Sir Bors was always with him, but he never changed his secular clothing, because he purposed him to go again into the realm of Logris. Thus a year and two months lived Sir Percivale in the hermitage a full holy life, and then passed out of this world ; and Sir Bors let bury him by his sister and by Sir Galahad in the spiritualities.   When Sir Bors saw that he was in so far countries, as in the parts of Babylon, he departed from Sarras, and armed him, and came to the sea and entered into a ship ; and so it befell him by adventure to come into the realm of Logris, and then he rode fast till he came to Camelot, where King Arthur was.   And then was there made great joy of him in the court ; for they deemed all that he had been dead, forasmuch as he had been so long out of the country.   And when they had eaten, King Arthur made great clerks to come before him, that they should chronicle the high adventures of the good knights.   When Sir Bors had told him of the adventures of the Sancgreal, such as had befallen him and his two fellows, that was Sir Galahad and Sir Percivale.   Then Sir Launcelot told the adventures of the Sancgreal that he had seen : all this was made in great books, and put in the armoury at Salisbury.   And anon Sir Bors said unto Sir Launcelot, " Sir Galahad, your son, saluted you by me, and after you, King Arthur and all the court, so did Sir Percivale ; for I buried them with mine own hands in the city of Sarras.   Also, Sir Launcelot, Sir Galahad prayeth you for to remember this unsteadfast world, as ye behight him when ye were together more than half-a-year."   " This is full true," said Sir Launcelot ; " now I trust to God his prayer shall avail me."   Then Sir Launcelot took Sir Bors in his arms and said, " Gentle cousin, ye are welcome to me, and all that ever I may do for you and yours, ye shall find me ready at all times, while I have life, and that I promise you faithfully, and never to fail you : and wit ye well, gentle cousin, Sir Bors, that you and I will never depart in sunder whilst that our lives may last."   " Sir," said he, " I will as ye will."

———◆———

<h2 style="text-align:center">THE BOOK OF SIR MADOR.</h2>

I.

OW after that the quest of the Sancgreal was fulfilled, and that all the knights that were left alive were come again to the Round Table, as the book of the Sancgreal maketh mention, then was there great joy in the court, and especially King Arthur and Queen Guenever made great joy of the remnant that were come home : and passing glad was the King and the Queen of

Sir Launcelot and of Sir Bors, for they had been passing long away in the quest of the Sancgreal. Then Sir Launcelot began to resort unto Queen Guenever again, and forgot the promise and the profession that he made in the quest; had not Sir Launcelot been in his privy thoughts and in his mind set inwardly to the Queen, as he was in seeming outward unto God, there had no knight passed him in the quest of the Sancgreal, but ever his thoughts were privily upon the Queen. And so they loved together more hotter than they had done before, and had such privy meetings together; and many in the court spake of it, and most especially Sir Agravaine, and Sir Gawaine's brother, for he was ever open-mouthed. So it befell that Sir Launcelot had many resorts of ladies and damsels, that daily resorted unto him, which besought him to be their champion. And in all such manners of right Sir Launcelot appealed him daily to do for the pleasure of our Lord Jesu Christ; and always as much as he might he withdrew him from the company and fellowship of Queen Guenever, for to eschew the slander and the noise. Wherefore, the Queen waxed wroth and angry with Sir Launcelot; and, upon a day, she called Sir Launcelot unto her chamber, and said to him thus: " Sir Launcelot, I see and feel daily that thy love beginneth for to slack, thou hast no joy to be in my presence, but ever thou art out of this court, and quarrels and matters thou hast now-a-days for ladies and gentlewomen, more than ever they were wont to have in time past." "Ah, madam," said Sir Launcelot, " in this ye must have me excused for divers causes; one is, that I was but late in the quest of the Sancgreal, and I thank God of his great mercy, and never of my deserving, that I saw in my quest as much as ever saw any sinful man, and so was it told me: and if I had not had my privy thoughts to return to your love again as I do, I had seen as great mysteries as ever saw my son, Sir Galahad, Sir Percivale, or Sir Bors; and therefore, madam, I was but late in that quest. Wit ye well, madam, it may not be yet lightly forgotten the high service in whom I did my diligent labour: also, madam, wit ye well that there be many men that speak of our love in this place, and have you and me greatly in await, as Sir Agravaine and Sir Mordred; and wit ye well, madam, I dread them more for your sake than for any fear that I have of them myself, for I may happen to escape and rid myself in a great need, whereas ye must abide all that will be said to you. And then, if that ye fall in any distress through wilful folly, then is there none other remedy or help but by me and my blood. And wit ye well, madam, the boldness of you and me will bring us unto great shame and slander, and that were me loth to see you dishonoured ; and that is the cause that I take upon me more for to do for damsels and maidens than ever I did before. Men should understand my joy and my delight is to have to do for damsels and maidens."

II.

ALL this while the Queen stood still, and let Sir Launcelot say what he would ; and, when he had all said, she break out on weeping, and she sobbed and wept a great while : and when she might speak she said, "Sir Launcelot, now I understand that thou art a false, recreant knight, and lovest and holdest other ladies, and of me thou hast disdain and scorn. For wit thou well," said she, "now I understand thy falsehood ; and, therefore, I shall never love thee any more, and never be thou so hardy to come in my sight. And right here I charge thee, that thou never come more within this court ; and I forbid thee my fellowship, and, upon pain of thy head, that thou see me no more." Right so Sir Launcelot departed with great heaviness, that unless he might sustain himself for great dole-making. Then he called Sir Bors, Sir Ector de Maris, and Sir Lionel, and told them how the Queen had forbidden him the court ; and so he was in will to depart into his own country. "Fair knight," said Sir Bors de Ganis, "ye shall not depart out of this land by mine advice. Ye must remember in what honour ye are renowned, and called the most noble knight of the world, and many great matters ye have in hand ; and women, in their hastiness, will do oftentimes that which sore repent them. And, therefore, by my advice, ye shall take your horses, and ride to the hermitage beside Windsor, which sometime was a good knight, whose name is Sir Brastias; and there shall ye abide, till I send you word of better tidings." "Fair cousin," said Sir Launcelot, "wit ye well that I am full loth to depart out of this realm ; but the Queen hath forbidden me so highly, that me seemeth she will never be my good lady as she hath been in times past." "Say ye never so," said Sir Bors ; "for many times beforetime she hath been wrath with you, and, after it, she was the first that repented it." "Ye say well," said Sir Launcelot ; "for now will I do by your counsel, and take my horse and my harness, and ride to the hermit, Sir Brastias : and there will I rest me, until I hear some manner of tidings from you. But, fair cousin, I pray you, get me the love of my lady,

Queen Guenever, and ye may."   "Sir," said Sir Bors, "ye need not to move me of such matters ; for well ye wot I will do what I may please to you."   And then the noble knight, Sir Launcelot, departed suddenly with a right heavy cheer, that none earthly creature wist of him where he was become, but only Sir Bors.   So, when Sir Launcelot was departed, the Queen made no manner of outward sorrow in showing to any of his blood, nor yet to none other ; but wit ye well that inwardly she took great thought : but she bore it out with a proud countenance, as though she felt no thought nor danger.

III.

AND then the Queen let make a privy dinner in the city of London, unto the knights of the Round Table ; and all was to show outward that she had a great joy in all other knights of the Round Table, as she had in Sir Launcelot.   All only at that dinner she had Sir Gawaine and his brethren; that is to say, Sir Agravaine, Sir Gaheris, Sir Gareth, and Sir Mordred.   Also there was Sir Bors de Ganis, Sir Blamor de Ganis, Sir Bleoberis de Ganis, Sir Galihud, Sir Galihodin, Sir Ector de Maris, Sir Lionel, Sir Palomides, and his brother, Sir Safre ; la Cote mal Tail, Sir Persuant, Sir Ironside, Sir Brandiles, Sir Kaye the seneschal, Sir Mador de la Port, Sir Patrice a knight of Ireland, Sir Aliducke, Sir Astomore, and Sir Pinell le Savage, the which was cousin unto Sir Lamoracke de Galis, the good knight, the which Sir Gawaine and brethren slew by treason. And so these knights should dine with the Queen in a privy place by themselves ; and there was made a great feast of all manner of dainty meats and drinks.   But Sir Gawaine had a custom that he used daily at dinner and at supper, that he loved well all manner of fruits, and in especial apples and pears ; and, therefore, whosoever dined or feasted, Sir Gawaine would commonly purvey for good fruit for him : and so did the Queen ; for, to please Sir Gawaine, she let purvey for him of all manner of fruits.   For Sir Gawaine was a passing hot knight of nature ; and this Sir Pinell hated Sir Gawaine, because of his kinsman, Sir Lamoracke de Galis : and, therefore, for pure envy and hate, Sir Pinell poisoned certain apples for to poison Sir Gawaine withal.   And so this was well unto the end of the meat ; and so it befell, by misfortune, that a good knight, named Sir Patrice, cousin unto Sir Mador de la Port, took one of the poisoned apples : and, when he had eaten it, he swelled till he burst ; and there Sir Patrice fell down dead suddenly among them. Then every knight leaped from the board, ashamed, and enraged for wrath nigh out of their wits ; for they wist not what to say, considering that Queen Guenever made the feast and dinner, they all had suspicion upon her. "My lady, the Queen," said Sir Gawaine, "wit ye well, madam, that this dinner was made for me : for all folks, that know my conditions, understand well that I love fruit ; and now I see well I had been near slain : therefore, madam, I dread me least ye will be shamed." Then the Queen stood still, and was right sore abashed, that she wist not what to say. "This shall not be ended so," said Sir Mador de la Port ; "for here have I lost a full noble knight of my blood : and, therefore, upon this shame and despite I will be revenged to the uttermost." And thereupon Sir Mador appealed Queen Guenever of the death of his cousin, Sir Patrice. Then stood they all still, that none of them would speak a word against him ; for they had a great suspection unto Queen Guenever, because she let make the dinner. And the Queen was so sore abashed, that she could none otherwise do, but wept so heartily, that she fell in a swoon. With this noise and sudden cry came unto them King Arthur, and marvelled greatly what it might be ; and, when he wist of their trouble, and the sudden death of that good knight, Sir Patrice, he was a passing heavy man.

IV.

AND ever Sir Mador stood still before King Arthur, and ever he appealed Queen Guenever of treason. For the custom was such at that time, that all manner of shameful death was called treason. "Fair lords," said King Arthur, "me repenteth sore of this trouble, but the cause is so, we may not have to do in this matter ; for I must be a rightful judge, and that repenteth me that I may not do battle for my wife ; for, as I deem, this deed came never of her, and therefore I suppose we shall not be all destitute, but that some good knight shall put his body in jeopardy, rather than she should be burnt in a wrong quarrel. And, therefore, Sir Mador, be not so hasty ; for it may happen she shall not be all friendless: and, therefore, desire thou the day of battle, and she shall purvey her of some good knight, which shall answer you, or else it were to me great shame, and unto all my court." "My gracious lord," said Sir Mador, "ye must hold me excused : for, though ye be our King in that degree, ye are but a knight as we are, and ye are sworn unto knighthood as we are : and, therefore, I pray you, that ye will not be displeased ; for there is none of the twenty knights that were bidden for to come unto this dinner, but all they have great suspection unto the Queen. What say ye all, my lords?" said Sir Mador. Then they answered by-and-by, and said, that they "could not excuse the Queen ; for why she made the dinner : and either it must come by her, or by her servants." "Alas!" said the Queen, "I made this dinner for a good intent, and never for any evil (so God help me in my right!) as I was never purposed to do such evil deeds, and that I report me unto God." "My lord, the King," said Sir Mador, "I require you heartily, as ye be a righteous king, give me a day that I may have justice." "Well," said King Arthur, "I give you a day this day fifteen days, that ye be ready armed on horseback in the meadow beside Westminster ; and, if it so fall that there be any knight to encounter with you, there may ye do your best, and God speed the right : and, if it so fall that there be no knight at that day, then must my Queen be burnt, and there shall ye be ready to have her judgment." "Well, I am answered," said Sir Mador ; and every knight went where it liked him. So, when the King and the Queen were together, the King asked the Queen how this case befell. Then answered the Queen, "So God me help, I wot not how, or in what manner." "Where is Sir Launcelot?" said King Arthur ; "and he were here, he would not grudge to do battle for you." "Sir," said the Queen, "I cannot tell you where he is ; but his brother, and all his kinsmen, deem that he is not within this realm." "That sore repenteth me," said King Arthur ; "for and he were here, he would full soon stint this strife. Then I will counsel you," said the King, "that ye go unto Sir Bors, and pray him to do that battle for you for Sir Launcelot's sake : and, upon my life, he will not refuse you. For right well I perceive," said King Arthur, "that none of all those twenty knights, without more, that were with you in fellowship together at your dinner, where Sir Patrice was so traitorously slain, that will do battle for you, nor none of them will say well of you ; and that shall be great slander for you in this court." "Alas!" said the queen, "I cannot do withal : but now I miss Sir Launcelot ; for, and he were here, he would put me full soon unto my heart's ease." "What aileth you," said King Arthur, "that ye cannot keep Sir Launcelot on your side? For wit ye well," said King Arthur, "whosoever hath the noble knight, Sir Launcelot, on his part, hath the most man of worship in the world on his side. Now, go your way," said the King unto the Queen, "and require Sir Bors to do battle for you for Sir Launcelot's sake."

V.

So the Queen departed from the King, and sent for Sir Bors into her chamber; and when he was come, she besought him of succour. "Madam," said he, "what would ye that I do? for I may not with my worship have to do in this matter, because I was at the same dinner, for dread that any of those knights would have me in suspection. Also, madam," said Sir Bors, "now miss ye Sir Launcelot; for he would not have failed you, neither in right, nor yet in wrong, as ye have well proved when ye have been in danger; and now have ye driven him out of this country, by whom ye and we all were daily worshipped. Therefore, madam, I greatly marvel me how ye dare for shame require me to do any thing for you, insomuch as ye have chased him out of your country, by whom I was borne up and honoured." "Alas! fair knight," said the Queen, "I put me wholly in your grace; and all that is done amiss I will amend, as ye will counsel me." And therewith she kneeled down upon both her knees, and besought Sir Bors to have mercy upon her, "for I shall have a shameful death, and thereto I never offended." Right so came King Arthur, and found the Queen kneeling before Sir Bors. Then Sir Bors took her up, and said, "Madam, ye do to me great dishonour." "Ah! gentle knight," said King Arthur, "have mercy upon my Queen, for I am now in a certain that she is now untruly defamed; and, therefore, courteous knight," said the King, "promise her to do battle for her: I require you for the love of Sir Launcelot." "My lord," said Sir Bors, "ye require me of the greatest thing that any man may require me; and wit ye well if I grant to do battle for the Queen, I shall wrath many of my fellowship of the Round Table; but, as for that," said Sir Bors, "I will grant my lord, for my lord Sir Launcelot's sake, and for your sake, I will at that day be the Queen's champion, unless that there come by adventure a better knight than I am to do battle for her." "Will ye promise this," said the King, "by your faith?" "Yes, sir," said Sir Bors, "of that will I not fail you, nor her both: but if that there come a better knight than I am, then shall he have the battle." Then was the King and the Queen passing glad, thanked him heartily, and so departed.

So then Sir Bors departed secretly upon a day, and rode unto Sir Launcelot there as he was with the hermit by Sir Brastias, and told him of all his adventures. "Ah! Jesu," said Sir Launcelot, "this is happily come as I would have it, and therefore I pray you make you ready to do battle; but look that ye tarry till ye see me come as long as ye may, for I am sure Sir Mador is a hot knight, if he be chafed, for the more ye suffer him, the hastier will he be to do battle." "Sir," said Sir Bors, "let me deal with him; doubt ye not ye shall have all your will." Then departed Sir Bors from him, and came unto the court again. Then was it noised in all the court that Sir Bors should do battle for the Queen; wherefore many knights were greatly displeased with him, that he should take upon him to do battle in the Queen's quarrel; for there were but few knights in the court but that they deemed the Queen was in the wrong, and that she had done that treason. So Sir Bors answered thus unto his fellows of the Round Table, "Wit ye well, my fair lords, it were shame unto us all, and we suffered to see the most noble queen of the world for to be shamed openly, considering that her lord and our lord is the man of most worship of the world, and the most christened; and he hath always worshipped us all in all places." Many knights answered him again, and said, "As for our most noble King Arthur, we love him and honour him as well as ye do; but as for Queen Guenever, we love her not, for because she is a destroyer of good knights." "Fair lords," said Sir Bors, "me seemeth, ye say, not as ye should say, for never yet in all my days knew I, nor heard say, that ever she was a destroyer of any good knight; but at all times, as far as I ever could know, she was always a maintainer of good knights; and always she hath been large and free of her goods to all good knights, and the most bounteous lady of her gifts and her good grace that ever I saw, or heard speak of; and therefore it were great shame (said Sir Bors) unto us all to our most noble King's wife, if we suffer her to be shamefully slain: and wit ye well (said Sir Bors) I will not suffer it; for I dare say so much the Queen is not guilty of Sir Patrice's death, for she ought him never none evil will, nor none of the twenty knights that were at that dinner; for I dare well say that it was for good love she had us to dinner, and not for no malice, and that I doubt not shall be proved hereafter; for howsoever the game goeth, there was treason among some of us." Then some said to Sir Bors, "We may well believe your words." And so some of them were well pleased, and some were not pleased.

VI.

THE day came on fast until the even that the battle should be. Then the Queen sent for Sir Bors, and asked him "how he was disposed." "Truly, madam," said he, "I am disposed in likewise as I promised you ; that is to say, I shall not fail you, unless by adventure there come a better knight than I to do battle for you ; then, madam, am I discharged of my promise." "Will ye," said the Queen, "that I tell my lord, King Arthur, thus?" "Do as it shall please you, madam," said Sir Bors. Then the Queen went unto the King, and told him the answer of Sir Bors. "Have ye no doubt," said the King, "of Sir Bors, for I call him now one of the best knights of the world, and the most profitablest man ; and this is past forth until the morrow." And the King and the Queen, and all the knights that were there at that time, drew them to the meadow beside Winchester, whereas the battle should be. And so when the King was come with the Queen, and many knights of the Round Table, then the Queen was put there in the constable's ward, and there was made a great fire about the iron stake, that and Sir Mador de la Port had the better she should be burnt ; such a custom was used in those days, that neither for favour, nor for love, nor for affinity, there should be none other but right wise judgment as well upon a King as upon a knight, as well upon a Queen as upon another poor lady.

So in the meanwhile came in Sir Mador de la Port, and took the oath before the King, that Queen Guenever did this treason unto his cousin, Sir Patrice, and unto his oath he would prove it with his body, hand for hand, who that would say the contrary thereto. Right so came Sir Bors de Ganis, and said, "that as for Queen Guenever she is in the right, and that will I make good with my hands, that she is not culpable of this treason that is put upon her." "Then make thee ready," said Sir Mador, "and we shall soon prove whether thou be in the right or I." "Sir," said Sir Bors, "wit ye well I know thee for a good knight, not for then I shall not fear thee so greatly, but I trust unto Almighty God, my Maker, I shall be able enough to withstand thy malice ;. but thus much have I promised my lord, King Arthur, and my lady, the Queen, that I shall do battle for her in this case to the uttermost, only that there came a better knight than I am, and discharged me." "Is that all," said Sir Mador ; "either come thou off and do battle with me, or else say nay." "Take your horse," said Sir Bors, "and as I suppose ye shall not tarry long, but that ye shall be answered." Then either departed to their tents, and made them ready to mount upon horseback as they thought best. And anon Sir Mador de la Port came into the field with his shield on his shoulder, and a spear in his hand, and so rode about the place, crying unto King Arthur, "Bid your champion come forth and he dare." Then was Sir Bors ashamed, and took his horse, and came to the list end ; and then was he ware whereas came out of a wood there fast by, a knight, all armed at all points, upon a white horse, with a strong shield and of strange arms ; and he came riding all that he might run. And so he came to Sir Bors, and said, "Fair knight, I pray you, be not displeased, for here must a better knight than ye are have this battle ; therefore I pray you to withdraw you ; for I would ye knew I have had this day a right great journey, and this battle ought to be mine, and so I promised you when I spake with you last, and with all my heart I thank you for your good will." Then Sir Bors rode unto King Arthur, and told him how there was a knight come that would have the battle for to fight for the Queen. "What knight is he ?" said King Arthur. "I cannot show you," said Sir Bors, "but such a covenant made he with me for to be here this day. Now, my lord," said Sir Bors, "here am I discharged."

VII.

THEN the King called unto the knight, and asked him "if he would fight for the Queen ?" Then he answered unto the King, "Therefore came I hither ; and, therefore, Sir King," he said, "tarry me no longer, for I may not tarry ; for anon as I have finished this battle, I must depart hence, for I have to do many matters elsewhere : for wit ye well," said that knight, "this is dishonour unto you, all knights of the Round Table, to see and know so noble a lady and so courteous a Queen, as Queen Guenever is, thus to be rebuked and shamed among you." Then marvelled they all what knight that might be, that so took the battle upon him ; but there was not one that knew him but if it were Sir Bors. "Then," said Sir Mador de la Port unto the King, "now let me wit with whom I shall have to do withal." And then they rode to the list's end, and there they couched their spears, and ran the one against the other with all their mights : and Sir Mador's spear break all to pieces : but Sir Launcelot's spear held, and bear Sir Mador's horse and all backward to the ground, and had a great fall ; but mightily and suddenly he avoided his horse, and dressed his shield before him, and then drew his sword, and bade that other knight alight and do battle with him on foot. Then that knight descended lightly from his horse like a valiant man, and put his shield afore him, and drew out his sword. And so they came eagerly to battle, and either gave other many sad strokes, tracing and traversing, racing and foyning, and hurtling together with their swords, as they had been two wild boars.

Thus were they fighting nigh an hour; for this Sir Mador was a full strong knight, and mightily proved in many strong battles. But, at the last, the knight smote Sir Mador grovelling upon the ground, and the knight stepped near him for to have pulled Sir Mador flat-long upon the ground. And therewith, all suddenly, Sir Mador arose; and, in his arising, he smote that knight through the thigh, that the blood ran out right fiercely. And when he felt himself so wounded, and saw his blood, he let him arise upon his feet, and then he gave him such a buffet upon the helm that he fell flat-long to the ground. And therewith he strode to him, for to have pulled off his helm from his head : and then Sir Mador prayed that knight to save his life ; and so he yielded him as an overcome knight, and released the Queen of his quarrel. " I will not grant thee life," said the knight, " but only that you freely release the Queen for ever, and that no manner of mention be made upon Sir Patrice's tomb that ever Queen Guenever consented to that treason." "All this shall be done," said Sir Mador ; " and clearly I discharge my quarrel for ever." Then the knights' porters of the list took up Sir Mador, and led him to his tent ; and the other knight went straight to the stair-foot, whereas King Arthur sat. And by that time was the Queen come unto the King, and either kissed other lovingly. And, when the King saw that knight, he stooped unto him, and thanked him ; and in likewise did the Queen : and then the King prayed him to put off his helm, and to rest him, and to take a sup of wine. And then he put off his helm to drink, and then every knight knew that he was the noble knight, Sir Launcelot. As soon as the King wist that, he took the Queen by the hand, and went unto Sir Launcelot, and said, " Gramercy ! of your great travail that ye have had this day for me, and for my Queen." " My lord," said Sir Launcelot, " wit ye well that I ought of right ever to be in your quarrel, and in my lady the Queen's quarrel, to do battle ; for ye are the man that gave me the high order of knighthood ; and that day my lady, your Queen, did me great worship, or else I had been shamed. For that same day ye made me knight, through my hastiness I lost my sword, and my lady, your Queen, found it, and lapped it in her train, and gave me my sword when I had need thereof, or else had I been shamed among all knights. And, therefore, my lord, King Arthur, I promised her at that day ever to be her knight in right or in wrong." "Gramercy," said King Arthur, "for this journey : and wit you well," said King Arthur, "I shall acquit you of your goodness." And ever the Queen beheld Sir Launcelot, and wept so tenderly that she sank almost down upon the ground for sorrow that he had done to her so great goodness, whereas she had showed him great unkindness. Then the knights of his blood drew unto him, and there either of them made great joy of other ; and so came all the knights of the Round Table that were there at the time, and he welcomed them ; and then Sir Mador was had to leechcraft, and Sir Launcelot was healed of his wound : and then was there made great joy and mirth in the court.

VIII.

AND so it befell that the Damsel of the Lake, which was called Nimue, the which wedded the good knight, Sir Pelleas ; and so she came to the court, for ever she did great goodness unto King Arthur, and to all his knights, through her sorcery and enchantments. And so when she heard how the King was angry for the death of Sir Patrice, then she told it openly that she was never guilty ; and there she disclosed by whom it was done, and named him Sir Pinell, and for what cause he did it, there it was openly disclosed : and so the Queen was excused, and the knight, Sir Pinell, fled into his country. Then was it openly known that Sir Pinell empoisoned the apples of the feast, to the intent to have destroyed Sir Gawaine, because Sir Gawaine and his brethren destroyed Sir Lamoracke de Galis, to whom Sir Pinell was cousin unto. Then was Sir Patrice buried in the church of Winchester, in a tomb, and thereupon written, "Here lieth Sir Patrice of Ireland, slain by Sir Pinell le Sauvage, that empoisoned apples to have slain Sir Gawaine ; and, by misfortune, Sir Patrice eat one of those apples, and then suddenly he burst." Also there was written upon the tomb, that Queen Guenever was appealed of treason of the death of Sir Patrice by Sir Mador de la Port : and there was made mention how Sir Launcelot fought with him for Queen Guenever, and overcame him in plain battle : and this was writ upon the tomb of Sir Patrice in excusing of the Queen. And then Sir Mador sued daily and long to have the Queen's good grace : and so, by the means of Sir Launcelot, he caused him to stand in the Queen's grace, and all was forgiven.

THE BOOK OF ELAINE.

I.

THUS it passed forth until our Lady-day, the assumption, and within fifteen days of that feast, King Arthur let cry a great joust and tournament that should be at that day at Camelot, that is, Winchester : and the King let cry that he, and the King of Scotland, would joust against all that would come against them. And when this cry was made, thither came many knights : so there came thither the King of Northgalis, and King Anguish of Ireland, and the king with the hundred knights, and Sir Galihud, the haughty prince, and the King of Northumberland, and many other noble dukes and earls of divers countries. So King Arthur made him ready to depart to these jousts, and would have had the Queen with him, but at that time she would not go, she said, for she was sick, and might not ride at that time. "Then me repenteth," said the King, "for these seven years ye saw not such a fellowship together, except at Whitsuntide, when Sir Galahad departed from the court." "Truly," said the Queen unto the King, "ye must hold me excused; I may not be there, and that me repenteth." And many deemed that the Queen would be there, because of Sir Launcelot du Lake, for Sir Launcelot would not ride with the King, for he said that he was not whole of the wound the which Sir Mador had given him ; wherefore the King was passing heavy and wrath, and so departed toward Winchester with his fellowship. And so, by way, the King lodged in a town called Astolat, which is now, in English, called Guildford ; and there the King lay in the castle. So, when the King was departed, the Queen called Sir Launcelot unto her, and thus she said, "Sir Launcelot, ye are greatly to blame, thus to hold you behind my lord ; what trow ye what your enemies and mine will say and deem ? nought else but, See how Sir Launcelot holdeth him ever behind the

King, and so doth the Queen, for that they would have their
pleasure together, and thus will they say," said the Queen unto
Sir Launcelot, "have ye no doubt thereof." "Madam," said
Sir Launcelot to the Queen, " I allow your wit, it is of late come
since ye were wise ; and, therefore, as at this time I will be
ruled by your counsel, and this night I will take my rest, and
to-morrow betimes will I take my way towards Winchester :
but, wit ye well," said Sir Launcelot unto Queen Guenever,
"that at those jousts I will be against the King and all his
fellowship." "Ye may there do as ye list," said Queen Guenever,
"but by my counsel ye shall not be against your King and your
fellowship, for therein are many hardy knights of your blood,
as ye wot well enough it needeth not for to rehearse them."
"Madam," said Sir Launcelot, "I pray you that ye be not displeased with me, for I will take the adventure that God will send
me." And so, on the morrow, Sir Launcelot went to the church
and heard mass, and after broke his fast, and took his leave of
the Queen, and so departed ; and then he rode so long till he
came to Astolat, that now is called Guildford. And there it
happened him in the eventide he came unto a baron's place
which hight Sir Bernard of Astolat ; and as Sir Launcelot
entered into his lodging, King Arthur espied him as he walked in
a garden beside the castle how he took his lodging, and knew him
full well. "It is well said," quoth King Arthur to all the knights
that were there with him, "in yonder garden, beside the castle,
I have espied a knight which will full well play his play at the
jousts, towards which we go : I understand he will do many
deeds of arms." "Who is that, we pray you tell us ?" said the
knights that were there at that time. "Ye shall not know for
me," said the King, "at this time :" so the King smiled, and
went to his lodging. So as Sir Launcelot was in his lodging
and his chamber unarming him, the old baron and the hermit
came unto him, making him reverence, and welcomed him in the
best manner that they could ; but the old knight knew not Sir
Launcelot. "Fair sir," said Sir Launcelot to his host, "I
would pray you to lend me a shield that were not openly known,
for mine is too much known." "Sir," said his host, "ye shall
have your desire, for me seemeth ye be one of the likeliest
knights of the world ; and, therefore, I shall show you friendship.
Sir, wit ye well, I have two sons, which were but late made
knights, and the eldest hight Sir Tirre, and he was hurt the
same day that he was made knight, that he may not ride ; and
his shield ye shall have, for that is not known, I dare say,
but here, and in no place else : and my youngest son hight Sir

Lavaine, and if it please you, he shall ride with you unto these jousts : and he is of his age strong and mighty—for much my heart giveth unto you that ye should be a noble knight ; therefore, I beseech you, tell me your name," said Sir Bernard. "As for that," said Sir Launcelot, "ye must hold me excused as at this time, and if God give me grace to speed well at the jousts, I shall come again and tell you : but I pray you heartily," said Sir Launcelot, "in anywise let me have your son, Sir Lavaine, with me, and that I may have his brother's shield." "Also this shall be done," said Sir Bernard. This old baron had a daughter at that time, that was called the fair maid of Astolat, and ever she beheld Sir Launcelot wonderfully ; and she cast such a love unto Sir Launcelot, that she could not withdraw her love, wherefore she died ; and her name was Elaine le Blaunch. So thus as she came to and fro, she was so hot in her love, that she thought Sir Launcelot should wear upon him at the jousts a token of hers. "Fair damsel," said Sir Launcelot, "and if I grant you that, ye may say I do more for your love than ever I did for lady or damsel." Then he remembered him that he would ride unto the jousts disguised, and for because he had never before that time borne no manner of token of no damsel ; then he bethought him that he would bear one of hers, that none of his blood thereby might know him. And then he said, "Fair damsel, I will grant you to wear a token of yours upon my helmet ; and, therefore, what it is, show me." "Sir," said she, "it is a red sleeve of mine, of scarlet, well embroidered with great pearls ;" and so she brought it him. So Sir Launcelot received it, and said, "Never or this time did I so much for no damsel." And then Sir Launcelot betook the fair damsel his shield in keeping, and prayed her to keep it until he came again. And so that night he had merry rest and great cheer, for ever the fair damsel Elaine was about Sir Launcelot all the while that she might be suffered.

II.

So upon a day, in the morning, King Arthur and all his knights departed ; for the King had tarried there three days to abide his knights. And so when the King was ridden, Sir Launcelot and Sir Lavaine made them ready for to ride, and either of them had white shields, and the red sleeve Sir Launcelot let carry with him. And so they took their leave of Sir Bernard, the old baron, and of his daughter, the fair maid of

Astolat ; and then they rode so long till that they came to
Camelot, which is now called Winchester. And there was great
press of knights, dukes, earls, and barons, and many noble
knights. But there was Sir Launcelot privily lodged, by the
means of Sir Lavaine, with a rich burgess, that no man was
aware what they were. And so they sojourned there till our
Lady-day, the assumption, as the great feast should be. So
then trumpets began to blow unto the field, and King Arthur
was set on high upon a scaffold, to behold who did best : but
King Arthur would not suffer Sir Gawaine to go from him, for
never had Sir Gawaine the better if Sir Launcelot were in the
field ; and many times was Sir Gawaine rebuked when Sir
Launcelot came into any jousts disguised. Then some of the
kings, as King Anguish of Ireland, and the King of Scotland,
were that time turned upon King Arthur's side. And then upon
the other part was the King of Northgalis, and the King with
the hundred knights, and the King of Northumberland, and Sir
Galahalt, the haughty prince. But these three kings, and this
one duke, were passing weak to hold against King Arthur's part,
for with him were the most noble knights of the world. So
then they withdrew them either party from other, and every man
made him ready in his best manner to do what he might. Then
Sir Launcelot made him ready, and put on his red sleeve upon
his head, and fastened it : and Sir Launcelot and Sir Lavaine
departed out of Winchester privily, and rode unto a little leaved
wood behind the party that held against King Arthur's part, and
there they held them still till the parties smote together :
and then came the King of Scotland, and the King of Ireland,
on King Arthur's part. And against them came the King
of Northumberland ; and the King with the hundred knights
smote down the King of Northumberland, and also the King
with the hundred knights smote down King Anguish of
Ireland. Then Sir Palomides, that was on King Arthur's part,
encountered with Sir Galahalt, and either of them smote down
other, and either party helped their lords on horseback again.
So there began a strong assail on both parties ; and there came
in Sir Brandiles, Sir Sagramore le Desirous, Sir Dodinas le
Sauvage, Sir Kaye, the seneschal ; Sir Griflet le fife de Dieu,
Sir Mordred, Sir Meliot de Logris, Sir Ozanna le ever Hardy,
Sir Safre, Sir Epinogris, and Sir Galleron of Galway : all these
fifteen knights of the Round Table. So these, with other more,
came in together, and beat back the King of Northumberland
and the King of Wales. When Sir Launcelot saw this, as he
halted in a little wood, he said unto Sir Lavaine, " See yonder

is a company of good knights, and they hold them together as boars that were chased with dogs." "That is truth," said Sir Lavaine.

III.

"Now," said Sir Launcelot, "and ye will help me a little, ye shall see yonder fellowship, which chased now these men of our side, that they shall go as fast backward as they went forward." "Sir, spare not," said Sir Lavaine, "for I shall do what I may." Then Sir Launcelot and Sir Lavaine came in at the thickest of the press, and there Sir Launcelot smote down Sir Brandiles, Sir Sagramore, Sir Dodinas, Sir Kaye, and Sir Griflet, and all this he did with one spear. And Sir Lavaine smote down Sir Lucas the butler, and Sir Bediver. And then Sir Launcelot got another great spear, and there he smote down Sir Agravaine, Sir Gaheris, Sir Mordred, and Sir Meliot de Logris. And Sir Lavaine smote down Ozanna le ever Hardy. And then Sir Launcelot drew out his sword, and then he smote on the right hand and on the left ; and by great force he unhorsed Sir Safre, Sir Epinogris, and Sir Galleron. And the knights of the Round Table withdrew them back, after they had gotten their horses as well as they might. "O mercy, Jesu," said Sir Gawaine, "what knight is that I see yonder, that doth so marvellous deeds of arms in the fields?" "I wot well who is that," said King Arthur, "but all this time I will not name him." "Sir," said Sir Gawaine, "I would say it were Sir Launcelot, by the riding, and by his buffets that I see him deal. But always me seemeth it should not be he, because he beareth the red sleeve upon the helm, for I wist him never yet bear token at no jousts of lady or gentlewoman." "Let him be," said King Arthur, "for he will be better known, and do more, or he depart." Then the party that were against King Arthur were well comforted, and they held them together, which beforehand were sore rebuked. Then Sir Bors, Sir Ector de Maris, and Sir Lionel called unto them the knights of their blood, as Sir Blamore de Ganis, Sir Bleoberis, Sir Aliduke, Sir Galihud, Sir Galihodin, and Sir Bellangere le Beuse : so these nine knights of Sir Launcelot's kin thrust in mightily, for they were all noble knights ; and they, of great hate and despite that they had to him, thought to rebuke those noble knights, Sir Launcelot and Sir Lavaine, for they knew them not. And so they came hurtling together, and smote down many knights of Northgalis and of Northumberland. And when Sir Launcelot saw them fare so he got a spear in his hand, and there encountered with them all

at once ; Sir Bors, Sir Ector de Maris, and Sir Lionel smote
him all at once with their spears.

And with force of themselves they smote Sir Launcelot's
horse unto the ground, and by misfortune Sir Bors smote Sir
Launcelot through the shield into the side, and the spear break,
and the head abode still inside. When Sir Lavaine saw his
master lie upon the ground, he ran to the King of Scotland, and
smote him to the ground ; and by great force he took his horse,
and, maugre them all, he made him to mount upon that horse.
And then Sir Launcelot did maugre them all, he made him to
mount upon that horse ; and then Sir Launcelot got him a great
spear in his hand, and there he smote Sir Bors, both horse and
man, to the ground : and in the same wise he served Sir Ector
and Sir Lionel. And Sir Lavaine smote down Sir Blamore de
Ganis ; and then Sir Launcelot began to draw his sword, for he
felt himself so sore hurt, that he weened there to have had his
death ; and then he smote Sir Bleoberis such a buffet upon the
helm, that he fell down to the ground in a swoon ; and in the
same wise he served Sir Aliduke and Sir Galihud. And Sir
Lavaine smote down Sir Bellangere, that was the son of Sir
Alisaunder Lorphelin. And by that time Sir Bors was horsed,
and then he came with Sir Ector and Sir Lionel, and they three
smote with their swords upon Sir Launcelot's helmet ; and when
he felt their buffets, and his wound, that was grievous, then he
thought to do what he might while he might endure ; and then
he gave Sir Bors such a buffet, that he made him to bow his
head passing low, and therewithal he raised his helm, and might
have slain him, and so pulled him down. And in the same
manner of wise he served Sir Ector and Sir Lionel : for he
might have slain them ; but, when he saw their visages, his
heart might not serve him thereto, but left them there lying.
And then after he hurtled in among the thickest press of them
all, and did there marvellous deeds of arms that ever any man
saw or heard speak of ; and alway the good knight, Sir Lavaine,
was with him. And then Sir Launcelot, with his sword, smote
and pulled down more knights, and the most part were of the
Round Table. And Sir Lavaine did full well that day, for he
smote down ten knights of the Round Table.

IV.

"AH ! mercy Jesu," said Sir Gawaine unto King Arthur, "I
marvel what knight he is with the red sleeve ?" "Sir," said
King Arthur, "he will be known or he depart." And then the

King let blow unto lodging, and the prize was given by heralds to the knight with the white shield, and that bear the red sleeve. Then came the King with the hundred knights, the King of Northgalis, and the King of Northumberland, and Sir Galahalt, the haughty prince, and said unto Sir Launcelot, "Fair knight, God thee bless, for much have ye done this day for us ; therefore, we pray you, that ye will come with us, that ye may receive the honour and the prize, as ye have worshipfully deserved it." "My fair lords," said Sir Launcelot, "wit ye well, if I have deserved thanks, I have sore bought it, and that me repenteth, for I am like never to escape with my life ; therefore, fair lords, I pray you that ye will suffer me to depart where me liketh, for I am sore hurt, I take no force of none honour ; for I had liefer to rest me than to be lord of all the world." And therewith he groaned piteously, and rode a great gallop away from them, until he came under a wood's side ; and when he saw that he was from the field nigh a mile, that he was sure he might not be seen, then he said, with a high voice, "O gentle knight, Sir Lavaine, help me, that this truncheon were out of my side, for it sticketh so sore, that it almost slayeth me." "O, mine own lord," said Sir Lavaine, "I would fain help you, but it dreads me sore, and I draw out the truncheon, that ye shall be in peril of death." "I charge you," said Sir Launcelot, "as ye love me, draw it out." And therewith he descended from his horse, and so did Sir Lavaine ; and forthwith Sir Lavaine drew the truncheon out of his side : and Sir Launcelot gave a great shriek, and a marvellous ghastly groan, and his blood burst out nigh a pint at once, that at the last he sunk down upon his buttocks and swooned, pale and deadly. "Alas," said Sir Lavaine, "what shall I do now?" And then he turned Sir Launcelot into the wind, but so he lay there nigh half-an-hour, as he had been dead. And so at last Sir Launcelot cast up his eyes, and said, "O, Sir Lavaine, help me, that I were upon my horse ; for here, fast by, within these two miles, is a gentle hermit, which sometime was a noble knight, and a great lord of possessions, and for great goodness he hath taken him unto wilful poverty, and hath forsaken his possessions, and his name is Sir Bawdewine of Britain, and he is a full noble surgeon, and a right good leech. Now, let see, help me up, that I were there ; for always my heart giveth me that I shall not die of my cousin-german's hands." And then with great pain Sir Lavaine helped him upon his horse, and then they. rode a great gallop together ; and ever Sir Launcelot bled, that it ran down to the earth. And so, by fortune, they came unto that hermitage, the which was under a wood, and a great cliff on the other side, and a fair water running under it.   And then Sir Lavaine beat on the gate with the end of his spear, and cried, "Let me in, for Christ's sake."   And then came a fair child to them, and asked them what they would.   "Fair son," said Sir Lavaine, "go and pray thy lord, the hermit, for God's sake, to let in a knight which is right sore wounded ; and this day, tell thy lord, that I saw him do more deeds of arms than ever I heard say that any man did."   So the child went in lightly, and then he brought the hermit, that was a passing good man. So when Sir Lavaine saw him, he prayed him, for God's sake, of succour.   "What knight is he?" said the hermit, "is he of the house of King Arthur or not?"   "I wot not," said Sir Lavaine, "what he is, nor what is his name ; but well I wot I saw him do marvellously this day, as of deeds of arms."   "On whose part was he?" said the hermit.   "Sir," said Sir Lavaine, "he was this day against King Arthur, and there he won the prize of all the knights of the Round Table."   "I have seen the day," said the hermit, "I would have loved him the worse, because he was against my lord King Arthur ; for I was some-time one of the fellowship of the Round Table : but now, I thank God, I am otherwise disposed.   But where is he? Let me see him."   Then Sir Lavaine brought the hermit where the most noble knight, Sir Launcelot, was.

V.

AND when the hermit beheld him, as he sat leaning upon his saddle-bow, ever bleeding piteously ; and alway the knight hermit thought that he should know him, but he could not bring him to knowledge, because he was so pale for bleeding. "What knight are ye?" said the hermit, "and where were ye born?"   "Fair lord," said Sir Launcelot, "I am a stranger, and a knight adventurous, that laboureth throughout many realms, for to win worship."   Then the hermit advised him better, and saw, by a wound on the cheek, that he was Sir Launcelot.   "Alas!" said the hermit, "mine own lord, why hide ye your name from me ; forsooth, I ought to know you of right, for ye are the most noble knight of the world.   For well I know you for Sir Launcelot."   "Sir," said he, "sith ye know me, help me and ye may, for Christ's sake ; for I would be out of this pain at once, either to death or to life."   "Have ye no doubt," said the hermit, "ye shall live, and fare right well." And so the hermit called to him two of his servants: and so he and his servants bear him into the hermitage, and lightly unarmed him, and laid him in his bed. And then anon the hermit stenched the blood, and then he made him to drink good wine; so by that Sir Launcelot was right well refreshed, and came to himself again. For, in those days, it was not the guise of hermits, as it now is in these days: for there were no hermits in those days, but that they had been men of worship and of prowess; and those hermits held great households, and refreshed people that were in distress. Now turn we unto King Arthur, and leave we Sir Launcelot in the hermitage. So when the Kings were together, on both parties, and the great feast should be holden, King Arthur asked the King of Northgalis, and his fellowship, where was the knight that bare the red sleeve, "bring him before me, that he may have his land and honour, and the prize, as it is right." Then spake Sir Galahalt, the haughty prince, and the King with the hundred knights, "We suppose that knight is mischieved, and that he is never like to see you, nor none of us all; and that is the most greatest pity that ever we wist of any knight." "Alas!" said King Arthur, "how may this be, is he so hurt? What is his name?" said King Arthur. "Truly," said they all, "we know not his name, nor from whence he came, nor whither he would." "Alas!" said King Arthur, "these be to me the worst tidings that ever came to me these seven years; for I would not, for all the lands I have, to know, and wit it were so, that noble knight were slain." "Know ye him?" said they all. "As for that," said King Arthur, "whether I know him or not, ye shall not wit for me what he is; but Almighty Jesu send me good tidings of him." And so they said all. "By my head," said Sir Gawaine, "if it be so that the good knight be so hurt, it is great damage and pity to all this land, for he is one of the noblest knights that ever I saw in a field handle a spear or a sword; and, if he may be found, I shall find him, for I am sure that he is not far from this town." "Bear you well," said King Arthur, "and ye may find him; without that he be in such a plight that he may not bestir himself." "Jesu defend," said Sir Gawaine, "but I shall know what he is and if I may find him." Right so, Sir Gawaine took a squire with him, and rode upon two hackneys, all about Camelot, within six or seven miles. But as he went, so he came again, and could hear no word of him. Then within two days King Arthur, and all the fellowship, returned to London again; and so, as they rode by the way, it happened Sir Gawaine, at Astolat, to lodge with Sir Bernard, where Sir Launcelot was lodged. And so, as Sir Gawaine was in his chamber, for to take his rest, Sir Bernard, the old baron, came to him, and also his fair daughter, Elaine, for to cheer him, and to ask him what tidings he knew, and who did best at the tournament at Winchester. "So God help me," said Sir Gawaine, "there were two knights, which bear two white shields, but the one of them bear a red sleeve upon his head, and certainly he was one of the best knights that ever I saw joust in the field. For, I dare make it good," said Sir Gawaine, "that one knight with the red sleeve smote down forty valiant knights of the Round Table, and his fellow did right well and worshipfully." "Now, blessed be God," said the fair maid of Astolat, "that the good knight sped so well; for he is the man in the world the which I first loved, and truly he shall be the last man that ever after I shall love." "Now, fair maid," said Sir Gawaine, "is that good knight your love?" "Certainly," said she, "wit ye well he is my love." "Then know ye his name?" said Sir Gawaine, "Naturally," said the maid, "I know not his name, nor from whence he came : but, to say that I love him, I promise God and you that I love him." "How had ye knowledge of him first?" said Sir Gawaine.

VI.

THEN she told him, as ye have heard before, and how her father betook him her brother to do him service, and how her father lent him her brother Sir Tirre's shield, and here with her he left his own shield. "For what cause did he so?" said Sir Gawaine. "For this cause," said the damsel; "for his shield was too well known among many noble knights." "Ah, fair damsel," said Sir Gawaine, "please it you for to let me have a sight of that shield." "Sir," said she, "it is in my chamber, covered with a case, and if it will please you to come in with me ye shall see it." "Not so," said Sir Bernard unto his daughter, "let send for it." So when the shield was come Sir Gawaine took off the case ; and, when he beheld that shield, he knew anon that it was Sir Launcelot's shield, and his own arms. "Ah! Jesu mercy," said Sir Gawaine, "now is my heart more heavier than ever it was before." "Why?" said the damsel, Elaine. "For I have a great cause," said Sir Gawaine; "is that knight that owneth that shield your love?" "Yes, truly," said she, "my love he is : God would that I were his love." "So God me speed!" said Sir Gawaine, "fair damsel, ye love the most honourable knight of the world, and the man of most worship." "So me thought ever," said the damsel, "for never or that time, for no knight that ever I saw, loved I never none erst." "God grant," said Sir Gawaine, "that either of you may rejoice other, but that is in a great adventure. But truly," said Sir Gawaine unto the damsel, "ye may say ye have a fair grace; for why? I have known that noble knight this fourteen years, and never or that day, I or none other knight, I dare make it good, saw nor heard that ever he bear token or sign of no lady nor gentlewoman, nor maid at any jousts nor tournament; and therefore, fair maid," said Sir Gawaine, "ye are much beholden to give him thanks. But I dread me," said Sir Gawaine, "ye shall never see him in this world, and that is great pity as ever was of earthly knight." "Alas!" said she, "how may this be; is he slain?" "I say not so," said Sir Gawaine; "but wit ye well that he is grievously wounded by all manner of signs, and by men's sight more likelier to be dead than to be alive, and wit ye well, he is the noble knight, Sir Launcelot; for by his shield I know him." "Alas!" said the fair maid, Elaine, "how may it be? what was his hurt?" "Truly," said Sir Gawaine, "the man in the world that loveth him best hurt him so, and I dare say," said Sir Gawaine, "and that knight that hurt him knew the very certain that he had hurt Sir Launcelot, it would be the most sorrow that ever came to his heart." "Now, fair father," said Elaine, "I require you give me leave to ride and to seek him, or else I wot well I shall go out of my mind, for I shall never stint till that I have found him and my brother, Sir Lavaine." "Do as ye think best," said her father, "for me right sore repenteth of the hurt of that noble knight." So the maid made her ready before Sir Gawaine, mak'ng great dole. Then on the morrow Sir Gawaine came unto King Arthur, and told him how he had found Sir Launcelot's shield in the keeping of the fair maid of Astolat. "All that I knew," said King Arthur, "and that caused me I would not suffer you to have to do at the great jousts. For I espied him," said King Arthur, "when he came into his lodging, full late in the evening, in Astolat; but marvel have I," said King Arthur, "that ever he would bear any sign of any damsel, for or now I never heard say nor knew that ever he bear any token of no earthly woman." "By my head," said Sir Gawaine, "the fair maid of Astolat loveth Sir Launcelot marvellously well, but what it meaneth I cannot say; and she is ridden after him for to seek him."

So King Arthur and all his court came to London, and there Sir Gawaine openly disclosed unto all the court that it was the noble knight, Sir Launcelot, that jousted best.

VII.

AND when Sir Bors heard that, wit ye well he was a heavy and a sorrowful man, and so were all his kinsmen. But when Queen Guenever wist that Sir Launcelot bear the red sleeve of the fair maid of Astolat, she was nigh out of her mind for anger and wrath : and then she sent for Sir Bors de Ganis, in all the haste that might be. So when Sir Bors came afore the Queen, she said unto him, "Ah ! Sir Bors, have ye heard say how falsely Sir Launcelot hath betrayed me?" "Alas ! madam," said Sir Bors, "I am afraid he hath betrayed himself and us all." "No force," said the Queen, "though that he be destroyed, for he is but a false, traitorous knight." "Madam," said Sir Bors, "I beseech you say not so, for wit ye well I may not hear such language of him." "Why, Sir Bors," said the Queen, "should I not call him a traitor, when he bear the red sleeve upon is head at Winchester, at the great tournament?" "Madam," said Sir Bors, "that red sleeve-bearing repenteth me sore ; but I dare say he did it to none evil intent, but for this cause he bear the red sleeve, that none of us that be of his blood should know him. For or then he nor one of us all, never knew that ever he bear token or sign of maid, lady, or gentlewoman." "Fie on him," said the Queen, "notwithstanding for all his pride and boldness, yet there ye proved yourself his better." "Nay, madam," said Sir Bors, "say ye never more so, for he beat me and my fellows, and might have slain us, if he had liked." "Fie on him," said Queen Guenever, "for I heard Sir Gawaine say, before my lord Arthur, that marvel it were to tell the great love that is between the fair maid of Astolat and him." "Madam," said Sir Bors, "I may not warn Sir Gawaine to say what it pleased him ; but I dare say, as for my lord, Sir Launcelot, that he loveth no lady, gentlewoman, nor maid, but all he loveth in like much ; and therefore, madam," said Sir Bors, "ye may say what ye will that I will haste me to seek him and find him wheresoever he be, and God send me good tidings of him."

And so leave we them there, and speak we of Sir Launcelot, that lay in great peril. So as the fair maid Elaine came to Winchester, she sought there all about, and by fortune Sir Lavaine was ridden to play him and to enchase his horse. And anon as fair Elaine saw him, she knew him, and then she cried aloud unto him : and when he heard her, anon he came unto her, and then she asked her brother, "How fareth my lord, Sir Launcelot?" "Who told you, sister, that my lord's name was Sir Launcelot?" Then she told him how Sir Gawaine by his shield knew him. So they rode together till they came unto the hermitage, and anon she alighted : so Sir Lavaine brought her unto Sir Launcelot, and when she saw him lie so sick and pale in his bed, she might not speak, but suddenly she fell unto the ground in a swoon, and there she lay a great while. And when she was relieved, she sighed, and said, " My lord, Sir Launcelot, alas ! why go ye in this plight ? " and then she swooned again. Then Sir Launcelot prayed Sir . Lavaine to take her up, and to bring her to him. And when she came to herself again, Sir Launcelot kissed her, and said, " Fair maid, why fare ye thus, ye put me to pain ; wherefore make ye no more such cheer, for and ye be come to comfort me, ye be right welcome, and of this little hurt that I have, I shall be full hastily whole by the grace of God. But I marvel," said Sir Launcelot, " who told you my name ? " Then the fair maid told him all how Sir Gawaine was lodged with her father, " and there by your shield he discovered your name." " Alas ! " said Sir Launcelot, " me sore repenteth that my name is known, for I am sure that it will turn to anger." And then Sir Launcelot compassed in his mind that Sir Gawaine would tell Queen Guenever how he bear the red sleeve, and for whom, that he wist well that it would turn to great anger. So this maid, Elaine, never went from Sir Launcelot, but watched him day and night, and gave such attendance upon him, there was never woman did more kindlier for man than she did. Then Sir Launcelot prayed Sir Lavaine to make espies in Winchester for Sir Bors, if he came there, and told him by what token he should know him, by a wound in his forehead. " For well I am sure," said Sir Launcelot, " that Sir Bors will seek me, for he is the good knight that hurt me."

VIII.

Now turn we unto Sir Bors de Ganis, that came to Winchester to seek after his cousin, Sir Launcelot : and so when he came to Winchester, anon there were men that Sir Lavaine had made to lie in watch for such a man, and anon Sir Lavaine had warning thereof. And then Sir Lavaine came to Winchester and found Sir Bors, and there he told him what he was, and what his name was. " Now, courteous knight," said Sir Bors, " I require you that ye will bring me unto my lord, Sir Launcelot." " Sir," said Sir Lavaine, " take your horse, and within this hour ye shall see him." And so they departed and came unto the hermitage, where Sir Launcelot was ; and when Sir Bors saw Sir Launcelot lie in his bed all pale and discoloured, anon Sir Bors lost his countenance, and for kindness and for pity he might not speak, but wept full tenderly a great while. And then when he might speak, he said unto him thus : " O, my lord, Sir Launcelot ! God bless you, and send you hasty recovery ; and full heavy am I of my misfortune, and of mine unhappiness, for now I may call myself unhappy, and I dread and fear me that God is greatly displeased with me, that he would suffer me to have such a shame for to hurt you, that are all our leader and all our worship, and therefore I call myself unhappy. Alas ! that ever such a captive knight as I am should have power, by unhappiness, to hurt the most noble knight of all the world, where I so shamefully set upon you, and overcharged you ; and whereas ye might have slain me, ye saved me, and so did not I, for I and my blood did to you our uttermost. I marvel," said Sir Bors, "that my heart or blood would serve me, wherefore my lord, Sir Launcelot, I ask you mercy." "Fair cousin," said Sir Launcelot, "ye are right heartily welcome, and wit ye well ye say overmuch to please me, which pleaseth me not ; for why I have the same I sought, for I would with pride have overcome you every each one, and there in my pride I was nigh slain, and that was through mine own default, for I might have given you warning of my being there, and then had I not been hurt : for it is an old saying, 'There is a hard battle whereas kin and friendship do battle either against other, there may be no mercy, but mortal war.' Therefore, fair cousin," said Sir Launcelot, "let this speech overpass, and all shall be welcome that God sendeth ; and let us leave of this matter, and let us speak of some rejoicing. For this that is done may not be undone, and let us find some remedy how soon that I may be whole." Then Sir Bors leaned upon his bed's side, and there he told Sir Launcelot how the Queen was passing wrath with him, because he wore the red sleeve at the great jousts. And there Sir Bors told him all how Sir Gawaine discovered it by his shield, which he left with the fair maid of Astolat. "Then is the Queen wroth," said Sir Launcelot, "and therefore am I right heavy, for I deserved no wrath ; for all that I did was because that I would not be known." "Knight, so excused I you," said Sir Bors ; "but all was in vain : for she said more largelier to me than I to you now. But is this she," said Sir Bors, "that is so busy about you, that men call the Fair Maid of Astolat ?" "She it is," said Sir Launcelot, "which, by no manner of means, I can put from me." "Why should ye put her from you?" said Sir Bors, "she is a passing fair damsel, and well beseen, and well taught; and, would to God, fair cousin," said Sir Bors, "that ye could love her. But, as to that, I may not, nor dare not, counsel you; but I see well," said Sir Bors, "by her diligence about you, that she loveth you entirely." "That me repenteth," said Sir Launcelot. "Sir," said Sir Bors, "she is not the first that hath lost her pain upon you, and that is the more pity." And so they talked of many other things more; and so, within four or five days, Sir Launcelot was big and strong again.

IX.

THEN Sir Bors told Sir Launcelot how that there was sworn a great tournament and jousts between King Arthur and the King of Northgalis, that should be upon Allhallowmas-day, beside Winchester. "Is that truth?" said Sir Launcelot; "then shall ye abide still with me a little while, until that I be whole; for I feel myself right big and strong." "Blessed be God," said Sir Bors. Then they abode there almost a month together; and ever this fair maid, Elaine, did her diligence and labour night and day unto Sir Launcelot, that there was never child more meeker unto the father, nor wife unto her husband, than was that fair maid of Astolat; wherefore, Sir Bors was greatly pleased with her. So upon a day, by the assent of Sir Launcelot, Sir Bors and Sir Lavaine made the hermit to go seek in woods for diver herbs; and so Sir Launcelot made fair Elaine for to gather herbs for him to make him a bane. In the meanwhile Sir Launcelot made him to arm him at all points, and there he thought for to assay his armour and his spear for his hurt or not. And, when he was upon his horse, he spurred him fiercely; and the horse was passing lusty and fresh, because he was not laboured a month before: and then Sir Launcelot couched his spear in the rest. So that courser leapt mightily, when he felt the spurs, and him that was upon him, the which was the noblest knight in the world; he steered him rigorously, and he stiffly and stably kept still the spear in the rest. And therewith Sir Launcelot strained himself so straightly with so great a force to get his horse forward, that the bottom of the wound broke, both within and without; and therewith the blood came out so fiercely, that he felt himself so feeble that he might not sit upon his horse. And then Sir Launcelot cried unto Sir Bors, "Ah! Sir Bors, and Sir

Lavaine, help me ; for I come unto mine end." And therewith he fell down on the one side unto the ground, like a dead corpse. And then Sir Bors and Sir Lavaine came to him, making out of measure great sorrow ; and so, by fortune, the maid Elaine heard their sorrow and dole, and then she came thither. And, when she found Sir Launcelot there armed in that place, she cried and wept as she had been mad ; and then she kissed him, and did what she might to awake him. And then she rebuked her brother and Sir Bors, and called them both false traitors, and why they would take him out of his bed ? There she cried, and said she would appeal them of his death. With this came the holy hermit, Sir Bawdewine of Britain ; and, when he found Sir Launcelot in that plight, he said but little ; but wit ye well he was right wrath. And then he said to them, "Let us have him in." And so they all bear him into the hermitage, and unarmed him, and laid him in his bed ; and evermore his wound bled piteously, but he stirred no limb of his body. Then the knight-hermit put a thing in his nose, and a little deal of water in his mouth ; and then Sir Launcelot awakened out of his swoon. And then the hermit staunched his bleeding ; and, when he might speak, he asked Sir Launcelot why he put his life in jeopardy. "Sir," said Sir Launcelot, "for because I weened I had been strong enough ; and also Sir Bors told me that there should be at Allhallowmas a great joust between King Arthur and the King of Northgalis : and, therefore, I thought to assay myself, if I might be there or not." "Ah ! Sir Launcelot," said the hermit, "your heart and your courage will never be done, until your last day. But ye shall do now by my counsel. Let Sir Bors depart from you, and let him do at that tournament what he may. And, by the grace of God," said the knight-hermit, "by that the tournament be done, and ye come hither again, Sir Launcelot shall be as whole as ye, so that he will be ruled by me."

X.

AND then Sir Bors made him ready to depart from Sir Launcelot ; and then Sir Launcelot said, "Fair cousin, Sir Bors, recommend me unto all them unto whom I ought to recommend me unto ; and I pray you enforce yourself at that joust, that ye may be best for my love ; and here shall I abide you, at the mercy of God, till ye come again." And so Sir Bors departed, and came to the court of King Arthur, and told them in what place he had left Sir Launcelot. "That me repenteth," said the King; "but, sith he shall have his life, we all may thank God." And there Sir Bors told the Queen in what great jeopardy Sir Launcelot was, when he would assay his horse. "And all that he did, madam, was for the love of you, because he would have been at this tournament." "Fie on him, recreant knight!" said the Queen; "for wit ye well I am right sorry and he shall have his life." "His life shall he have," said Sir Bors; "and who that would otherwise (except you, madam), we that be of his blood should help to shorten their lives. But, madam," said Sir Bors, "ye have been oftentimes displeased with my lord, Sir Launcelot; but at all times, at the end, ye find him a true knight." And so he departed; and then every knight of the Round Table that was there present at that time made them ready to be at the jousts of Allhallowmas · and thither drew many knights of many countries. And, as Allhallowmas drew near, thither came the King of Northgalis, and the King with the hundred knights, and Sir Galahalt, the haughty prince of Surluse; and thither came King Anguish of Ireland, and the King of Scotland. So these three knights came on King Arthur's part. And so that day Sir Gawaine did great deeds of arms, and began first; and the heralds numbered that Sir Gawaine smote down twenty knights. Then came in at that same time Sir Bors de Ganis, and he was numbered that he had smitten down twenty knights; and, therefore, the prize was given between them both: for they began first, and longest endured. Also Sir Gareth did that day great deeds of arms: for he smote down and pulled down thirty knights: but, when he had done these deeds, he tarried not, but so departed; and, therefore, he lost his prize. And Sir Palomides did great deeds of arms that day; for he smote down twenty knights. But he departed suddenly; and men deemed that Sir Gareth and he rode together on some adventure.

So when this tournament was done, Sir Bors departed, and rode till he came to Sir Launcelot, his cousin, and then he found him walking on his feet; and there either made great joy of other. And so Sir Bors told Sir Launcelot of all the jousts, like as ye have heard. "I marvel," said Sir Launcelot, "that Sir Gareth, when he had done such deeds of arms, that he would not tarry." "Thereof we marvelled all," said Sir Bors; "for, but if it were you, or Sir Tristram, or Sir Lamoracke de Galis, I saw never knight bear down so many in so little a while as did Sir Gareth; and anon he was gone we wist not where." "By my head," said Sir Launcelot, "he is a noble knight and a

16

mighty man, and well breathed. And if that he were strongly assayed," said Sir Launcelot, "I would deem that he were good enough for any man that beareth life. And he is a gentle knight, courteous, true, and bounteous, meek and mild ; and in him is no manner of malice, but plain, faithful, and true." So then they made them ready to depart from the hermit. And so, upon a day, they took their horses, and took Elaine le Blaunch with them ; and, when they came to Astolat, there they were well lodged, and had great cheer of Sir Bernard, the old baron, and of Sir Tirre, his son. And so, on the morrow, when Sir Launcelot should depart, fair Elaine brought her father with her, and her two brethren, Sir Tirre and Sir Lavaine, and thus she said :—

XI.

"My lord, Sir Launcelot, now I see that ye will depart, fair and courteous knight, have mercy upon me, and suffer me not to die for your love." "What would you that I did ?" said Sir Launcelot. "I would have you unto my husband," said the maid Elaine. "Fair damsel, I thank you," said Sir Launcelot ; "but certainly," said he, "I cast me never to be married." "Then, fair knight," said she, "will ye be my love ?" "Jesu defend me !" said Sir Launcelot ; "for then should I reward your father and your brother full evil for their great goodness." "Alas !" said she, "then must I needs die for your love." "Ye shall not," said Sir Launcelot ; "for wit ye well, fair damsel, that I might have been married and I had would ; but I never applied me to be married. But because, fair damsel, that ye will love me as ye say ye do, I will, for your good love and kindness, show you some goodness ; and that is this : That wheresoever ye will set your heart upon some good knight that will wed you, I shall give you together a thousand pounds yearly to you and to your heirs. Thus much will I give you, fair maid, for your kindness, and always while I live to be your own knight." "Of all this," said the damsel, "I will none ; for but if ye will wed me, or else be my love at the least, wit ye well, Sir Launcelot, my good days are done." "Fair damsel," said Sir Launcelot, "of these two things ye must pardon me." Then she shrieked shrilly, and fell down to the ground in a swoon ; and that gentlewoman bear her into her chamber, and there she made ever much sorrow. And then Sir Launcelot would depart ; and there he asked Sir Lavaine what he would do? "What should I do," said Sir Lavaine, "but follow you, but if ye drive me from you." Then came Sir Bernard unto Sir Launcelot, and said unto him thus : " I cannot see but that my daughter, Elaine, will die for your sake." "I may not do thereto," said Sir Launcelot, "for that me sore repenteth. For I report me unto yourself, that my proffer is fair ; and me repenteth," said Sir Launcelot, "that she loveth me as she doth. I was never the causer of it : for I report me unto your son, I early nor late proffered her bounty nor fair behests. And as for me," said Sir Launcelot, "I dare do all that a good knight should do, that she is a clean maid for me, both for deed and for will ; and I am right heavy of her distress ; for she is a full fair maid, good and gentle, and right well taught." "Father," said Sir Lavaine, "I dare make it good that she is a clean maid as for my lord, Sir Launcelot ; but she doth as I do. For, sithence that I first saw my lord, Sir Launcelot, I could never depart from him ; nor nought I will, and I may follow him." Then Sir Launcelot took his leave ; and so they departed, and came to Winchester. And when King Arthur wist that Sir Launcelot was come whole and sound, the King made great joy of him ; and so did Sir Gawaine and all the knights of the Round Table, except Sir Agravaine and Sir Mordred. And also Queen Guenever was waxed wrath with Sir Launcelot, and would by no means speak with him, but estranged herself from him : and Sir Launcelot made all the means that he might to speak with the Queen, but it would not be.

Now speak we of the fair maid of Astolat, which made such sorrow day and night, that she never slept, eat, nor drank ; and always she made her complaint unto Sir Launcelot. So when she had thus endured about ten days, that she felt that she must needs pass out of this world. Then she shrove her clean, and received her Creator ; and ever she complained still upon Sir Launcelot. Then her ghostly father bade her leave such thoughts. Then said she, "Why should I leave such thoughts ? am I not an earthly woman ? and all the while the breath is in my body, I may complain. For my belief is, that I do none offence, though I love an earthly man ; and I take God unto record, I never loved any but Sir Launcelot du Lake, nor never shall : and a maiden I am, for him and for all other. And sith it is the sufferance of God that I shall die for the love of so noble a knight, I beseech the high Father of heaven for to have mercy upon my soul ; and that mine innumerable pains which I suffer may be allegiance of part of my sins. For our sweet Saviour, Jesu Christ," said the maiden, "I take thee to record, I was never greater offender against thy laws, but that I loved this noble knight, Sir Launcelot, out of all measure: and of myself, good Lord! I might not withstand the fervent love, wherefore I have my death." And then she called her father, Sir Bernard, and her brother, Sir Tirre; and heartily she prayed her father that her brother might write a letter like as she would indite it. And so her father granted it her. And, when the letter was written, word by word, as she had devised, then she prayed her father that she might be watched until she were dead. "And while my body is whole let this letter be put into my right hand, and my hand bound fast with the letter until that I be cold; and let me be put in a fair bed, with all the richest clothes that I have about me. And so let my bed, with all my rich clothes, be laid with me in a chariot to the next place whereas the Thames is; and there let me be put in a barge, and but one man with me, such as ye trust, to steer me thither, and that my barge be covered with black samite over and over. Thus, father, I beseech you let be done." So her father granted her faithfully that all this thing should be done like as she had devised. Then her father and her brother made great dole; for, when this was done, anon she died. And so, when she was dead, the corpse, and the bed, and all, were led the next way unto the Thames; and there a man, and the corpse and all, were put in a barge on the Thames: and so the man steered the barge to Westminster, and there he rode a great while to and fro or any man discovered it.

XII.

So, by fortune, King Arthur and Queen Guenever were speaking together at a window: and so as they looked into the Thames, they espied the black barge, and had marvel what it might mean. Then the King called Sir Kaye, and showed him it. "Sir," said Sir Kaye, "wit ye well that there is some new tidings." "Go ye thither," said the King unto Sir Kaye, "and take with you Sir Brandiles and Sir Agravaine, and bring me ready word what is there." Then these three knights departed and came to the barge, and went in; and there they found the fairest corpse, lying in a rich bed, that ever they saw, and a poor man sitting in the end of the barge, and no word would he speak. So these three knights returned unto the King again, and told him what they had found. "That fair corpse will I see," said King Arthur. And then the King took the Queen by the hand, and went thither. Then the King made the barge to be holden fast; and then the King and the

Queen went in with certain knights with them ; and there they saw a fair gentlewoman, lying in a rich bed, covered unto her middle with many rich clothes, and all was cloth of gold : and she lay as though she had smiled. Then the Queen espied the letter in the right hand, and told the King thereof. Then the King took it in his hand, and said, "Now I am sure this letter will tell what she was, and why she is come hither." Then the King and the Queen went out of the barge ; and the King commanded certain men to wait upon the barge. And so when the King was come within his chamber, he called many knights about him, and said "that he would wit openly what was written within that letter." Then the King broke it open, and made a clerk to read it. And this was the intent of the letter :—

"Most noble knight, my lord, Sir Launcelot. du Lake, now hath death made us two at debate for your love. I was your love, that men called the Fair Maiden of Astolat ; therefore unto all ladies I make my moan. Yet for my soul that ye pray, and bury me at the least, and offer me my mass penny. This is my last request : and a clean maid I died, I take God to my witness. Pray for my soul, Sir Launcelot, as thou art a knight peerless." This was all the substance of the letter. And when it was read, the Queen and all the knights wept for pity of the doleful complaints. Then was Sir Launcelot sent for ; and when he was come King Arthur made the letter to be read to him. And when Sir Launcelot had heard it, word by word, he said, "My lord, King Arthur, wit you well that I am right heavy of the death of this fair damsel. God knoweth I was never causer of her death by my will ; and that I will report me unto her own brother here, he is Sir Lavaine. I will not say nay," said Sir Launcelot, "but that she was both fair and good ; and much was I beholden unto her : but she loved me out of measure." "Ye might have showed her," said the Queen, "some bounty and gentleness, that ye might have preserved her life." "Madam," said Sir Launcelot, "she would none other way be answered, but that she would be my wife, or else my love ; and of these two I would not grant her ; but I proffered her for her good love, which she showed me, a thousand pounds yearly to her and her heirs, and to wed any manner of knight that she could find best to love in her heart. For, madam," said Sir Launcelot, "I love not to be constrained to love ; for love must arise of the heart, and not by constraint." "That is truth," said King Arthur and many knights ; "love is free in himself, and never will be bound ; for where he is bound, he loseth himself. Then," said the King unto Sir Launcelot, "it will be your worship that ye oversee that she be buried worshipfully." "Sir," said Sir Launcelot, "that shall be done as I can best devise." And so many knights went thither to behold the fair dead maid. And on the morrow she was richly buried, and Sir Launcelot offered her mass penny; and all the knights of the Round Table that were there, at that time, offered with Sir Launcelot. And then, when all was done, the poor man went again with the barge. Then the Queen sent for Sir Launcelot, and prayed him of mercy, for because she had been wrath with him causeless. "This is not the first time," said Sir Launcelot, "that ye have been displeased with my counsels; but, madam, ever I must suffer you, but what sorrow that I endure, ye take no force." So this passed forth all that winter, with all manner of hunting and hawking, and jousts and tourneys were many between many great lords. And ever, in all manner of places, Sir Lavaine got great worship, that he was nobly renowned among many of the knights of the Round Table. Thus it passed on until Christmas, and every day there were jousts made for a diamond, that whosoever joust best should have a diamond. But Sir Launcelot would not joust, but if it were a great joust cried: but Sir Lavaine jousted there all the Christmas passing well, and most was praised; for there were but few that did so well as he; wherefore all manner of knights deemed that Sir Lavaine should be made a knight of the Round Table, at the next high feast of Pentecost.

So after Christmas King Arthur let call to him many of his knights, and there they advised them together to make a part, and a great tournament and jousts. And the King of Northgalis said unto King Arthur, "that he should have on his part King Anguish of Ireland, and the King with the hundred knights, and the King of Northumberland, and Sir Galahalt, the haughty prince." So these four Kings, and this mighty duke, took a part against King Arthur and the knights of the Round Table. And the cry was made of the day, and jousts should be beside Westminster on Candlemas-day; whereof many knights were full glad, and made them ready to be at that joust in the freshest manner that they could. Then Queen Guenever sent for Sir Launcelot; and, when he was come, she said to him in this manner: "I warn you that ye ride no more in no jousts nor tournament, but that your kinsmen may know you; for at these jousts that shall be, ye shall have of me a sleeve of cloth of gold; and I pray you, for my sake, enforce yourself so there, that men may speak of your worship: but I charge you, as ye will have my love, that ye warn your kinsmen, that ye will bear

that day the sleeve of cloth of gold upon your helmet."
"Madam," said Sir Launcelot, "your desire shall be done."
And so either made of other great joy. And when Sir Launcelot saw his time, he told Sir Bors, "that he should depart, and no more with him but Sir Lavaine, unto the good hermit that dwelled in the forest of Windsor, whose name was Sir Brastias, and there he thought to rest him, and to take all the ease that he might, because he would be fresh at that day of jousts." When Sir Launcelot and Sir Lavaine were ready, they departed, that no creature wist where he was become, but the noble men of his blood. And so when he was come unto the hermitage, wit you well he had good cheer; and so daily Sir Launcelot would go to a well, fast by the hermitage, and there he would lie down and see the well spring and bubble, and sometimes he slept there. So at that time there was a lady dwelled in that forest, and she was a great huntress, and daily she used to hunt; and always she bear her bow with her; and no men went never with her, but always women, and they were shooters, and could well kill a deer, but at the stalk and at the trest; and they daily bear bows and arrows, horns, and wood knives, and many good hounds they had, both for the string and for a bait. So it happened that this lady, the huntress, had baited her hounds for the bow, at a barren hind; and this barren hind took her flight over heaths and woods. And ever this lady and part of her gentlewomen coursed the hind, and checked it by the noise of the hound, for to have met with the hind at some water. And so it happened that the said hind came to the well, whereas Sir Launcelot was sleeping and slumbering. And so the hind, when she came to the well, for heat she went to the soil, and there she lay a great while; and the hound came fast after, and made a cast about, for she had lost the perfect scent of the hind. Right so there came the lady huntress, which knew by her hound that the hind was at the soil in that well: and there she came stiffly, and found the hind. And anon she put a broad arrow in her bow, and shot at the hind, and overshot the hind, and, by misfortune, the broad arrow smote Sir Launcelot in the thick of the buttock over the barbs. When Sir Launcelot felt himself so hurt, he hurtled up woodly, and saw the lady which had smitten him. And then when he saw she was a woman, he said thus: "Lady, or damsel, what that thou be, in an evil time bear thou a bow, the devil made thee a shooter."

XIII.

"Now mercy, fair sir," said the lady, "I am a gentlewoman that used here in this forest hunting, and our Lord knoweth I saw you not; but as here is a barren hind at the soil in the well, and I weened to have done well, but my hand swerved." "Alas!" said Sir Launcelot, "now have ye mischieved me." And so the lady departed. And Sir Launcelot as well as he might drew out the arrow, and the head abode still in his buttock, and so went weakly unto the hermitage, ever bleeding as he went. And when Sir Lavaine and the hermit espied that Sir Launcelot was hurt, wit ye well they were passing heavy; but Sir Launcelot nor the hermit wist not how he was hurt, nor by whom: and then were they wrath out of measure. Then, with great pain, the hermit got out the arrow-head out of Sir Launcelot's buttock, and much of his blood he shed at that time, and the wound was passing sore, and right unhappily smitten; for the wound was in such a place that Sir Launcelot might not sit in a saddle. "Ah! mercy, Jesu," said Sir Launcelot, I call myself the most unhappiest knight that liveth; for ever when I would fainest have worship, there befalleth me ever some unhappy thing. Now, so Jesu me help," said Sir Launcelot, "and if no man would but God, I shall be in the field upon Candlemas-day at the joists, whatsoever fall of it." So all that might be gotten to heal Sir Launcelot was had. So when the day was come, Sir Launcelot let devise that he was arrayed, and Sir Lavaine and their horses, as though they had been Saracens,

And so they departed, and came nigh to the field. The King of Northgalis, with a hundred knights with him; and the King of Northumberland also brought with him a hundred good knights; and King Anguish, of Ireland, brought with him a hundred good knights, ready to joust; and Sir Galahalt, the haut prince, brought with him a hundred good knights; and the King with the hundred knights brought with him as many; and all these were proved knights. And then came in King Arthur's part: and there came in the King of Scotland, with a hundred knights; and King Urience, of Core, brought with him a hundred good knights; and King Howel, of Britain, brought with him a hundred knights; and King Chalaunce, of Clarence, brought with him a hundred knights; and King Arthur himself came into the field with two hundred knights, and the most part were knights of the Round Table, which were proved noble knights. And there were old knights set upon scaffolds, to judge with the Queen who did best.

XIV.

THEN they blew unto the field, and there the King of Northgalis encountered with the King of Scotland, and there the King of Scotland had a fall. And the King of Ireland smote down King Urience, and the King of Northumberland smote down King Howel, of Britain; and Sir Galahalt, the haut prince, smote down King Chalaunce, of Clarence. And at that King Arthur was waxed wrath, and ran to the King with the hundred knights, and there King Arthur smote him down; and after, with that same spear, King Arthur smote down three other knights; and then, when his spear was broken, King Arthur did passing well. And so therewithal came Sir Gawaine and Sir Gaheris, Sir Agravaine and Sir Mordred, and there every each of them smote down a knight. And Sir Gawaine smote down four knights. And then there began a full strong meddle: for then there came in the knights of Sir Launcelot's blood, and Sir Gareth, and Sir Palomides with them, and many knights of the Round Table: and they began to hold the four kings and the mighty duke so hard, that they were discomfited. But their duke, Sir Galahalt, the haut prince, was a noble knight, and by his mighty prowess of arms he held the knights of the Round Table straight enough. All these doings saw Sir Launcelot, and then he came into the field with Sir Lavaine, as it had been thunder. And then Sir Bors, and the knights of his blood, espied Sir Launcelot, and said unto them all, "I warn you, beware of him with the sleeve of gold upon his head, for he himself is Sir Launcelot du Lake." And for great goodness Sir Bors warned Sir Gareth. "I am well assayed," said Sir Gareth, "that I may know him in the same array." "That is the good and gentle knight, Sir Lavaine," said Sir Bors. So Sir Launcelot encountered with Sir Gawaine, and there, by force, Sir Launcelot smote down Sir Gawaine and his horse to the ground; and likewise he smote down Sir Agravaine and Sir Gaheris, and also he smote down Sir Mordred, and all this was done with one spear. Then Sir Lavaine met with Sir Palomides, and either met other so hard and so fiercely, that both their horses fell to the ground, and then they were horsed again. And then met Sir Launcelot with Sir Palomides, and there Sir Palomides had a fall. So Sir Launcelot, or ever he stinted, as fast as he might get spears, he smote down thirty knights, and the most of them were knights of the Round Table. And ever the knights of his blood withdrew them, and made them to do in other places where Sir Launcelot came not. And then King Arthur was wrath, when he saw Sir Launcelot do such deeds. Then the King called unto Sir Gawaine, Sir Mordred, Sir Kaye, Sir Griflet, Sir Lucas, the butler; Sir Pedivere, Sir Palomides, and Sir Safre, his brother, and so King Arthur, with these nine knights, made them ready for to set upon Sir Launcelot and upon Sir Lavaine. All this espied Sir Bors de Galis, and Sir Gareth of Orkney. "Now I dread me sore," said Sir Bors, "that my lord Sir Launcelot will be hard matched." "By my head," said Sir Gareth, "I will ride unto my lord Sir Launcelot for to help him, befall of me what may, for he is the same man that made me knight." "Ye shall not do so," said Sir Bors, "by my counsel, unless that ye were disguised." "Ye shall see me disguised," said Sir Gareth, "and that anon."

And therewith he espied a Welsh knight where he was to rest himself; and he was sore hurt before by Sir Gawaine, and to him Sir Gareth rode, prayed him of his knighthood for to lend him his shield for his. "I will well," said the Welsh knight. And when Sir Gareth had his shield, it was green, with a maiden that seemed in it. Then Sir Gareth came driving as fast as he might unto Sir Launcelot, and said thus unto him, "Sir knight, keep thyself, for yonder cometh King Arthur, with nine noble knights with him, to put you to rebuke; and so am I come to bear you fellowship for old love ye have shown me." "Gramercy," said Sir Launcelot. "Sir," said Sir Gareth, "encounter with Sir Gawaine, and I shall encounter with Sir Palomides, and let Sir Lavaine match with King Arthur; and when we have delivered them, let us three hold us steadily together." Then came King Arthur with his nine knights with him, and Sir Launcelot encountered with Sir Gawaine, and gave him such a buffet, that the arson of his saddle broke, and Sir Gawaine fell to the earth. Then Sir Gareth encountered with the good knight, Sir Palomides, and he gave him such a buffet, that both his horse and he dashed to the earth. Then encountered King Arthur with Sir Lavaine, and there either of them smote other to the earth, horse and all, that they lay a great while.

Then Sir Launcelot smote down Sir Agravaine, Sir Gaheris, and Sir Mordred. And then Sir Gareth smote down Sir Kaye, Sir Safre, and Sir Griflet; and when Sir Lavaine was horsed again, he smote down Sir Lucas, the butler, and Sir Pedivere; and then there began a great throng of good knights. Then Sir Launcelot hurtled and pulled off helms, so that at that time there might none sit him a buffet with his spear nor his sword. And Sir Gareth did such deeds of arms, that all men marvelled what knight he was with the green shield, for he smote down that day and pulled down more than thirty knights. And Sir Launcelot marvelled greatly when he beheld Sir Gareth do such deeds what knight he might be ; and Sir Lavaine pulled down and smote down twenty knights. Also Sir Launcelot knew not Sir Gareth, for and Sir Tristram de Lyons or Sir Lamoracke de Galis had been alive, Sir Launcelot would have deemed that he had been one of them twain.

So ever as Sir Launcelot, Sir Gareth, and Sir Lavaine fought ; and, on the other side, Sir Bors, Sir Ector de Maris, Sir Lionel, Sir Bleoberis, and Sir Galihud, Sir Galihodin, Sir Pelleas, with more others of King Ben's blood, fought on another part, and held the King with the hundred knights, and also the King of Northumberland, right straight and right hardy.

XV.

So this jousting and the tournament endured long, till it was almost night ; for the knights of the Round Table relieved ever unto King Arthur, for the King was wrath out of measure, but he and his knights might not prevail this day. Then Sir Gawaine said unto King Arthur, "I marvel where all this day Sir Bors de Galis, and his fellows of Sir Launcelot's blood be ; I marvel me all this day greatly that they be not about you ; it is for some cause," said Sir Gawaine. "By my head," said Sir Kaye, "Sir Bors is yonder all this day upon the right hand of the field, and there he and his blood done more worshipfully than we do." "It may well be," said Sir Gawaine, "but I dread me always of guile ; for, upon pain of my life," said Sir Gawaine, "this knight with the red sleeve of gold is Sir Launcelot himself, I see well by his riding, and by his great strokes given ; and the other knight in the same colour is the good young knight, Sir Lavaine. Also, that knight with the green shield is my brother, Sir Gareth, and yet he hath disguised himself, for no man can make him to be against Sir Launcelot, because he made him knight." "By my head," said King Arthur, "nephew, I believe you, therefore tell me now what is your best counsel." "Sir," said Sir Gawaine, "ye shall have my best counsel : let blow unto lodging, for and if he be Sir Launcelot, and my brother, Sir Gareth, with him, with the help of that good young knight, Sir Lavaine, trust me truly it will be no boot to strive with them, but if we should fall ten or twelve upon one knight, and that were no worship, but shame." "Ye say truth," said the King, "and for to say sooth," said the King, "it were shame to us, so many as

we be, to set upon them any more; for, wit ye well," said
King Arthur, "they be three good knights, and, namely, that
knight with the red sleeve of gold;" so then they blew unto
lodging.   But forthwithal King Arthur let send unto the four
kings, and unto the mighty duke, that the knight with the sleeve
of cloth of gold depart not from them, but that the King
may speak with him.   Then forthwithal King Arthur alighted
and unarmed him, and gat him a little hackney, and rode after
Sir Launcelot, for ever he had an eye upon him.   And so they
found him among the four kings and the duke.   And there
King Arthur prayed them all unto supper, and they answered
with a good will.   And so when they were all unarmed, King
Arthur knew Sir Launcelot, .Sir Lavaine, and Sir Gareth.
"Ah, Sir Launcelot," said King Arthur, "this day ye have hated
me and my knights."   So they went unto King Arthur's lodging
altogether; and the prize was given unto Sir Launcelot; and by
heralds they named him that he had smitten down fifty knights,
and Sir Gareth thirty-five, and Sir Lavaine twenty-four knights.
Then Sir Launcelot told the King and the Queen how the
lady huntress shot him in the forest of Windsor, in the buttock,
with a broad arrow, and how the wound thereof was that
time six inches deep, and also in like long.   And King Arthur
blamed Sir Gareth, because he left his fellowship and held with
Sir Launcelot.   "My lord," said Sir Gareth, "he made me a
knight, and when I saw him so hard bestead, me thought it was
my worship to help him, because I saw him do so much, and
so many noble knights against him.   And when I understood
that he was Sir Launcelot du Lake, I shamed me to see so
many knights against him alone."   "Truly," said King Arthur
unto Sir Gareth, "ye say well, and worshipfully have ye done,
and to yourself great worship; and all the days of my life,"
said King Arthur unto Sir Gareth, "wit ye well, I shall love
you and trust you the better: for ever," said King Arthur, "it
is a worshipful knight's deed for to help another worshipful
knight, when he seeth him in great danger; for, ever a worshipful man will be loth to see a worshipful man shamed: and he
that is of no worship, and fareth with cowardice, never shall he
show gentleness, nor no manner of goodness, whereas he seeth
a man in any danger; for then ever a coward will show no
mercy, and always a good knight will do ever to another knight
as he would be done unto himself."   So then there were made
great feasts to kings and dukes, and revel, game, and play, and
all manner of nobleness was used : and he that was courteous,
true, and faithful unto his friend, was that time cherished.

THE BOOK OF THE QUEEN'S MAYING.

I.

AND thus it passed on from Candlemas until after Easter, that the month of May was come, when every lusty heart beginneth to blossom, and to bring forth fruit. For, like as herbs and trees bring forth fruit, and flourish in May, in likewise every lusty heart, that is in any manner a lover, springeth and flourisheth in lusty deeds; for it giveth unto all lovers courage that lusty month of May in some thing, for to constrain him in some manner of thing, more in that month than in any other month, for divers causes; for then all herbs and trees renew a man and woman. And, in likewise, lovers call again to their mind old gentleness and old service, and many kind deeds that were forgotten by negligence. For, like as winter rasure doth always rase and deface green summer; so fareth it by unstable love in a man, and in woman, for in many persons there is no stability. For we may see all day a little blast of winter's rasure, anon we shall deface and put away true love for little or naught, that cost much thing; this is no wisdom nor stability, but is feebleness of nature, and great disworship, whosoever useth this. Therefore, like as May month flowereth and flourisheth in many gardens, so in likewise let every man of worship flourish his heart in this world; first unto God, and next unto the joy of them that he promiseth his faith unto. For there was never worshipful woman, but they loved one better than another. And worship in arms may never be defiled. But first, reserve the honour unto God; and secondly, the quarrel must come of thy lady; and such love I call virtuous love. But now-a-days men cannot love, may not endure by reason; for where they be soon accorded, and hasty heat soon cooleth; right so fareth love now-a-days, soon hot, soon cold. This is no stability, but the old love was not so. Men and women could love together seven years, and no lusts were between them; and then was love truth and faithfulness. And so in likewise was love used in King Arthur's days; wherefore, I liken love now-a-days unto summer and winter: for, like as the one is hot and the other cold, so fareth love now-a-days. Therefore, all ye that be lovers, call unto your remembrance the month of May, like as did Queen Guenever, for whom I make here a little mention, that while she lived she was a true lover, and there she had a good end.

II.

Now it befell in the month of lusty May that Queen Guenever called unto her knights of the Round Table, and she gave them warning, that early in the morning she should ride a-maying into woods and fields beside Westminster; "And I warn you that there be none of you but that he be well horsed, and that ye all be clothed in green; and I shall bring with me ten ladies, and every knight shall have a lady behind him, and every knight shall have a squire and two yeomen, and I will that ye and all be well horsed." So they made them ready in the freshest manner, and these were the names of the knights: Sir Kaye, Sir Agravaine, Sir Brandiles, Sir Sagramore, Sir Donidas, Sir Ozanna, Sir Ladinas, Sir Persuant, Sir Ironside, and Sir Pelleas. And those ten knights made them ready in the most freshest manner to ride with the Queen. So on the morrow they took their horses and rode a-maying with the Queen in great joy and delight; and the Queen purposed to have been again with the King at the furthest by ten of the clock, and so was her purpose at that time. Then there was a knight, the which hight Sir Meliagraunce, and he was son unto King Bagdemagus; and this knight had at that time a castle of the gift of King Arthur, within seven miles of Westminster. And this knight, Sir Meliagraunce, loved passing well Queen Guenever, and so he had done long and many years; and he had laid long in wait for to steal away the Queen, but evermore he forbear, because of Sir Launcelot du Lake, for in nowise he would meddle with the Queen if Sir Launcelot were in her company, or else and he were near hand her; and that time there was such a custom, that the Queen rode never without a great fellowship of men of arms about her; and there were many good knights, and the most part were young men that would have worship, and they were called the Queen's knights, and never in no battle, tournament, or jousts, they never bear none of them no manner of knowledge of their own arms, but plain white shields, and thereby they were called the Queen's knights. And then when it happened any of them to be of great worship by his noble deeds, then at the next high feast of Pentecost, if there were any slain or dead, as there was no year that failed but some were dead, then was there chosen in their stead that were dead the most men of worship, that were called the Queen's knights. And thus they came up all first, or they were renowned men of worship, both Sir Launcelot and all the remnant of them. But this knight, Sir Meliagraunce, had full well espied the Queen and her purpose, and how Sir Launcelot was not with her, and how she had no men of arms with her, but the ten knights all arrayed in green for maying. Then he purveyed him twenty men of arms, and a hundred archers to destroy the Queen and her knights, for he thought that time was the best season to take the Queen.

III.

So as the Queen had mayed and all her knights, all were bedecked with herbs and flowers, in the best manner and freshest. Right so came out of a wood Sir Meliagraunce, with eight score men well armed, as they should fight in battle of arrest, and bade the Queen and her knights abide, for maugre there heads they should abide. "Traitor knight," said Queen Guenever, "what thinkest thou to do? wilt thou shame thyself? Bethink thee how thou art a king's son, and knight of the Round Table, and thou to be about for to dishonour the noble king that made thee knight; thou shamest the high order of knighthood and thyself! And me, I let thee wit, shalt thou never shame, for I had rather cut my throat in twain, rather than thou shouldest dishonour me." "As for all this language," said Sir Meliagraunce, "be it as it may, for wit ye well, madam, that I have loved you many years, and never or now could I get you at such advantage as I do now, and therefore I will take you as I find you." Then spake the ten knights all with one voice, and said, "Sir Meliagraunce, wit ye well ye are about to jeopard your worship to dishonour, also ye cast for to jeopard our persons; howbeit we be unarmed, ye have us at a great advantage, for it seemeth by you that ye have laid watch on us; but rather than ye should put the Queen to shame and us all, we had as leave to depart from our lives, for and if we otherwise did we were shamed for ever." Then Sir Meliagrance said, "Dress you as well as ye can, and keep the Queen." Then the ten knights of the Round Table drew their swords, and the others let run at them with their spears; and the ten knights manly abode them, and smote away their spears, that no spear did them harm. Then they lashed together with their swords, and anon Sir Kaye, Sir Griflet, Sir Agravaine, Sir Dodinas, and Sir Ozanna were smitten to the earth with grimly wounds. Then Sir Brandiles and Sir Persaunt, Sir Ironside and Sir Pelleas, fought long, and they were full sore wounded; for these knights, or ever they were laid to the ground, slew forty men of the best of them. So when the Queen saw her knights thus dolefully wounded, and needs must be slain at the last, then for pity and sorrow she cried and said, " Sir Meliagraunce, slay not my knights, and I will go with thee upon this covenant, that thou save them, and suffer them to be no more hurt ; with this, that they be led with me wheresoever thou leadest me, for I will rather slay myself than I will go with thee, unless that these, my noble knights, may be in presence." " Madam," said Sir Meliagraunce, " for your sake they shall be led with you into my castle, with that ye will be ruled and ride with me."

Then Queen Guenever prayed the four knights to leave their fight, and she and they would not depart. "Madam," said Sir Pelleas, "we will do as ye do ; for as for me, I take no force of my life nor death." For Sir Pelleas gave such buffets there, that no armour might hold them.

IV.

THEN by the Queen's command they left battle, and dressed the wounded knights on horseback, some sitting and some athward, that it was pity to behold them. And then Sir Meliagraunce charged the Queen and all the knights, that none of her fellowship should depart from her ; for full sore he dreaded Sir Launcelot du Lake, lest he should have any knowledge. All this espied the Queen, and privily she called unto her a child of her chamber, which was swiftly horsed, to whom she said, " Go thou, when thou seest thy time, and bear this ring unto Sir Launcelot du Lake, and pray him as he loveth me that he will come and see me, and that he rescue me if ever he will have joy of me, and spare not thou thy horse," said the Queen, " neither for water nor yet for land." And so the child espied his time, and lightly he mounted upon his horse, and smote him with his spurs, and so departed from them as fast as ever his horse might run. And when Sir Meliagraunce saw the child so flee, he understood well it was by the Queen's command, for to warn Sir Launcelot. Then they that were best horsed chased him, and shot at him ; but the child went from them all. And then Sir Meliagraunce said unto Queen Guenever, " Madam, ye be about to betray me ; but I shall ordain for Sir Launcelot, that he shall not lightly come at you." And then he rode with her and they all to his castle, in all the haste that they might ; and by the way Sir Meliagraunce laid in an ambushment the best archers that he might get in his country, to the number of thirty, for to wait upon Sir Launcelot, charging them, that if they saw such a manner of knight come by the way upon a white horse, in anywise to slay his horse ; but in no manner of wise not to have to do with him bodily, for he is overhard to be overcome. So this was done, and they were come to his castle ; but in nowise the Queen would never let none of the ten knights and her ladies be out of her sight, but alway they were in her presence : for that Sir Meliagraunce durst make no masteries for dread of Sir Launcelot, insomuch as he deemed that he had warning. So when the child was departed from the fellowship of Sir Meliagraunce, within a while he came to Westminster, and anon he found Sir Launcelot ; and when he had told his message, and delivered him the Queen's ring, "Alas !" said Sir Launcelot, "now am I shamed for ever only that I may rescue that noble lady from dishonour." Then eagerly he asked his armour, and ever the child told Sir Launcelot how the ten knights fought marvellously, and how Sir Pelleas, Sir Ironside, Sir Brandiles, and Sir Persaunt of Inde fought strongly, but mainly Sir Pelleas ; for there was none might withstand him, and how they all fought till at the last they were laid to the earth. And then the Queen made appointment for to save their lives, and went with Sir Meligraunce. "Alas !" said Sir Launcelot, "that·that most noble knight should be destroyed ; I had rather," said Sir Launcelot, "than all the realm of France, that I had been there well armed." So when Sir Launcelot was all armed and upon his horse, he prayed the child of the Queen's chamber for to warn Sir Lavaine how suddenly he was departed, and for what cause ; and pray him that, as he loveth me, that he will hie him fast after me, and that he stint not till that he come to me unto the castle whereas Sir Meliagraunce abideth or dwelleth. "For there," said Sir Launcelot, "shall he hear of me, if I be a man living ; and rescue the queen, and the ten knights, the which full traitorously have been taken, that shall I prove upon his head, and all them that holdeth with him."

V.

THEN Sir Launcelot rode as fast as he might, and then he took the water at Westminster bridge, and made his horse for to swim over the Thames to Lambeth. And then within a while he came to the place whereas the ten knights had fought with Sir Meliagraunce. And then Sir Launcelot followed the trace until he came unto a wood, and there was a straight way, and therein the thirty archers bade Sir Launcelot to turn again and follow no longer the trace. "What command have ye thereto," said Sir Launcelot, "to cause me, that am a knight of the Round Table, to leave my right way?" "This way shalt thou leave, or else thou shalt go it upon thy feet; for wit thou well, thy horse shall be slain." "That is little mastery," said Sir Launcelot, "for to slay my horse; but as for myself, when my horse is slain, I give right nought for you, not and ye were five hundred more." So then they shot Sir Launcelot's horse, and smote him with many arrows. And then Sir Launcelot avoided his horse and went on foot; but there were so many ditches and hedges between them and him, that he might not meddle with one of them. "Alas! for shame," said Sir Launcelot, "that ever one knight should betray another knight; but it is an old saying, 'A good man is never in danger but when he is in danger of a coward.'" Then Sir Launcelot went awhile on foot, and then was he foul cumbered with his armour, shield, and spear, and all that belonged to him; wit ye well he was full sore annoyed, and full loth he was to leave any thing that belonged unto him, for he dread right sore the treason of Sir Meliagraunce. And then by fortune there came by a chariot, the which came thither for to fetch wood. "Tell me, carter," said Sir Launcelot, "what I shall give thee for to suffer me to leap into the chariot, and that thou bring me unto a castle within these two miles." "Thou shalt not come within my chariot," said the carter; "for I am sent for to fetch wood for my lord, Sir Meliagraunce." "With him would I fain speak," said Sir Launcelot. "Thou shalt not go with me," said the carter. Then Sir Launcelot leapt to him, and gave him such a buffet, that he fell to the ground stark dead. Then the other carter, his fellow, was afraid, and thought to have gone the same way, and then he cried and said, "Fair lord, save my life, and I will bring you where you will." "Then I charge thee," said Sir Launcelot, "that thou drive me and this chariot even unto Sir Meliagraunce Castle." "Leap up into the chariot," said the carter, "and ye shall be there anon." So the carter drove forth as fast as he could; and Sir Launcelot's horse followed the chariot with more than forty arrows broad and rough in him. And more than an hour and a-half Queen Guenever was in a bye window waiting with her ladies, and espied an armed knight standing in a chariot, "See, madam," said a lady, "whereas rideth in a chariot a goodly armed knight; I suppose that he rideth to hanging." "Where?" said the Queen. And then the Queen espied by his shield that he was there himself, Sir Launcelot du Lake. And then she was aware where came his horse after that chariot. "Alas!" said the Queen, "now I see well and prove, that well is him that hath a trusty friend. Ah! most noble knight," said Queen Guenever, "I see well that thou hast been hard bestead, when thou ridest in a cart." Then she rebuked that lady that likened him to ride in a chariot to hanging. "It was foul mouthed," said the Queen, "and evil likened, so for to liken the most noble knight in the world in such a shameful death. Oh! Jesu, defend him and keep him," said the Queen, "from all mischievous end." By this was Sir Launcelot come unto the gate of the castle, and he descended down, and cried, that all the castle rang of it : "Where art thou, false traitor, Sir Meliagraunce, and knight of the Round Table? Now come forth here, thou false traitor knight, thou and thy fellowship with thee, for here I am, Sir Launcelot du Lake ; I shall fight with thee." And therewithal he bear the gate wide open upon the porter, and smote him under his ear with his gauntlet, that his neck brake asunder.

VI.

So when Sir Meliagraunce heard that Sir Launcelot was come, he ran to the Queen, and fell upon his knees, and said, "Mercy, madam! now I put me wholly in your grace." "What aileth you now?" said Queen Guenever : "forsooth, ye might well wit that some good knight would revenge me, though my lord King Arthur wist not of this your work." "Madam," said Sir Meliagraunce, "all that is done amiss on my part shall be amended, right as yourself will devise, and wholly I put me in your grace." "What would ye that I did ?" said the Queen. "I would no more," said Sir Meliagraunce, "but that ye would take into your own hands, and that ye will rule my lord, Sir Launcelot ; and such cheer as may be made him in this poor castle ye and he shall have until to-morrow. And then may ye and all your knights and ladies return to Westminster, and my body, and all that I have, shall I put into your rule." "Ye say well," said the Queen ; "and better is peace than always war ; and the less strife is made, the more is my worship." Then the Queen and her ladies went down unto the knight, Sir Launcelot, which stood wroth out of measure in the inner court for to abide battle, and ever he said, "Thou traitor knight, come forth here!" Then the Queen came unto him, and

said, "Sir Launcelot, why be ye so moved?"   "Ah! madam,"
said Sir Launcelot, "wherefore ask ye me that question?   Me
seemeth," said Sir Launcelot, "ye ought to be more displeased
than I am, for ye have the hurt and the dishonour; for wit ye
well, madam, my hurt is but little for the killing of a mare's son,
but the despite grieveth me much more than all my hurt."
"Truly," said Queen Guenever, "ye say truth: but heartily I
thank you," said the Queen, "but ye must come in with me
peaceably, for all things is put in my hands, and all that is evil
shall be for the best, for the knight full sore repenteth him for
the misadventure that is befallen him."   "Madam," said Sir
Launcelot, "sith it is so that ye are accorded with him; as for
me, I may not be against it, howbeit Sir Meliagraunce hath
done full shamefully to me and full cowardly.   Madam," said
Sir Launcelot, "if I had wist that ye would have been so soon
accorded with him, I would not have made such haste to you."
"Why say you so?" said the Queen: "do you forethink yourself of your good deeds?   Wit ye well," said the Queen, "I
accorded never unto him for favour, nor love that I have unto
him, but for to lay down every shameful noise."   "Madam,"
said Sir Launcelot, "ye understand full well that I was never
willing nor glad of shameful slander nor noise; and there is
neither king, queen, nor knight that beareth life, except my
lord King Arthur and you, madam, that should let me, but that
I should make Sir Meliagraunce's heart full cold or I depart from
hence."   "That wot I well," said the Queen, "but what will ye
more; ye shall have all things ruled as ye like to have it."
"Madam," said Sir Launcelot, "so that ye be pleased, I care
not; as for my part, ye shall full soon please."   Right so the
Queen took Sir Launcelot by the bare hand, for he had put off
his gauntlet, and so she went with him to her chamber.   And
then she commanded him to be unarmed; and then Sir
Launcelot asked where the ten knights were, that were sore
wounded.   So she showed them unto Sir Launcelot, and there
they made great joy of his coming; and Sir Launcelot made
great dole for their hurts, and bewailed them greatly.   And
there Sir Launcelot told them how cowardly and traitorously
Sir Meliagraunce had set archers to slay his horse, and how he
was fain to put himself in a chariot.   Thus they complained the
one unto the other: and full fain they would have been revenged,
but they appeased themselves because of the Queen.   Then Sir
Launcelot was called many a day after Le Chevalier du Chariot,
and did many deeds, and great adventures he had.

And so leave we off this tale of Chevalier du Chariot, and

return we unto our tale. So Sir Launcelot had great cheer with the Queen ; and then Sir Launcelot made a promise with the Queen, that the same night he should come into a window, outward into a garden, and that window was barred with iron. And there Sir Launcelot promised for to meet her, when all folks were asleep. So then came Sir Lavaine driving to the gate, crying, "Where is my lord, Sir Launcelot du Lake?" Then was he forthwith sent for, and when Sir Lavaine saw Sir Launcelot he said, "My lord, I found well how ye were hard bestead, for I have found your horse, the which was slain with arrows." "As for that," said Sir Launcelot, "I pray you, Sir Lavaine, speak ye of other matters, and let this pass ; and we shall right it another time, when we best may."

VII.

THEN the knights that were wounded were searched, and soft salves were laid to their wounds, and so it passed on till supper time ; and all the cheer that might be made them, there it was showed unto the Queen and her knights. Then, when season was, they went to their chamber : but in no wise the Queen would not suffer the wounded knights to be from her, but that they were laid within draughts, upon beds and pillows, that she herself might see to them, that they lacked nothing. So when Sir Launcelot was in his chamber, that was assigned unto him, he called unto him Sir Lavaine, and told him, that that night he must go speak with his lady, Dame Guenever. "Sir," said Sir Lavaine, "let me go with you, and it please you; for I dread me sore of the treason of Sir Meliagraunce." "Nay," said Sir Launcelot, "I thank you ; I will have no person with me at this time." And then Sir Launcelot took his sword in his hand, and privily went unto a place whereas he had espied a ladder beforehand, and that he took under his arm, and bear it through the garden, and set it up in a window, and there anon the Queen was ready to meet him ; and then they made either to other their complaints of divers things : and then Sir Launcelot wished that he might come in. "Wit ye well," said the Queen, "I would as fain as ye that ye might come in." "Would ye, madam," said Sir Launcelot, "with your heart that I were with you?" "Yea, truly," said the Queen. "Now shall I prove my might," said Sir Launcelot, "for the love of you." And then he set his hand upon the bars of iron, and pulled at them with such a great might, that he break them clean out of the stone walls ; and therewithal one of the bars of iron cut the brawn of Sir

Launcelot's hand throughout to the bone, and then he leapt into the chamber to the Queen. "Make ye no noise," said the Queen, "for my wounded knights lie here fast by me." And so, to pass forth upon this tale, Sir Launcelot took no force of his hurt hand, but took his pleasure and his liking until it was in the dawning of the day; and wit ye well he slept not, but watched. And when he saw the time that he might tarry no longer, he took his leave, and departed at the window, and put it together again as well as he might, and so departed and came to his own chamber. And there he told Sir Lavaine how he was hurt. Then Sir Lavaine dressed his hand, and staunched it, and put upon it a glove, that it should not be espied. And so the Queen lay long in her bed, until it was nine of the clock. Then Sir Meliagraunce went to the Queen's chamber, and found her ladies there ready clothed. "Jesu, mercy!" said Sir Meliagraunce, "what aileth you, madam, that ye sleep thus long?" And so forthwithal he opened the curtains for to behold her; and then was he ware where she lay, and all the sheet and pillow was all bloody, with the blood of Sir Launcelot's hurt hand: and when Sir Meliagraunce espied that blood, then he deemed in himself that she was false unto the King, and that some of the wounded knights had been with her all that night. "Ah! madam," said Sir Meliagraunce, "now I have found you false traitoress unto my lord, King Arthur; for now I prove it well, that it was not for nought that ye laid these wounded knights within the bounds of your chamber. Therefore I will accuse you of treason before my liege lord, King Arthur, and now I have proved you, madam, with a shameful deed, and that they be all false, or some of them, and that I will make good; for a wounded knight this night hath been with you." "That is false," said the Queen, "and that I report me to them all." Then, when the ten knights heard Sir Meliagraunce's words, they spake all with one voice, and said to Sir Meliagraunce, "Thou sayest falsely, and wrongfully puttest upon us such a deed; and that we will make good, any of us, choose which thou list of us, when we are whole of our wounds." "Ye shall not," said Sir Meliagraunce, "say nay, with proud language: for here ye may all see," said Sir Meliagraunce, "that by the Queen this night a wounded knight hath lain." Then were they all ashamed when they saw that blood. And wit ye well that Sir Meliagraunce was passing glad that he had the Queen at such advantage, for he deemed that should hide his treason. So in this rumour came in Sir Launcelot, and found them all at a great array.

VIII.

"AHA! what array is this?" said Sir Launcelot. Then Sir Meliagraunce told him what he had found, and showed him the Queen's bed. "Truly," said Sir Launcelot, "ye did not your part, nor knightly, to touch a queen's bed, the while it was drawn, and she lying therein. For I dare say, and make good, that my lord King Arthur himself would not have displaced her curtains, she being within her bed, unless that it had pleased him to have lain down by her; and therefore have ye done unworshipfully and shamefully to yourself." "I wot not what you mean," said Sir Meliagraunce: "but well I am sure there hath one of her wounded knights lain with her this night; and therefore I will prove it, by my hands, that she is a traitoress unto my lord, King Arthur." "Beware what ye do," said Sir Launcelot, "for and ye say so, and that he will prove it, it shall be taken at your hands." "My lord, Sir Launcelot," said Sir Meliagraunce, "be you aware also what ye do; for though ye are never so good a knight, as wot ye well that ye are renowned the best knight of the world, yet should ye be advised to do battle in a wrong quarrel. For God will have a stroke in every battle that is done." "As for that," said Sir Launcelot, "God is to be dreaded. But as to that I say nay plainly, that this night there was none of these ten wounded knights with my lady, Queen Guenever, and that will I prove with my hands, that ye say untruly in that now." . "Hold!" said Sir Meliagraunce, "here is my glove, that she is a traitoress unto my lord, King Arthur." "And I receive your glove," said Sir Launcelot. And so they were sealed with their signets, and delivered to the ten knights. "Upon what day shall we do battle together?" said Sir Launcelot. "This day eight days," said Sir Meliagraunce, "in the field beside Westminster." "I am agreed," said Sir Launcelot. "But now," said Meliagraunce, "sith it is that we must do battle together, I beseech you, as ye are a noble knight, await me with no treason, nor no villainy, in the meanwhile." "Nor none for you, so God me help," said Sir Launcelot: "ye shall right well wit I was never of these conditions, for I report me unto all knights that ever knew me, I used never no treason; nor I loved never to be in the fellowship of no man that used treason." "Then let us go to dinner," said Sir Meliagraunce, "and after dinner ye and the Queen, and ye all, may ride unto Westminster." "I will well," said Sir Launcelot. And then Sir Meliagraunce said unto Sir Launcelot, "Please it you to see the features of this castle?" "With a good will," said Sir

Launcelot. And then they went together from chamber to chamber : for Sir Launcelot dreaded no perils. For ever a man of worship and of prowess dreadeth always perils least ; for they ween that every man is as they be ; but always he that dealeth with treason putteth a man oft in great danger. So it befell upon Sir Launcelot that no peril dreaded. And, as he went with Sir Meliagraunce, he trod on a trap, and the board rolled, and therewith Sir Launcelot fell down more than ten fathom into a cave, upon straw. And then Sir Meliagraunce departed, and made semblance as though he had not wist where he was. And when Sir Launcelot was thus missed, they marvelled where he was become ; and then Queen Guenever, and many of them, deemed that he was departed, as he was wont to do suddenly. For Sir Meliagraunce made suddenly to put out of the way Sir Launcelot's horse, that they might all understand that Sir Launcelot was departed suddenly. So it past forth until after dinner, and then Sir Lavaine would not stint until that he had ordained horse-litters for the wounded knights, that they might be laid in them ; and so with the Queen, and them all, both ladies and gentlewomen, and many other went to Westminster. And the knights told unto King Arthur how Sir Meliagraunce had appealed the Queen of high treason ; and how Sir Launcelot had received the glove of him, and this day eight days they shall do battle together afore you. " By my head," said King Arthur, " I am afraid that Sir Meliagraunce hath taken upon him a great charge : but where is Sir Launcelot ?" said the King. " Sir," said they all, " we wit not where he is ; but we deem he is ridden to some adventures, as he is oftentimes wont to do, for he hath Sir Lavaine's horse." " Let him be," said the king ; "he will be found, but if he be trapped with some treason."

IX.

Now return we unto Sir Launcelot, lying within that cave, in great pain. And every day there came a lady and brought him his meat and his drink, and wooed him to have his love ; and ever the noble knight, Sir Launcelot, said her nay. " Sir Launcelot," said she, " ye are not wise, for ye may never come out of this prison, but if ye have my help ; and also your lady, Queen Guenever, shall be burnt in your default, unless that you be there at the day of battle." " God defend it," said Sir Launcelot, "that she should be burnt in my default ; and if that be so," said Sir Launcelot, "that I may not be there, it shall be well understood, of both the King and of the Queen, and with all men of worship, that I am dead, or sick, or else in prison ; for all men that know me will say for me, that I am in some evil case, if I be not there that day : and well I wot there is some good knight, either of my blood, or else some other that loveth me, that will take my quarrel in hand ; and, therefore," said Sir Launcelot, "wit ye well that ye shall not fear me : and if there were no more women in this land but you, I would not have your love." "Then art thou shamed and destroyed for ever," said the lady. "As for world's shame," said Sir Launce-lot, "Jesu defend me ; and as for my distress, it is welcome whatsoever it be that God sendeth me." So she came unto Sir Launcelot that same day that the battle should be, and said to him, "Sir Launcelot, me thinketh ye are too strong hearted ; but wouldest thou kiss me once, I would deliver thee and thine armour, and the best horse that is within Sir Meligraunce's stable." "As for to kiss you," said Sir Launcelot, "I may do that and loose no worship ; and wit you well, and I understand there was any disworship for to kiss you, I would not do it" Then he kissed her, and then she gat him, and brought him to his armour. And when he was armed she brought him to a stable, whereas stood twelve good coursers, and bade him choose the best. Then Sir Launcelot looked upon a white courser which liked him best ; and anon he commanded the keeper fast to saddle him with the best saddle of war that was there : and so it was done as he commanded. Then gat he his spear in his hand, and his sword by his side, and commended the lady to God, and said, "Lady, for this good deed I shall do you service, if ever it be in my power."

X.

Now leave we Sir Launcelot galloping all that he might, and speak we of Queen Guenever that was brought to a fire to have been burnt ; for Sir Meliagraunce was sure him thought that Sir Launcelot should not be at that battle ; and, therefore, he ever cried upon King Arthur for to do him justice, or else for to bring forth Sir Launcelot. Then was the King and all the court full sore abashed and shamed, that the Queen should be burnt in the default of Sir Launcelot. "My good lord, King Arthur," said Sir Lavaine, "ye may right well understand that it is not well with my lord, Sir Launcelot, for and he were alive, so that he be not sick or in prison, wit ye well that he would be here, for never heard ye that ever he failed his part for whom he should do battle for; and, therefore, now," said Sir Lavaine, "my lord, King Arthur, I beseech you give me license to do battle here this day for my lord and master, and for to save my lady, the Queen." "Gramercy, gentle knight, Sir Lavaine," said King Arthur, "for I dare say that that Sir Meliagraunce putteth upon my lady, Queen Guenever, is wrong; for I have spoken with all the ten wounded knights, and there is not one of them, and he were whole, and able to do battle, but that he would prove upon Sir Meliagraunce's body that it is false that he putteth upon the Queen." "So shall I," said Sir Lavaine, "in defending of my lord, Sir Launcelot, and ye will give me leave." "Now I give you leave," said King Arthur, "and do your best; for I dare well say there is some treason done to Sir Launcelot." Then was Sir Lavaine horsed, and suddenly at the list's end he rode to perform this battle. And right as the heralds should cry, "*Laissez les aller,*" right so came in Sir Launcelot, driving with all the force of his horse. And so King Arthur cried, "Go and abide." Then was Sir Launcelot called before King Arthur on horseback, and there he told openly before the King, and all them that were present, how Sir Meliagraunce had served him first and last. And when the King and the Queen and all the lords knew of the treason of Sir Meliagraunce, they were all ashamed on his behalf. And then was Queen Guenever sent for, and set by the King in great trust of her champion. And so then there was no more to say, but Sir Launcelot and Sir Meligraunce dressed them unto battle, and took their spears, and so they came together as thunder, and there Sir Launcelot bore him down quite over his horse's croup: and then Sir Launcelot alighted and dressed his shield on his shoulder, with his sword in his hand: and Sir Meligraunce in the same wise dressed him unto Sir Launcelot. And there they smote many strokes together; and at the last Sir Launcelot smote him such a buffet upon the helm, that he fell on the one side to the ground, and then he cried upon him aloud, "Most noble knight, Sir Launcelot du Lake, I pray you save my life, for I yield me unto you; and I beseech you, as ye be a knight and fellow of the Round Table, slay me not, for I yield me as an overcome knight; and, whether I shall live or die, I put me in the King's hands and yours." Then Sir Launcelot wist not what to do, for he had rather than all the good of the world he might have been revenged upon Sir Meliagraunce. And then Sir Launcelot looked towards Queen Guenever if he might espy, by any sign or countenance, what he should have done : and then the Queen wagged her head upon Sir Launcelot, as though she should say, Slay him.   Full well knew Sir Launcelot, by the wagging of the head, that she would have had him dead.   Then Sir Launcelot bade him "arise for shame, and perform that battle to the uttermost." "Nay," said Sir Meliagraunce, "I will never arise until that ye take me as yielden and recreant." "I shall proffer you large proffers," said Sir Launcelot ; "that is to say, I shall unarm my head, and the left quarter of my body, all that may be unarmed, and I shall let bind my left hand behind me, so that it shall not help me ; and right so I shall do battle with you." When Sir Meliagraunce heard that, he started up on his legs, and said on high, "My lord, King Arthur, take heed to this proffer, for I will take it, and let him be disarmed and bound according unto his proffer." "What say ye," said King Arthur unto Sir Launcelot ; "will ye abide by your proffer?" "Yea, my lord," said Sir Launcelot, "I will never go from that I have once said."   Then the knights' porters of the field disarmed Sir Launcelot, first his head, and after his left arm, and his left side ; and then they bound his left arm behind his back, without shield or any thing, and then were they put together.   Wit ye well, there was many a lady and knight marvelled that Sir Launcelot would jeopard himself in such wise.   Then Sir Meliagraunce came with his sword all on high, and Sir Launcelot showed him openly his bare head, and the bare left side ; and when he weened to have smitten him upon the head, then lightly he avoided the left leg and the left side, and put his right hand and his sword to that stroke, and so put it aside with great sleight ; then, with great force, Sir Launcelot smote him upon the helmet such a buffet, that the stroke carved the head in two parts.   Then there was no more to do, but he was drawn out of the field ; and, at the instance of the knights of the Round Table, the King suffered him to be buried, and the mention made upon him, and for what cause he was slain.   And then the King and the Queen made much of Sir Launcelot, and more he was cherished than ever he was before.

And so leave I here off this tale, and overskip great books of Sir Launcelot du Lake, what great adventures he did when he was called Le Chevalier du Chariot : for because of despite of those knights and ladies that called him the knight that rode in the chariot, like as he had been judged to the gallows. Therefore, in despite of all them that named him so, he was carried in a chariot twelve months ; for, but little after he had slain Sir Meliagraunce in the Queen's quarrel, he never in twelve months came on horseback ; and he did, in those twelve months, more than forty battles : and, because I have lost the very matter of Le Chevalier du Chariot, I depart from the tale of Sir Launcelot, and here I go unto the death of King Arthur, and that caused by Sir Agravaine.

----◆----

THE BOOK OF SIR LAUNCELOT AND THE KING.

I.

AT that season of the merry month of May, when every heart flourisheth and rejoiceth ; for, as the season is lusty to behold and comfortable, so man and woman rejoice, and be glad of summer coming with her fresh flowers : for winter, with his rough winds and blasts, causeth a lusty man and woman to cower, and sit by the fire. So in this season, as the month of May, it happened there befell a great misfortune, the which stinted not till the flower of chivalry of all the world was destroyed and slain : and all was long of two unhappy knights, the which were named Sir Agravaine and Sir Mordred, that were brethren unto Sir Gawaine ; for these two knights, Sir Agravaine and Sir Mordred, had ever a privy hate unto the Queen, Dame Guenever, and unto Sir Launcelot ; and, daily and nightly, they ever watched upon Sir Launcelot. So it mishappened Sir Gawaine and his brethren were in King Arthur's court ; and then Sir Agravaine said thus openly, and not in counsel, that many knights might hear it, " I marvel that we all be not ashamed both to see and know how Sir Launcelot cometh daily and nightly to the Queen, and all we know it so ; and it is shamefully suffered of us all, that we all should suffer so noble a King, as King Arthur is, so to be ashamed." Then spake Sir Gawaine, and said, " Brother, Sir Agravaine, I pray you and charge you, have no such matter any more before me ; for wit you well," said Sir Gawaine, " I will not be of your counsel." " So God me help," said Sir Gaheris and Sir Gareth, " we will not be known, brother Sir Agravaine, of your deeds." " Then will I," said Sir Mordred. " I believe that well," said Sir Gawaine ; " for ever unto all unhappiness, brother Sir Mordred, thereto will ye grant : and I would that ye left all this, and made you not so busy ; for I know well enough," said Sir Gawaine, "what will befall of it." "Fall of it what fall may," said Sir Agravaine, "I will disclose it unto the King." "Ye shall not do it by my counsel," said Sir Gawaine ; "for, if there arise any war and wrath between Sir Launcelot and us, wit you well, brother, there will many kings and great lords hold with Sir Launcelot. Also, brother Sir Agravaine," said Sir Gawaine, "ye must remember how oftentimes Sir Launcelot hath rescued the King and the Queen ; and the best of us all had been full cold at the heart-root, had not Sir Launcelot been a better knight than we, and that hath he proved himself so oft : and, as for my part," said Sir Gawaine, "I will never be against Sir Launcelot for one day's deed, as when he rescued me from King Carados, of the Dolorous Tower, and slew him, and saved my life. Also, brothers Sir Agravaine and Sir Mordred, in likewise Sir Launcelot rescued you both, and threescore and two, from Sir Torquine. Me thinketh, brother, such kind deeds and kindness should be remembered." "Do as ye list," said Sir Agravaine ; "for I will hide it no longer." With these words came to them King Arthur. "Now, brother, stint your noise," said Sir Gawaine. "We will not," said Sir Agravaine and Sir Mordred. "Will ye so ?" said Sir Gawaine ; "then God speed you ; for I will not hear your tales, nor be of your counsel." "Nor more will I," said Sir Gareth and Sir Gaheris : "for we will never say evil of that man ; for because," said Sir Gareth, "Sir Launcelot made me knight, by no manner ought I to say evil of him." And therewith they three departed, making great dole. "Alas !" said Sir Gawaine and Sir Gareth, "now is the realm whole mischief, and the noble fellowship of the Round Table shall be dispersed." So they departed.

II.

AND then King Arthur asked them what noise they made ? "My lord," said Sir Agravaine, "I shall tell you which I may keep no longer. Here is I and my brother, Sir Mordred, brake unto my brother, Sir Gawaine, Sir Gaheris, and Sir Gareth. Now this we know all, that Sir Launcelot holdeth your Queen, and hath done long ; and we be your sister's sons, and we may suffer it no longer : and we know all, that ye are the King that made him knight ; and, therefore, we will prove it that he is traitor to your person." "If it be so," said King Arthur, "wit ye well he is none other ; but I would be loth to begin such a thing but if I might have proofs upon it : for I tell you Sir

Launcelot is a hardy knight, and all ye know he is the best knight among us all. And but, if he be taken with the deed, he will fight with him that bringeth up the noise, and I know no knight that is able to match with him : therefore, and it be sooth as ye say, I would he were taken with the deed." For King Arthur was loth thereto, that any noise should be upon Sir Launcelot and his Queen ; for the King had a deeming, but he would not hear of it, for Sir Launcelot had done so much for him and for his Queen so many times, that wit ye well King Arthur loved him passingly well. "My lord," said Sir Agravaine, "ye shall ride to-morrow on hunting, and doubt not Sir Launcelot will not go with you ; then when it draweth towards night, ye may send the Queen word that ye will lie out all that night : and so may ye send for your cooks, and then upon pain of death we shall take him that night with the Queen, and either we shall bring him to you dead or quick." "I will well," said the King : "then I counsel you," said the King, "take with you sure fellowship." "Sir," said Sir Agravaine, "my brother Sir Mordred and I will take with us twelve knights of the Round Table." "Be well ware," said King Arthur, "for I warn you ye shall find him full weighty." "Let us deal," said Sir Agravaine.

So on the morrow King Arthur rode on hunting, and sent word unto the Queen that he would lie out all that night. Then Sir Agravaine and Sir Mordred gat unto them twelve knights, and hid themselves in a chamber in the castle of Carlisle, and thus were their names ; first, Sir Colgrevaunce, Sir Mador de la Port, Sir Gingaline, Sir Melior de Logris, Sir Petipace, of Winchelsea ; Sir Galleron, of Galway ; Sir Melion, of the Mountain ; Sir Astamore, Sir Gromore Somor Jour, Sir Curselaine, Sir Florence, Sir Lovell. So these twelve knights were with Sir Mordred and Agravaine ; and all they were of Scotland, either of Sir Gawaine's kin, either well-willers of his brethren. So when the night came, Sir Launcelot told Sir Bors how he would go that night and speak with Queen Guenever. "Sir," said Sir Bors, "ye shall not go this night by my counsel." "Why?" said Sir Launcelot. "Sir," said Sir Bors, "I always dread me much of Sir Agravaine, which waiteth you daily for to do you shame and us all, and never gave my heart against you going that ever ye went to the Queen so much as now ; for I mistrust that the King is out this night from the Queen, because peradventure he hath lain some watch for you and the Queen, and therefore I dread me sore of treason." "Have ye no doubt," said Sir Launcelot, "for I shall go, and come again, and make no tarrying." "Sir," said Sir Bors, "that me sore repenteth, for I dread me greatly that your going out this night shall wrath us all." "Fair nephew," said Sir Launcelot, "I marvel me much why ye say thus, sithence the Queen hath sent for me ; and wit ye well that I will not be such a coward, but that she shall understand I will see her good grace." "God speed you well," said Sir Bors, "and send you safe and sound again."

III.

So Sir Launcelot departed, and took his sword underneath his arm ; and so that noble knight went forth in his mantle, and put himself in great jeopardy : and so he passed till he came unto the Queen's chamber. And then Sir Launcelot was lightly put into the chamber ; and thus as the Queen and Sir Launcelot were together, there came Sir Agravaine and Sir Mordred, with twelve knights with them of the Round Table, and with a crying voice they said thus : "Traitor knight, Sir Launcelot du Lake, now art thou taken ;" and thus they cried with a loud voice, that all the court might hear it : and they all were fourteen, armed at all points, as they should fight in a battle. "Alas !" said Queen Guenever, "now are we mischieved both." "Madam," said Sir Launcelot, "is here any armour within your chamber that I might cover my body withal, and if there be any, I pray you heartily let me have it, and I shall soon stint their malice by the grace of God." "Truly," said the Queen, "I have none armour, shield, sword, or spear, where, I dread me sore our long love is come to a mischievous end ; for I hear by their noise there be many valiant knights, and well I wot they be surely armed, against them ye may not resist, wherefore ye are like to be slain, and then shall I be burnt ; for, and ye might escape them," said the Queen, "I would not doubt but that ye would rescue me in what danger soever I stand in." "Alas !" said Sir Launcelot, "in all my life was I never thus bestood, that I should be thus shamefully slain for lack of mine armour." But always Sir Agravaine and Sir Mordred cried, "Traitor knight, come out of the Queen's chamber ; for, wit thou well, thou art so beset, that thou shalt not escape." "O Jesu mercy," said Sir Launcelot, "this shameful cry and noise we might not suffer; for better were death at once than thus to endure this pain." Then he took the Queen in his arms and kissed her, and said, "Most noble Christian Queen, I beseech you, as ye have ever

been my special good lady, and I at all times your true and poor
knight to my power, and as I never yet failed you in right, nor
yet in wrong, since the first day that King Arthur made me
knight, that ye will pray for my soul if that I be slain ; for well
I am assured, that Sir Bors, my nephew, and all the remnant of
my kin, with Sir Lavaine and Sir Urre, that they will not fail
you for to rescue you from the fire ; and, therefore, mine own
lady, recomfort yourself whatsoever come of me, that ye go with
Sir Bors, my nephew, and Sir Urre, and they will do you all the
pleasure they can or may, that ye shall live like a queen upon
my lands."   " Nay, Sir Launcelot," said the Queen, " wit thou
well I will never live a day after thy days ; but, and thou be
slain, I will take my death as meekly, for Jesu Christ's sake, as
ever did any Christian Queen."   " Well, madam," said Sir
Launcelot, " since it is so that the day is come that our love
must depart, wit you well that I shall sell my life as dear as I
may ; and a thousandfold," said Sir Launcelot, " I am more
heavier for you than for myself.   And now I had rather than to
be lord of all Christendom, that I had sure armour upon me,
that men might speak of my deeds or I were slain."   " Truly,"
said Queen Guenever, " I would, and it might please God, that
they would take me and slay me, and suffer you to escape."
" That shall never be," said Sir Launcelot ; " God defend me
from such a shame, but Lord Jesu be thou my shield and mine
armour."

IV.

AND therewithal Sir Launcelot wrapped his mantle round
about his arm well and surely ; and by then they had gotten
a great form out of the hall, and therewithal they dashed at the
chamber door.   "Fair lords," said Sir Launcelot, " leave your
noise and your dashing, and I shall set open the door, and then
may ye do with me what it liketh you to do."   " Come off then,"
said they all, " and do it, for it availeth thee not to strive against
us all, and therefore let us into the chamber, and we shall save
thy life until thou come to King Arthur."   Then Sir Launcelot
unbarred the door, and with his left hand he held it open a
little, so that but one man might enter at once.   And so anon
there came in a striding good knight, and a big man, and a
large, which was called Sir Colgrevaunce, of Gore ; and he, with
a sword, struck at Sir Launcelot mightily, and he put aside the
stroke, and gave him such a buffet upon the helm, that he
fell down dead, grovelling within the chamber door ; and

then Sir Launcelot, with his great might, drew that dead knight within the chamber door ; and then Sir Launcelot, with the help of the Queen and her ladies, was lightly armed in Sir Colgrevaunce's armour.   And ever stood Sir Agravaine and Sir Mordred crying, "Traitor knight, come out of the Queen's chamber." "Let be your noise," said Sir Launcelot unto Sir Agravaine, "ye shall not prison me this night ; and, therefore, do ye by my counsel ; go ye all from this chamber door, and make no such crying, and such manner of slander as ye do ; for I promise you by my knighthood, and ye will depart and make no more noise, I shall, as to-morrow, appear before you all, and before the King, and then let it be seen which of you will accuse me of treason : and there I shall answer you as a knight ought to do, that hither I came for no manner of evil, and that I will prove and make good with mine own hands." "Fie on thee, false traitor," said Sir Agravaine and Sir Mordred, "we will have thee maugre thy head, and slay thee if we list, for we will let thee to wit that we have the choice of King Arthur to save thee or to slay thee." "Ah, sirs," said Sir Launcelot, "is there none other grace with you, then keep yourself." So then Sir Launcelot set the chamber door wide open, and mightily and knightly he strode among them ; and anon, at the first buffet, he slew Sir Agravaine, and twelve of his fellows, within a little while after, he had laid them to the cold earth ; and there was none of all the twelve that might stand with Sir Launcelot a buffet. Also, Sir Launcelot wounded Sir Mordred, and he fled with all his might. And then Sir Launcelot returned again unto the Queen and said, "Madam, now wit ye well that all our true love is brought unto end ; for now will King Arthur ever be my foe ; and therefore, madam, and if it like you that I may have you with me, and I shall save you from all manner of ill adventures and danger." "That is not best," said the Queen ; "me seemeth now ye have done so much harm, it will be best ye hold you still with this ; and if ye see that as to-morrow they will put me unto the death, then may ye rescue me as ye think best." "I will well," said Sir Launcelot, "for have ye no doubt while I am living I shall rescue you." And then he kissed her, and either gave other a ring ; and so there he left the Queen, and went to his lodging.

V.

So, when Sir Bors saw Sir Launcelot, he was never so glad of his home-coming as he was at that time. " Jesu, mercy," said Sir Launcelot, " what may this mean?" " Sir," said Sir Bors, " after that ye were departed from us, we all, that be of your blood and your well-willers, were so dreaming, that some of us leapt out of our beds naked ; and some, in their dreams, caught naked swords in their hands ; therefore," said Sir Bors, " we deem there is some great strife at hand. And then we all deemed that ye were betrayed with some treason : and, therefore, we made us thus ready, what need soever ye had been in." " My fair nephew," said Sir Launcelot unto Sir Bors, " now shall ye wit all, that this night I was more harder bestead than ever I was in my life, and yet I escaped." And so he told them all how, and in what manner, as ye have heard before. " And therefore, my fellows," said Sir Launcelot, " I beseech you all that ye will be of good heart, in what need soever that I stand in, for now is war come to us all." " Sir," said Sir Bors, " all is welcome that God sendeth us, and we all have had much wealth with you and much worship, and therefore we will take the woe with you as we have taken the wealth." And therefore they said all, which were many knights, " Look that ye take no discomfort, for there is no band of knights under heaven but that we shall be able to grieve them as much as they may us ; and, therefore, discomfort not yourself by no means, and ye shall gather together those that we love, and that loveth us, and what ye will have done shall be done ; and therefore, Sir Launcelot," said they, " we will take the woe with the wealth." " Gramercy," said Sir Launcelot, " of your good comfort ; for in my great distress, my fair nephew, ye comfort me greatly, and much I am beholden unto you ; but this, my fair nephew, I would that ye did in all haste that ye may, or it be four days, that ye will look in their lodgings, that been lodged here nigh about the King, which will hold with me, and which will not, for now I would fain know which were my friends from my foes." " Sir," said Sir Bors, " I shall do what I may ; and, or it be seven of the clock, I shall wit of such as ye have said before, who will hold with you or not." Then Sir Bors called to him Sir Lionel, Sir Ector de Maris, Sir Blamor de Ganis, Sir Bleoberis de Ganis, Sir Galahautine, Sir Galihodine, Sir Galihud, Sir Menadewke, with Sir Villiers the Valiant, Sir Hebes le Renomes, Sir Lavaine, Sir Urre of Hungary, Sir Neroveus, and Sir Plenorius, these two Sir

Launcelot made knights, and the one of them he won upon
a bridge, and therefore they would never be against him. And
Sir Harry le Fife de Lake, and Sir Selises of the Dolorous
Tower, and Sir Melias de Lile, and Sir Bellangere le Beuse,
which was Sir Alisaunder, Lorphelin's son, because his mother,
Dame Alis la Beale Pilgrim, was of kin unto Sir Launcelot, he
held with him. So there came Sir Palomides, and Sir Safre,
his brother, to hold with Sir Launcelot, and Sir Clegis of
Sadocke, and Sir Dinas, and Sir Clarius of Claremount. So
these two-and-twenty knights drew them together, and anon
they were armed and on horseback, and promised Sir Launcelot
to do what he would. Then there fell to them what of North
Wales, and what of Cornwall, for Sir Lamoracke's sake, and for
Sir Tristram's sake, to the number of fourscore good and valiant
knights. "My lords," said Sir Launcelot, "wit ye well that I
have been ever, sithence I came into this country, well witling
unto my lord, King Arthur, and unto my lady, Queen Guenever,
unto my power ; and this night, because my lady, the Queen,
sent for me to speak with her, I suppose it was by treason ;
howbeit I dare largely excuse her person, notwithstanding I was
thereby aforecast nigh slain, but as Jesu provided me, I escaped
all their malice :" and then that noble knight, Sir Launcelot, told
them all how he was hard bestead in the Queen's chamber, and
how and in what manner he escaped from them. "And therefore," said Sir Launcelot, "wit ye well, my fair lords, I am sure
there is naught but war unto me and mine ; and for because I
have slain this night these knights, as Sir Agravaine, Sir
Gawaine's brother, and at the least twelve of his fellows, and for
this cause now I am sure of mortal war. These knights were
sent and ordained by King Arthur to betray me, and therefore
the King will in his hate and malice judge the Queen to the fire,
and that may I not suffer, that she should be burnt for my sake.
For and I may be heard and suffered, and so taken, I will fight
for the Queen, that she is a true lady unto her lord ; but the
King in his heat, I dread me, will not take me as I ought to be
taken."

VI.

"My lord Sir Launcelot," said Sir Bors, "by mine advice ye
shall take the woe with the wealth, and take it patiently, and
thank our Lord God for it. And sithence it is fallen as it is, I
counsel you to keep yourself ; for if ye will yourself, there is no
fellowship christened of knights that shall do you any wrong.

Also, I will counsel you, my lord Sir Launcelot, that and my lady, Queen Guenever, be in distress, insomuch as she is in pain for your sake, that ye knightly rescue her.   And if ye did otherwise, all the world will speak of your shame to the world's end, insomuch as ye were taken with her   Whether ye did right or wrong, it is now your part to hold with the Queen, that she be not slain and put to a mischievous death, for and the Queen die so, the shame shall be yours."   "Oh, good Lord Jesu! defend me from shame," said Sir Launcelot, "and keep and save my lady the Queen from villainy and from shameful death, and that she never be destroyed in my default.   And therefore, my fair lords, ye that be of my kin and my friends," said Sir Launcelot, "what will ye do?" Then they said all, "We will do as ye will do yourself."   "I put this to you," said Sir Launcelot, "that if my lord, King Arthur, by evil counsel, will to-morrow in his heat put my lady the Queen to the fire, there to be burnt, now I pray you counsel me what is best to be done."   Then they said all at once, with one voice, "Sir, we think that the best that ye may do is this: that ye knightly rescue the Queen, inasmuch as she shall be burnt it is for your sake: and it is to be supposed that if ye might be handled, ye should have the same death, or else a more shamefuller death.   And, sir, we say all, that many times ye have rescued the Queen from death, for other men's quarrels, us seemeth it is more your worship that ye rescue the Queen from this peril, so much as she hath it for your sake."   Then Sir Launcelot stood still and said, "My fair lords, wit ye well that I would be loth to do that thing that should dishonour you or my blood.   And wit ye well I would be right loth that my lady the Queen should die a shameful death: but and it be so that ye will counsel me for to rescue her, I must do much harm or I rescue her; and peradventure I shall there destroy some of my best friends, which would repent me much.   And peradventure there be some, and they could well bring it about, or disobey my lord, King Arthur, they would full soon come to me, the which I were loth to hurt; and if so be that I should rescue her, where should I keep her?"   "That shall be the least care of us all," said Sir Bors. "How did the noble knight, Sir Tristram, by your good will? Did not he keep with him la beale Isoud nigh three years in Joyous Gard, the which was done by both your advices, and that same place is your own.   And in likewise may ye do as ye list, and take the Queen lightly away, if it be so that the King will judge her to be hurt; and in Joyous Gard ye may keep her long enough, until the heat of the King be past, and then shall ye bring again the Queen unto the King with great worship ; and then, peradventure, ye shall have thanks for her bringing home again, where other shall have maugre." "That is hard to do," said Sir Launcelot ; "for by Sir Tristram I may have a warning : for when by means of the treaty Sir Tristram brought again la beale Isoud unto King Marke, from Joyous Gard, look what fell on the end, how shamefully that false traitor (King Marke) slew that noble knight as he sat harping before his lady, la beale Isoud, with a sharp grounded lance-head thrust him behind to the heart. It grieveth me," said Sir Launcelot, "to speak of his death, for all the world may not find such a knight." "All this is truth," said Sir Bors, "but there is one thing shall courage you and us all. Ye know well that King Arthur and King Marke were never like of conditions, for there was never yet man that could prove King Arthur untrue of his promise." So, to make short tale, they were all consented that for better or worse, if it were so that the Queen were on the morrow brought to the fire, shortly they all would rescue her. And so, by the advice of Sir Launcelot, they put them all to an ambushment in a little wood as nigh Carlisle as they might, and there they abode still for to wit what the King would do.

VII.

Now turn we again unto Sir Mordred, which when he was escaped from the noble knight, Sir Launcelot, he anon gat his horse and mounted upon him, and rode straight to King Arthur, sore wounded, and beaten, and all bebled. And there he told the King all how it was, and how they were all slain but he. "Jesus, mercy ! how may this be ?" said the King ; "did ye take him in the Queen's chamber." "Yea, so God me help," said Sir Mordred, "there we found him unarmed, and there he slew Sir Colgrevaunce, and armed him in his armour ; and all this he told the King from the beginning to the ending."

"Ah ! Jesus mercy," said the king, "he is a marvellous knight of prowess. Alas ! me sore repenteth," said the King, "that ever Sir Launcelot should be against me ; now I am sure the noble fellowship of the Round Table is broken for ever, for with him will hold many a noble knight : and now it is befallen so," said King Arthur, "that I may not with my worship but that the Queen must suffer death." So then there was made great ordinance in this heat, that the Queen must be judged to death. And the law was such in those days, that whatsoever they were, of what estate or degree, if that they were found guilty of treason, there should be none other remedy but death, and either the men or the taking with the dead should be the causer of their hasty judgment. And right so was it ordained for Queen Guenever; because Sir Mordred was escaped sore wounded, and the death of twelve knights of the Round Table: these proofs and experiences caused King Arthur to command the Queen to the fire there to be burnt. Then spake Sir Gawaine, and said, "My lord, King Arthur, I would counsel you, and not to be overhasty, but that ye would put in respite this judgment of my lady, the Queen, for many causes. One is, though it were so that Sir Launcelot were found in the Queen's chamber, yet it might be so that he came thither for none evil. For ye know, my lord," said Sir Gawaine, "that the Queen is much beholden to Sir Launcelot, more than to any other knight alive: for oftentimes he hath saved her life, and done battle for her, when all the court refused the Queen. And, peradventure, she sent for him for goodness, and for none evil, to reward him for the good deeds he had done to her in time past; and, peradventure, my lady, the Queen, sent for him to that intent, that Sir Launcelot should come to her good grace privily and secretly, weening to her that it was best so to do, in eschewing and dreading of slander. For oftentimes we do many things that we ween it is for the best, and yet peradventure it turneth to the worst: for I dare say," said Sir Gawaine, "that my lady, your Queen, is to you both good and true. And as for Sir Launcelot," said Sir Gawaine, "he will make it good upon any knight living, that will put upon himself any villainy or shame; and in likewise he will make good for my lady, Dame Guenever." "That I believe well," said King Arthur, "but I will not that way with Sir Launcelot, for he trusteth so much upon his hands and his might, that he doubteth no man; and therefore, for the Queen, he shall never fight more, for she shall have the law. And if that I may get Sir Launcelot, wit ye well he shall have a shameful death." "Jesu defend," said Sir Gawaine, "that I may never see it." "Wherefore say ye so?" said King Arthur unto Sir Gawaine: "for truly ye have no great cause to love Sir Launcelot, for this night last past he slew your own brother, Sir Agravaine, a full good knight; and also he had almost slain your other brother, Sir Mordred; and also there he slew twelve good knights; and also, Sir Gawaine, remember you how he slew two sons of yours, Sir Florence and Sir Lovel." "My lord," said Sir Gawaine, "of all this I have knowledge, of whose death I repent me sore: but insomuch as I gave them warning,

and told my brethren and my sons beforehand what would fall
in the end, insomuch as they would not do by my counsel, I will
not meddle me thereof, nor revenge me nothing of their deaths,
for I told them it was no boot to strive with Sir Launcelot,
howbeit I am sorry of the death of my brother and of my sons,
for they were the causers of their own death. For oftentimes I
warned my brother, Sir Agravaine, and told him the perils the
which be now befallen."

VIII.

THEN said the noble King Arthur to Sir Gawaine, "My dear
nephew, I pray you that ye will make you ready in your best
array, with your brethren, Sir Gaheris and Sir Gareth, to bring
my Queen to the fire, there to have her judgment, and receive
her death." "Nay, my most noble lord," said Sir Gawaine,
"that will I never do in my life : for wit you well, that I
will never be in place where so noble a queen, as is my lady
Queen Guenever, shall take such a shameful ending. For
wit ye well," said Sir Gawaine, "that my heart will never
serve me to see her die ; and it shall never be said that ever
I was of your counsel of her death." "Then," said King
Arthur unto Sir Gawaine, "suffer your brothers, Sir Gaheris
and Sir Gareth, to be there." "My lord," said Sir Gawaine,
" wit you well that they will be loth to be there present, because
of many adventures which be like to fall there ; but they are
young, and full unable to say you nay." Then spake Sir
Gaheris, and the good knight, Sir Gareth, unto King Arthur,
"Sir, ye may well command us to be there, but wit ye well
it shall be sore against our will ; but and we be there by your
straight commandment, ye shall plainly hold us there excused :
we will be there in peaceable wise, and bear no harness of
war upon us." "In the name of God," said the King, "then
make you ready, for she shall soon have her judgment."
"Alas !" said Sir Gawaine, "that ever I should endure to
see this woeful day." So Sir Gawaine turned him and wept
heartily, and so he went into his chamber. And then the
Queen was led forth without Carlisle, and there she was
despoiled unto her smock ; and so then her ghostly father
was brought to her, to be shriven of her misdeeds. Then there
was weeping and wailing, and wringing of hands, of many lords
and ladies. But there was but few, in comparison, that would
bear any armour, for to strengthen the death of the Queen.

Then was there one which Sir Launcelot had sent unto that
place, for to espy what time the Queen should go unto her
judgment ; and anon, as he saw that the Queen was despoiled
unto her smock, and also that she was shriven, then he gave Sir
Launcelot . warning thereof. Then was there spurring and
plucking up of horses. And right so they came to the fire,
and who that stood against them there, they were slain ; there
might none withstand Sir Launcelot : so all that bear arms, and
withstood them, there were they slain many a noble knight.
For there was slain Sir Belias le Orgulous, Sir Sagwardes, Sir
Griflet, Sir Brandiles, Sir Aglouvaile, Sir Tor, Sir Gauter, Sir
Guillimere, Sir Reinolds, three brethren, Sir Damas, Sir Priamus,
Sir Kaye, the stranger, Sir Driaunt, Sir Lambegus, Sir Herminde,
Sir Pertelopoe, Sir. Perimone's two brethren, which were called
the green knight and the red knight. And at this rushing and
hurtling, as Sir Launcelot through here and there, it mishappened him to slay Sir Gaheris, and the noble knight, Sir
Gareth, for they were unarmed and unaware. For Sir Launcelot smote Sir Gareth and Sir Gaheris upon the brain-pans,
wherethrough they were both slain in the field. Howbeit,
in very truth, Sir Launcelot saw them not ; and so were they
found dead among the thickest of the press. Then, when Sir
Launcelot had thus done, and had put them to flight all they
would withstand him, then he rode straight unto Queen
Guenever, and made a kirtle and a gown to be cast upon her,
and then he made her to be set behind him, and prayed her to
be of good cheer. Wit ye well that the Queen was glad that
she was escaped from death : and then she thanked God and
Sir Launcelot. And so he rode his way with the Queen
unto Joyous Gard, and there he kept her as a noble knight
should do. And many great lords and kings sent Sir Launcelot
many good knights ; and many noble knights drew unto Sir
Launcelot. When this was known openly, that King Arthur
and Sir Launcelot were at debate, many knights were glad of
their debate, and many knights were sorry of their debate.

IX.

Now turn we again to King Arthur, that, when it was told
him how and in what manner of wise the Queen was taken
away from the fire, and when he heard of the death of his noble
knights, and in special of Sir Gaheris and Sir Gareth's death,
then the King swooned for pure sorrow : and, when he was

revived, he said, "Alas! that ever I bare any crown upon my head, for I have now lost the fairest fellowship of noble knights that ever held Christian king together. Alas! my good knights be slain away from me : now, within these two days, have I lost forty knights, and also the noble fellowship of Sir Launcelot and his blood, for now I may never more hold them together with my worship. Alas! that ever this war began. Now, fair fellows," said the King, "I charge you that no man tell Sir Gawaine of the death of his two brethren ; for I am sure," said the King, "when Sir Gawaine heareth that Sir Gareth, his brother, is dead, he will nigh go out of his mind. Oh, merciful Jesu!" said the King, "why slew he Sir Gareth and Sir Gaheris. For I dare say, as for Sir Gareth, he loved Sir Launcelot above all earthly men." "That is truth," said some knights ; "but they were slain in the hurtling, as Sir Launcelot thrang in the thick of the press ; and, as they were unarmed, he smote them, and wist not whom he smote, and so unhappily they were slain." "The death of them," said King Arthur, "will cause the greatest mortal war that ever was. I am sure, wist Sir Gawaine that Sir Gareth were slain, I should never have rest of him till that I had destroyed Sir Launcelot's kin and himself both, or else he to destroy me, and therefore wit you well that his heart was never so heavy as it is now ; and much more greater sorrow for my good knights' loss than for the loss of my Queen ; for queens might have enough, but such a fellowship of good knights shall never be together in no company. And now I dare say," said the King, "that there was never Christian king that held such a fellowship together. Alas! that ever Sir Launcelot and I should be at debate. Ah! Agravaine! Agravaine!" said the King, "Jesu forgive it thy soul, for thine evil will that thou and thy brother, Sir Mordred, had unto Sir Launcelot, hath caused all this sorrow." And ever, among these complaints, King Arthur wept and swooned.

Then there came one unto Sir Gawaine, and told him the Queen was laid away with Sir Launcelot, and nigh twenty-four knights slain. "Oh, Jesu! defend my brethren," said Sir Gawaine, "for full well wist I that Sir Launcelot would rescue her, or else he would die in the field : and so, for to say the truth, he had not been a man of worship if he had not rescued the Queen that day, insomuch as she should have been burnt for his sake. And as in that," said Sir Gawaine, "he hath done but knightly, and as I would have done myself, and I had stood in like case. But where are my brethren ?" said Sir Gawaine ; "I marvel that I hear not of them." "Truly," said the man,

"your two brethren, Sir Gareth and Sir Gaheris, be slain."
"Jesu defend!" said Sir Gawaine, "for all the good in the
world, I would not that they were slain, and in especial Sir
Gareth." "Sir," said the man, "he is slain, and that is great
pity." "Who slew him?" said Sir Gawaine. "Sir," said the
man, "Sir Launcelot slew them both." "That may I not
believe," said Sir Gawaine, "that he slew my brother, Sir Gareth;
for I dare say my brother Sir Gareth loved him better than me,
and all his brethren, and the King both. Also, I dare say, and
if Sir Launcelot had desired my brother, Sir Gaheris, to have
been with him, he would have been with him against the King,
and us all, and therefore I may never believe that Sir Launcelot
slew my brother." "Sir," said the man, "it is noised that he
slew him."

X.

"ALAS!" said Sir Gawaine, "now is all my joy gone," and
then he fell down in a swoon, and long he lay there, as he had
been dead; and then, when he arose out of his swoon, he cried
out so ruefully, and said, "Alas!" And right so Sir Gawaine
ran unto the King, crying and weeping, "Oh, King Arthur, mine
uncle, my good brother, Sir Gaheris, is slain, and my brother,
Sir Gareth, also, the which were two noble knights." Then the
King wept, and he both, and they fell down in a swoon. And
when they were revived again, Sir Gawaine spake and said,
"Sir, I will go see my brother, Sir Gareth." "Ye may not see
him," said the King, "for I caused him to be buried, and Sir
Gaheris both. For I well understood that he would make over
much sorrow; and the sight of Sir Gareth should have caused
you double sorrow." "Alas! mine own lord," said Sir
Gawaine, "who slew my brother, Sir Gareth? mine own good
lord, I pray you that you will tell me." "Truly," said the King,
"I shall tell you as it is told me: Sir Launcelot slew him and
Sir Gaheris both." "Alas!" said Sir Gawaine, "neither of
them bear none arms against him." "I wot not how it was,"
said the King, "but, as it is said, Sir Launcelot slew them both
in the thickest of the press, and knew them not, and therefore
let us make a remedy for to revenge their deaths."

"My most gracious lord, and my uncle," said Sir Gawaine,
"wit you well that now I shall make you a promise, the which
I shall hold by my knighthood, that from this day I shall never
fail Sir Launcelot, until the one of us has slain the other, and
therefore I require you, my lord and my King, dress you unto the

war : for, wit you well, I shall be revenged upon Sir Launcelot. And, therefore, as ye will have my service and my love, now haste you thereto, and assay your friends ; for I promise unto God," said Sir Gawaine, "that for the death of my brother, Sir Gareth, I shall seek Sir Launcelot throughout seven kings' realms, but I shall slay him, or else he shall slay me." "Ye shall not need to seek him so far," said the King ; "for, as I heard say, Sir Launcelot will abide me and you in Joyous Gard, and much people draweth unto him, as I hear say." "That may I full well believe," said Sir Gawaine ; "but, my lord, assay your friends, and I will assay mine." "It shall be done," said the King ; "and, as I suppose, I shall be big enough to draw him out of the highest tower of his castle." So then King Arthur sent letters and writs throughout all England, both in the length and in the breadth, for to assemble all his knights. And so unto King Arthur drew many knights, dukes, and earls, so that he had a great host. And, when they were assembled, the King informed them all how Sir Launcelot had bereft him of his Queen. Then the King and all his host made them ready to lay siege about Sir Launcelot, where as he lay within Joyous Gard. Thereof heard Sir Launcelot, and pursued him of many a good knight ; for with him held many knights, some for his own sake, and some for the Queen's sake. Thus they were on both parties well furnished and garnished of all manner of things that belonged to the war. But King Arthur's host was so big, that Sir Launcelot would not abide him in the field : for he was full loth to do battle against the King. But Sir Launcelot drew him to his strong castle, with all manner of victuals, and as many noblemen as might suffice, both within the town and the castle. Then came King Arthur and Sir Gawaine, with a huge host, and laid a siege about Joyous Gard, both at the town and at the castle ; and there they made full strong war on both parties. But in nowise Sir Launcelot would not ride out nor go out of the castle of a long time, neither would he suffer none of his good knights to issue out, neither none of the town, nor of the castle, until fifteen weeks were past.

XI.

So it befell on a day in harvest that Sir Launcelot looked over the walls, and spake on high to King Arthur and Sir Gawaine : "My lords, both wit ye well it is in vain that ye labour at this siege, for here win ye no worship, but dishonour and maugre ; for, and it list me come out myself and my good knights, I should full soon make an end of this war." "Come forth," said King Arthur unto Sir Launcelot, "and thou darest, and I promise thee I shall meet thee in the midst of the field." "God defend me," said ·Sir Launcelot, "that ever I should encounter with the most noble King that made me a knight." "Fie upon thy fair language," said the King ; "for wit thou well, and trust it, that I am thy mortal foe, and ever will be to my dying day ; for thou hast slain my good knights and the noble men of my blood, which I shall never recover again ; also thou hast holden my Queen many winters, and since like a traitor taken her from me by force." "My most noble King," said Sir Launcelot, "ye may say what ye will ; for wit you well that with yourself I will not strive : but whereas ye say that I have slain your good knights, I wot well that I have done so, and that me sore repenteth, but I was enforced to do battle with them in saving of my life, or else I must have suffered them to have slain me ; and as for my lady, Queen Guenever (except your person of your highness, and my lord, Sir Gawaine), there is no knight under heaven that dare make it good upon me, that ever I was a traitor unto your person ; and where it pleaseth you to say that I have holden my lady, your Queen, years and winters, unto that I shall make answer, and prove it upon any knight that beareth life (except your person, and Sir Gawaine), that my lady, Queen Guenever, is a true lady unto your person, and that will I make good with my hands ; howbeit it hath liked her good gráce to have me in charity, and to cherish me more than any other knight; and unto my power I have deserved her love again : for oftentimes, my lord, ye have consented that she should be burnt and destroyed in your heat, and then it fortuned me to do battle for her, and, on that I departed from her adversaries, they confessed their untruths, and she full worshipfully excused. And at such times, my lord Arthur," said Sir Launcelot, "ye loved me, and thanked me when I saved your Queen from the fire, and then ye promised me for ever to be my gracious lord, and now me thinketh ye reward me full evil for my good service. And, my good lord, me seemeth that I had lost a part of my worship in my knight-hood if I had suffered my lady, your Queen, to have been burnt, insomuch as she should have been burnt for my sake : for since I have done battles for your Queen in other quarrels than in mine own, me seemeth now I had more right to do battle for her in a right quarrel ; and, therefore, my good and gracious lord," said Sir Launcelot, "take your Queen unto your good grace, for she is both fair, true, and good." "Fie on thee, false, recreant knight," said Sir Gawaine; "I let thee to wit that my lord, mine uncle, King Arthur, shall have his Queen, and thee maugre thy visage, and slay you both, where it shall please him." "It may well be," said Sir Launcelot; "but wit ye well, my lord, Sir Gawaine, and me list to come out of this castle, ye should win me and the Queen more harder than ever ye won a strong battle." "Fie upon thy proud words," said Sir Gawaine; "as for my lady, the Queen, I will never say of her shame. Ah! thou false, recreant knight, what cause hadst thou to slay my good brother, Sir Gareth, that loved thee more than all thy kin? Alas! thou madest him knight with thine hands; why slewest thou him that loved thee so well?" "For to excuse me," said Sir Launcelot, "it helpeth me not; but, by Jesu," said Sir Launcelot, "and by the faith that I owe unto the high order of knighthood, I should, with as good a will, have slain my nephew, Sir Bors de Ganis, at that time. But alas! that ever I was so unhappy," said Sir Launcelot, "that I had seen Sir Gareth and Sir Gaheris." "Thou liest, false, recreant knight," said Sir Gawaine, "thou slewest him in despite of me; and, therefore, wit thou well that I shall make war unto thee, all the while that I may live." "That me sore repenteth," said Sir Launcelot, "for well I understand that it helpeth me not to seek for none accordment whiles that ye, Sir Gawaine, are so mischievously set; and if ye were not, I would not doubt to have the good grace of my lord, King Arthur." "I believe it well, false, recreant knight," said Sir Gawaine, "for thou hast many long days overlaid me, and us all, and hast destroyed many of our good knights." "Ye say as it pleased you," said Sir Launcelot, "and yet may it never be said on me, and openly proved, that ever I before cast of reason slew a good knight, as ye, my lord, Sir Gawaine, have done; and so did I never, but in my own defence, and that I was driven thereto in saving of my life." "Ah! false knight," said Sir Gawaine, "that thou meanest by Sir Lamoracke; but wit thou well that I slew him." "Ye slew him not yourself," said Sir Launcelot, "for it had been overmuch for you to have slain him, for he was one of the best knights christened of his age, and it was great pity of his death."

XII.

THEN said Sir Gawaine unto Sir Launcelot, "Sith thou upbraidest me of Sir Lamoracke, wit thou well I shall never leave thee till I have thee at such advantage, that thou shalt not escape my hands." "I trust you well enough," said Sir Launcelot, "that if ye may get me, I shall have but little mercy." But King Arthur would have taken his Queen again, and would have been accorded with Sir Launcelot, but Sir Gawaine would not suffer him by no manner of means. And then Sir Gawaine made many men to blow upon Sir Launcelot, and all at once they called him "False, recreant knight." Then when Sir Bors de Ganis, Sir Ector de Maris, and Sir Lionel heard this outcry, they called unto them Sir Palomides, and Sir Safre, his brother, and Sir Lavaine, with many other more of their blood ; and all they went unto Sir Launcelot, and to him they said thus : "My lord, Sir Launcelot, wit ye well that we have great scorn of the great rebukes that we heard Sir Gawaine say unto you, wherefore we beseech you, and charge you as ye will have our service, keep us no longer within these walls ; wit you well, we will ride into the field, and do battle with them ; for ye fare as a man that was afraid : and for all your fair speech, it will not avail you ; for wit ye well, Sir Gawaine will not suffer you to be accorded with King Arthur : and, therefore, fight for your life and your right, and ye dare." "Alas !" said Sir Launcelot, " for to ride out of this castle, and do battle, I am full loth to do it." Then Sir Launcelot spake on high unto King Arthur and Sir Gawaine : "My lords, I require you and beseech you, since I am thus required and conjured to ride into the field, that neither you, nor my lord, King Arthur, nor you, Sir Gawaine, come not into the field." "What shall we do then?" said Sir Gawaine; "is not this the King's quarrels with thee to fight, and it is my quarrel to fight with thee, Sir Launcelot : because of the death of my brother, Sir Gareth." "Then must I needs unto battle," said Sir Launcelot : "now wit ye well, my lord, King Arthur, and Sir Gawaine, ye will repent it, whensoever I do battle with you." And so then they departed either from the other ; and then on the morrow either party made them ready for to do battle, and great purveyance was made on both sides ; and Sir Gawaine let purvey many knights for to wait upon Sir Launcelot, for to overset him, and to slay him. And on the morrow, at nine in the morning, King Arthur was ready in the field with three great hosts ; and then Sir Launcelot's fellowship came out at three gates, in full good array : and Sir Lionel came in the foremost battle, and Sir Launcelot came in the middle battle, and Sir Bors came out at the third gate. Thus they came in order and rule as valiant knights ; and always Sir Launcelot charged all his knights in any wise to save King Arthur and Sir Gawaine.

XIII.

THEN came forth Sir Gawaine from the knights' host, and he came before and proffered to joust ; and Sir Lionel was a fiery knight, and lightly he encountered with Sir Gawaine, and there Sir Gawaine smote Sir Lionel throughout the body, that he dashed unto the earth as he had been dead : and then Sir Ector de Maris, and many others, bear him unto the castle. Then began a great stir, and much people was there slain. And ever Sir Launcelot did what he might to save the people on King Arthur's part ; for Sir Palomides, and Sir Bors, and Sir Safre overthrew many knights, for they were deadly knights ; and Sir Blamor de Ganis, and Sir Bleoberis de Ganis, with Sir Bellangere le Breuse, these six knights did much damage and hurt. And ever King Arthur was nigh about Sir Launcelot for to have slain him ; and Sir Launcelot suffered him, and would not strike again. So Sir Bors encountered with King Arthur, and there with a spear Sir Bors smote him down to the ground ; and so he alighted and drew his sword, and said unto Sir Launcelot, "Shall I make an end of this war." And he meant for to have slain King Arthur. "Not so hardy," said Sir Launcelot, "upon pain of thy head that thou touch him no more ; for I will see that most noble King that made me a knight neither slain nor shamed." And therewithal Sir Launcelot alighted from his horse, and took up the King, and horsed him again, and said unto him thus : "My lord, Arthur, for God's love stint this strife, for ye may get here no worship, and I would do mine uttermost, but ever I forbear you ; and ye nor none of yours forbeareth me. My lord, remember what I have done in many places, and now I am evil rewarded." When King Arthur was again on horseback, he looked upon Sir Launcelot, and then the tears burst out of his eyes, thinking on the great courtesy that was in Sir Launcelot, more than in any other man : and therewith the King rode forth his way, and might no longer behold him, and said to himself, "Alas ! that ever this war began." And then either parties of the battles withdrew them for to rest them, and buried the dead bodies, and to the wounded men they laid soft salves. And thus they endured that night till on the morrow; and, on the morrow, by undern, they made them ready to do battle: and then Sir Bors led them forward. So on the morrow came Sir Gawaine, as grim as any bear, with a spear in his hand. And when Sir Bors saw him, he thought to revenge his brother, Sir Lionel, of the despite that Sir Gawaine had done him the other day: and so they that knew either other feutred their spears, and, with all the might of their horses and themselves, they met together so furiously, that either bear other through, and so they fell both to the ground: and then the battles joined together, and there was great slaughter on both sides. Then Sir Launcelot rescued Sir Bors, and sent him into the castle. But neither Sir Gawaine nor Sir Bors died not of their wounds, for they were both holpen. Then Sir Lavaine and Sir Urre prayed Sir Launcelot to do his pain, and fight as they done, "for we see that ye forbear and spare, and that doth much harm; therefore, we pray you, spare not your enemies, no more than they do you." "Alas!" said Sir Launcelot, "I have no heart to fight against my lord, King Arthur, for always me seemeth I do not as I ought to do." "My lord," said Sir Palomides, "though ye spare them all this day, they will never give you thanks; and if they may get you at any vantage, ye are but dead." So then Sir Launcelot understood well that they told him truth, and then he strained himself more than he did aforehand, and because that his nephew, Sir Bors, was sore wounded. And then, within a little while, by even-song time, Sir Launcelot and his party better stood: for their horses went in blood above their foot-locks, there was so much people slain on both parties: and then, for pity, Sir Launcelot withdrew his knights, and so did King Arthur's part; and then Sir Launcelot and his party entered into their castle, and either party buried the dead bodies, and put salve to the wounded men.

So when Sir Gawaine was hurt, they, on King Arthur's party, were not half so orgulous and proud as they were before to do battle. Of this war was noised through all Christendom; and, at the last, it was noised before the Pope; and he considering the great goodness of King Arthur and Sir Launcelot, which was called the most noble knight of the world, wherefore the Pope called unto him a noble clerk, that at that time was there present, which was the Bishop of Rochester. And the Pope gave him bulls, under lead, unto King Arthur of England, charging him, upon pain of interdicting of all England, that he take his Queen, Dame Guenever, to him again, and accord with Sir Launcelot.

XIV.

So when this Bishop was come to Carlisle he showed the King these bulls; and when the King understood the bulls, he wist not what to do: gladly he would accord with Sir Launcelot, but Sir Gawaine would not suffer him: but as for to have the Queen again, thereto he agreed, but in no wise Sir Gawaine would not suffer the King to accord with Sir Launcelot; but as for the Queen she consented. And then the Bishop had of the King his great seal, and his assurance, as he was a true anointed King, that Sir Launcelot should come and go safe, and that the Queen should not be reproved of the King, nor of none other, for nothing done before time past: and of all these appointments the Bishop brought with him assurance and writing to show Sir Launcelot. So when the Bishop came to Joyous Gard, there he showed Sir Launcelot how the Pope had written unto King Arthur, and unto him; and there he told him of the perils, if he withheld the Queen from the King. "It was never my thought," said Sir Launcelot, "for to withhold the Queen from my lord, King Arthur; but insomuch as she would have been dead for my sake, me seemeth it was my part to save her life, and put her from that danger till better recover might come; and now I thank God that the Pope hath made her peace: for God knoweth," said Sir Launcelot, "I would be a thousand-fold more gladder to bring her again than I was of her taking away; with this that I may be sure for me and mine to come safe, and go safe, and that the Queen shall have her liberties as she had before, and never for nothing that hath been surmised before this time, that she never from this day stand in no peril: for else," said Sir Launcelot, "I dare adventure me for to keep her from a harder shower than ever I kept her." "That shall not need," said the Bishop, "for to dread you so much; for wit you well the Pope must be obeyed: and if it were not the Pope's worship, and my poor honesty, ye were distressed, neither the Queen, neither in peril, nor shamed." And then he showed Sir Launcelot all his writings, both from the Pope and from King Arthur. "This is sure enough," said Sir Launcelot; "for full well I dare trust my lord's own writing, and his seal; for he was never yet shamed of his promise: therefore," said Sir Launcelot unto the Bishop, "ye shall ride unto the King before me, and recommend me unto his good grace, and let him have knowledge that this same day eight days, by the grace of God, I myself shall bring my lady, Queen Guenever, unto him. And ye may say unto my

most redoubted lord, King Arthur, that I will say largely for my
lady, the Queen, that I shall expect none for dread, nor fear,
but the King himself, and my lord, Sir Gawaine, and that is
more for King Arthur's love than for himself." So the Bishop
departed, and came to the King at Carlisle, and told him
all how Sir Launcelot had answered him ; and then the tears
burst out of King Arthur's eyes.   Then Sir Launcelot purveyed
him a hundred knights, and they all were clothed in green
velvet, and their horses trapped to the heels ; and every knight
held a branch of olive in his hand, in token of peace ; and the
Queen had with her twenty gentlewomen following her in
the same wise, and Sir Launcelot had twelve coursers following
him : and upon every courser sat a young gentleman, and they
all were arrayed in green velvet, with girdles of gold about their
quarters, and their horses trapped in the same wise down to the
heels, with many clasps, and set with stones and pearls in gold,
to the number of a thousand ; and Queen Guenever and Sir
Launcelot were clothed in white cloth of gold tissue.   And
right so as ye have heard, he rode with the Queen from Joyous
Gard unto Carlisle ; and so Sir Launcelot rode throughout
Carlisle, and so into the castle, that every man might behold :
and wit you well there was many a weeping eye : and then
Sir Launcelot alighted and avoided his horse, and took the
Queen, and led her whereas King Arthur sat in his seat, and
Sir Gawaine sat before him, and many other great lords.   So,
when Sir Launcelot saw the King and Sir Gawaine, then he
led the Queen by the arm, and then he kneeled down and
the Queen both.   Wit you well then there was many a bold
knight with King Arthur that wept as tenderly as though they
had seen all their kin before them.   So King Arthur sat still,
and said not a word ; and, when Sir Launcelot saw his
countenance, he arose and took up the Queen with him : and
thus spake he unto the most noble King Arthur full knightly,
and like a man of great honour.

XV.

" MY most redoubted lord, ye shall understand that, by the
Pope's commandment and yours, I have brought unto you my
lady, the Queen, as right requireth ; and if there be any knight,
of whatsoever degree he be (except your person), that will say, or
dare to say, but that she is true and clean unto you, I here
myself, Sir Launcelot, will make it good upon his body, that she

is a true lady unto you. But liars ye have listened unto, and that has caused great hate between you and me ; for the time hath been, my lord, King Arthur, that ye had been greatly pleased with me, when I did battle for my lady, your Queen ; and full well ye know, my most noble lord and King, that she has been put unto great wrong or this time. And sith it pleased you, at many times, that I should fight for her, me seemeth, my good lord, I had more cause to rescue her from the fire, insomuch as she should have been burnt for my sake : for they that told you those tales were liars, and so it fell upon them. For by likelihood, had not the might of God been with me, I might never have endured against fourteen knights, and they armed and before purposed, and I unarmed and not purposed. For I was sent for unto my lady, your Queen, I wot not for what cause ; but I was not so soon within the chamber door, but anon Sir Agravaine and Sir Mordred called me false traitor and recreant knight." "They called thee right," said Sir Gawaine. "My lord, Sir Gawaine," said Sir Launcelot, "in their quarrel they proved themselves not in the right." "Well, well, Sir Launcelot," said King Arthur, "I have given thee no cause to do me as thou hast done ; for I have worshipped thee and thine more than all my knights." "My good lord and King," said Sir Launcelot, "so ye be not displeased, ye shall understand that I and mine have often done better service than any other knights in divers places ; and, where ye have been full hard bestead, divers times I have myself rescued you from many dangers ; and even unto my power I was glad for to please you and my lord, Sir Gawaine, both in jousts and in tournaments, and in battles set both on horseback and on foot I have often rescued you and my lord, Sir Gawaine, and more of your knights, in divers places. For now I will make my avaunt," said Sir Launcelot, "I will that ye all wit that yet I found never any manner of knight, but that I was overhard for him ; and I had done mine uttermost, thanked be God. Howbeit, I have been matched with good knights, as Sir Tristram and Sir Lamoracke ; but ever I had a favour to them, and a deeming what they were. And I take God to record," said Sir Launcelot, "I was never wrath nor greatly heavy with any knight, and I saw him busy about to win worship ; and full glad I was ever when I found any knight that might endure me on horseback and on foot. Howbeit, Sir Carados, of the Dolorous Tower, was a full noble knight, and a passing strong man, and that ye know, my lord, Sir Gawaine : for he might full well be called a noble knight, when he by fine force pulled you out of your

saddle, and bound overthwart his horse before him to his saddle-
bow. And there, my lord, Sir Gawaine, I rescued you, and slew
him before your face : and I found his brother, Sir Torquine,
in likewise leading Sir Gaheris, your brother, bound before him ;
and there I rescued your brother, and slew that Sir Torquine,
and delivered forty-four of my lord Arthur's knights out of
prison. And now, I dare say," said Sir Launcelot, "I met
never with so strong knights, nor so well fighting, as was Sir
Carados and Sir Torquine ; for I fought with them to the uttermost. And, therefore," said Sir Launcelot unto Sir Gawaine,
"me seemeth that ye ought of right for to remember this ; for,
and I might have your good will, I would trust to God to have
my lord King Arthur's good grace."

XVI.

"THE King may do as he will," said Sir Gawaine ; "but wit
thou well, Sir Launcelot, thou and I shall never be accorded
while we live : for thou hast slain three of my brethren, and
twain of them thou slewest traitorously and piteously ; for they
bore no harness against thee, nor none would bear." "God
would they had been armed," said Sir Launcelot ; "for then
had they been alive. And wit ye well, Sir Gawaine, as for Sir
Gareth, I love none of my kinsmen so much as I do him ;
and ever while I live," said Sir Launcelot, "I will bewail Sir
Gareth's death. Not all only for the great fear that I have of
you, but many causes causeth me to be sorrowful : one is, for I
made him knight ; another is, I wot well he loved me above all
earthly knights ; and the third is, he was passing noble, true,
virtuous, and gentle, and well-conditioned ; the fourth is, I
wist well anon, as I heard that Sir Gaheris was dead, that I
should never after have your love, but everlasting war between us.
And also I wist well that ye would cause my lord, King Arthur,
for ever to be my mortal foe : and, as Jesu be my help," said
Sir Launcelot, "I slew never Sir Gareth nor Sir Gaheris by my
will. But alas ! that they were unarmed that unhappy day !
But this much I offer you," said Sir Launcelot, "if it may
please the King's good grace, and you, my lord, Sir Gawaine :
and first I shall begin at Sandwich, and there shall I go in my
shirt and barefoot ; and, at every ten miles' end, I will found
and cause to make a house of religion, of what order ye will
assign me, with a holy convent to sing and to read day and
night in especial, for Sir Gareth and Sir Gaheris' sake, and

this shall I perform from Sandwich unto Carlisle, and every house shall have sufficent livelihood ; and this shall I perform while I have any livelihood in Christendom : and there is none of all these religious places but they shall be performed, furnished, and garnished, in all things as a holy place ought to be, I promise you faithfully. And this, Sir Gawaine, me thinketh were more fair, and better unto their souls, than that my most noble lord Arthur and you should war on me ; for thereby shall ye get none avail.". Then all the knights and ladies that were there wept as they had been mad ; and the tears fell upon King Arthur's cheeks. "Sir Launcelot," said Sir Gawaine, "I have well heard thy speech and thy great proffers ; but wit thou well (let the King do as it shall please him), I will never forgive thee my brethren's death, and in especial the death of my brother, Sir Gareth : and, if mine uncle, King Arthur, will accord with thee, he shall lose my service ; for wit thou well, that thou art both false to the King and to me." "Sir," said Sir Launcelot, "he beareth not the life that may make that good ; and if that ye, Sir Gawaine, will charge me with so high a thing, ye must pardon me ; for then needs must I answer you." "Nay," said Sir Gawaine, "we are past that as at this time, and that caused the Pope ; for he hath charged mine uncle, the King, that he shall take the Queen again, and for to accord with thee, Sir Launcelot, as for this season ; and, therefore, thou shalt go safe, Sir Launcelot, as thou camest : but in this land thou shall not abide past fifteen days—such warning I give thee. So the King and we were consented and accorded or thou camest hither ; and else," said Sir Gawaine, "wit thou well that thou shouldest not have come hither, but if it were maugre thy head : and, if that it were not for the Pope's commandment, I should do battle with my body against thy body, and prove it unto thee that thou hast been false unto mine uncle, King Arthur, and to me both ; and that shall I prove upon thy body, when thou art departed from hence, wheresoever I find thee."

XVII.

THEN Sir Launcelot sighed, and therewith the tears fell on his cheeks, and then he said these words :—"Alas ! most noble Christian realm, whom I have loved above all other realms, and in thee have I gotten a great part of my worship, and now I shall depart in this wise. Truly me repenteth that ever I came into this realm, that I should be thus shamefully banished

undeserved and causeless. But fortune is so variable, and the
wheel so mutable, that there is no constant abiding; and that
may be proved by many old chronicles of noble Hector, and
Troylus, and Alisaunder, the mighty conqueror, and many
other more, when they were most in their royalty they alighted
lowest: and so it fareth by me," said Sir Launcelot; "for in
this realm I have had worship, and by me and mine all the
whole Round Table hath been increased more in worship by
me and my blood than by any other. And, therefore, wit
thou well, Sir Gawaine, I may live as well upon my lands
as any knight that is here; and if ye, my most renowned
King, will come upon my lands with your nephew, Sir
Gawaine, for to war upon me, I must endure you as well as I
may. But as for you, Sir Gawaine, if that ye come there, I
beseech you and require you, charge me not with treason nor
felony; for, and ye do, I must answer you." "Do thou thy
best," said Sir Gawaine; "therefore, hie thee fast that thou
were gone : and wit thou well, we shall soon come after, and
break the strongest castle that thou hast upon thy head."
"That shall not need," said Sir Launcelot, "for, and I were as
orgulous proudly and set as ye are, wit ye well I should meet
with you in the midst of the field." "Make ye no more ado,"
said Sir Gawaine, "but deliver the Queen from thee, and
get thee lightly out of this court.". "Well," said Sir Launcelot,
"and I had wist of this short answer, I would have advised me
twice or I had come hither ; for, and the Queen had been so
dear to me as ye noise her, I durst have kept her from the
fellowship of the best knights under heaven." And then Sir
Launcelot said unto Queen Guenever, in hearing of the King
and all the knights, "Madam, now I must depart from you and
this noble fellowship for ever; and sithence it is so, I beseech
you pray for me, and send me word if ye be noised with any
false tongues; lightly, my lady, let me have knowledge; and,
if any knight's hands may deliver you by battle, I shall deliver
you." And so therewith Sir Launcelot kissed the Queen ; and
then he said openly, that all they that were there might hear
him, "Now let me see what he be in this, that dare say the
Queen is not true unto my lord, King Arthur ; let see who will
speak, and he dare speak." And therewith he brought the
Queen unto the King, and then Sir Launcelot took his leave
and departed ; and there was neither King, duke, nor earl,
baron nor knight, lady nor gentlewoman, but that they all wept
as people out of their wits, except Sir Gawaine. And so,
when the noble knight, Sir Launcelot, took his horse for to ride

out of Carlisle, there was sobbing and weeping for pure dole of his departing; and so he took his way to Joyous Gard, and afterwards he called it the Dolorous Gard; and thus Sir Launcelot departed from the court for ever. And so, when he came to Joyous Gard, he called of his fellowship unto him, and asked them what they would do? Then they answered altogether with one voice, that they would do as he would do. "My fair fellows," said Sir Launcelot, "I must depart out of this most noble realm; and now I shall depart it grieveth me sore at my heart, for I shall depart with no worship; for a banished man departeth never out of any realm with worship. And that is my heaviness; for ever I fear, after my days, that they shall chronicle upon me that I was banished out of this realm; and else, my fair lords, be ye sure, and I had not dread shame, my lady, Dame Guenever, and I should never have parted asunder." Then spake many noble knights—as Sir Palomides, Sir Safre, his brother; and Sir Bellanger le Breuse, and Sir Urre, with Sir Lavaine, and with many others: "Sir, and ye be so disposed for to abide in this country, we will never fail you; and, if ye list not to abide in this country, there is none of the good knights that be here will fail you for divers causes. One is this:—All we that be not of your blood shall never be welcome to the court of King Arthur; and, since it liketh us to take part with you in your distress and heaviness in the realm, wit you well it shall like us all well for to go in other countries with you, and there to take such part as ye do." "My fair lords," said Sir Launcelot, "I well understand you, and as I can I thank you; and ye shall understand as to such livelihood as I am born unto: I shall depart it with you in this manner of wise; that is to say, that I shall depart all my livelihood and all my lands freely among you: and I myself will have as little as any of you; for I have sufficient that may belong to my person: I will ask none other rich array, and I trust to God to maintain you on my lands as well as ever were maintained any knights." Then spake all the knights at once, "He have shame that will leave you; for we all understand in this realm will be now no quiet, but ever strife and debate, now the fellowship of the Round Table is broken: for by the noble fellowship of the Round Table was King Arthur borne up, and by their nobleness the King and all his realm was in quietness and in rest: and a great part," said they all, "was because of your great nobleness."

XVIII.

"TRULY," said Sir Launcelot, "I thank you for your good saying, howbeit I wot well in me was not all the stability of this realm; but in that I might I did my endeavours; and well I am sure I knew many rebellious in my days, which by me were peaced. I trow we all shall hear of them in short space, and that me sore repenteth. For ever I dread me," said Sir Launcelot, "that Sir Mordred will make republic, for he is passing envious, and applieth him to trouble." So they were accorded to go with Sir Launcelot unto his lands: and, for to make short tale, they made ready and payed all that would ask them. And well a hundred knights departed with Sir Launcelot at once, and made their vows, that they would never depart from him for weal nor for woe: and so they shipped at Cardiff, and sailed unto Benwicke (some men call it Beyon, and some men call it Beaund, whereas the wine of Beaune is).

But, for to say the truth, Sir Launcelot and his nephews were lords of the realm of France, and of all the lands that belonged unto France, he and his kindred rejoiced it through Sir Launcelot's noble prowess: and then Sir Launcelot stuffed and furnished and garnished all his good towns and castles. Then all the people of those lands came unto Sir Launcelot on feet and hands: and so when he had established all these countries, he shortly called a parliament; and there he crowned Sir Lionel King of France; and he made Sir Bors to be crowned King of all King Claudas's lands; and Sir Ector de Maris, which was Sir Launcelot's youngest brother, he crowned him King of Benwicke, and also King of all Guian, which was Sir Launcelot's own land; and he made Sir Ector prince of them all: and thus he parted his honour. Then Sir Launcelot rewarded his noble knights, and many more, that me seemeth it were too long to rehearse.

XIX

So leave we Sir Launcelot in his lands, and his noble knights with him, and return we again unto King Arthur and Sir Gawaine, that made a great host ready, to the number of threescore thousand, and all things was ready for their shipping to pass over the sea; and so they shipped at Cardiff. And there King Arthur made Sir Mordred chief ruler of all England; and also he put Queen Guenever under his governance, for because Sir Mordred was King Arthur's son, he gave him the rule of all his land, and of his Queen. And so King Arthur passed over the sea, and landed upon Sir Launcelot's land; and there he burnt and wasted, through the vengeance of Sir Gawaine, all that they might overrun. When these tidings came unto Sir Launcelot, that King Arthur and Sir Gawaine were landed upon his lands, and that they made great destruction and waste, then spake Sir Bors and said, " My lord, Sir Launcelot, it is great shame that we suffer them thus to ride over our lands; for wit ye well, suffer ye them as long as ye will, they will do you no favour, and they may handle you." Then said Sir Lionel, which was ware and wise, " My lord, Sir Launcelot, I will give you this counsel—let us keep our strong walled town until they have hunger and cold, and blow on their nails, and then let us freshly set upon them, and cut them down as sheep in the field, that all aliens may take example for ever how they land upon our lands." Then spake King Bagdemagus unto Sir Launcelot: " Sir, your courtesy will hurt us all, and your courtesy hath caused all this sorrow; for and they thus override our lands, they shall, by process of time, bring us all to nought, whilst we thus hide us in holes." Then said the good knight, Sir Galihud, to Sir Launcelot, " Sir, here be knights come of kings' blood that will not long droop, and they were without the walls; and therefore give us leave, as we are knights, to meet them in the field, and we shall slay them, that they shall curse the time that ever they came into this country." Then spake the seven brethren of North Wales, and they were seven noble knights, as a man might seek in seven lands or he might find such noble knights; then they spake all with one voice, " Sir Launcelot, for Christ's sake let us ride out with Sir Galihud, for we have been never wont to cower in castles nor in towns." Then spake Sir Launcelot, which was master and governor of them all, " My fair lords, wit you well I am full loth to ride out with my knights, for shedding of Christian men's blood; and yet, my lords, I understand we are full bare to sustain any boast a while: for the mighty warriors that other whiles made King Claudas and my father, King Ban, and mine uncle, King Bors, for to obey. Howbeit we will keep our strong walls, and I shall send a messenger unto my lord, King Arthur, desiring him to take a treaty; for better is peace than always war." So Sir Launcelot sent forth a damsel, and a dwarf with her, requiring King Arthur to leave his war upon his lands; and so she start upon a palfrey, and the dwarf ran by her side. And when she came unto the pavilion of King Arthur, there she alighted; and there met her a knight, whose name was Sir·Lucan, the butler, that said, "Fair damsel, come ye from Sir Launcelot du Lake?" "Yea," said she, "therefore come I hither to speak with my lord, King Arthur." "Alas!" said Sir Lucan, "my lord, King Arthur, would love Sir Launcelot, but Sir Gawaine will not suffer him." And then he said, "I pray to God, damsel, ye may speed well, for all we that are about the King would that Sir Launcelot did best of any knight living." And so with this Lucan led the damsel unto King Arthur, where he sat with Sir Gawaine, for to hear what she would say. So when she had told her tale, the water began to run out of King Arthur's eyes ; and all the lords were right glad to advise the King to be accorded with Sir Launcelot, save all only Sir Gawaine, and he said, " My lord, mine uncle, what will ye do? will ye now turn again, now ye are past thus far upon this journey? all the world will speak of your villainy." "Nay," said King Arthur, "wit ye well, Sir Gawaine, I will do as ye will advise me, and yet me seemeth," said King Arthur, "his fair proffers were not good to be refused ; but since that I am come so far upon this journey, I will that ye give the damsel her answer, for I may not speak to her for pity."

XX.

THEN Sir Gawaine said unto the damsel thus : " Damsel, ye shall say unto Sir Launcelot, that it was but idle labour now to send to mine uncle ; for tell him, and he would have made any labour for peace, he should have made it or this time, for tell him that now it is too late : and say that Sir Gawaine sendeth him word, and that I promise him by the faith I owe to God, and unto the order of knighthood, that I shall never leave him till he hath slain me or I him." So the damsel wept and departed, and there were many weeping eyes ; and so Sir Lucan brought the damsel unto her palfrey. And so she came unto Sir Launcelot, whereas he was among all his knights ; and, when Sir Launcelot had heard this answer, then the tears ran down by his cheeks : and then his noble knights that stood about him said, " Sir Launcelot, wherefore make ye such cheer? think what ye are, and what men we are, and let us noble knights match them in the midst of the field." " That may lightly be done," said Sir Launcelot, "but I was never so loth to do battle ; there, I pray you fair sirs, as ye love me, be ruled as I will have you, for I will always flee that noble King that made me knight : and, when I may no farther, I must needs defend me, and that will be the more worship for me, and every one of us, than to compare with the noble King, whom we all have served." Then they held their language, and as at that night they took their rest ; and on the morrow, early in the dawning of the day, as the knights looked out, they saw how the city of Benwicke was besieged round about, and fast they began to set up ladders ; and then they defied them out of the town, and beat them mightily from the walls. Then went forth Sir Gawaine, well armed at all points, upon a stiff steed, and he came before the chief gate, crying on high, "Sir Launcelot ! where art thou ? Is there not one of you proud knights that dare break a spear with me ? " Then Sir Bors made him ready, and came forth out of the town : and there Sir Gawaine encountered with Sir Bors, and so he smote Sir Bors down from his horse, and almost he had slain him, and anon Sir Bors was rescued and borne into the town. Then there came forth Sir Lionel, brother unto Sir Bors, and thought to revenge him, and either feutred their spears and ran together, and there they met right spitefully : but Sir Gawaine was so fiery, that he smote Sir Lionel down, and wounded him there passing sore ; and then Sir Lionel was rescued and borne into the town. And thus Sir Gawaine came every day, and failed not but that he smote down one knight or other. So thus they endured well half a-year, and much slaughter of people there was on both parties. Then it befell upon a day that Sir Gawaine came before the gates armed at all pieces, upon a great courser, with a great spear in his hand : and then he cried with a loud voice, "Where art thou now, thou false traitor, Sir Launcelot ! why dost thou hide thyself within holes and walls like a coward ? Look out now, thou false traitor knight, and here I shall revenge upon my body the death of my three brethren." All this language heard Sir Launcelot, and his kin, every deal, and then his knights drew about him, and they said all at once unto Sir Launcelot, " Sir Launcelot, now ye must defend you like a knight, or else ye be shamed for ever ; for now ye be called upon treason, it is time for you to stir, for ye have slept over long, and slept over-much." "So God me help," said Sir Launcelot, "I am right heavy of Sir Gawaine's words, for now he chargeth me with a great charge ; and, therefore, I wot it as well as ye, that I must defend me, or else to be a recreant knight." Then Sir Launcelot commanded to saddle his strongest horse, and bid fetch his armour, and bring all unto the gate of the tower : and then Sir Launcelot spake on high unto King Arthur, and said, "My lord, and noble King, which made me knight, wit you well that I am right heavy for your sake, that ye thus sue upon me, and always

I forbear you ; for, and I would have been revengeful, might
I have met you in the midst of the field, and there to have
made your boldest knights full tame : and now I have forborne
you half a-year, and have suffered you and Sir Gawaine to do
what ye would, and now must I needs defend myself, insomuch
as Sir Gawaine hath appealed me of treason, the which is
greatly against my will, that ever I should fight against any of
your blood : but now I may not forsake it, I am driven thereto
as best to obey." Then Sir Gawaine said unto Sir Launcelot,
"Sir Launcelot, and thou darest do battle, leave thy babbling,
and come off, and let us ease our hearts." Then Sir Launcelot
began to arm him lightly, and mounted upon his horse ; and
either of the knights gat great spears in their hands, and the
host without stood still apart, and the noble knights came out
of the city by a great number, insomuch, that when King Arthur
saw the number of men and knights, he marvelled, and said to
himself, "Alas ! that ever Sir Launcelot was against me, for now
I see that he hath forborne me." And so the covenant was
made, there should no man come nigh them, nor deal with
them, till that one were dead or yielden.

XXI.

THEN Sir Gawaine and Sir Launcelot departed a great way
in sunder, and then they came together with all their horses'
might, as fast they might run, and either smote other in the
midst of their shields ; but the knights were so strong, and
their spears so big, that their horses might not endure their
buffets : and so their horses fell to the earth. Then they
avoided their horses, and dressed their shields before them ;
then they strode together, and gave many sad strokes upon
divers places of their bodies, that the blood burst out of many
places. Then had Sir Gawaine such a grace and gift, which a
holy man had given him, that every day in the year, from nine
in the morning till high noon, his might increased those three
hours as much as thrice his own strength, and that caused Sir
Gawaine to win great honour : and for his sake, King Arthur
made an ordinance, that all manner of battles, for any quarrels
that should be done before King Arthur, they should begin at
nine in the morning. And all this was done for Sir Gawaine's
sake, that by likelihood, if that Sir Gawaine were on the one
party, he should have the better hand in battle, while that
his strength endured three hours ; but there were but few
knights that time living that knew this vantage that Sir

Gawaine had, but King Arthur all only. Then Sir Launcelot fought with Sir Gawaine; and when Sir Launcelot felt his might evermore increase, Sir Launcelot had of him great wonder, and dread him sore to be shamed; for he weened, when he felt Sir Gawaine double his strength, that he had been fiend, and none earthly man; wherefore, Sir Launcelot traced, and traversed, and covered himself with his shield, and kept his might and his breath during three hours; and that while Sir Gawaine gave him many sad brunts, and many strokes, that all knights that beheld Sir Launcelot marvelled how he might endure him. But full little understood they the travail that Sir Launcelot had for to endure him. And then when it was past noon, Sir Gawaine had no more but his own might. Then, when Sir Launcelot felt him so come down, then began he to stretch himself up, and stood near Sir Gawaine, and said to him these words: "My lord, Sir Gawaine, now I feel that ye have done, now my lord, Sir Gawaine, I must do my part, for many great and grievous strokes I have endured you this day with pain." Then Sir Launcelot began to double his strokes, and gave Sir Gawaine many a buffet upon the helmet, that he fell down on his side, and then Sir Launcelot withdrew him from him. "Why withdrawest thou thyself?" said Sir Gawaine, "now turn again, traitor knight, and slay me; for, and thou leave me thus, when I am whole I shall do battle with thee again." "Sir, I shall endure you by the grace of God," said Sir Launcelot; "but wit you well, Sir Gawaine, I will never smite a felled knight." And so Sir Launcelot went into the city, and Sir Gawaine was borne into one of King Arthur's pavilions: and anon there was leeches brought to him, which searched his wound, and salved it with soft ointments. And then Sir Launcelot said, "Now have good day my lord, the King, for wit ye well ye shall win no worship at these walls; and, if I would bring out my knights, there should many a man die. Therefore, my lord, King Arthur, remember you of old kindness, and, howsoever I fare, Jesu be your guide in all places."

XXII.

"ALAS!" said the King, "that ever this unhappy war began; for ever Sir Launcelot forbeareth me in all places, and in likewise my kin, and that is seen this day by my nephew, Sir Gawaine." Then King Arthur fell sick, for sorrow of Sir Gawaine, that was so sore hurt, and because of the war between him and Sir Launcelot. So then they of King Arthur's part kept the siege with little war and small force, and they within kept their walls, and defended them when need was. Thus Sir Gawaine lay sick about three weeks in his tent, with all manner of leech-craft that might be had ; and, as soon as Sir Gawaine might go and ride, he armed him all points, and start upon a courser, and got a spear in his hand. And so he came riding before the chief gate of Benwicke, and there he cried on high, "Where art thou, Sir Launcelot? come forth, thou false traitor knight, and recreant, for I am here : Sir Gawaine will prove this that I say on thee." All this language Sir Launcelot heard, and then he said thus : "Sir Gawaine, me repenteth of your foul saying, that ye will not cease of your language. For wit ye well, Sir Gawaine, I know your might, and all that ye may do." "And well ye wot," said Sir Gawaine, "that ye may not greatly hurt me. Come down, thou traitor knight, and make it good, contrary with thy hands, for it mishappened me, the last battle, to be hurt of thy hands, therefore wit thou well that I am come this day to make amends. For I ween this day to lay thee as low as thou laidest me." "Jesu defend me," said Sir Launcelot, "that ever I should be so far in your danger as ye have been in mine : for then my days were at an end. But, Sir Gawaine," said Sir Launcelot, "ye shall not think that I tarry long ; but since that ye so unknightly call me of treason, ye shall have both your hands full of me." And then Sir Launcelot armed him at all points, and mounted upon his horse, and gat him a great spear in his hand, and rode out at the gate ; and both the hosts were assembled, of them without and of them within, and stood in array full manly ; and both parties were charged for to hold them still, to see and behold the battle of these two noble knights : and then they laid their spears in their rests, and they ran together as thunder, and Sir Gawaine break his spear upon Sir Launcelot in a hundred pieces unto his hand ; and Sir Launcelot smote him with a greater might, that Sir Gawaine's horse's feet raised, and so the horse and he fell to the earth. Then Sir Gawaine full quickly avoided his horse, and put his shield before him, and eagerly drew his sword, and bid Sir Launcelot alight, "traitor knight, for though this mare's son hath failed me, wit thou well, that a king's son, and a queen's son, shall not fail thee." Then Sir Launcelot avoided his horse, and dressed his shield before him, and drew his sword, and so they stood together, and gave many sad strokes, that all men on both parties had thereof passing great wonder. But when Sir Launcelot felt Sir Gawaine's might so marvellously increase, he then withheld his courage and his wind, and kept himself wondrous covered from his might; and under his shield he traced, traversed, here and there, for to break Sir Gawaine's strokes and his courage. And Sir Gawaine enforced him with all his might and power to destroy Sir Launcelot; for ever as Sir Gawaine's might increased, right so increased his wind and his evil will. Thus Sir Gawaine did great pain unto Sir Launcelot three hours continually, that Sir Launcelot had great pain to defend himself; and after that the three hours were passed, then Sir Launcelot felt verily that Sir Gawaine was come to his own proper might and strength, and that his great power was done. Then Sir Launcelot said unto Sir Gawaine, "Now have I well proved you twice, that ye are a full dangerous knight, and a wonderful man of your might, and many wonderful deeds have you done in your days; for by your might increasing ye have deceived many a noble and valiant knight; and now I feel that ye have done your mighty deed. Now, wit you well, I must do my deeds:" and then Sir Launcelot stood near Sir Gawaine, and doubled his strokes, and Sir Gawaine defended him mightily. But, nevertheless, Sir Launcelot smote such a stroke upon Sir Gawaine's helm, and upon the old wound, that Sir Gawaine sunk down upon his one side in a swoon: and anon, as he was awake, he raved and foamed at Sir Launcelot there, as he lay, and said, "Traitor knight, wit thou well that I am not yet slain; come thou near, and perform this battle to the uttermost." "I will no more do than I have done," said Sir Launcelot; "for when I see you on foot, I will do battle with you all the while I see you stand on your feet; but, for to smite a wounded man that may not stand, God defend me from such a shame." And then he turned him and went his way toward the town; and Sir Gawaine evermore calling him traitor knight, and said, "Wit thou well, Sir Launcelot, when I am whole, I shall do battle with thee again, for I shall never leave thee till that one of us be slain."

Thus, as this siege endured, and as Sir Gawaine lay sick near a month, and when he was well recovered, and ready within three days to do battle again with Sir Launcelot, right so came tidings unto King Arthur from England, that made King Arthur and all his host to remove.

THE BOOK OF THE MORTE D' ARTHUR.

I.

AS Sir Mordred was ruler of all England, he caused letters to be made, as though they came from beyond the sea, and the letters specified that King Arthur was slain in battle with Sir Launcelot ; wherefore Sir Mordred made a parliament, and called the lords together, and there he made them to chuse him King, and so he was crowned at Canterbury, and held a feast there fifteen days. And afterward he drew him to Winchester, and there he took Queen Guenever, and said plainly that he would wed her, which was his uncle's wife, and his father's wife : and so he made ready for the feast, and a day prefixed that they should be wedded. Wherefore Queen Guenever was passing heavy, but she durst not discover her heart ; but speak fair, and agreed to Sir Mordred's will. Then she desired of Sir Mordred for to go to London, for to buy all manner of things that belonged unto the wedding : and, because of her fair speech, Sir Mordred trusted her well enough, and gave her leave to go ; and, when she came to London, suddenly, in all haste possible, she stuffed it with all manner of victuals, and well garnished it with men, and so kept it. Then, when Sir Mordred wist and understood how he was deceived, he was passing wrath out of measure. And, to make short tale, he went and laid a mighty siege about the Tower of London, and made many great assaults thereat, and threw many great engines unto them, and shot great guns. But all might not prevail Sir Mordred. For Queen Guenever would never, for fair speech, nor for foul, trust to come in his hands again. And then came the Bishop of Canterbury, the which was a noble clerk, and a holy man, and thus he said to Sir Mordred, " Sir, what will ye do? will ye first displease God, and after shame yourself, and all knighthood? Is not King Arthur your uncle, no further but your mother's brother, and on her himself King Arthur begat you upon his own sister, therefore how may ye wed your father's wife? Sir," said the noble clerk, " leave this opinion, or else I shall curse you with book, bell, and candle." " Do thy worst," said Sir Mordred, " wit thou well that I utterly defy thee." " Sir," said the bishop, " I shall not fear me to do that I ought to do. Also, whereas ye noise that my lord King Arthur is slain, it is not so ; and therefore ye will make an

abominable work in this land." " Peace ! thou false priest," said
Sir Mordred, "for and thou chafe me any more, I shall make
thy head to be stricken off." So the bishop departed, and did
the curse in the most orgulous wise that might be done. And
then Sir Mordred sought the Bishop of Canterbury, for to have
slain him. And when the bishop heard that, he fled, and took
part of his goods with him, and went nigh unto Glastonbury, and there he was a religious hermit in a chapel, and lived
in poverty, and in holy prayers. For well he understood that a
mischievous war was near at hand. Then Sir Mordred sought
upon Queen Guenever, by letters and messages, and by fair
means and foul, for to have her come out of the Tower of London.
But all this availed him not, for she answered him shortly,
openly and privily, that she had lever slay herself than to be
married with him. Then came word to Sir Mordred, that King
Arthur had raised the siege from Sir Launcelot, and that he
was coming homeward with a great host, for to be avenged
upon Sir Mordred. Wherefore Sir Mordred made to write
letters unto all the barony of this land, and much people drew
unto him ; for then was the common voice among them, that
with King Arthur was none other life but war and strife, and
with Sir Mordred was great joy and bliss. Thus was King
Arthur deprived, and evil said of ; and many there were that
King Arthur had made up of nought, and had given them lands,
might not say of him then a good word.

Lo ! we all Englishmen see what a mischief here was : for he
that was the noblest knight and king of the world, and most
loved the fellowship of noble knights and men of worship, and
by him they were all upholden. Now, might not we Englishmen hold us content with him ; lo ! this was the old custom
and usage of this land. And also men say, that we of this land
have not yet lost nor forgotten the custom and usage. Alas !
alas ! this is a great default of us Englishmen, for there may
nothing please us no term. And so fared the people at that
time. For they were better pleased with Sir Mordred than
they were with King Arthur ; and much people drew unto Sir
Mordred, and said they would abide with him, for better and
for worse. And so Sir Mordred drew with great haste toward
Dover, for there he heard say that King Arthur would arrive ;
and so he thought to beat his own father from his lands : and
the most part of all England held with Sir Mordred, the people
were so new-fangled.

II.

AND so, as Sir Mordred was at Dover, with his host, there came King Arthur, with a great many ships, galleys, and carracks ; and there was Sir Mordred ready, waiting upon his landing, to hinder his own father to land upon the land that he was king of. Then was there launching of great boats and small, and all were full of noble men of arms ; and there was much slaughter of gentle knights, and many a full bold baron was laid full low, on both parties. But King Arthur was so courageous, that there might no manner of knight let him to land, and his knights fiercely followed him ; and so they landed, maugre Sir Mordred and all his power : and put Sir Mordred back, that he fled, and all his people. So when this battle was done, King Arthur let bury his people that were dead : and then was the noble knight, Sir Gawaine, found in a great boat, lying more than half dead. When King Arthur wist that Sir Gawaine was laid so low, he went unto him, and there the King made sorrow out of measure, and took Sir Gawaine in his arms, and thrice he swooned : and then he came to himself again, and said, "Alas ! my sister's son, here now thou liest, the man in the world that I loved most ; and now is my joy gone. For now, my nephew, Sir Gawaine, I will discover me unto your person : in Sir Launcelot and you I most had my joy and mine affiance, and now have I lost my joy of you both, wherefore all mine earthly joy is gone from me." "My uncle, King Arthur," said Sir Gawaine, "wit you well, that my death's-day is come, and all is through mine own hastiness and wilfulness ; for I am smitten upon the old wound that Sir Launcelot du Lake gave me, of the which I feel that I must die ; and if Sir Launcelot had been with you as he was, this unhappy war had never begun, and of all this I myself am causer : for Sir Launcelot and his blood, through their prowess, held all your cankered enemies in subjection and danger. And now," said Sir Gawaine, "ye shall miss Sir Launcelot : but, alas ! I would not accord with him, and therefore," said Sir Gawaine, "I pray you, fair uncle, that I may have paper, pen, and ink, that I may write unto Sir Launcelot a letter with mine own hands." And when paper and ink was brought, Sir Gawaine was set up, weakly, by King Arthur, for he had been shriven a little before, and he wrote thus :

"UNTO SIR LAUNCELOT, flower of all noble knights that ever I heard of or saw in my days.

"I, Sir Gawaine, King Lot's son, of Orkney, sister's son unto the noble King Arthur, send unto thee, greeting, and let thee have knowledge, that the tenth day of May I was smitten upon the old wound which thou gavest me before the city of Benwicke ; and through the same wound thou gavest me I am come unto my death-day, and I will that all the world wit that I, Sir Gawaine, knight of the Round Table, sought my death, and not through thy deserving, but it was mine own seeking ; wherefore I beseech thee, Sir Launcelot, for to return again unto this realm, and see my tomb, and pray some prayer, more or less, for my soul. And that same day that I wrote this letter I was hurt to the death in the same wound, the which I had of thy hands, Sir Launcelot. For of a nobler man might I not be slain. Also, Sir Launcelot, for all the love that ever was between us, make no tarrying, but come over the sea in all the haste that thou mayest, with thy noble knights, and rescue that noble King that made thee knight, that is my lord and uncle, King Arthur, for he is full straitly bestood with a false traitor, which is my false brother, Sir Mordred, and he hath let crown himself king, and he would have wedded my lady, Queen Guenever ; and so had he done, if she had not put herself in the Tower of London. And so the tenth day of May last past, my lord and uncle, King Arthur, and we, all landed upon them at Dover, and there we put that false traitor, Sir Mordred, to flight ; and there it misfortuned me for to be stricken upon thy stroke. And, at the date of this letter was written, but two hours and a-half before my death, written with mine own hand, and so subscribed with part of my heart's blood, and I require thee, as thou art the most famous knight of the world, that thou wilt see my tomb."

And then Sir Gawaine wept, and also King Arthur wept, and then they swooned both ; and when they awaked both, the King made Sir Gawaine to receive his Saviour. And then Sir Gawaine prayed the King to send for Sir Launcelot, and to cherish him above all other knights. And so, at the hour of noon, Sir Gawaine betook his soul into the hands of our Lord God. And there the King let bury him in a chapel within the castle of Dover : and there, yet unto this day, all men may see the skull of Sir Gawaine, and the same wound is seen that Sir Launcelot gave him in battle. Then was it told to King Arthur that Sir Mordred had pitched a new field upon Barendown, and on the morrow the King rode thither to him, and there was a great battle between them, and much people were slain on both parts ; but at the last King Arthur's party stood best, and Sir Mordred and his party fled unto Canterbury.

III.

AND then the King searched all towns for his knights that were slain, and made to bury them ; and those that were sore wounded he caused them to be salved with soft salves. Then much people drew unto King Arthur, and said that Sir Mordred warred on King Arthur wrongfully. And then the King drew him and with his host down unto the sea-side, westward, unto Salisbury, and there was a day assigned between King Arthur and Sir Mordred, and they should meet upon a down beside Salisbury, and not far from the sea-side ; and this day was assigned upon a Monday after Trinity Sunday, whereof King Arthur was passing glad, that he might be avenged upon that traitor, Sir Mordred. Then Sir Mordred raised much people about London, for they of Kent, Sussex, and Surrey, Essex, and Suffolk, and of Norfolk, held for the most part with Sir Mordred, and many a noble knight drew unto Sir Mordred, and unto King Arthur ; but they that loved Sir Launcelot drew unto Sir Mordred.

And so, upon Trinity Sunday, at night, King Arthur dreamed a right wonderful dream, and that was this : that him thought he sat upon a scaffold in a chair, and the chair was fast unto a wheel, and thereupon sat King Arthur, in the richest cloth of gold that might be made ; and the King thought there was under him, far from him, a hideous and a deep black water, and therein was all manner of serpents and worms, and wild beasts, foul and horrible ; and suddenly the King thought that the wheel turned upside down, and that he fell among the serpents and wild beasts, and every beast took him by a limb : and then the King cried, as he lay in his bed and slept, "Help!"

And then knights, squires, and yeomen awaked the King, and then he was so amazed, that he wist not where he was ; and then he fell in a slumbering again, not sleeping, nor through waking. So King Arthur thought there came Sir Gawaine unto him verily, with a number of fair ladies with him ; and so, when King Arthur saw him, he said, "Welcome, my sister's son, I weened thou hast been dead, and now I see thee alive ; much am I beholden unto Almighty Jesu. Oh! fair nephew, and my sister's son, what be these ladies that be come hither with you?" "Sir," said Sir Gawaine, "all these be the ladies for whom I have fought when I was a man living ; and all these are those that I did battle for in a rightwise quarrel, and God hath given them that grace at their great prayer, because I did battle for them, that they should bring me hither to you ; thus much hath

God given me leave for to warn you of your death ; for and ye fight as to-morrow with Sir Mordred, as both ye have assigned, doubt ye not ye must be slain, and the most part of your people, on both parties : and for the great grace and goodness that Almighty Jesu hath unto you, and for pity of you, and many more other good men, that there should be slain, God hath sent me unto you, of His most special grace, for to give you warning, that in no wise ye do battle as to-morrow, but that ye take a treaty for a month's day, and proffer him largely, so as to-morrow to be put in a delay ; for within a month shall come Sir Launcelot, with all his noble knights, and shall rescue you worshipfully, and slay Sir Mordred and all that ever will hold him." Then Sir Gawaine and all the ladies vanished. And anon the King called upon his knights, squires, and yeomen, and charged them lightly to fetch his noble lords and wise bishops unto him ; and when they were come, the King told them his vision, what Sir Gawaine told him, and warned him, that if he fought on the morrow he should be slain. Then the King commanded Sir Lucan, the butler ; and his brother, Sir Bedivere ; and two bishops with them, and charged them in any wise if they might take a treaty for a month with Sir Mordred ; and spare not to proffer him lands and goods, as much as ye think best. So then they departed and came to Sir Mordred, where he had a grimly host of a hundred thousand men, and thereby entreated Sir Mordred long time ; and, at the last, Sir Mordred was agreed to have Cornwall and Kent by King Arthur's days, and after the days of King Arthur to have all England to his obeisance.

IV.

So then were they condescended that King Arthur and Sir Mordred should meet between both their hosts, and every each of them should bring fourteen persons ; and then came this word unto King Arthur. "And then," said he, "I am glad that this is done." And so he went into the field ; and when King Arthur should depart, he warned all his host, "that and they saw any sword drawn, look that ye come on fiercely, and slay that traitor, Sir Mordred, for in nowise trust him." In likewise Sir Mordred did warn his host, "that if ye see any manner of sword drawn, look that ye come on fiercely, and so slay all that ever standeth before you ; for in nowise I will not trust for this treaty, for I know well that my father will be avenged upon me."

And so they were agreed and accorded thoroughly, and wine was set, and they drank. Right so came an adder out of a little heath bush, and stung a knight on the foot. And when the knight felt him stung, he looked down and saw the adder, and then he drew his sword to slay the adder, and thought of none other harm. And when the hosts on both parties saw that sword drawn, they blew beames, trumpets, and horns, and shouted grimly. And so both hosts dressed them together, and King Arthur took his horse, and said, "Alas! this unhappy day:" and so rode he to his part. And so Sir Mordred did in likewise, and never was there seen a more dolefuller battle in no Christian land : for there was but rushing and riding, foining and striking, and many a grim word was there spoken either to other, and many a deadly stroke. But alway King Arthur rode throughout the battle of Sir Mordred many times, and did there right nobly as a noble King should do ; and at all times he never fainted. And Sir Mordred that day put him in devoir and in great peril, and thus they fought all the long day, and never stinted till the noble knights were laid to the cold ground. And ever they fought still till it was nigh night, and by that time was there a hundred thousand laid dead upon the down. Then was King Arthur wrath out of measure, when he saw his people so slain from him. Then the King looked about him, and then was he ware that of all his host, and of his good knights, were left no more alive but two knights ; that were Sir Lucan, the butler, and Sir Bedivere, his brother, and they were right sore wounded. "Jesu mercy," said King Arthur, "where are all my noble knights become? Alas! that ever I should see this doleful day: for now," said King Arthur, "I am come unto mine end. But would to God that I wist where that traitor, Sir Mordred, is, which hath caused all this mischief?" Then was King Arthur aware where Sir Mordred leaned upon his sword among a great heap of dead men. "Now give me my spear," said King Arthur to Sir Lucan, "for yonder I have espied the traitor which hath wrought all this woe." "Sir, let him be," said Sir Lucan, "for he is unhappy ; and if ye pass this unhappy day, ye shall be right well revenged upon him. My good lord, remember well your dream that ye had this night, and what the spirit of Sir Gawaine told you this night ; yet God of his great goodness hath preserved you hither, therefore, for God's sake, my lord, leave off by this ; for, blessed be God, ye have won the field, for here we be three alive, and with Sir Mordred is none alive, and if ye leave off now this wicked day of destiny is done."

"Betide me death, betide me life," said the King ; "now I see him yonder alone, he shall never escape my hands, for at better advantage shall I never have him." "God speed you well," said Sir Bedivere. Then King Arthur gat his spear in both his hands, and ran toward Sir Mordred, crying, "Traitor, now is thy death-day come." And when Sir Mordred heard King Arthur, he ran unto him with his sword drawn in his hand, and there King Arthur smote Sir Mordred under the shield, with a foin of his spear, throughout the body more than a fathom. And when Sir Mordred felt that he had his death wound, he thrust himself with all the might that he had up to the end of King Arthur's spear with his sword, that he held in both his hands, on the side of the head, that the sword pierced the helmet and the brain-pan. And therewith Sir Mordred fell down stark dead to the earth, and the noble King Arthur fell in a swoon to the earth, and there he swooned oftentimes. And Sir Lucan and Sir Bedivere oftentimes heaved him up, and so weakly they laid him between them both unto a little chapel, not far from the sea-side. And when the King was there, he thought him well eased. Then heard they people cry in the field. "Now go thou, Sir Lucan," said the King, "and do me to write what betokeneth that noise in the field." So Sir Lucan departed, and he was grievously wounded in many places ; and so, as he went, he saw and hearkened by the moonlight, how the pilfers and robbers were come into the field, for to pilfer and rob many a noble knight of broaches and beads, of many a good ring, and of many a rich jewel. And who that were not dead all out, there they slew them for to have their harness, and their riches. And when Sir Lucan understood this work, he came unto the King as soon as he might, and told him all that he had heard and seen. "Therefore, by mine advice," said Sir Lucan, "it is best that we bring you unto some town." "I would it were so," said the King.

V.

"But I may not stand, my head acheth so. Ah ! Sir Launcelot," said King Arthur, "this same day have I sore missed thee ; alas ! that ever I was against thee, for now have I my death, whereof Sir Gawaine warned me in my dream." Then Sir Lucan took up King Arthur on the one part, and Sir Bedivere on the other part, and in the lifting the King swooned. And Sir Lucan fell in a swoon with that lift, that therewith the noble knight's heart burst. And when King Arthur came to himself again, he beheld Sir Lucan how he lay foaming at the mouth. "Alas!" said King Arthur, "this is unto me a full heavy sight for to see this noble duke so to die for my sake; for he would have holpen me, that had more need of help than I have. Alas! he would not complain him, his heart was so set for to help me. Now, Jesu, have mercy upon his soul." Then Sir Bedivere wept for the death of his brother. "Leave this weeping and mourning," said King Arthur, "for all this will not avail me; for wit thou well I might live myself, the death of Sir Lucan would grieve me evermore. But my time hieth fast," said King Arthur unto Sir Bedivere, "therefore take thou Excalibur, my good sword, and go with it unto yonder water-side; and when thou comest there, I charge thee, throw my sword into that water, and come again and tell me what thou shalt see there." "My lord," said Sir Bedivere, "your command shall be done, and lightly bring you word again." And so Sir Bedivere departed, and by the way he beheld that noble sword, where the pommel and the haft were all of precious stones. And then he said to himself, "If I throw this rich sword into the water, thereof shall never come good, but harm and loss." And then Sir Bedivere hid Excalibur under a tree, and as soon as he might, he came again unto King Arthur, and said he had been at the water, and had thrown the sword into the water. "What sawest thou there?" said the King. "Sir," said he, "I saw nothing but waves and wind." "That is untruly said of thee," said King Arthur, "therefore go thou lightly and do my command, as thou art to me life and dear, spare not but throw it in." Then Sir Bedivere returned again, and took the sword in his hand; and then he thought it sin and shame to throw away that noble sword: and so after he hid the sword, and returned again, and told to the King that he had been at the water and done his command. "What saw ye there?" said the King. "Sir," said he, "I saw nothing but the water lap and waves wan." "Ah! traitor, untrue," said King Arthur, "now hast thou betrayed me two times, who would have weened that thou that hast been unto me so self and dear, and thou art named a noble knight, and wouldest betray me for the rich sword. But now go again lightly, for thy long tarrying putteth me in great jeopardy of my life, for I have taken cold; and but if thou do as I command thee, and if ever I may see thee, I shall slay thee with mine own hands, for thou wouldest for my rich sword see me dead." Then Sir Bedivere departed, and went to the sword, and lightly took it up and went to the water's side, and there he bound the girdle about the belts. And then he threw the sword into the water as far as he might, and there came an arm and a hand above the water, and met it and caught it, and so shook it thrice and brandished. And then the hand vanished away with the sword in the water.

So Sir Bedivere came again to the King, and told him what he had seen. "Alas!" said the King, "help me from hence; for I dread me I have tarried over long." Then Sir Bedivere took King Arthur upon his back, and so went with him to the water's side; and, when they were at the water's side, even fast by the bank hovered a little barge, with many fair ladies in it: and among them all was a queen, and all they had black hoods; and they wept and shrieked when they saw King Arthur.

"Now put me into the barge," said the King. And so he did softly, and there received him three queens with great mourning; and so these three queens sat them down, and in one of their laps King Arthur laid his head. And then that queen said, "Ah! dear brother, why have ye tarried so long from me? Alas! this wound on your head hath taken overmuch cold." And so then they rowed from the land; and Sir Bedivere beheld all those ladies go from him. Then Sir Bedivere cried, "Ah! my lord Arthur, what shall become of me now ye go from me, and leave me here alone among mine enemies?" "Comfort thyself," said King Arthur, "and do as well as thou mayest; for in me is no trust for to trust in: for I will into the vale of Avilion, for to heal me of my grievous wound; and, if thou never hear more of me, pray for my soul." But evermore the queens and the ladies wept and shrieked, that it was pitiful for to hear them: and, as soon as Sir Bedivere had lost the sight of the barge, he wept and wailed, and so took the forest, and so he went all the night; and, in the morning, he was aware, between two hills, of a chapel and a hermitage.

VI.

THEN was Sir Bedivere glad, and thither he went; and, when he came into the chapel, he saw where lay a hermit grovelling upon all fours there, fast by a tomb newly graven. When the hermit saw Sir Bedivere he knew him well; for he was, but a little before, Bishop of Canterbury, that Sir Mordred had banished away. "Sir," said Sir Bedivere, "what man is there buried that ye pray so fast for?" "My fair son," said the hermit, "I wot not verily but by deeming; but this night, at midnight, here came a great number of ladies, which brought this dead corpse, and prayed me to bury him ; and here they offered a hundred tapers, and gave me a hundred besants." "Alas !" said Sir Bedivere, "that was my lord, King Arthur, that here lieth buried in this chapel." Then Sir Bedivere swooned ; and, when he awoke, he prayed the hermit that he might abide with him here still, to live with fasting and prayers; "For from hence will I never go," said Sir Bedivere, "by my will ; but all the days of my life here to pray for my lord, King Arthur." "Ye are welcome to me," said the hermit ; "for I know you better than ye ween that I do : for ye are that bold Bedivere, and the noble duke Sir Lucan, the butler, was your own brother."

Then Sir Bedivere told the hermit all as ye beard before. So Sir Bedivere abode there still with the hermit, which had been before the Bishop of Canterbury: and there Sir Bedivere put upon him poor clothes, and served the hermit full lowly in fasting and in prayers. This of King Arthur I find no more written in my copy of the certainty of his death : but thus was he led away in a barge, wherein were three queens : that one was King Arthur's sister, Morgan le Fay ; the other was the Queen of Northgalis ; and the third was the Queen of the Waste Lands. And there was Nimue, the chief Lady of the Lake, which had wedded Sir Pelleas, the good knight. And this lady had done much for King Arthur ; for she would never suffer Sir Pelleas to be in any place whereas he should be in danger of his life : and so he lived to the uttermost of his days with her in great rest. More of the death of King Arthur could I never find, but that ladies brought him unto the burials. And such one was buried here, that the hermit bare witness, that sometimes was Bishop of Canterbury: but yet the hermit knew not of a certain that it was verily the body of King Arthur. For this tale Sir Bedivere, knight of the Round Table, made it plainly to be written.

VII.

SOME men yet say, in many parts of England, that King Arthur is not dead ; but had by the will of our Lord Jesu Christ into another place : and men say that he will come again, and he shall win the holy cross. I will not say that it shall be so ; but rather I will say, that here in this world he changed his life. But many men say that there is written upon his tomb this verse :—

Hic jacet Arthurus rex quondam, rexque futurus.

Thus leave we here Sir Bedivere with the hermit, that dwelled that time in a chapel beside Glastonbury, and there was his hermitage ; and so they lived in prayers, and fastings, and great abstinence.   And when Queen Guenever understood that her lord, King Arthur, was slain, and all the noble knights, Sir Mordred and all the remnant, then she stole away, and five ladies with her : and so she went to Almesbury, and there she let make herself a nun, and wore white clothes and black : and great penance she took, as ever did sinful lady in this land, and never creature could make her merry, but lived in fastings, prayers, and alms deeds, that all manner of people marvelled how virtuously she was changed. Now leave we Queen Guenever in Almesbury, that was a nun in white clothes and in black, and there she was abbess and ruler as reason would : and turn we from her, and speak we of Sir Launcelot du Lake.

VIII.

And when he heard in his country that Sir Mordred was crowned king in England, and made war against King Arthur, his own father, and would not let him to land in his own land. Also it was told Sir Launcelot how that Sir Mordred had laid siege about the Tower of London, because the Queen would not wed him.   Then was Sir Launcelot wondrous wrath, and said to his kinsmen, "Alas! that double traitor, Sir Mordred! now I repent me that he escaped my hands ; for much shame hath he done to my lord, King Arthur : for I feel, by the letter of Sir Gawaine, that my lord, King Arthur, is right hard bestead. Alas!" said Sir Launcelot, "that ever I should live to hear that most noble King, that made me knight, thus to be overset with his subjects in his own realm : and this doleful letter, that my lord, Sir Gawaine, hath sent me before his death, praying me to see his tomb, wit ye well his doleful words shall never go from my heart.   For he was a full noble knight that ever was born ; and in an unhappy hour was I born, that ever a wretch should have that mishap to slay Sir Gawaine, and Sir Gaheris, the good knight, and mine own friend, Sir Gareth, that noble knight.

"Alas! may I say, that I am unhappy," said Sir Launcelot, "that ever I should do thus unhappily! Alas! might I never have hap to slay that traitor, Sir Mordred?" "Leave your complaints," said Sir Bors, "and first revenge you of the death of Sir Gawaine, and it will be well done that ye go to see Sir Gawaine's tomb ; and, secondly, that ye revenge my lord, King Arthur, and Queen Guenever." "I thank you," said Sir Launcelot, "for ever ye will my worship."

Then they made them ready in all the haste that might be, with ships and galleys, with Sir Launcelot and his host, for to pass into England : and so he passed over the sea, and arrived at Dover ; and there he landed with seven kings, and the number of their men of arms was hideous to behold.   Then Sir Launcelot inquired of the men of Dover where King Arthur was become?

Then the people told him how that he was slain with Sir Mordred, and a hundred thousand died upon a day ; and how Sir Mordred gave King Arthur there the first battle at his landing, and there was the good knight, Sir Gawaine, slain ; and, on the morrow, Sir Mordred fought with King Arthur upon Barendown, and there King Arthur put Sir Mordred to the worst.   "Alas !" said Sir Launcelot, "this is the heaviest tidings that ever came to me.   Now, fair sir," said Sir Launcelot, " I beseech you show me the tomb of Sir Gawaine."

And then certain people of the town brought him to the castle of Dover, and showed him the tomb of Sir Gawaine. Then Sir Launcelot kneeled down and wept, and prayed full heartily for his soul ; and that night he made a dole.   And all they that would come had as much flesh and fish, wine and ale, as they might eat and drink ; and every man and woman had twelvepence, come who would.   Thus, with his own hands, dealed he his money in a mourning gown ; and ever he wept, and prayed them to pray for the soul of Sir Gawaine.   And, on the morrow, all the priests and clerks that might be gotten in the country were there, and sung mass of requiem.   And there Sir Launcelot offered first, and he offered a hundred pounds : and then the seven kings offered forty pounds each ; and the offering endured from the morning to night : and Sir Launcelot lay two nights upon his tomb in prayers and in weeping ; then, on the third day, Sir Launcelot called unto him the kings, dukes, earls, barons, and knights, and thus he said—" My fair lords, I thank you all of your coming hither into this country with me : but we come too late, and that shall repent men while I live ; but against death there may no man rebel.   But sith it is so," said Sir Launcelot, " I will myself ride and seek my lady, Queen Guenever ; for, as I heard say, she hath had much pain and great disease : and I have heard say, that she is fled to the west country.   Therefore, ye all shall abide me here ; and, but if I come again within fifteen days, then take your ships, and depart into your countries ; for I will do as I have said to you."

———

IX.

Then came Sir Bors de Ganis, and said, "My lord, Sir Launcelot, what think ye to do? Now to ride in this realm, wit thou well ye shall find few friends." "Be as it may," said Sir Launcelot, "keep you still here; for I will forth on my journey, and neither man nor child go with me." So it was no boot to strive; but he departed and rode westward, and there he sought seven or eight days, and at the last he came upon a nunnery. And then was Queen Guenever aware of Sir Launcelot as he walked in the cloister; and, when she saw him there, she swooned three times, that all the ladies and gentlewomen had work enough for to hold the Queen up. So, when she might speak, she called the ladies and gentlewomen unto her: "Ye marvel, fair ladies, why I make this cheer. Truly," said she, "it is for the sight of yonder knight which is yonder; wherefore, I pray you all to call him unto me." And when Sir Launcelot was brought unto her, then she said, "Through this knight and me all the wars were wrought, and the death of the most noble knights of the world; for through our love that we have loved together is my most noble lord slain: therefore, wit thou well, Sir Launcelot, I am set in such a plight to get my soul's health; and yet I trust, through God's grace, that after my death for to have the sight of the blessed face of Jesu Christ, and at the dreadful day of doom to sit on his right side: for as sinful creatures as ever was I are saints in heaven.

"Therefore, Sir Launcelot, I require thee, and beseech thee heartily, for all the love that ever was between us two, that thou never look me more in the visage; and furthermore I command thee, on God's behalf, right straightly that thou forsake my company, and that unto thy kingdom shortly thou return again, and keep well thy realm from war and wreck. For as well as I have loved thee, Sir Launcelot, now mine heart will not once serve me to see thee; for through me and thee are the flower of kings and knights destroyed, therefore, Sir Launcelot, go thou unto thy realm, and there take thee a wife, and live with her in joy and bliss; and I beseech you heartily pray for me unto our Lord God, that I may amend my misliving."

"Now, sweet madam," said Sir Launcelot, "would ye that I should now return again into my country, and there to wed a lady? Nay, madam, wit ye well that I will never while I live; for I shall never be so false to you of that I have promised, but the same destiny that ye have taken you unto I will take me unto, for to please God, and especially to pray for you."

"If thou wilt do so," said the Queen, "hold thy promise; but I may not believe but that thou wilt return to the world again." "Ye say well," said he; "yet wist me never false of my promise, and God defend but that I should forsake the world like as ye have done; for in the quest of the Sancgreal I had forsaken the vanities of the world, had not your lord been: and if I had done so at that time with my heart, will, and thought, I had passed all the knights that were in the quest of the Sancgreal, except Sir Galahad, my son. And, therefore, my lady, Dame Guenever, since ye have taken you unto perfection, I must needs take me unto perfection of right. For I take record of God in you have I had mine earthly joy; and if I had found you so disposed now, I had cast me for to have had you into mine own realm and country.

X.

"But since I find you thus disposed, I endure you faithfully that I will take me to penance, and pray, while my life lasteth, if I may find any good hermit, either grey or white, that will receive me; wherefore, madam, I pray you kiss me once, and never more." "Nay," said the Queen, "that shall I never do; but abstain you from such things." And so they departed; but there was never so hard-hearted a man but he would have wept to see the sorrow that they made: for there was a lamentation as though they had been stung with spears, and many times they swooned. And the ladies bare the Queen to her chamber, and Sir Launcelot awoke, and went and took his horse, and rode all day and all that night in a forest, weeping; and at the last he was aware of a hermitage, and a chapel that stood between two cliffs, and then he heard a little bell ring to mass, and thither he rode, and alighted, and tied his horse to the gate, and heard mass. And he that sung the mass was the Bishop of Canterbury; both the bishop and Sir Bedivere knew Sir Launcelot, and they spake together after mass. But when Sir Bedivere had told him his tale all whole, Sir Launcelot's heart almost burst for sorrow; and Sir Launcelot threw away his armour, and said, "Alas! who may trust this world."

And then he kneeled down on his knees, and prayed the bishop for to shrive him and assoil him: and then he besought the bishop that he might be his brother. Then the bishop said, "I will gladly." And then he put a habit upon Sir Launcelot; and there he served God, day and night, with prayers and fastings.

Thus the great host abode at Dover; and then Sir Lionel took fifteen lords with him, and rode to London to seek Sir Launcelot; and there Sir Lionel was slain, and many of his lords. Then Sir Bors de Ganis made the great host to go home again unto their own country; and Sir Bors, Sir Ector de Maris, Sir Blamor, Sir Bleoberis, and with more other of Sir Launcelot's kin, took on them to ride through all England to seek Sir Launcelot.

So Sir Bors rode so long till he came unto the same chapel where Sir Launcelot was; and so Sir Bors heard a little bell that rung to mass, and there he alighted, and heard mass. And when mass was done, the bishop, Sir Launcelot, and Sir Bedivere came unto Sir Bors; and when he saw Sir Launcelot in that manner of clothing, then he prayed the bishop that he might be in the same suit : and so there was a habit put upon him, and there he lived in prayers and fasting. And within half-a-year there was come Sir Galihud, Sir Galihodin, Sir Bleoberis, Sir Villiers, Sir Clarrus, and Sir Galahautine: so these seven noble knights abode there still. And when they saw that Sir Launcelot had taken him unto such perfection, they had no list to depart, but took such a habit as he had. Thus they endured in great penance five years, and then Sir Launcelot took the habit of priesthood, and twelve months he sung the mass. And there was none of these other knights but that they read in books, and helped for to sing mass, and ring bells, and did lowly all manner of service. And so their horses went where they would; for they took no regard in worldly riches : for when they saw Sir Launcelot endure such penance, in prayer and fasting, they took no force what pain they endured, for to see the noblest knight of the world take such abstinence, so that he waxed full lean. And thus upon a night there came a vision unto Sir Launcelot, and charged him, in remission of all his sins, to haste him toward Almesbury, "and by that time thou come there thou shall find Queen Guenever dead; and, therefore, take thy fellows with thee, and also purvey thee a horse-bier, and bring you the corpse of her, and bury it by her lord and husband, the noble King Arthur." So this vision came thrice unto Sir Launcelot in one night.

XI.

THEN Sir Launcelot rose up ere it was day, and told the hermit thereof. "It is well done," said the hermit; "look that ye disobey not this vision." Then Sir Launcelot took his seven fellows with him, and on foot they went from Glastonbury, the which is little more than thirty miles : and thither they came within two days, for they were weak and feeble to go. And when Sir Launcelot was come to Almesbury, within the nunnery, Queen Guenever died but half-an-hour before ; and the ladies told Sir Launcelot, that Queen Guenever had told all ere she died, "that Sir Launcelot had been a priest near twelve months, and hither he cometh, as fast as he may, for to fetch my corpse ; and beside my lord, King Arthur, he shall bury me." Wherefore the Queen said, in hearing of them all, "I beseech Almighty God, that I may never have power to see Sir Launcelot with my worldly eyes." "And this," said all the ladies, "was ever her prayer all those two days, until she was dead." Then Sir Launcelot saw her visage ; but he wept not greatly, but sighed. And so he did all the observance of the service himself, both the dirge at night, and the mass on the morrow ; and there was ordained a horse-bier : and so with a hundred torches ever burning about the corpse of the Queen. And ever Sir Launcelot with his seven fellows went about the bier, singing and reading many a holy and devout orision, and frankincense upon the corpse incensed. Thus Sir Launcelot and his seven fellows went on foot from Almesbury until they came to Glastonbury ; and when they were come to the chapel and the hermitage, there she had a dirge with great devotion ; and on the morrow the hermit, that was sometime Bishop of Canterbury, sung the mass of requiem, with great devotion ; and Sir Launcelot was the first that offered, and then offered all his seven fellows : and then she was wrapped in seared cloths of reins, from the top to the toe, in thirty fold, and then she was put in a web of lead, and after in a coffin of marble. And when she was put into the earth, Sir Launcelot swooned, and lay long upon the ground, while the hermit came and awaked him, and said, "Ye are to blame, for ye displease God with such manner of sorrow-making." "Truly," said Sir Launcelot, "I trust I do not displease God, for he knoweth well mine intent, for my sorrow was not, nor is not for any rejoicing of sin ; but my sorrow may never have an end. For when I remember and call to mind her beauty, her bounty, and her nobleness, that was as well with her King, my lord Arthur, as with her ; and also when I saw the corpse of that noble King, and noble Queen, so lie together in that cold grave, made of earth, that sometime were so highly set in most honourable places, truly mine heart would not serve me to sustain my wretched and careful body also. And when I remember me how I, through my default, and through my presumption and pride, that they were both laid full low, the which were peerless that ever were living of Christian people. Wit ye well," said Sir Launcelot, "this remembered of their kindness, and of mine unkindness, sunk and impressed so in my heart, that all my natural strength failed me, so that I might not sustain myself."

XII.

THEN Sir Launcelot, ever after, eat but little meat, nor drank, but continually mourned until he was dead ; and then he sickened more and more, and dried and dwindled away. For the bishop, nor none of his fellows, might not make him to eat, and little he drank, that he was soon waxed shorter by a cubit than he was, that the people could not know him. For evermore, day and night, he prayed, but needfully, as nature required ; sometimes he slumbered a broken sleep, and always he was lying grovelling upon King Arthur's and Queen Guenever's tomb ; and there was no comfort that the bishop, nor Sir Bors, nor none of all his fellows, could make him ; it availed nothing.

Oh ! ye mighty and pompous lords, shining in the glory transitory of this unstable life, as in reigning over great realms and mighty great countries, fortified with strong castles and towers, edified with many a rich city ; yea also, ye fierce and mighty knights, so valiant in adventurous deeds of arms ;— behold ! behold ! see how this mighty conqueror, King Arthur, whom in his human life all the world doubted ; see also, the noble Queen Guenever, which sometime sat in her chair, adorned with gold, pearls, and precious stones, now lie full low in obscure foss, or pit, covered with clods of earth and clay. Behold also this mighty champion, Sir Launcelot, peerless of all knighthood ; see now, how he lieth grovelling upon the cold mould ; now being so feeble and faint, that sometime was so terrible. How, and in what manner, ought ye to be so desirous of worldly honour so dangerous. Therefore methinketh this present book is right necessary often to be read ; for in it shall ye find the most gracious, knightly, and virtuous war, of the most noble knights of the world, whereby they gat a praising continually. Also me seemeth, by the oft reading thereof, ye shall greatly desire to accustom yourself in following of those gracious knightly deeds; that is to say, to dread God and to love righteousness, faithfully and courageously to serve your sovereign prince ; and the more that God hath given you the triumphal honour, the meeker ought ye to be, ever fearing the unstableness of this deceitful world. And so I pass over and turn again unto my matter.

So within six weeks after, Sir Launcelot fell sick, and lay in his bed, and then he sent for the bishop, that there was hermit, and all his true fellows. Then Sir Launcelot said, in dreary tone, " Sir Bishop, I pray you that ye will give me all my rights that belongeth unto a Christian man." " It shall not need you," said the hermit and his fellows ; " it is but a heaviness of your blood ye shall be well amended by the grace of God to-morrow."

" My fair lords," said Sir Launcelot, " wit ye well, my careful body will into the earth ; I have warning more than I will now say ; therefore, I pray you, give me my rights." So when he was houseled and eneled, and had all that a Christian man ought to have, he prayed the bishop that his fellows might bear his body unto Joyous Gard.

" Some men say Alnwick, and some men say to Bamborow ; howbeit," said Sir Launcelot " me repenteth sore ; but I made mine avow afore time, that in Toyous Gard I would be buried ; and, because of breaking of mine vow, I pray you all lead me thither." Then was there weeping and wringing of hands among all his fellows. So, at the season of the night, they went all to their beds ; for they all lay in one chamber. So after midnight, against day, the bishop that was hermit, as he lay in his bed asleep, he fell on a great laughter and therewith the fellowship awoke, and came unto the bishop, and asked him what he ailed ? " Ah ! Jesu, mercy," said the bishop," " why did ye awake me ? I was never in all my life so merry, and so well at ease." " Why, wherefore ?" said Sir Bors. " Truly," said the bishop, " here was Sir Launcelot with me, with more angels than ever I saw men upon one day ; and I saw the angels heave up Sir Launcelot towards heaven, and the gates of heaven opened against him." " It is but the troubling of dreams," said Sir Bors ; " for I doubt not Sir Launcelot aileth nothing but good." " It may well be," said the bishop ; " go ye to his bed, and then shall ye prove the truth."

So when Sir Bors and his fellows came to his bed, they found him stark dead, and he lay as he had smiled ; and the sweetest savour about him that ever they smelled. Then was there weeping and wringing of hands, and the greatest dole they made that ever made men. And on the morrow the bishop sung his mass of requiem, and after, the bishop and all those knights put Sir Launcelot in the same horse-bier that Queen Guenever was laid in, before that she was buried.

And so the bishop and they altogether went with the corpse of Sir Launcelot daily, till they came unto Joyous Gard, and ever they had a hundred torches burning about him.

And so, within fifteen days, they came to Joyous Gard, and there they laid his corpse in the body of the quire, and sung and read many psalters and prayers over him, and about him; and ever his visage was laid open and naked, that all folk might behold him. For such was the custom in those days, that all men of worship should so lie with open visage, till that they were buried. And right thus, as they were at their service, there came Sir Ector de Maris, that had sought seven years all England Scotland, and Wales, seeking his brother Sir Launcelot.

XIII.

AND when Sir Ector de Maris heard such noise and light in the quire of Joyous Gard, he alighted, and put his horse away from him, and came into the quire, and there he saw men sing the service lamentably. And all they knew Sir Ector, but he knew not them. Then went Sir Bors unto sir Ector, and told him how there lay his brother Sir Launcelot dead.

And then Sir Ector threw his shield, his sword, and his helm from him; and when he beheld Sir Launcelot's visage, he fell down in a swoon; and when he awoke, it were hard for any tongue to tell the doleful complaints that he made for his brother. "Ah! Sir Launcelot," said he, "thou wert head of all Christian knights. And now, I dare say," said Sir Ector, "that Sir Launcelot, there thou liest, thou were never matched of none earthly knight's hands; and thou wert the courtliest knight that ever bear shield: and thou wert the truest friend to thy lover that ever bestrode horse; and thou wert the truest lover of a sinful man that ever loved woman; and thou wert the kindest man that ever struck with sword; and thou wert the goodliest person that ever came among press of knights; and thou wert the meekest man, and the gentlest, that ever eat in hall among ladies; and thou wert the sternest knight to thy mortal foe that ever put spear in the rest.

Then there was weeping and dolor out of measure. Thus they kept Sir Launcelot's corpse above the ground fifteen days, and then they buried it with great devotion. And then at leisure they went all with the Bishop of Canterbury unto his hermitage, and there they were together more than a month. Then Sir Constantine (which was Sir Cador's son, of Cornwall) was chosen King of England; and he was a full noble knight, and worshipfully he ruled this realm.   And then this King Constantine sent for the Bishop of Canterbury, for he heard say where he was, and so he was restored unto his bishopric, and left that hermitage.   And Sir Bedivere was there ever still a hermit unto his life's end.   Then Sir Bors de Ganis, Sir Ector de Maris, Sir Galahautine, Sir Galihud, Sir Galihodin, Sir Blamor, Sir Bleoberis, Sir Villiers le Valiaunt, Sir Clarrus of Claremount, all these knights drew them to their countries : howbeit King Constantine would have had them with him, but they would not abide in this realm, and there they lived in their countries as holy men.   And some English books make mention, that they never went out of England after the death of Sir Launcelot, but that was favour of poets.

For Sir Bors, Sir Ector, Sir Blamor, and Sir Bleoberis went into the Holy Land, thereas Jesu Christ was both quick and dead, anon as they had established their lands.   For Sir Launcelot commanded them so to do, or ever he passed out of this world.   And these four knights did many battles upon the miscreants and Turks and there they died upon Good Friday for God's sake.

Here is the end of the whole book of King Arthur, and of his Noble Knights of the Round Table : that, when they were whole together, there was ever a hundred and forty ; also here is the end of the death of King Arthur.   I pray you all, gentlemen and gentlewomen, that read this book of King Arthur and his knights, from the beginning to the ending, pray for me, while I am alive, that God send me good deliverance.   And, when I am dead, I pray you all pray for my soul.   For this book was finished the ninth year of the reign of King Edward the Fourth, by Sir Thomas Malory, Knight, as Jesu help me, for his great might, as he is the servant of Jesu, both day and night.

Thus endeth this noble and joyous book, entitled *La Mort D' Arthur*, notwithstanding it treateth of the birth, life, and acts of the said King Arthur, and of his Noble Knights of the Round Table, and their marvellous conquests and adventures, the achieving of the Holy Sancgreal, and, in the end, the dolorous death and departing out of this world of them all.

NOTES.

A Note upon the more readily available works which the reader of
"King Arthur" will find useful may fitly be given here. We
omit the early editions of the *Morte D' Arthur*, confining ourselves to
the more important later reprints, beginning with Southey's edition,
which may have been suggested by the issue of two separate popular
versions, each issued in a couple of little volumes in painfully small
type, published in 1816.

1. *La Mort D' Arthure.*—Edited, with an Introduction, by Southey.
   2 vols., 4to, 1817. Longmans. [This is an exact reprint from a copy
   of the first edition by Caxton, in Earl Spencer's library, an omission
   of eleven leaves in that copy being unwittingly repeated.]

2. *The History of King Arthur.*—Edited from the text of the edition of
   1634, with Introduction and Notes by Thomas Wright, M.A., F.S.A.
   Second Edition, 3 vols., 8vo. Smith. 1866.

3. *Morte Darthur.*—The original edition of Caxton revised for modern
   use, with an Introduction by Sir Edward Strachey, Bart. The
   Globe Edition. Macmillan & Co. 1883. [The Introduction to
   this edition is admirable, and contains a great deal of most
   valuable information, together with a delightful "Essay on
   Chivalry."]

4. *Le Morte Arthur.*—(An early Fifteenth Century Poem). Edited from
   the Harleian MS. by F. J. Furnivall, M.A. Macmillan & Co.
   1864. [In addition to Mr. Furnivall's Introduction, this volume contains a very suggestive essay on "Arthur," by Herbert Coleridge.]

The reader may be also referred generally to the reprints of the Early English Text Society, in which will be found most interesting matter in prose and verse relating to Arthur, Merlin, and certain of the Arthurian Knights. Special attention may be drawn to *Sir Gawayne and The Green Knight*, an alliterative romance-poem of the Fourteenth Century, of a most fascinating character. For purposes of further investigation, it is only necessary to mention the Reading Room at the British Museum, where an invaluable treasury of the Arthurian and allied romances in old French and other versions is free to the student.

THE TEXT of the present volume is taken from the second work in the foregoing list, Mr. Wright's edition, the notes of which have also been largely used. The spelling has of course been revised throughout, and where there has seemed any doubt of the easy apprehension of old words, modern equivalents have been used. In a few instances also phrases which the squeamishness of these days might object to have been slightly altered, but on the whole the text may be taken as virtually that of the 1634 edition from which Mr. Wright printed. The main purpose of the revision has been to facilitate the reading of the book with pleasure.

Of the *Morte D' Arthur* as prepared by Malory, seven out of the twenty-one Books have been here omitted, in order, as was explained in the Introduction, to throw the Arthurian history proper into clearer and more coherent form—the history, that is, as complemented by the Quest of the Grail. The omitted books, dealing chiefly with pure knight-errantry, as in the romances of Sir Launcelot, Sir Beaumains, Sir Tristram, and other of the knights, it is intended to publish shortly as a companion volume of the CAMELOT CLASSICS. One book, however, dealing with Arthur's Roman War, being neither history nor good romance, is cast aside altogether; and the Book of Sir Bors in the portion dealing with the Quest of the Holy Grail, though interesting in itself, being largely a repetition of adventures chronicled of other knights also, is reserved for a still further use in the series.

NOTES.

REFERENCE LIST OF NAMES, Etc.

And.—Used constantly in the book in the sense of "if."

Aretted.—Reckoned.

Arthur.—Reference is made in the Introduction to the supposed mythical origins of the story of Arthur, and it is impossible to do more than remind the reader here of the vast and antique horizon which surrounds the romance centre of "many-towered Camelot." Of the historical Arthur it is difficult to speak exactly. He has been claimed for at least six different birth-places, and his bones lie pretty much at the mercy of the same localising imaginativeness. As to his supposed relationship to his mentor Merlin, the reader can turn to the note on that first of all the magicians. The note upon Excalibur may also be turned to for Arthur's possible prototype in the Sanskrit *Mahabharata*, the Prince Arjuna.

Assoil.—Absolve.

Assotted.—Besotted :—An old man's love dotage.

Avelyon.—Avallon, Avelon ; the famous Isle of Apples, on which Glastonbury was built.

Aventred.—To aventer, to couch spears.

Bamborough.—Sée Joyous Gard.

Barendowne.—This is, no doubt, meant for Barham Down, near Canterbury : a place well known to antiquaries on account of its early Anglo-Saxon cemetery, the existence of which, doubtless, gave rise to the notion of a battle having been fought there. (Wright.)

Beames.—Beume : a sort of trumpet.

Benwicke.—A French town, not to bo confused, of course, with Berwick in Northumberland. It has been explained variously in the text itself and elsewhere to be Beyon—Bayonne, Beaune, etc.

Besaunt.—A gold coin, named from Byzantium, or Constantinople, of which it is understood to have been the coinage. Its value varied at different times. (Wright.)

Beseen.—Adorned, arrayed.

Bleise.—Blaise, according to the legend of Merlin, was a hermit who had protected Merlin's mother from the fiend, and had undertaken his education. Merlin is afterwards supposed to have made Blaise his chronicler and father-confessor, reporting his feats of enchantment and the events in general of the time for purposes of record by Blaise.

Boot.—Help.

Brachet.—A kind of small hound, that hunted by scent.

Brast.—Broke.

Brawn.—The muscular, fleshy part of the limbs and extremities, as the palm of the hand.

Burgeneth.—Burgeon; bud, blossom.

Camelot.—In the "Globe Edition" of the *Morte D' Arthur*, the Introduction explains Camelot to be in Somersetshire, where the village of Queen-Camel (East Camel and West Camel), lies near the grass-grown remains of a castle, supposed to be Camelot, on the neighbouring hill, with the river Camel, crossed by Arthur's Bridge, running below. "Arthur's Well," writes Sir Edward Strachey, "still springs from the hill-side, and if Arthur's Hunting Causeway in the field below, Arthur's Round Table and Arthur's Palace within the camp, cannot still, as of old, be pointed out to the visitor, the peasant girl will still tell him that within that charmed circle they who look may see through golden gates a King sitting in the midst of his court." The name of the castle itself was gradually changed from Camelot successively to Camallate (Leland), Camellek, and at last Cadbury. Camelot has been identified with various other places, as with Winchester by Malory in the Book of Balin le Savage, and Caxton in his Prologue places it in Wales; but there can be little doubt that Queen-Camel, near South Cadbury, must be the shrine of the latter-day pilgrim who wishes to materially approach old-time Camelot.

CANDLEMAS.—The feast of Candles; a festival of the Roman Catholic Church in honour of the purification of the Virgin Mary, on the 2nd of February, and so called from the number of candles used.

CARBONEK.—It is difficult to localise the Castle of Carbonek at all. It has been identified by some writers with Monsalvat, but even this is mere conjecture.

CARDOILE.—The old form of Carlisle.

CARLION.—Caerleon-upon-Usk, the Isca Silurum of the Romans, the extensive ruins of which were celebrated at the time when the Arthurian romances were written. It was imagined to be the chief city of Arthur and the legendary British Kings of that time. (Wright.)

CARRACK.—A sort of small ship.

CERED CLOTHES.—Cerements; cered, *i.e.*, waxed, burial clothes.

CHILD.—Squire, or Young Knight.

CLEPED.—Yclept, called.

COURTELAGE.—Courtyard.

DEBONAIR.—Courteous.

DROMON.—A vessel of war.

DURESSE.—Bondage.

ELAINE.—Care must be taken not to confuse the various Elaines in the book—Elaine, King Pelleas's daughter and the mother of Sir Galahad; Elaine, the fair Maid of Astolat; Elaine, King Ban's wife, and Elaine, King Nentres's wife.

ENELED.—Anointed, with extreme unction. See "Hamlet."
"Unhousl'd, disappointed, unanel'd."
—Act 1. Sc. 1.

ERST.—Before.

EXCALIBUR.—King Arthur's celebrated magic sword may be indentified with certain other enchanted weapons of old-world myths, as perhaps with the holy bow, Gandiva, in the *Mahabharata*, versified by Mr. Edwin Arnold in his *Indian Idylls*, which a lady, Mrs. William Sharp, has pointed out to me. The whole episode of Arjuna's journey with his brother "to the far Lauchityan Sea," into which he casts the holy bow, Gandiva, has a curious parallelism to the casting into the water of Excalibur by Arthur's command at his death. "In the old metrical romance of Merlin," explains Mr. Wright, "this celebrated sword bore the following inscription:"—

Ich am y-hote Escalibore :
Unto a King fair tresore.

And it is added in explanation,

On Inglis is this writing ;—
" Kerve steel and yren and al thing."

Carve steel, and iron, and all things :—this seems to be the free interpretation of the name *Excalibur*.

FEWTER.—Put spear in rest.

FOINING.—Thrusting while fencing.

FORTHINK.—Repent, grieve.

GAD.—Spike or nob of iron or steel.

GALAHAD.—Sir Galahad is well-known through Tennyson's stirring lyric, and the whole story of the noblest of all the knights would make a delightful book by itself, excerpted from the *Morte D' Arthur*. It will be remembered that Sir Galahad took his name from his father Sir Launcelot, who was christened Galahad too.

GALFRIDUS.—Geoffrey of Monmouth.

GERFALCON.—Jer-falcon; the finest kind of falcon.

GISARM.—Two-edged battle-axe.

GLAIVE.—A long blade at the end of a lance.

GRAIL, THE HOLY,—The Sancgreall, or Saint Graal, was supposed to be the dish upon which the paschal lamb was served at the Last Supper, and in which Joseph of Arimathæa afterward received the blood from the wounds of Jesus at the Crucifixion. It was then, according to the legend, brought by Joseph to England; but like many other relics of the Roman Catholic Church, has a divided report as to its ultimate resting-place. The original vessel is said now to be in the cathedral of Genoa,—an emerald dish of hexagonal shape. Whatever its outward form and ultimate destination, however, this symbol of the knightly quest of the ideal has become one of the poet's special belongings, which will never cease to be religiously potent, let us hope, in his hands.

GRAMERCY. — Grand merci, great thanks!

GUENEVER.—Queen Guenever, known in the *Idylls of the King* as Guinevere, was called by Geoffrey of Monmouth, in whose *History* the first beginnings of most of the Arthurian legends are to be found, Guanhumara. In Geoffrey's *History* she is said to be of a noble Roman family, and the most beautiful woman of her time.

HANDSEL.—Earnest-money.

HARNESS.—Armour.

HAUBERK.—Coat of mail.

HAUT.—High, noble, as in "Haut Prince."

HIGHT.—Was called.

HOLT.—A wooded hill; sometimes a cliff.

HOUSLED.—To be houseled was to receive the sacrament.

HURTLE.—Dash.

JESSERAUNT.—The jesseraunt was a light coat of armour, usually made of small plates of metal overlapping each other, and having no sleeves.

JOURNEY.—Day's work.

JOYOUS GARD.—Various conjectures have been made about the site of Joyous Gard, Sir Launcelot's chief English castle, taking it to be Berwick, Alnwick, and Bamborough. So far as the evidence goes, Bamborough is perhaps the most likely situation of the three.

LARGESSE.—Bounty.

LATON.—A sort of amalgam, somewhat similar to brass.

LAUNCELOT.—Sir Launcelot was the favourite hero, above all the other knights, of the old romances. The *Roman de Lancelot du Lac* was told and re-told a hundred times in one way or another, in verse and prose. Malory seems to have followed closely an interesting copy in old French prose which can be seen at the British Museum.

LEACH.—Physician or Surgeon.

LET.—Hinder.

LEVER.—Rather.

LIEF.—Dear.

MAUGRE.—In spite of; sometimes also used to mean "misfortunate."

MERLIN.—Merlin,—magician and prime minister, the leading genius of the kingdom's destinies before and during part of King Arthur's reign, has never ceased to fascinate the popular imagination from the earliest times. His origin was said to be diabolical, but birth and death have been shrouded with infinite ingenuity of mystery. According to Geoffrey of Monmouth, Merlin had been court-magician from the time of Vortigern, whom he assisted with his magic in raising a castle in Salisbury Plain. As accounting for his extraordinary interest in the fortunes of a mere boy like the young King Arthur, a curious theory has been stated, making Arthur to be his illegitmate son by Igraine. The local traditions and legends of Merlin in certain parts of England and Wales are legion, and can only be thus referred to here.

MORGAN LE FAY.—The celebrated Queen-witch of the *Morte D' Arthur*, was, according to the old prose romance of Merlin, an illegitimate daughter of Igraine. On her mother's marriage with King Utherpendragon she was sent to a nunnery, which may account for her ill-will to her half-brother Arthur. At the nunnery she employed herself in studying evil spirits instead of good, out of sheer perversity apparently, thus through a girlish spite becoming an adept in witchcraft.

NE.—Ne is used constantly by Malory in the sense of *nor*.

ORGULE.—Pride. ORGULOUS.—Proud, haughty.

PAYNIMS.—Pagans.

PERDY.—Per Dieu,—Truly; 'i faith!

PRICKER.—A light rider. PRICKING.— Light riding.

PRISE.—The note blown on the horn at the stag's death.

QUESTING.—Baying, as hounds give tongue in hunting.

RASURE.—A cutting wind.

RECHATE.—Recheat; recall.

REDE.—Counsel, advise

SAMITE.—A rich silk, often interwoven with gold or silver thread.

SANCGREAL.—See GRAIL, HOLY !

SENDAL.—Cloth of Sendal was a fine sort of silk.

SIEGE.—Seat.

SITH, SITHEN.—Since.

SPERE.—Ask.

TEEN.—Grief.

WEREWOLF.—A man changed into a wolf by sorcery—a well known superstition, not yet extinct in some parts of Europe.

Printed by WALTER SCOTT, *Felling, Newcastle-on-Tyne.*

The Canterbury Poets.

NOW READY, PRICE ONE SHILLING,

SONNETS OF THIS CENTURY.

*With an Exhaustive and Critical Essay
on the Sonnet.*

By WILLIAM SHARP.

SONNETS BY

Lord Tennyson.

Robert Browning.

A. C. Swinburne.

Matthew Arnold.

Theodore Watts.

Archbishop Trench.

J. Addington Symonds.

W. Bell Scott.

Christina Rossetti.

Edward Dowden.

Edmund Gosse.

Andrew Lang.

George Meredith.

Cardinal Newman.

BY THE LATE

Dante Gabriel Rossetti.

Mrs. Barrett Browning.

C. Tennyson-Turner, etc.

And all the Best Writers of the Century.

" Mr. Sharp has produced a sonnet-book which represents the best craftsmanship of the nineteenth century, and supplies the public with an interesting guide to the technicalities of the subject."—*The Academy.*

London:
WALTER SCOTT, 24 Warwick Lane, Paternoster Row.

THE CAMELOT CLASSICS.

New Comprehensive Edition of the Leading Prose Writers.
Edited by ERNEST RHYS.

In SHILLING Monthly Volumes, Crown 8vo ; each Volume containing about 400 pages, clearly printed on good paper, and strongly bound in Cloth.

PROSPECTUS.

THE main idea in instituting this Edition is to provide the general reader with a comprehensive Prose Library after his own heart,—an Edition, that is to say, cheap, without the reproach which cheapness usually implies, comprising volumes of shapely form, well printed, well bound, and thoroughly representative of the leading prose writers of all time. Placed thus upon a popular basis, making the principle of literary selection a broadly human rather than an academic one, the Edition will, the Publisher hopes, contest not ineffectually the critical suffrages of the democratic shilling.

As in the CANTERBURY POETS issued from the same press, to which this aims at being a companion series, the *Editing* of the volumes will be a special feature. This will be entrusted to writers who will each, in freshly treated, suggestive Introductions, give just that account of the book and its author which will enable the significance of both in life and literature, and their relation to modern thought, to be readily grasped. And where, for the successful rescue of old-time books for modern reading, revision and selection are necessary, the editing will be done with careful zeal and with reverence always for the true spirit of the book. In the first volume a General Introduction by the Editor will appear, explaining more fully the bearing of the series, which, in course of time, it is hoped, will form

A COMPLETE PROSE LIBRARY FOR THE PEOPLE.

Vol. I. will be published on 1st March 1886.

The History of King Arthur
And the Quest of the Holy Grail.

BY SIR THOMAS MALORY. Edited by ERNEST RHYS.

To be followed on 1st April by

CONFESSIONS OF AN ENGLISH OPIUM-EATER,
Including " Levana " and " Rosicrucians."

BY THOMAS DE QUINCEY. With Introduction by WM. SHARP.

THE KENILWORTH LIBRARY.

Each Crown 8vo, from 300 to 500 pages, Strongly Bound in Elegant Cloth Binding, Coloured Edges.   Price 2s.

IMPORTANT ANNOUNCEMENT.

This Series of Popular Books, comprising many original Novels by new Authors, as well as the most choice works of Dickens, Lytton, Smollett, Scott, Ferrier, etc., etc., is now being brought out in an entirely new cover.   The books themselves will be considerably thicker, and each Volume will be Illustrated by six full-page engravings.   As hitherto the great objection to a Cheap Series of Books has been the loose Binding, an important feature of this Series will be the attention paid to this department.   They will be strongly sewn on Tape Bands, which will give them special value, either for Private or Public Libraries.

The following 20 Vols. of the Series are now ready, and will be followed by others shortly :—

Old Curiosity Shop	Ivanhoe
Pickwick Papers	Kenilworth
Nicholas Nickleby	Jacob Faithful
Oliver Twist	Roderick Random
Sketches by Boz	Peregrine Pickle
Barnaby Rudge	The Scottish Chiefs
Paul Clifford	The Inheritance
Eugene Aram	Ethel Linton
Ernest Maltravers	Hazel
Alice	A Mountain Daisy

LONDON:
WALTER SCOTT, 24 Warwick Lane, Paternoster Row.